The Second Calling

23.00

The Second Calling

A novel inspired by the life and work of
Jean Vanier

Hans S. Reinders

DARTON · LONGMAN + TODD

First published in 2016 by
Darton, Longman and Todd Ltd
1 Spencer Court
140 – 142 Wandsworth High Street
London SW18 4JJ

ISBN: 978-0-232-53217-3

A catalogue record for this book is available from the British Library

Illustrations by Jane Human.

Phototypeset by Kerrypress Ltd.
Printed and bound by Scandbook AB

The second call comes later, when we accept that we cannot do big or heroic things for Jesus; it is a time of renunciation, humiliation, and humility. We feel useless; we are no longer appreciated. If the first passage is made at high noon, under a shining sun, the second call is often made at night. We feel alone and are afraid because we are in a world of confusion.

Jean Vanier, Community and Growth

Those who come close to people in need do so first of all in a generous desire to help them and bring them relief; they often feel like saviours and put themselves on a pedestal. But once in contact with them, once touching them, establishing a loving a trusting relationship with them, the mystery unveils itself. At the heart of the insecurity of people in distress there is a presence of Jesus. And so they discover the sacrament of the poor and enter the mystery of compassion. People who are poor seem to break down the barriers of powerfulness, of wealth, of ability, and of pride; they pierce the armour the human heart builds to protect itself.

Jean Vanier, Community and Growth

Little did I know that I was on the road to an amazing discovery, a gold mine of truth, where the weak and the strong, the rich and the poor would be brought together in community and find peace, where those who were rejected could heal and transform those who rejected them.

Jean Vanier, Our Life Together

Contents

Part I

The New Assistant

1.

Sunflowers

'Sunflowers always turn to the sun, did you know that, Alonso?' They were overlooking the field full of yellow and green in front of them. 'This morning their heads turned that way.' The man pointed to the hills where the sun rises in the morning. Alonso gave him one of his broad smiles.

'Now they're looking at you. They want to know whether you are as happy as they are.' Alonso smiled again. A patch with hundreds of sunflowers stared him in the face with their big deep brown eye framed in golden leaves. His wide eyes looked happy. Then he took the man by his sleeve and pointed down the road. 'Uh, uh,' he murmured.

'Yeah, you're right, we need to go home.'

Ramón Jimenez was a frail middle-aged man with a typical Southern complexion. Had it not been for his funny worn-out straw hat, his dark eyes under his thick brows would have left the impression of a stern face. Compared with his light steps Alonso's gait in front of him was a bit strange, hesitant as it were. People who knew him called it his 'clumsy' walk. Alonso was shorter than his friend and clearly too heavy for his age. His feet seemed insecure about whether the road would carry his next step.

The road they had been walking on was a dusty trail in late August, meandering through fields that were full of olive trees. When they reached the crossroads where their path was going down the hill, Alonso again made his Platypus smile. There was a huge stone at the side of the road that apparently made him very excited.

'Boomm!' he shouted, making a gesture as if he summoned the stone to explode. Ramón stopped.

'Yes, Alonso. Boomm!' he repeated. 'The wagon nearly turned over, didn't it?' We were lucky that it didn't break down.'

Alonso nodded with excitement, as if he were going through the moment once again. 'Boomm! Boomm!' he shouted while making a jump in the air. A few months ago they had been visiting a music festival in Olivares, a village west of Seville. On their way home the people from Alonso's house crowded into a wagon taking them back to their own village, the village of Benacazón. They had been laughing and singing to the dark blue evening sky when all of a sudden their wagon had hit that same huge stone. It had been lying in the middle of the road then, but now it had been pushed aside. For a split second its passengers had found themselves floating in the air, which was an occasion for great excitement. Fortunately no one got hurt other than a few scratches. For weeks the adventure had been the story of the day.

'Come on, we need to go if we are to be in time for lunch!' Ramón pointed in the direction of the house to encourage Alonso to walk again. As they went along, he was thinking about the meeting he was to have in the pottery. Maria had made an appointment with a new assistant named Jonathan Harrison, a young man from the west coast of the United States, who had arrived about six weeks ago. It was Maria's task to supervise assistants. She had made it a rule that after six weeks a 'first-term' interview was to take place, and had asked Ramón to conduct these interviews. Jonathan Harrison had been assisting Antonio in the pottery. From what Ramón had heard he seemed to be doing quite well. Now that his first term as a new assistant was nearly over, the decision needed to be made about whether they wanted the young man to stay.

'Will you be back before lunch from your visit to Father Gilberto so that you can speak with him afterwards?'

'I think so. I will ask Alonso to join me. He can use some exercise. But he surely will want to be back in time not to miss his plate!' Ramón said smiling; he enjoyed the prospect of a pleasant morning.

When he was asked to join him for a walk Alonso had hugged him, which was his way of saying that he wanted to come. They had left before nine to visit Father Gilberto, a priest friend in Sanlúcar – Sanlúcar la Mayor to give it its full name. The air was still fresh, even though it was expected to be a hot day. It was a delightful morning

When Maria had briefed him about the young American she told him what she knew from Antonio's report.

'What do you make of him?' Ramón had asked her. 'Do we want him to stay?' She said that Jonathan seemed to have found his place in the pottery, but that there were some worries about him too.

'Antonio is quite pleased to have him, but he is less thrilled about his interest in Lucie. It seems as if he has made it his personal project to get her to actually work as a potter.'

'What's wrong with that?'

'You know what is wrong with that! It means pushing her around and making her do things she doesn't understand.'

The sun was really getting hot now that they were past the shady olive trees, approaching the railway. Ramón noticed that his companion was speeding up.

'Do you smell the kitchen already?' he joked. Alonso turned around with his big smile and put his hand on his belly. Ramón laughed.

'Your stomach wants to be filled again?'

When they were past the railway station of Benacazón they would soon be able to see the House of Bethany. The dusty dirt road turned into a wide lane with big oak trees, though still without a pavement.

There was laughter in the kitchen when they entered the house ten minutes later. Claire, who was in charge of preparing for lunch welcomed them. 'There you are!' To make their arrival known she called on Sylvia who was assisting her in the kitchen. 'Ramón has arrived with Alonso, we can start serving out the soup now.' Turning to the two men who had just arrived again, she said: 'We were just about to start without you.'

'Not without Alonso, I hope,' Ramón said.

'Why not? His belly could bear to skip a meal!'

'Did you hear that, Alonso? ...Where is he?'When he turned to the dining table, Alonso had already taken his chair – ready for a full plate of whatever the cook would serve for lunch this day.

'The walk from Sanlúcar has made me hungry too,' Ramón said.

'Let's hope there is a plate for you too, then. How was your walk?' Claire wanted to know. 'Did this fellow here behave himself?' She patted Alonso on his shoulder.

'Oh, yes. He is great company. We were watching sunflowers. Then he discovered the stone that almost knocked them off the road when they came back from Olivares.'

'Oh no, not that story again,' Claire said. She ordered everyone to the lunch table and asked Ramón to say a blessing. The ensuing meal was filled with gossip about what had happened that morning with the habitual joking and teasing of who had, and who hadn't, earned his or her meal.

'Alonso found the milestone that got you almost killed the other day,' Ramón said laughingly.

'No it didn't. It only gave us a sore butt.' He didn't hear who said it, but it caused a roar of laughter. Once again the story was the occasion for a merry excitement during their mealtime.

'That story gets crazier every time I hear it. Can we perhaps have lunch in an orderly manner?' Claire summoned the crowd with a loud voice, which was answered by more jokes and more laughter. Alonso listened while he ate a full plate of the pasta that was on the menu.

After lunch was finished Ramón went to the pottery for his appointment. He called upon his companion to join him again.

'Alonso, come we are going to Antonio.'

When they entered the workshop, Alonso saw a girl moving around and almost jumped upon her. It was Lucie Miles. The two of them seemed very fond of each other. Ramón stepped aside because the new assistant quickly moved in their direction, apparently intending to stop them.

'Enough, enough of this!' he said in a loud voice. 'Lucie watch yourself, you are ruining a day's work.' Ramón raised his brows. Then he turned to the young man.

'Jonathan, how are you?' he said, taking both his hands.

2.

Jonathan

Jonathan Harrison was not a sunflower. Sunflowers are inclined to turn to light, but Jonathan was more of a brooding type. Instead of living his life and enjoying it, he was still trying to figure out how to live it, and, particularly, what to do with it. This was not at all unusual for young men his age, especially when they were educated young men. In Jonathan's case there was also a father who didn't make finding one's own way any easier.

It was late June 1982, and a few weeks after his graduation from college, when his father had invited him into his office. It was on the top floor of an impressive high rise building in the San Francisco Bay area, in which a number of businesses and firms kept their offices. Peter Harrison was the owner of a health insurance company. When he had inherited it from his father, it had only been a small firm selling car insurance. As soon as the son took over, he changed the business to move into the expanding health insurance market. After a few years of hard work the change had become a huge success, which had been reflected lately in his impressive office with a mahogany desk, a leather sofa, broad windows, and an absolutely stunning view over the Bay. Jonathan remembered spending time with his grandfather quite well. A rather small, friendly man he had been there for his two grandsons of whom he was very fond. After he retired, his name was never mentioned in the firm, at least not by his own son, who didn't seem to think there was much in his father's life as a businessman that was worthwhile being remembered.

'Mostly sad,' Jonathan's mother answered when he had asked her how Grandpa Harrison's life had been. Financial problems had troubled him most of his life, and his marriage had not been very happy, being rebuked by a wife who cherished different expectations from the life they shared. But his wife had died young, only in her late thirties when she passed away.

When his grandfather had handed over the firm to his son Peter there were only a couple of administrative clerks on his payroll, two young women who fondly called him 'Boss Harrison.' Both of them were fired the next day after the old man had left the office. His son made no secret of the fact that he had different plans both for the firm and for the way he wanted to run it, making sure that nobody would dream of calling him 'Boss Harrison' as a pet name.

The firm had expanded, and ten years later Peter Harrison employed dozens of people, most of whom hardly dared to look him in the face as he arrived in the building each morning, followed by his chauffeur carrying his briefcase. Whatever else he was, Peter Harrison was never to be taken for granted. As a small boy Jonathan had looked up to his father and loved him, but at the same time he was often intimidated by the aloofness he saw in his face.

'Sit down, Jonathan,' his father said, watching his son looking out over the Bay. 'You know that one day all this will be yours. I am proud of you, son. Many people I know do not have a son to step into their shoes, but I do. Your mother and I consider ourselves to be very fortunate, having you seen grow up you the way you did. I have tried to raise you to become a strong man who will make his way in the world. It does seem to pay off, doesn't it? To teach your children to behave responsibly, I mean.'

Jonathan smiled. 'Thank you, dad, I am very grateful to you both.' By including his mother in this response he opposed his father claiming all the credit for the way their sons had been raised, as if Hannah Harrison's role had only been to follow her husband's instructions.

'When I think of my parents, simple folks as you know, you have every reason to be grateful,' said his father. The explanation that followed was not new to his son. As long as Jonathan could remember, his father never referred with scorn to his parents, but he never expressed any affectionate feelings for them either. 'I promised myself that life would be different for my kids,' his father said, 'so that they never would have to ask for something they knew they never would have.'

In this respect Peter Harrison had succeeded completely. Jonathan remembered his first bike that he had been given when he was five. When most kids were riding piggyback clinging to their father's shoulders, he was riding his first bike. Not because he wanted to, let alone asked for it, but because his father thought it was time that he learned how to go to school on a bicycle. In fact, Jonathan could not remember ever having asked anything for himself that his father had not already decided he should, or should not, have.

Untroubled characters turn to daylight when it shines upon their faces, but Jonathan Harrison's heart was too heavy to be lifted up to towards the sun. Had he been asked, he would not have been able to put words to the feeling that he carried deep down inside him. He loved a man, his father, who had never cared very much about him. This he had felt all his life, even when he had never put it into words. It had changed since he had left home to go to college, when he felt the day would come that he would stop pretending he didn't know that his father's heart was in his firm, not in his family.

That morning in late June 1982 the suffocating air in his father's office had been too much. Listening to his father explaining how he expected his oldest son to prepare for taking over the firm in another ten years Jonathan felt all the energy seeping out of his body. The moment of squarely opposing his father had not yet arrived, but the prospect of having to face him every day in his own territory was more than his son could bear. When he packed his bag the next day it was not because he had made a resolution. He just ran to escape a future that was imposed upon him.

Two weeks later Jonathan Harrison found himself in the city of Seville. He had paid for his airfare to Madrid with the money he had earned during his years in college, a fact that would have made his father proud, if only he had been able to understand why he had done it. In spite of the determination to go away, however, there had not been an even remotely defined plan for what he wanted to do.

So why Spain, and why Seville? Jonathan had no clue, other than that he had taken Spanish language classes in college. They had read a text about Seville being the centre of the 'real' Spain before the Castilian kings took over, which meant its culture had to be very old. Another thing that attracted him was the tradition of gypsy music for which the city was famous. The fire of the passionate flamenco music appealed to him as it felt like the opposite of the iron cage of control that his father had prepared for him.

After wandering around for a week in Seville, he had met a guy from Boston in a bar. He told him he had been around for a month looking for work to earn some 'cash'. One of the things he had heard was from someone telling him about a place in a village a few miles down the road. 'From what I was told I think it is a kind of spiritual community. At any rate they're not very formal about hiring and they are short of people. They seem to need someone for their pottery. But it is like an internship, so it doesn't pay much,' the guy from Boston had said. 'If you don't mind that, you could give 'em a call.'

For the time being money was not his main concern, so Jonathan decided to call the House of Bethany, as the place was named. The runaway son proved himself to be no coward. Without so much as realizing it, he was his father's son after all. To his surprise he found himself invited to come for a job interview. It was a small spiritual community, just like he had been told, and the pottery was their workshop. It would turn out to be the place where Jonathan

Harrison was destined to make a few important discoveries about himself.

When he arrived the next day a woman in her forties received him. Her name was Maria. She seemed to be in charge of recruiting and supervising new people - 'assistants' she called them. After friendly introductions the interview started. Maria turned out to be a tough nut to crack.

'Why do you want to work here?' she asked him.

'Because for the moment it seems for me the place to be.'

'How so?' Maria had noticed his hesitation, which he hated. He wanted to appear self-contained.

'Look,' he said a bit too aggressively, 'it is important for people to go their own way, isn't it?'

'Oh, sure, if they know what that way is. Do you?'

Jonathan felt as if she was looking right through him. No shadow of a doubt in her voice. Behind her he saw the oval mirror in his father's office.

'That's what I am about to find out, and this seems as good a place as any to do so,' he said, alarmed by his own boldness. He could not have expressed less interest in what their community was about. Prepared for being sent away, he reached for his bag.

'We're not done yet, unless you want to leave right now?' said Maria, faintly smiling. Unsure what to answer, he looked her in the eye. 'Not really.'

'Good.'

'Does it mean I can stay?'

'It means we're not done yet. Not many people who come here express their self-interested motive as clearly as you do,' she said.

'Oh ... What do they express then?' he responded.

'That's not our business right now. Important for us, at least at this moment, is that you are clear about what you want to do here. You are coming here to find out about yourself, which is okay. You got at least that much straightened out, which is more than most new assistants can say for themselves.'

Surprised at her frankness Jonathan thought it wise to keep silent. 'You know we are sharing our lives with vulnerable people here,' Maria continued. He nodded vaguely. The guy from Boston who had mentioned the place had said something about 'handicapped people' without knowing exactly what that was supposed to mean.

'It means that you will work with people for whom assistants who are too much busy with themselves can be dangerous. Do you understand?'

'Yes, I do.'

'Good.'

'Did you ever work in a pottery?'

'No. Why?'

'Because that is where I would like you to start. We're short of people there. But it's not my call. Antonio is in charge of the workshop. I will ask him to see you tomorrow at nine for an interview.'

Jonathan nodded, but didn't say a word.

'We have a rule about new assistants. They are invited to stay for two weeks. If they have not left by then, they are invited to stay another month. After that Ramón will speak with them to see if they can stay for a longer stretch of time.'

'Who is Ramón?'

'He is the founder of this community. You will get to know him soon enough.' Looking at him with a serious expression, she added: 'And he will soon get to know you.'

When he left Maria's office, Jonathan felt he had not just had a job interview. She had been figuring out what he was about. 'That makes two of us,' he said to himself. Reading his character, that's what she had been doing. Not too unhappy with his own candour, he was wondering whether this would be the right time to write a letter to his parents.

3.

The Pottery

Antonio was an artist from Galicia. Broad-shouldered with a grey apron over his heavy belly, he looked like a man who was used to physical work. Jonathan liked him the moment he saw him, but was unsure why. Apart from his physical appearance as a craftsman, Antonio's face was that of an ancient Spanish nobleman. His oval-shaped face framed by long dark curls falling on his shoulders had piercing black eyes that looked into the world without any sign of emotion. When they fell upon you, you would feel they saw right through you. The short salt-and-pepper beard around his mouth was flanked by a dimple on both cheeks. The dimples prevented his gaze from being completely terrifying.

'Antonio.' That was all he said in response to Jonathan's introduction of himself. With his black eyes measuring up the newcomer, he sat down on a chair in his office. 'Office' was perhaps not an adequate name for what looked more like a storage room for materials. A few boxes containing clay were placed in the corner behind the desk; a dirty coffee mug on the table, which besides a phone also had papers with sketches on them. A shelf against the wall displayed a few jars, apparently made in the pottery. A filing cabinet against the opposite wall completed the inventory.

'Sit down,' said Antonio grabbing a second chair for Jonathan. His tone was not unfriendly, but the young man failed to notice this, inadvertently intimidated as he was by self-composed men who seemed to know exactly what they were about. 'So you want to work here.' The words were spoken as if to conclude an interview that had not even begun.

'Maria suggested that the pottery is a place where I might be useful given that you are short of assistants.'

'We'll see about useful,' Antonio said, 'but being short of assistants is true enough. Did you ever work in a pottery before?' Shaking slightly with his curly head he anticipated Jonathan's answer.

'No, I am afraid not, Sir.'

'Nothing to be afraid of, young man, unless you continue calling me "Sir".'

'I won't.'

'Good.'

'What do you want me to do?' Jonathan asked, having understood that this was not going to be a long interview.

Antonio looked him straight in the eye. 'For the rest of the week: use your eyes, and try not to get in the way. Coming Monday I want a report about what you have seen. We'll meet here at ten.' Antonio got up from his chair to leave the room, but turned around just before he passed the door and stuck out his hand. 'Welcome,' he said. They shook hands, and that was it.

When they entered the workshop, a woman in a wheelchair approached them. 'Hi, Antonio! I brought us some cookies to have with our coffee.' She spoke with agitation, showing some red marks in her neck. She seemed quite nervous.

'You make my day, sweetheart,' Antonio responded affectionately, which made Jonathan wonder about his first impression of the man. 'But there is work to do today. Can you finish that bowl you have been working on? It looks good, and we should get it done so that it can be baked at the end of the day.'

'You think so?' Happy with his compliment, the woman turned around her wheelchair, and went to a cupboard where unfinished pottery seemed to be stored.

'Wait a minute, wait a minute,' Antonio said, 'there is someone new that I want to introduce you to.' He winked to Jonathan to come over.

'This is …'

'Jonathan, Sir, my name is Jonathan.'

Antonio pretended not to have heard the address. 'This is Sofia,' he said and turned to the woman. 'I will leave him with you, don't fall in love with him.' He grinned and went to his office. The woman blushed. 'Don't be silly.'

'Hi,' she said turning to the newcomer. 'I like your name.'

'Thank you.'

'I hope you will like it here. I do.'

'I hope so too. May I know your name?'

'Oh … of course, I am Sofia Recuenco.'

'I am pleased to meet you, Sofia.'

She blushed and smiled. Then, after a moment of silence, she asked, 'Do you know pottery?'

'No, I haven't had the experience so far.'

'It doesn't matter. Antonio will teach you. He taught me a lot. He is a good teacher. But you shouldn't call him 'Sir'. He doesn't like that. And don't call him "Tonio", he doesn't like that either.'

'I will try to remember.' He looked into her face, and noticed she had sad eyes. There seemed to be a lot of pain hidden behind her smile.

'I will go to work now. You can come and watch if you want. I will show you how it's done.'

'Maybe I should.'

In the meantime three other people had entered the workshop. Two of them who came in together were holding hands, which looked a bit strange. Later that day he was to find out that the smaller of the two, Joaquin, was blind. He was of a relatively short, slender appearance, much shorter at any rate than his companion, a big guy by the name of Fernando. Fernando had a flat face, as if somebody had tried to push his nose into his head. He had friendly, albeit somewhat dull eyes. His mouth seemed to be chewing constantly, with his large tongue sticking out, as if it didn't fit in properly. Antonio welcomed them. Fernando remained silent; Joaquin greeted him. Number three was Alfredo. He had a hunchback, and could only with difficulty raise his head to see what was in front of him.

'Good morning, Alfredo!' said Antonio coming back from his office.

'Good morning, Antonio.'

'Ready for a day's work?'

'Yes I am.'

'First we have a coffee, sit down, sit down,' Antonio responded while making an effort to assist Alfredo. 'Let me pull down the back of your chair a bit, so that you can look this young fellow here in the face.' Sitting down the man appeared in a much more comfortable position. 'His name is Jonathan, he is coming to assist us for a few weeks.'

'Hi, Jonathan.'

'I am pleased to meet you,' Jonathan made it sound much more formal than he had intended.

'A well-behaved young man, as you can see,' Antonio commented with a touch of irony in his voice. 'We can use that here!'

'If you mean yourself, I agree,' Alfredo retorted.

'Thank you for the compliment.' Antonio laughed. 'Come on people, let's have a coffee before we start working.' The two men sat down besides Alfredo. Sofia hurried to pull up her wheelchair and place herself beside Jonathan. Antonio saw it and blinked.

After a few minutes the door of the workshop opened again and another young man came in. As he approached the table, Jonathan noticed that he was probably older than he looked at first sight.

'Pascal, you're late,' Antonio greeted him, not unfriendly.

'Yes, I know. I had to run an errand for Ramón. He needed paper for his old typewriter.'

'Is he still using that machine?'

'Yes, he is.'

'People hate change, what can you say.' Antonio was a man of outspoken opinion. 'Talk about change, this here is your new colleague, Jonathan. Jonathan, this is Pascal, the master potter of this workshop. He knows everything there is to learn in this trade.'

'I don't know about master potter,' the boy responded, 'but I will be happy to tell you about what we do here.'

'Do here? We make art, young man, didn't I teach you that?' Antonio said. Then he pulled up another chair, and poured Pascal a cup of coffee.

4.

The Princess of Light

Half an hour later, when Jonathan sat beside Sofia to watch her work on her bowl that needed finishing, the door of the workshop was opened again. Two more people came in. The first was a young woman, almost a girl, whose walk was like a flittering bird. Her feet seemed to barely touch the ground.

An elderly woman followed behind her. 'Can I have your coat, dear,' the lady spoke, 'so that I can hang it away, and put on your apron?' The young woman began to unzip her coat, but she got stuck with her zipper. 'Here, let me do that for you,' the woman said and took off the coat.

When her younger companion saw Antonio, she turned around and flittered his way. 'This is Lucie,' he said to Jonathan stretching out his arms. 'This is our Lucia, the princess of light.' He bowed his head and spoke graciously as if announcing royalty.

Jonathan watched her intently. What a curious person, he thought. To disprove Antonio's description of the 'princess of light', Lucie responded with a gloomy face. She doesn't really look at us, Jonathan noticed.

'Your highness is in the right mood today, I hope,' Antonio jested, 'to devote her precious time to art?'

Jonathan felt immediately intrigued by this person. Thus far she had not spoken a word. She went round the workshop very briefly touching a table here and there, when all of a sudden the older woman hurried in her direction.

'No, Lucie, don't! Leave it there! Don't drop it!' But she was too late. Quick as lightning Lucie had turned to the table with the empty coffee mugs, where she took one and dropped it on the granite floor. It broke into pieces.

'Your highness is in the mood of breaking rather than making art?' Antonio said with a pleasant sense of humour. Probably not a bad thing to have here, Jonathan thought. The artist's wit seemed to feed on irony and sarcasm, for he had hardly spoken a serious word since they had met.

Lucie was led to a chair and sat down without a sound. 'She doesn't speak,' Sofia informed him, 'and she is difficult to handle. I hate it when she smashes things. She once broke a vase that I made. It was done on purpose. I hated her.' Jonathan nodded that he understood, but made no comment. What a strange idea to have a person like Lucie in a workshop like this!

'How do you think this bowl is coming out?' Sofia wanted to know, eager to get his attention back. 'Do you think it's finished?'

'You should know, since you're the potter here.'

'I will go and ask Antonio whether it's finished,' Sofia responded. Since Lucie's entrance her mood had clearly changed. She seemed nervous, almost scared. Pulling her wheelchair out, she turned around leaving her bowl on her desk. 'Please, watch it. I do not want her to smash this one also.'

'I will.'

He watched Sofia wheel over to Antonio who was busy inspecting a couple of jars that were shelved in the corner of the workshop. He could now see that she was clearly overweight; probably because of insufficient physical exercise. More than before her face and neck seemed reddened. Asking Antonio's opinion was apparently not to be taken lightly, but perhaps Sofia was a young woman who always had a reason for anxiety.

After sharing a cup of coffee with Lucie, the woman who had accompanied her left. Wondering what would happen next, Jonathan took his time to observe her. He noticed that she picked a scrap of paper from the floor, put it in her mouth and took it out again. She used her saliva to shape it into a little ball, the size of a small marble. She laid it in the palm of her hand and then moved her hand in small circles to make it roll. This she kept doing for a few minutes. When she finally got up – her empty coffee mug still on the table in front of her – she came his way. Aware of his assignment he moved his chair in the direction of Sofia's bowl in order not to be taken by surprise.

Standing right in front of him Lucie did not look at him, nor did she show any interest in the bowl. Instead her gaze was fixed upon something in his clothes. She bent over, her face much too close to his, and pulled the cord that came out of the hood of his sweater. Then he noticed what kept her eyes fixed: the cord had a bead at its end.

'Is it the bead that you want?' he asked. Instead of paying attention to him, she pulled the cord to see if the bead would come off. 'That won't go Lucie, unless you want to break the cord.' It appeared that was the plan. She put the bead in her mouth and tried to cut the cord with her teeth. 'Ho, ho,' he protested, but without sufficient resolve, his voice sounding more surprised than firm.

'Lucie! Stop that immediately!' From a distance Antonio had followed what happened and now was with a few quick steps behind her to grasp her hand. 'Leave it, you don't ruin people's clothes.' His grasp was firm and squeezed the blood out of Lucie's knuckles. She let go. Then she uttered a deep sigh, and Jonathan saw the tension in her upper body relax.

'Good girl,' Antonio said.

'Pascal!' The young man, who was wedging a loaf of clay, responded immediately by calling her: 'Lucie, come over here.' She went over. 'Take a chair and see if you can help me with wedging this loaf of clay.'

'You need to be very direct and firm with Lucie,' Antonio said with a soft voice, 'otherwise she will make a mess out of you any time she wants something from you. If you don't, you will learn that the hard way.'

'I think I just did.'

'Wait till she really gets frustrated, then you will see something else. Lucie's biggest problem is her absolute lack of patience. When the good Lord was passing out the virtue of patience to his creatures, she was last in line. That's how my mother – God bless her soul – would have put it. In this respect Lucie is just like a newborn infant. Anything she wants, she wants right here and now. If you don't pay attention, anything she can lay her hands on might end up in pieces instantaneously.'

'Like the coffee mug.'

'Yes. For Lucie coffee mugs mean coffee, and when she finds one empty, she throws it away, like trash. It's her way of communicating that she wants coffee, which, if we would let her, she would have all day. What you saw this morning was a mistake on my part. The rule is: no empty mugs on the table. I simply didn't pay attention.'

'What about using disposable mugs, like the ones you get out of a coffee machine?'

'We have been thinking about it, of course, but we decided not to go that way. Once you start to think in terms of what Lucie can break or ruin, you will find yourself creating all kinds of barriers to stop her. We don't want that. There is nothing wrong with taking precautions, but there is a subtext that I don't like. It says: "Watch out for Lucie!" In no time you will find everybody behaving towards her in order to control her. We want Lucie to be loved. That means she needs guidance, not control. There is a fine line between the two, which you will have to find out.'

'I wondered …' said Jonathan, but Antonio foresaw what was coming and interrupted: 'Whether the pottery is the right place for her to work?'

'Yes.'

'Same story. The underlying question is whether you believe that she will be able to adapt herself to the place. The predictable answer is that she will not. Therefore we prefer to turn the question around and ask ourselves: how can we adapt the place so that Lucie can just be herself.'

'I see.'

'You do? That's hopeful because many days I don't!' Antonio said, displaying his usual love of sarcasm again. 'I cannot number the days I have asked myself that same question.' Then, in a more grave tone, 'Sometimes it's just too hard. Not always, but sometimes it is. At least she has her own apartment, which helps to keep her away from bothering the others too much, when necessary.'

Jonathan had noticed a door at the far end of the pottery that was mostly open, and that seemed to connect it with another space he hadn't figured out yet. He asked Antonio what it was.

'You mean the space behind the door over there?' You haven't seen it? Let me show you.' He turned away towards Pascal to call the girl.

'Lucie, dear, come you have a visitor. Pascal I am going to borrow her from you, so that she may show her apartment to our friend here. Lucie, come. Show Jonathan where your bed is.'

The girl came over, but again, as Jonathan noticed, without any sign that she was responding to something. When she went past Antonio without looking, he grabbed her arm.

'Here, take Jonathan with you. He wants to see your apartment.'

When the young man stuck out his hand, she took it, and slowly moved towards the door.

'Is this all yours?' he asked her, looking around in what appeared like a spacious living room with a couch and a table. 'And a kitchen too, I see.' Then she took his sleeve and moved towards an open slide door, accessing her bedroom.

'Well, you surely must be a princess to have this luxurious place all to yourself!'

'Wait till you see her servants busy tidying her grace's quarters!' Antonio had followed them and stood in the door smiling. Lucie dropped Jonathan's arm to pick up a scrap of paper from the floor, after which she had no attention left for her visitor.

'You're dismissed,' Antonio commented dryly, 'at least for the moment.' His sarcasm could not hide that he had a weaker side too. 'I love that girl,' he continued in a softer voice, 'but I can assure you it will take some exercise to learn how to do that. It doesn't come easy.'

'Is there a family?'

'She came to live with us after her mother died. That was about five years ago when she was fourteen. Her father could not keep her at home because taking care of her had largely been his wife's job. How she managed to do that for so long escapes me, but he could and would not do it. He found a home for her in one of those places they call mental hospitals. He chose it because it was pretty close to where they lived. But after a while he took her from there. The place was entirely geared up to control their patients. At one point she was drugged to keep her quiet, and then she stopped eating. When they finally resolved to tube feed her, her father had enough and took her home. That story has repeated itself till she came to live with us.'

'And you have not sent her away.'

Antonio raised a brow. The young man had a kind of frankness about him that he liked, so he responded without trying to be funny. 'Thus far we have managed and she seems to be doing all right. The father is thrilled, and made significant contributions to realizing the plan for the apartment, for which he is grateful to the present day. He regrets he cannot see Lucie as often as he would like to. He lives in Zaragoza, which is hundreds of miles away.'

He paused for a moment, again measuring up the young man in front of him. Then he continued, 'Anyway, if you happen to be looking for a challenge I can congratulate you,' he said, 'You have found it.'

Without knowing it Antonio had hit upon a nerve. At home challenges always had meant to Jonathan not to disappoint his father. Here was a very different one, something he chose on his own account, and it didn't seem like it would be a piece of cake either.

5.

Dinner

Dinner was not just an occasion to eat, Jonathan had noticed. More than a meal, it was a celebration. Claire did the blessing of the food in which she praised the gifts that Mother Earth had produced for this day. She also included Philippe for picking the vegetables, and Sylvia for preparing the stew.

Listening to Claire's blessing Jonathan was carried away to his parents' house, the place he grew up, with Josh, his younger brother. Before their evening meal started his dad had said grace all right, but Jonathan had never experienced it the way he did here. For all he remembered his father could have read the weather forecast without anybody noticing the difference.

Claire's blessing was something else. 'When we eat, we remember whose gifts we are enjoying, and who prepared them for us.' She made it sound sacramental, like when the minister in Church back home when Jonathan was a small boy had invited them to the meal saying: 'Come to the table, for all things are prepared.' None of these things had ever been spoken about at home, at least not as long as he had been there.

As soon as they had said 'Amen,' there was the noisy exchange of what the day had brought. He picked up from the conversation at the table that Antonio had had a bad afternoon. With Pascal and Alfredo being absent, and Fernando and Joaquin working in the house with Claire, he had been on his own with Sofia, and Lucie. 'Not my strongest team.' Jonathan felt disappointed. Not only was his name left out – there was also no recognition of the fact that he had tried to keep Lucie busy. Whatever gifts there were recognized at the dinner table, the presence of a new assistant was apparently not one of them.

Fortunately there were other stories clamouring for people's attention. The one told by Claire turned out to be particularly entertaining. It was about the woman who had accompanied Lucie to the pottery. Later that morning she had asked Claire if she could see her. Even though it was none of her business, not officially at least, Claire had agreed to see her, mainly because they were from the same part of Andalusia. It turned out that the woman wanted to quit being a volunteer.

'Oh, I am sorry to hear this. Why is that?' Claire had asked her.

'This morning she broke again a coffee mug.'

'How awful. It must be frustrating given how much attention you give her. But you know, it happens to everybody. Antonio told me he forgot to take the coffee mugs from the table. You couldn't help it.' Claire had tried to change her mind by comforting her about the smashed coffee mug.

This had been of no avail, however, for something else had happened that by far exceeded a broken mug. It turned out that after lunchtime the woman had taken Lucie to her home, not more than fifteen minutes down the road from Bethany at the other side of the railway station. She had forgotten her purse and couldn't go shopping without it. Taking Lucie with her for a quick stop at her house to look for her purse, something had happened to really make her snap. Lucie had molested her dog.

'*What* did she do?' Maria asked.

'Molested her dog. That's what she said.'

'But how?'

'I am not sure,' Claire said, 'but it seems that pulling the dog's ears has been part of it!'

'That's what dog ears are for, isn't it?' Antonio commented, but his joke was lost in the general consternation about Lucie's behaviour.

'That's a cruel thing to do!' Sofia said, ready to identify with the dog's feelings, or any other feelings that Lucie Miles might have hurt.

'Was it a small dog with small ears?' Pascal wanted to know.

'Oh, stop it Pascal, you're awful!' Maria responded.

'Huh, am I?'

'It doesn't matter what size the dog was! You know that!'

Antonio's sense of humor was awakened. 'Of course it matters! Big dog ears give a much better pull!' Claire barely succeeded in keeping her face neutral.

'What happened next?' Maria wanted to know.

Claire explained that apparently the dog had been one of those tiny creatures that some people hardly recognize as dogs. 'It seems that Lucie had picked up the dog and then had thrown it to the ground.'

'Like a coffee mug!' Pascal could not help himself saying. Antonio chuckled.

'Boomm!' said Alonso. Whether or not he understood what he had just said, this comment was too much, of course. The entire crowd burst out in exuberant laughter. Even Maria, trying to maintain a straight face, could not help smiling.

Jonathan observed the scene with much amusement. When he looked at Lucie, he noticed that she had no clue that her behaviour was the occasion for all the excitement. What had she actually been doing in the woman's kitchen, he wondered. Would she know the difference between throwing a mug and throwing a little dog on the floor?

'I am sorry I told you this story,' said Claire.

'No, no,' Antonio said, 'I had my doubts about this volunteer lady all along.'

'That's why I shouldn't have told you. We need to treasure them, because we haven't all that many volunteers.'

'We need to treasure them when they know what people need. This lady clearly had no clue about who Lucie is.'

'Didn't she?'

'No. This morning as she came in, she would take off Lucie's coat, put her on a chair, pour her a coffee, as if she was a non-person, incapable of doing anything herself.'

'Is she then?' Claire asked.

'How can you even ask such a question?' Antonio responded, truly indignant.

All this was very revealing to Jonathan. He had kept quiet the whole time, not to invite any comments on his opinion. One thing was crystal clear to him. If his stay here were to be a success, Lucie Miles would be his *pièce de résistance*. Wisely Jonathan did not communicate this idea. Several people in the room would have explained that he could not have been more wrong in picking his target.

6.

The Next Day

'Good morning everyone!' Jonathan intended it to sound relaxed but wasn't sure he succeeded. This would be his first official day in the pottery. Since Antonio had not given him any particular assignment, other than to use his eyes and stay out of the way, he was unsure how to figure out for himself what to do.

'Good morning.' Antonio and Pascal, both of who were standing by the kiln, replied. Of the others only Sofia and Alfredo were present. No Lucie yet, Jonathan noticed. The other two men were absent. Today was their second day of the week working in the house with Claire.

'Jonathan would you be so kind as to make coffee?' Antonio asked. 'Sofia will tell you where you find everything.'

Since he had different aspirations for his own contribution to the workshop, he was not excited by the idea of being the coffee maid, but Sofia saw an opportunity.

'Oh, sure, I am glad to assist you!' she spoke with a red-cheeked smile towards him that was clearly meant to be endearing. 'The coffee machine is in the office, where we also have a drawer that has the mugs, and the coffee and sugar. Cream is in the fridge in the hall. Come let me show you.'

Antonio saw with a twinkle in his eyes that the plan worked. This kid might be very useful, but he needed to learn a few things in order to understand what this place was about. Antonio had seen a number of new assistants coming and going, and had developed an eye for what they were up to. This young American seemed to be the 'I do it my way' type. 'Maybe later you will,' Antonio said to himself, 'but not right now.'

Sofia led Jonathan into the office to prepare the early morning coffee when Alfredo got up from his chair. 'Antonio, do you have a minute?'

'Yes, sure, I will be with you in a second.' He finished the plan with Pascal for the pieces that were to be fired in the kiln that day, and then turned to Alfredo. 'What's up, Sir?'

Alfredo did not mind being addressed in this way. On the contrary, his disfigured body had made him feel undignified, which he made up for by comporting himself in a somewhat formal manner. There were no jackets and ties to be found in the entire community, but Alfredo was the exception. He wore them every day.

'I need to speak to you about my back. It's hurting when I try to sit straight enough to see what I am doing at the wheel.'

'That's awful! I am sorry I haven't noticed. Has this been going on for some time?'

'A few weeks. I haven't had the same trouble in the house, only here in the workshop.'

'You think it's working at the wheel, then?'

'Yes, I do.'

'What can we do about it?'

'I don't know.'

'Would it help if we place the wheel differently?'

'Perhaps.'

'We could lower the wheel, but then you will only be able to see what you're doing from above, which is not what you want as a potter.'

'No,' Alfredo agreed, 'Then I could not see how the shape of what I am making comes out.'

'Right.'

'Let me think of something. I may have an idea.'

'What is it?'

'Well, something I must have seen somewhere. It's a potter's wheel that is set into motion horizontally, like this.' Antonio moved his hand from left to right before Alfredo's face.

'Huh? How can I then use my feet?'

'You don't need to use your feet. It can be made to turn on electricity. It is switched on and off with a big button, like the ones they use for electric doors, so you can handle the speed with your elbow.'

'That's pretty smart.'

'It is pretty smart. You and I are going to re-invent the wheel!' Antonio joked.

Sofia and Jonathan had brought in the coffee. Pascal left his work at the kiln and joined them. 'Who is going to re-invent what?' he wanted to know.

'Antonio and I,' said Alfredo with noticeable pride, 'we are going to make a new type of potter's wheel.'

'What type?'

'It's hard to explain, you will see when it's ready.'

'You're making me curious.'

'I have to talk with Diego, the handyman,' Antonio said, 'he knows how to do this kind of thing. As of today: no wheel-job for you anymore, Alfredo. You must spare your back. All right?' Then, turning to the others, 'What other stories do we have this morning, people? Did everybody sleep well?'

'No news from Lucie?' Jonathan asked. His question brought back the hilarious moment at the dinner table the night before, when Claire told how Lucie had thrown the volunteer's dog on the floor like a coffee mug.

'Nothing so far,' Antonio replied. 'I asked Claire. Someone will be assisting her in the afternoon, but we might have to miss her this morning.'

'I am glad,' Sofia whispered. Everybody pretended not to have heard her comment.

Jonathan saw that his plan to devote his time to Lucie that morning was not going to work, which annoyed him. He anticipated excitement on Sofia's part imagining that she would have him all for herself, and he resolved that this was not going to happen.

'Maybe I can join Alfredo, and learn from him today,' he said cheerfully but not being entirely honest. Sofia's face showed disappointment, as he had anticipated.

'You do that,' said Antonio, which settled the matter. They all went to work while Antonio cleared the empty coffee mugs from the table.

'Alfredo, what is your plan for this morning?' Jonathan asked.

'I have nothing going, since I finished my bowl yesterday. It's going to be baked in the kiln today, I think.'

'No new project?'

'I was thinking about an Andalusian vase, you know, they are about this high,' Alfredo explained, indicating a size of seven or eight inches. 'They are decorated very colourfully, so I first need to make a drawing of how it is going to look.'

'Do you always work from a drawing?'

'Not always, but when you are making something that you don't do too often, it's better to have a clear picture in your head of what you want it to look like. In that case a drawing will help.'

'I would love to learn what an Andalusian vase looks like.' This time Jonathan seemed genuinely interested. Sitting together behind a drawing would allow him to learn a lot about the workshop, which would be good for his report.

'Let's ask Antonio,' Alfredo suggested, 'I think he has books with examples of different pots, and jars, and stuff like that. We will find ideas.'

A few minutes later they were drawing. Antonio had found an old catalogue from an exhibit of Andalusian pottery by a gallery in Seville. 'Bring it back to me as soon as you have found something.' Alfredo had picked a fine specimen in blue, a typical colour for the kind of vase he had in mind. The decorations were elegant geometrical motifs in white.

'How do you know about these vases?' Jonathan wanted to know.

'My family is from Seville. I saw them quite often when I was a boy.'

'How was your childhood? Did you…'

'Did I always have my hump?'

'Yes.'

7.

The Path of Humility

'I was born with a disease that runs through the family from my mother's side,' said Alfredo as he began his first sketch of the vase he had in mind. Jonathan followed his example. Being together at work, the balance of intimacy and distance proved just right for what turned out to be a painful question.

'How did your father react?' Jonathan asked.

'He hated it, saw it as a sign of weakness.'

Jonathan barely managed not to ask himself what his own father's response to such a condition would have been. 'What kind of man was your father?'

'A carpenter from Seville. Broad-shouldered and strong headed who couldn't bear having me for a son; a working class man. As a teenager, I suffered from fatigue because of my trouble standing and sitting straight, so I frequently had to lie down. My father took it as a sign of laziness. "Born a gentleman taking his *siesta*, I suppose?" he would say with biting sarcasm.'

He went on: 'At other times, when he saw me sitting with my head down because of my aching spine, he would yell: "Don't slouch! A man holds his head up!" Then to my mother "That boy of yours will not grow up a man". Afterwards my mother would cry because of being humiliated in this way. "It's not your fault, mother," I would say to comfort her.'

Jonathan saw Alfredo was biting his lip, but couldn't say whether this was because he was concentrating on his drawing. Alfredo's vase came out nicely, an oval body narrowing at its neck to widen again towards the rim. 'You must have done this before,' Jonathan said with admiration in his voice.

'Yes, Antonio taught me how to sketch from a picture.'

They concentrated on their work for a while. Then Jonathan asked: 'Was there anyone in your home to comfort you?'

'I don't think anyone ever did. My family on mother's side were farmers; women running the household, busy as bees, men working in the fields, strong as oxen. To them I was simply Alfredo with the hump who was trouble for his parents. Nobody ever asked me what it was to be in that deformed body of mine.'

'Did you go to school?'

'For a year or two, yes. But school was even worse than home.' His schoolmates had been cruel, Alfredo explained. 'No one called me Alfredo, my nickname was Quasimodo, as in the famous story by Victor Hugo that was made into a movie.'

'How did they know that?'

'Somebody must have told them, perhaps one of the teachers. Or someone had seen the movie.'

'Did the schoolteachers not tell them to leave you alone?'

'Not really. When my classmates forced me to join them in boys' games, like running, they knew I could not do it because it caused me a lot of pain when I tried, but no teacher told them to stop.'

'How was your own teacher?'

'She was the devil.'

'She?'

'A nun. We had nuns the first three years. Her name was Mother Philomena. She had her special ways of making me miserable before my classmates. 'Alfredo, how many lamps are hanging from the ceiling?' she would ask. It was probably meant as an exercise, both physical and intellectual at the same time. On every occasion she would make me feel that I was less than the other boys.'

'How?'

'There were small tasks that would allow you to leave the classroom for a few minutes as a reward. I was never chosen. "No Alfredo," she would say when I volunteered to bring her a glass of water, "you wouldn't be able to carry a glass of water without spilling half of it." Grinning classmates made the rebuke in such remarks all the more painful.'

'Did your mother never take you to see a doctor?'

'For my hump? In her family they had known it for ages. It was taken to be a sign of rejection by God. "Nothing comes from nothing," they would say. My mother believed so herself, even if she had no clue what her offense had been.'

'Did you love her?'

'Oh, yes, very much so. After my father had one of his angry outbursts about me and had taken it out on her, she would say to me: "You are my humiliation." She didn't mean to make me feel bad, but that hurt me more than my back ever did.'

'I can imagine,' said Jonathan softly. 'It must have left a mark.'

'It has. I was going down the path of humility,' Alfredo said, laying down his pencil. He looked at the result with satisfaction in his eyes. Then he turned to Jonathan, 'but I have to tell you that I only discovered this afterwards. At the time I was going through it, I had no clue that life could be different, even for someone like me.'

Vaguely aware that it was not only Alfredo's life he was interested in, Jonathan was not yet done with his questions. 'What changed it?' he wanted to know.

'When I was sixteen, the situation at home became untenable. My father didn't want me as an apprentice so I had to work in the fields also, but I couldn't. "Then we must find a place where they can take care of you," he said. "We can't feed those who do not work." My mother was heartbroken about his cruelty, but she could not stop him since she believed it was her fault to begin with. Then a nephew of my mother came by and suggested asking if I could come here, to this community. She did, and I was invited to come. It took a few years before I began to see what they had done to me.'

'Then you have already been here for some time?'

'Seven years now.'

'That means you're only twenty-three. I thought you were much older. A retired gentleman.'

'I guess that's what humiliation does to a person. It does not make you any younger at any rate; that I can tell. Here I have learned what it is to be accepted as a person in my own right. It is dignifying. That probably explains this,' Alfredo said holding up his tie.

They were quiet for a few minutes and concentrated on their drawing, which Alfredo had managed to work on while he was talking. Jonathan had achieved much less on his paper. He felt tired; tired and very old.

8.

An Unexpected Visitor

'My mother is coming to visit!' Sofia came hurrying into the workshop with a face that was even more agitated than usual. At lunch Claire had informed her of a phone call she had received an hour ago. It had been Sofia's mother telling her that she would drop in from Seville this afternoon.

'I am very glad for you,' Antonio said with a frown, 'When is she coming?'

'Around three o'clock.'

'Is it in our book?'

'No,' Sofia replied with a gracious smile, knowing that Antonio wasn't too keen of these kinds of surprises of her mother's. 'But I have finished my bowl already,' pretending that she assumed this to be his main concern.

'Oh, that's all right.' He made no further comments.

'I need to go to the bathroom,' Sofia announced and turned around her wheelchair. 'You do that,' Antonio responded.

When she had left his office he went to inform Jonathan who had been watching the scene. 'She gets all agitated and nervous about her mother visiting, especially when it's one of her spontaneous raids.'

'How come?'

'Because of the kind of woman her mother is.'

'What is she like, then?'

'I never met anyone so beholden to herself as that woman; entirely obsessed with having things her way. Every other day she is on the phone with Claire to complain about this, that or the other. She thinks she is always right about everything, which drives everybody crazy. Her air is pretentious, with manners as if she were from a noble family, Mrs Recuenco, whereas in truth she is a bus driver's daughter from Sants, which is one of the poorer districts of Barcelona. Of course, her demeanour has affected Sofia. The mother is everything the daughter is not.'

'Like what?'

'Sofia is not pretentious to begin with.'

'What else?'

'I hate to admit,' Antonio said with irritation in his voice, 'but she is a beautiful woman. You will see for yourself when she walks in this afternoon. Tall, a classy appearance, and a lovely face. It's hard not to be taken in by her.'

Jonathan could not help thinking why you would hate to admit that a woman is beautiful. He was about to ask Antonio whether Sofia's mother had taken him in too, but then decided it would be better to keep quiet. He wondered what had passed between them. There was no sign of his habitual sarcasm or irony in the artist's voice, only anger.

'How does she affect her daughter?'

'She kills her with love.'

Jonathan raised his eyebrows.

'You didn't know people could do that? Suffocating affection, that's what it is. She is constantly worried about Sofia. One minute she tells you how special her daughter is, the next she will break down sobbing because her daughter's life is so difficult, and then she is all kisses and hugs over the poor girl. The woman is a narcissist, begging for attention in everything she does. In the meantime there is hardly any space for Sofia for not having to try to be her mother's daughter.'

As he spoke, Antonio watched Sofia rolling her wheelchair in again. She was all excitement and anxiety. 'Are my clothes okay?' she wanted to know. Her mother hated stains on her dress. 'Is there any dirt on my wheelchair?'

'No, Sofia, you look fine.'

Jonathan was curious to see what Mrs Recuenco would be like, but he volunteered to work with Lucie who came to the workshop after lunch. An unexpected visitor meant a lot of diversion from what otherwise might have been a quiet afternoon.

'Look closely after Lucie,' Antonio said to him. 'Lucie does not like unexpected visits from anyone, and what is more, Mrs Recuenco hates Lucie.'

The incident when Lucie had smashed a piece of her daughter's pottery had led to a furious reaction with the result that her relations with the workshop had cooled down for a while. 'That horrible place,' she had called it, complaining about the incident in a meeting with Claire, 'one cannot even be sure that one's child is safe there.'

That was one thing shared by both mother and daughter, then, Jonathan thought. Perhaps expressing her dislike of Lucie was part of Sofia's devotion to her mother. His plan was to see whether he could make Lucie ignore the visitor altogether, which under normal circumstances should not be too difficult. He only had to figure out a way for her to be absorbed by her little paper balls, rolling them in the palm of her hand. To that end he chose a table in the far corner, away from the entrance, and placed Lucie with her back to the door.

A few minutes later there were agitated footsteps in the hall that announced the entry of Sofia's mother. Jonathan had just succeeded in getting Lucie's attention for the scraps of paper that he had deliberately dropped on the floor. Determined not to pay attention to the woman in order not to get Lucie distracted, he could not help himself from turning his head to get a glimpse of her. She was indeed a ravishing beauty. Coloured pins pulled up her long blonde hair in a way that must have taken her a long time to achieve. Her dress was simple but very elegant. Her make-up was meticulous. The one thing Jonathan didn't like were her brows, painted black, in a way he thought was too dark for her fair complexion. He turned his back to hide that he had been looking at her, but Mrs

Recuenco was not the kind of woman to be oblivious to the fact that her entrance was noticed.

'Hello everybody!' she said with a radiant smile. 'I am so glad to drop by, since I was in the neighbourhood. I know you hate unexpected visitors, Antonio, but I could not resist seeing my darling. And seeing you of course! Do I see a new face? Who is that young man?' She was about to come over, when Antonio, quite rudely, pointed his finger in the direction of her daughter Sofia who had been ready to receive her mother's embrace.

'Oh, of course. That can wait. Hi, my sweet angel, how are you? Is mama's baby doing well?' Bowing down she gave Sofia her cheek, but didn't kiss her. Then she turned away from her daughter to greet Pascal. More timid than Jonathan had seen him before, Pascal stood near the kiln, and muttered something that sounded like a greeting.

'He is going to bake the bowl that I just finished, mother.' Her daughter spoke softly with a tear in her eyes.

'Is he now? He is so accomplished, our Pascal, I bet Antonio would not know what to do without him.' Just in time to prevent Sofia from starting to cry, she turned to her. 'Mama is very proud of you, girl.' It was said in such a condescending way that it made Jonathan shudder. Her daughter took it as a great compliment, and seemed very happy. 'If you have given up expecting more, you will end up being satisfied with very little,' Jonathan thought to himself. Filling the workshop with her overwhelming charm, Mrs Recuenco was not a pleasant woman.

Antonio asked Pascal to make some coffee for their guest, but she managed to turn this to her own advantage too. 'Oh, no, please don't bother. You don't want to treat me as a guest, do you dear? After all this is just a quick stop to say hello.' The artist gave the boy a sign to leave the coffee. Turning back to Mrs Recuenco, he offered her a chair without saying anything.

Apparently Antonio was determined to step in for Sofia, and balance the scales of justice between daughter and mother. As affectionate as he was to the one, so rude he was to the other. Once again Jonathan could not help wondering what had happened between them.

As she sat down, asking Antonio about how her daughter was doing, Sofia moved her wheelchair to be at her side.

'What about asking her?' Antonio responded.

'You know she is always so anxious to see me that I hardly get a word out of her.' From the little he had seen of her Jonathan knew that Sofia's face was dropping from being spoken to in this belittling manner. But her mother was not done yet. Without directing herself to anyone in particular, she said, 'Oh, how much my late husband and I have hoped she would be able to walk again some day, when her legs would be strong enough.'

Antonio shrugged his shoulders. 'Well Sofia, how does that make you feel?' he said, refusing talk about the girl in her presence as if she wasn't there.

'I would have been so happy,' she said in her usual nervous tone, 'and it would make mama very happy too.' Her high-pitched giggle sounded like she was laughing at a joke from the devil. Clearly, the poor girl anticipated her next failure to make her mother proud of her.

They chatted a few moments till Mrs Recuenco decided that enough time had been spent on her daughter's wellbeing. She got up and turned to Jonathan, who was working hard to keep Lucie focused on her ritual. That was about to end now.

'I think we have not met before?' She approached him with a beautiful smile.

'No, ma'am, we haven't. I am Jonathan.'

'My name is Carina.'

'Pleased to meet you, ma'am.' He shook hands with her, noticing the grin on Antonio's face behind her back when he kept their introduction as formal as he could.

In the meantime Lucie had got up and was no longer focused on her little paper balls. She turned towards Mrs Recuenco and had her eyes fixed on the woman's dress. Remembering her attack on his hooded sweater, Jonathan saw a disaster in the making. He noticed that the dress had red wooden beads as buttons, separated by about an inch from each other.

He made a step forward to place himself between the girl and the woman. 'Come this way, Lucie,' he said, but Lucie had noticed the beads already. Not foreseeing what was coming Mrs Recuenco took offense at his move. 'You will allow me to greet Lucie, won't you, Jonathan,' she said in her sweetest voice, stinging like a needle, and stepped aside so that her dress came fully within Lucie's reach. The girl stretched her hand, and held a couple of beads in her tight fist, and with a firm pull the dress was torn apart.

'Oooh, you…!' Before anyone knew what was happening, Mrs Recuenco's eyes flashed with rage and she raised her hand, but this time Jonathan was alert. 'No, Mrs Recuenco,' he said very firmly. With a resolute look in his eyes Jonathan had grasped her hand to protect the girl. Surprised at his own strength he held it till she gave way. Sofia was very much alarmed when she saw what happened. Her mother sank down on a chair, holding her torn dress together, and cried. 'How awful, my dress … completely ruined! Are you at all competent to control this girl?'

All this time Antonio had been silent, but now he stepped forward. 'I am sorry, Mrs Recuenco. This man tried to protect you, but you would not pay attention. You have no one to blame but yourself.'

'Oh shut up you boorish man, you will never fail to accuse me!' she yelled at him, losing her temper completely. Watching the complete collapse of her mother's charm Sofia started crying. She felt that her mother's disgrace would somehow reflect upon her, and that Jonathan would dislike her because of her mother.

Antonio did not respond to her outburst, and said: 'I think you had better go now. I should have been wiser and not allowed this kind of surprise visit. I am sorry for your daughter, Mrs Recuenco, but no more unexpected appearances in the pottery.'

9.

Buddies

Fernando and Joaquin entered the workshop together, hand in hand as Jonathan had noticed before. He realized that so far he had not paid much attention to them. When he saw them coming in, something came into his mind that he had not noticed the first day. What was this blind young man doing in a pottery? Since he had seen Joaquin working with a loaf of clay, he conjectured he must be the craftsman of the two. Fernando's role appeared to be quite limited. 'He leads his friend like a guide dog is leading his master,' Jonathan thought, the point of the comparison not being that Fernando was the dog, but that his role was to guide Joaquin to where he needed to be.

His conjecture proved to be right. Joaquin was indeed a blind potter. Jonathan wondered how that could be. How could he make something he could not see, and still be in control of its shape?

'Who said you need your eyes to be in control of a shape?' Antonio said when he asked him.

'What else is there?'

'What about your hands? I have to admit I didn't know this either until I tried to let Joaquin work at the wheel. He does with his fingers what you and I do with our eyes.'

'How does that work?'

'What do I know? I am not a psychologist.'

When he watched Joaquin working at the potter's wheel, Jonathan saw what Antonio meant. Turning his wheel, Joaquin drew a perfect round shape with his hands out of the chunk of clay he was working with. He wetted his fingers to keep it soft and smooth, and kept the wheel turning with his foot. Fernando was sitting beside him. Once again Jonathan noticed his large tongue moving back and forth in and out his mouth as if it was trying to find space to get in. Somehow Fernando did not look like he was made for the art of pottery. His eyes were fixed on Joaquin's hands, but they didn't seem to notice anything in particular.

'I could use a bit more of that clay, Fernando.' Joaquin spoke softly as if not to disturb his friend in his daydream, and held his hand out. Fernando responded by giving him what he asked for. His big hands took a piece of clay from the loaf that he had in a bucket in front of him, and put it in Joaquin's hand.

'Another non-speaker,' Jonathan said to himself. When he checked with Antonio, he turned out to be right again. 'Not a single word. No one has ever heard a sound from his mouth, as far as I know. Lucie can get mad sometimes, and she might scream like you're standing next to an airplane with its engine running. But not Fernando, he is as silent as a lamb.' Jonathan noticed the odd mix of metaphors in this description. Looking at Fernando one hardly got the impression of a lamb.

'He has never as much as hurt a fly in his life,' Antonio said looking at the man. 'He is peace on earth incarnate, a man of good will, if there ever was one. Just the right kind of man for a friend whose life has been far from peaceful.'

Then he told Jonathan the story of Joaquin Morales. His mother had been infected with rubella during her pregnancy. As a toddler he was found to be blind because of his mother's previous infection. Feeling guilty, his mother, who was single, desperately wanted to find a husband. She wanted to be able to afford a special school for her son to be educated. When she believed she had found the man she thought she was looking for, he turned out to be a brutally violent monster. Joaquin never spoke of his past, but what was known about it was enough to suggest it must have been horrifying. 'A blind boy can't see, can he?' his stepfather used to say whenever he beat his mother up in front of her son.

When his mother had had enough, she took her son and left, but she had no means of subsistence. Roaming the slums of Seville, they barely managed to survive. The following winter his mother fell ill with pneumonia. Without timely access to medical care her fate was sealed. She died that same winter at the age of only thirty-five. It was for Joaquin the worst period in his young life. As a homeless child, he was taken in by one of the older religious orders that remained in the city, and after a while they contacted the House of Bethany to see whether they had a place for him to live. They accepted the boy. His mother's attempt to get him an education would not be in vain after all, even though it might not have come about in the way she had hoped for.

'Another story of a mother and her unfortunate son,' Jonathan said to himself. From what he had heard so far, fathers turned out to be unstable figures. Since Joaquin's stepfather had disappeared, there had been no other man in his life. The task of male bonding had remained completely unknown territory. Perhaps this was why the appearance of Fernando was such a big deal. They met in the pottery. Without having an idea what to do with the blind boy, Antonio placed him at Fernando's table. He connected with the big man, although no one exactly knew how. From the very first day, Fernando accompanied him to the dining hall for lunch.

'How did Fernando come to live in the community?' Jonathan wanted to know.

'One day a farmer knocked on the door. He pointed to the boy he had with him and said: "Too dumb for anything". That was all. Andalusian farmers don't waste words on things that cannot be changed, I guess,' Antonio said. 'The son came to live with us, and we never saw the father again.'

'Does this mean you know nothing about Fernando's story?'

'Nothing whatsoever.'

Jonathan thought how awkward it must be not to know anything of the young man's background even though he was living with them in the same house. 'Not only awkward, but sad, 'Antonio responded when Jonathan said so. 'For each of our members to know their story is to know what to pay attention to.'

'Is Fernando…?' Jonathan hesitated.

'As dumb as his father said he was?'

'Yes.'

'With regard to formal education his father proved to be right. We haven't been able to teach Fernando very much, but that doesn't matter too much here. What matters is his character. For Joaquin he is as reliable as a German shepherd. They have been buddies since Joaquin came to Bethany, which must have been about two years now.'

From what Antonio told him Jonathan guessed that Joaquin was five years youger than he was. Was what had made him run from San Francisco really so unbearable that he had to leave? When he was a boy *his* father had taken him to school every day.

'What horrible experiences these guys have been through.'

'Yes, they have. But now they are inseparable. As a matter of fact it took a violent incident to make that happen. Going for a walk one day into the fields behind the house they were stopped by a drunken man on the dirt road leading to the olive groves. We knew that man; he was from Benacazón. He was making fun of Joaquin and laid his hand upon his arm so as to have a laugh with him. Fernando did not make a sound, but just took the man's hand in his fist and squeezed it till the man almost fainted. When he finally let go of that fist, he put Joaquin's hand on his own arm, and walked on.'

'Since that day they have been together. Joaquin feels secure in a way he has probably never felt since his stepfather's violence. As for Fernando, it is hard to tell what he feels, since he communicates very little. There is something so down to earth about that man that it almost makes me envy him.'

Jonathan raised his brows, but said nothing.

'I mean the peace he seems to carry within him. Think about it. One day you receive a hand from a boy who apparently needs you, and you take it. That is how it has been ever since, every single day.'

10.

Sons and Their Mothers

The first three days in the pottery had passed, and Jonathan spent the following Saturday in the House of Bethany in Benacazón. Anticipating what to do, he considered taking the bus to Seville for a late August night in the city, perhaps to listen to some music. But then he decided not to. There was too much to think about that made him feel like wanting to be on his own.

His mother's birthday would be the following week, which would be the first occasion to let them know that he had moved from the city and found a job. While in Seville he had only once made a quick phone call, telling them that he was doing all right. That was now about two weeks ago. The response he received was as expected. His mother was sick to death about his sudden leave, his father was angry. Jonathan had fumbled a few sentences together to explain but it had been of no use.

Considering what he had experienced the last three days, it struck him that the difference with their life in California could not have been greater. He was a rich kid from San Francisco, facing the future of an abundant life. The people here hardly had a life at all before they came to this place. While he was immersed in these thoughts he arrived at a conclusion. He would send his mother a gift for her birthday; that was the least he could do. For the time being he was content with the fact that he had found himself a job. Bridging the gap with his former life was a task that could wait till later. The main part of it would be the reconciliation with his dad, which was not something to look forward to.

Going back to the stories he had heard, he reflected how they were about abusive fathers, be it in very different ways. But he saw that the real question in these stories concerned the place of mothers. The one had delivered her son into the hands of a child molester; the other had been too weak to oppose an abusive father because she believed to be guilty of her son's condition. Inadvertently Jonathan was drawn to think about his own mother. What had her role been in their family? How had it been different?

The question brought back memories from home. Jonathan began to wonder why he had had to run. What had there been to be afraid of? He had never been dumped, let alone been abused. He realized that a decisive moment had taken place when something changed in his relationship with his mother. There was a time she had been his safe haven, the one he could always turn to. The intimate conversations between them were his sanctuary, a space where his father was denied access. She was gentle and kind, and always made him feel that she understood his worries; worries about losing friends, about girls, about failing to perform well in school, or living up to his father's expectations. Without being aware of it, he had regarded his mother as a companion to endure the one tower of strength in their lives, named 'dad'. But this had all changed when one day he attempted to stand up to his father.

The occasion had been a conversation about the company. 'My job is to sell to our customers what they want to hear our company is doing,' Jonathan's father said with a grin on his face.

'What do our customers want to hear then, dear?' his mother asked somewhat naively.

'That their health is our top priority, and that we will go the extra mile to make sure they get value for money. Pay your insurance premium, and we will make sure you get the best possible treatment in case you or one of your loved ones gets sick. That's the message.'

'That's what health insurers ought to be doing, isn't it dear? You always said so,' she said, knowing he would be pleased to find his views supported. Looking back at this conversation Jonathan realized his mother hardly ever spoke her own mind about anything, not just because of her gentleness. It was because she was afraid of her husband.

'You're absolutely right, dear,' her husband said while he put his napkin beside his plate, indicating that the conversation was over as far as he was concerned.

'We had a discussion about our healthcare system in our social studies class.' Jonathan said it timidly, being aware that he was approaching dangerous territory.

His father looked annoyed, but seeing his wife's encouraging face looking at their son, he turned around feigning interest in his remark: 'What did you learn?'

'We watched a video-taped TV show about how healthcare insurance companies operate, making American healthcare much more expensive than it need be.' A deep frown appeared on his father's face. Jonathan continued: 'They try to find fault with their customers as soon as they get sick and need their healthcare bills paid for. Issues in their medical history that are not reported the right way are used to block their treatment. Small print in their contracts is used against them. Then they are dumped.'

'Health reform propaganda,' his father retorted in a dismissive tone.

'Mr Milner our social studies teacher said their top priority is profit for their shareholders, not their customers' health.' Jonathan was well aware that he was crossing a line.

'Mr Milner must be an expert on the subject.' His father's voice was loaded with disgust. 'Let me tell you this, son. If there were no people to invest their money in healthcare, there would be no insurance to begin with,' he said. 'Besides, people who buy health insurance should not sign contracts they don't understand.'

Then Jonathan's mother turned to her son. 'It cannot be that bad, dear,' she wanted it to sound reassuring, which was how she had always tried to keep them happy, reassuring that all would be well somehow, or someday. 'Don't you think it would be all over the news if it were true that healthcare insurers were abandoning their clients?'

With a big smile his father sensed victory. 'Exactly,' he said joining his wife, 'that is why health insurance companies are troubling themselves to inform their customers correctly and ask for their opinion about the services to have received.'

'But why do they teach this very different story then?' Her question was put in a way that even Jonathan was surprised. 'When it turns out that customers have been dumped, our company will correct the mistake, doesn't it dear?'

'Well, if there is a mistake. But most of the time our first job is to explain things correctly,' her husband attempted.

'Correctly meaning to tell the facts in such way that it doesn't hurt the company's interest, I guess?' Jonathan could not believe he had said this in front of his father, but he had. His father was quiet, but his face turned pale. Then Mr Harrison barked at his son,

'What do you think? It's a for-profit business remember? It does not only pay for your school, but also for the nice things we have here at home.' Looking alarmed by what she feared was about to happen, his wife tried to mitigate her son's question, and said: 'But surely the company does not dump people because it is in our interest, does it, dear?'

Mr Harrison was too deeply offended to cool down. Not because of what his son had suggested, but simply because he had dared to openly oppose his father. Now that his wife was seeming to take sides, he was furious.

'You're damn right it does! And if I were you I would not be too particular about how my husband's company makes its money because I would hate to see my luxurious life fall apart.'

Jonathan's mother fell silent. She could not believe what she just had heard. Being raised a Southern Baptist woman she would never have expected her husband to openly invite her to corrupt the integrity of her morals. 'Come finish your dinner,' she said to Jonathan.

He had never found out what happened that night, but the next day his mother was as sweet as cherry pie. She treated her husband in a way as if nothing had happened the evening before.

'Another coffee, my dear?' she asked him with a lovely smile the next morning at breakfast. That day Jonathan realized for the first time that his mother had admitted defeat, and that he would be opposing the tower of strength on his own.

11.

Jonathan's Report

The report Jonathan had to prepare for Antonio was weighing heavy on his mind. It was not so much the work that it would take. He had been given to understand that an oral account of what he had observed during his first three days would do. It did not have to be in writing. His main concern was that his impressions of the pottery were mixed up with feelings about his own history. He was aware of that. The question that kept him busy was how to go about dealing with this. Antonio would want to have his views about the people working in the pottery, but he might also want to know how Jonathan saw himself relating to his new colleagues.

When they met on Monday morning Antonio fired a question at him right away. 'Jonathan, tell me, do people back home know you're here?' Though he didn't refer to his parents directly, Jonathan knew who he meant.

'No, they don't. I called them when I stayed in Seville. This coming Wednesday is my mother's birthday; then I was going to call again to tell them I am in Benacazón. Not that this village would mean anything to them. They have never been to Spain.' He wanted it to sound indifferent, but the last remark made it sound silly.

'Why did you leave home?' Antonio wanted to know.

Jonathan was about to say that it was none of his business, but he saw that this was not an option. He kept his response as formal as possible. 'I finished college this spring, and I wanted to see Europe before going to work in my father's company.'

Antonio gave him one of his piercing looks but didn't say anything. He clearly understood that there was more to it than this. Being silent for a moment, he cleared his throat and then asked, 'What observations did you make in the pottery, last week?'

'I will start with Alfredo.'

Antonio nodded by way of approving.

'He seemed a very balanced person. He told me his story and it was quite painful, but the way he told it made clear to me that it's the story of his past. He found his dignity as a human person, that's how he put it. I noticed that you treat him in that way.'

'What way?'

'To pay him the respect he deserves by asking him for his opinion about things.'

'Go on.'

'Joaquin I find much harder to figure out.'

'To figure him out? What's that supposed to mean?' Clearly Antonio didn't like the expression.

'There is a kind of serenity hanging around him. I don't know whether that's the right word. I mean, he appears self-enclosed, as if he does not want you to approach him.'

'As far as I have noticed you didn't speak to him at all.'

'That's true. I wanted to, but somehow it felt inappropriate. I don't know why. Perhaps it is the way he is shielded.'

'Shielded?'

'The way Fernando is always near to him feels like being protective. As if he is saying, "Before you approach him, you have to go past me."'

Antonio nodded. 'That's an interesting way of putting it. We will need to look into this. Even though he is doing fine, I am sure he can do much more. The man has a lot of potential.' Taking this as encouragement Jonathan felt a little bit more secure.

'Go on.'

'Then there's Sofia. The way you explained her situation made it clear to me that she is a delicate person to work with. She has a habit of seeking security by making herself dependent upon other people's opinion of her, I guess.'

'Hmmm.'

'What about her mother?' Jonathan ventured to ask.

'What about her?'

'Well she said something to you when you defended me for preventing her from slapping Lucie's face, that sounded quite ... personal.'

'What did she say?'

'That you always found a way to blame her. What did she mean saying that?'

Antonio threw one of his stern looks at him, but then his face relaxed. 'Listen young man, the idea of this conversation is that I am asking you questions, not the other way around.' After a brief pause, 'Perhaps I will tell you at a later stage, but not right now. We want to make Maria happy and keep this interview formal, don't we?'

'Sure,' Jonathan responded, 'but I wasn't aware that it was part of the procedure. I assumed it was between you and me.' This was not quite true, of course, since Maria had explained to him the steps they would go through before a decision about his stay would be made. Was he trying to win Antonio's confidence, and if so, for what?

'Let's move on to Lucie.' Antonio said.

'To enable her to be herself in this place must be a hell of a job. That much I've seen. You made it a point of adjusting the environment to her rather than the other way around.' Jonathan said, but then hesitated to go on.

'Yes. And?'

'I wondered whether in that way you are sufficiently trying to get some activities out of her.' He expected signs of impatience with the view of a novice from Antonio, but he was mistaken. The response came in a neutral voice.

'How would you go about trying?'

'Everything she does seems to be impulse, so the trick seems to be how to develop her impulses into activities.'

'Hmmm,' Antonio made it sound as if he were astonished, but he refrained from making a comment on Jonathan's remarks. 'You know how to use your eyes, young man! Since that was your prime responsibility, it seems we have had a fruitful week.'

Happy with the compliment, Jonathan assumed the interview was done, but he was too quick.

'You didn't mention Pascal. You have not yet figured him out either?' It was said in a scornful tone, as if to make sure Jonathan would be reminded of his place.

'Sorry.'

'Don't be sorry. You haven't spoken much with Pascal, I believe. How come?'

'That's true. Frankly, since he is your right hand, my feeling was it would be better not to seem to be interfering.'

'I see. Well, let's finish here. I appreciate your observations, and your candour. Very much so.'

'Oh, thank you,' Jonathan said with relief.

When he was gone Antonio made a few notes to remember what he wanted to pass on to Maria from this conversation. Biting his pencil he was trying to make up his mind about the young American. 'Very bright, reliable, honest, as far as I can see at least, and a mind of his own. On the other hand, very closed about himself. We will see where this is going, we will see.'

Part II

Beads

12.

The Plan

When Jonathan left Antonio's office, he went to take over Lucie from Pascal, as had been agreed during coffee time earlier that morning. Lucie was wearing jeans, as usual, but had a bright red sweater on. Her hair was short and cut in a straight line, without much concern about how it looked, it seemed. Given her lack of patience, cutting Lucie's hair would probably be one of the more daunting tasks of her personal care.

'Hello, dear! Are we going to fight the bull today?' Jonathan said it with so much charm that Pascal turned around with a smile of surprise. The interview must have gone well. Indeed Jonathan's heart was much lighter. Antonio had been quite positive, he thought, apart from his usual display of irony and sarcasm, and even that could have been much worse.

Lucie did not respond at all, which was habitual, as Jonathan had learned during his first week. She would neither respond to greetings nor to goodbyes. 'It seems you and I are going to spend some time together today,' he said to her. In the corner of his eye he saw Sofia's face grow dark, and decided to cheer her up.

'Another pretty lady in the room this morning!' He said it with a big smile pointing at her colourful dress.

'Thank you, Jonathan,' Sofia giggled. 'When are you going to work with me again?'

'That's up to Antonio, you know. He is the boss.'

'I will ask him about tomorrow, then,' she said confidently.

Jonathan was about to say that he had other plans for tomorrow, but realized just in time that this would be the wrong move.

'You do that, girl,' he responded pleasantly. If the morning with Lucie went well, he would see Antonio and ask him about the rest of the week. Since his idea about Lucie seemed to be well received, Jonathan took Antonio's appreciation for his thought as a license to carry out his plan. He reckoned Antonio would want him to work with her just as he had set his mind on doing.

Jonathan had to admit to being pleasantly surprised about the way he had phrased his main idea. 'Since she seems to be acting from impulse, the task is to find out a way to change impulse into activity. Nicely done,' he said to himself. Antonio had not asked him about his college education, otherwise he would have found out that Jonathan had taken several psychology classes. Not that this would have been to his credit – the artist hated the idea of psychology as a science – but it would have explained the basis for how he had put his main idea.

In congratulating himself the young man took for granted the assumption that nobody had tried his idea before. In this he was too eager to prove himself to the artist. In fact he had told Antonio in so many words that his policy of reversed adjustment might have left Lucie without sufficient challenges. Antonio, however, had deliberately abstained from any comment. He was convinced that just maintaining herself in the social world entailed all the challenges that a person like Lucie needed. If this rookie thought otherwise, let him try his luck and see what happened.

Antonio's resolve was to watch closely how things went between them. He had not told Jonathan about his many attempts at doing exactly what Jonathan had suggested. Not because he didn't care, but because of a genuine curiosity. Maybe he would make a connection. The artist in him knew that one person's failure might be another person's success.

At any rate Jonathan felt free to work out his plan. The first thing was to expand his observations of Lucie. He had noticed her ritual with scraps of paper turned into little paper balls, but perhaps there were more of such ritual patterns. Then there was her way of moving. He had already observed a complex pattern. His first impression of a flittering bird was only partially correct. She could also move around in a slow, but steady way, wandering without any specific purpose. Jonathan wondered what to make of that.

There were questions about her mind also. He recalled the exchange between Claire and Antonio about Lucie related to the dog incident. Did the girl have any conception of what she was doing? Was there a difference between smashing a coffee mug, and throwing a tiny dog? Antonio had been truly upset by the question, but was the answer so obvious then?

Asking himself these questions, Jonathan at least understood that they were critical to his undertaking. If Lucie did not see the difference between a coffee mug and a dog, this meant whatever activity he would put before her could not count on her understanding.

'Lucie, let us see what we can do together. Would you mind sitting down here at this table with me?' Jonathan picked the same table they had been sitting at before. It stood in the corner of the workshop, right in front of the window. It seemed like the best place to keep the girl focused. He had found the lid of a container that could be used as a little tray. 'How many paper balls you think would fit into this tray? Let's find out.' On the table was a box with waste paper, which he put before her. 'Here, go ahead, you can make as many balls as you want.' So far, Lucie had never had more than two or three of her tiny paper balls in her hand. Jonathan wondered if she would be interested in making more.

It turned out that she wasn't. She took a scrap of paper out of the box, tore it to pieces, and threw them on the ground. When Jonathan picked up one of the pieces, wet it, and produced one of her little paper balls, she did not even look at it.

'Hmmm,' he said, 'you're not into this, are you?' Without paying attention, as far as he could tell, she got up and placed herself before the window, looking outside.

'So we need to work on your span of attention, then,' he said more to himself than to her. 'Lucie, please come here and sit at the table.' No response. 'Lucie, sit down here please.' He got up to make her notice what he was asking, and led her back to her chair, having no clue what to make of her behaviour. Was she ignoring him, or was she simply oblivious of any notion of an activity at all?

'I want you to make one of your paper balls, then you can go.' When she got up again, he stepped behind her to keep her on her chair. 'No, not yet, first a paper ball.' To get the idea across, he made another paper ball and held it before her. 'Now it's your turn.' She took the scrap of paper he held before her face, put it in her mouth to wet it, and started to roll.

'Very good, Lucie, you can put it in here.' He held the round tray before her. When she put it in, he placed the ones he had made also in the tray. 'The score is two to one. Not a big success, but it's a start. You can go now.' This time Lucie would not get up from her chair, so that Jonathan was a bit lost as to how to read her behaviour.

'This is not going to be easy.' Pascal had followed from a distance what had been going on. 'What is your plan?'

'I had two steps in mind. First to let her make a number of her little paper balls, and then used a sheet of board paper with glue on it, to make them stick. Just to see how she would go about it,' Jonathan said. Explaining it to the boy, however, he heard what an absurdly ambitious plan it was.

'It sounds like a nice idea,' was all that Pascal responded. There was no trace of criticism, or even doubt in his voice, although he probably had more than enough experience in trying to make Lucie perform some kind of activity. Jonathan took it as a sign to continue his experiment. He resolved to set the limit on six paper balls each before lunchtime.

13.

Sofia's Help

Had Antonio known, he would not have been very happy. The attempt to make Lucie part of an activity had not escalated, but it was designed to make her do things that she had no idea of. It would be only a matter of time before it went wrong. The young American made the classic mistake most new assistants made. They mostly acted on the premise that they had to lead rather than follow. Seasoned observers like Claire would have noticed that he was pushing Lucie around according to some preconceived plan of his own. If he persisted it would most likely end in violence. There was no point in trying to direct a person like Lucie, nor any other person for that matter, without learning to listen to what she had to say, even when she didn't say a word. But Jonathan had not yet learned this, and doing what he did he was bound to learn it the hard way.

Fortunately, from his current perspective at least, his boss didn't know what was going on because he was on an errand for the pottery. After a short break Jonathan intended to get Lucie at the table for the next round. But Pascal was not the only one who had been watching them.

'Perhaps I could help out?' Sofia wheeled into the corner where Jonathan and Lucie had been sitting. His first response was to be annoyed, but fortunately he turned to Sofia's face. When he looked into her imploring eyes, his mood changed. 'Why not?' he said to himself, 'I don't want her as an enemy.'

'That is very kind of you, Sofia,' he said, making room for her wheelchair at the table.

'I noticed that you were working with Lucie and that she did not obey you.'

'Obey me?' Jonathan had not perceived himself as giving orders.

'You told her to do things she didn't want to do. That's what I meant.' She spoke softly but there was none of her usual nervousness in her voice. Why not take on her offer and see where this would go?

'Ah, yes, I see you're right, I think I did. Did you also hear what the plan was, when I explained it to Pascal?'

'Only part of it. You want to make something out of these little balls she always makes?'

'Yes, that is the idea.'

'Don't you like it when she makes them and then let them roll in the palm of her hand? I don't like that she puts scraps of paper in her mouth.'

'I think she is more or less obsessed with these things, and I would like to see if that can be changed into something worthwhile,' he answered, ignoring the remark on Sofia's dislike.

'But what if it's only a game she plays?' It was a very sensible question that had not yet crossed Jonathan's mind.

'If it's a game, don't you think it is a silly game? Could we not change it into something meaningful?'

Sofia paused for a moment before she responded. 'I don't know. If it makes her anxiety go away, it may make her happy for a moment. I think people often don't know what makes other people happy.'

'Do you think Lucie is anxious?'

'Don't you? She flutters around like a bird that has her wing broken.'

Surprised at this observation, Jonathan realized he had not thought about Lucie in terms of her brokenness. 'What would her anxiety be about, you think?'

'Perhaps about herself. Perhaps she is anxious to know how to be Lucie.'

Jonathan did not know what to say. Sofia had spoken with a serenity he hadn't noticed in her before. What he didn't realize, at least not at that point, was that what she said described her own life as much as it did Lucie's. How to be the handicapped overweight daughter of a stunning woman like Mrs Recuenco? How was one to live, being everything your mother doesn't want you to be?

'I thought you hated her.'

'Hate Lucie? No, I don't hate her. I only hate it when she smashes things to pieces. Especially when she does it on purpose, as she sometimes does.'

This conversation only lasted for about five minutes, but it was long enough for Lucie to wander around in the workshop and disrupt the work first of Alfredo, and then Joaquin. When she approached the latter, his buddy Fernando got up from his chair to place himself between them. Not intimidated by the big man, Lucie only wanted to get to Joaquin who was working on the wheel. Just in time Jonathan noticed what was going on, and called her.

'Lucie, stop! Leave Joaquin alone. Stop, Lucie! Come over here!' Apparently his voice was resolute enough, even from the opposite corner where he stood, because she turned around, and came over.

'Good girl. It's time for our next round, and the good news is that Sofia is going to help us.' He had as yet no clue how, but the conversation they just had made him confident that it would work out fine. He pulled up a chair for Lucie to sit at their table, and then explained to Sofia the simple goal he had in mind. They would make twelve little paper balls, and glue them in three lines of four each on a sheet of board paper. But he didn't realize that his explanation left one question to be answered.

'What do you want me to do?' When Sofia had offered him help, he had not asked what she wanted to help him with, or what she proposed to do. So she asked him for instructions.

'Why not try to help Lucie produce another ball? The score so far is three, of which she made only one. Let's say that we are content when she produces four, then each of us would do the same number'.

There was a pleasantness in the 'we' that he used, which immediately brightened Sofia's face. But there seemed to be a hesitation too.

'I don't like putting paper in my mouth,' she said.

'Oh, yes, you mentioned that, didn't you? What can we do about it?'

'Instead of sticking it into our mouth, we could stick it in a pot of glue, that would do as well.'

'Brilliant! Then we do not need to glue the board paper. We can just stick them on it, since they're glued already.' No attention was paid to the fact that this would alter Lucie's habit of putting paper in her mouth. Since changing her impulsive habit into something useful was his aim, Jonathan failed to notice this detail.

Sofia radiated with joy over the warm reception of her idea. 'We will work well together, Jonathan.' It was the first time she had a touch of nervousness in her voice, to which he paid no attention. That she wanted an affirmation to know she was accepted also escaped him.

'Let's hope that Lucie agrees!' He said, and turned to the girl. 'Sofia is going to make paper balls with you.' Lucie showed no sign of response.

'Let me do one, so you can watch me,' Sofia proposed, and started to fumble a piece of paper together so that it could be dimpled in the glue pot. When she took it out, she started to roll it between the palms of her two hands. 'See? Just like you do it.' Neither Sofia not Jonathan perceived that what used to be an innocent game that Lucie played for herself because she liked it, now was changed in something else, something that promised to be the start of a new industry. It probably was hard to be Lucie and know how to live. But it might be infinitely harder to be Lucie and to be drawn into the world of meaningful activity as seen by other people.

14.

Hannah's Birthday

On Wednesday 17th July, Jonathan's mother, Hannah Harrison, would have her fiftieth birthday. He knew that given the custom in the family there would be a big party. He also knew that his parents would very much want him to be there. His mother, because she would miss him, his father, because he hated annoying questions about the absence of his oldest son. His brother Josh would miss him too, of that he was sure.

The 'little brother', as he fondly called him, was five years younger. Apart from occasional fights they had been getting along quite well. Josh was not as strong as he was, and at an early age Jonathan already was aware of the fact that his little brother would need his protection. Unfortunately the head of the family was not too keen on having a delicate child for a son. He preferred the strength of his firstborn. The positive side of this was that Josh was bound to become his mother's darling. Jonathan had never envied him for it, not really, although there had been regular fits of jealousy in his early years. 'Why are you telling me what I can't do when Josh does it all the time?' he would say. But on the whole the two brothers were very fond of one another.

Jonathan planned to make up for his absence from his mother's birthday by calling her. Since he assumed there would be many guests later in the day, he thought of a convenient moment when he could speak a little longer with her. She would probably be available in the morning. Given the nine hours time lapse between

Spain and the West coast this meant he would call her at seven in the evening.

Making phone calls in the House of Bethany was not an easy thing. There were rules. It was accepted that assistants, particularly those from abroad, wanted to call their loved ones every now and then. Since they did not earn much of a salary, using public phones was too expensive. He therefore had to sign up for the 'phone hour', where he was allowed a time slot of at most ten minutes between seven and nine in the evening. Early in the week he had secured for himself the first time slot on Wednesday night.

'Harrison residence.' It was his younger brother.

'Hey, Josh, dude, it's me.'

'Jonathan! Where are you? Still in Spain? You're calling on mam's birthday!'

'Sure I am calling on her birthday, what did you think? And yes, still in Spain. Hey listen, I am sorry but I have only ten minutes on a pay phone. Is mam there? She will tell you everything; that saves time. Take care, bro, I love you.'

'Love you too,' his brother responded warmly. Jonathan heard him yell through the house for his mother. 'Mam! It's Jonathan on the phone!'

Hannah Harrison came rushing to the phone; he could hear her taking a deep breath. 'Oh dear, oh dear, is it really you?'

'Yes, mother. I wish you a very happy anniversary! Your fiftieth, what a special day!' That was not a smart thing to say, but his mother was gracious enough not to burden him with a sense of guilt now that he was calling her.

'Thank you very much, Jonathan. But tell me about you. Where are you? What are you doing?' She was in tears, he could tell.

'Please don't cry, mother. I am fine. I am in a small village west of Seville in Spain, where I found myself a job in a pottery. It is part of a community where I am staying. I am really fine.'

'A pottery? You have never done anything like that before.'

'Yes I know, mother. But listen, I can only call you for ten minutes, so let me tell you as much as I can in that time, and you can tell Josh and dad all about it.'

'Oh. But why only ten minutes?'

'A rule of the house, but don't let us waste time on this.'

'Yes, sure, tell me about where you are.'

'Thanks, mother. The place where I am staying is part of a small community where all sorts of people are living together; different backgrounds, different ages, different abilities. I heard they needed people, and I went to see them. I was invited to stay and work in the pottery. Antonio, who is in charge, is an artist. It's really a good place for me, mother. I learn a lot, not only about pottery. Some of the people have been going through very rough times in their youth, things I didn't know were happening to people, horrible things.'

'What kind of things, Jonathan?'

'Violence, abuse, rejection, because they were not what their parents needed them to be. One guy is blind, another has a hunchback.'

'You mean handicapped people?'

'I guess that's what they are called, although I never heard that word used here. They're considered just people. They only need a little assistance.' Thinking about Lucie, he added 'Some need more than a little.'

'Are you going to be a potter then, like an artist?'

'For the time being, yes mother. As I said, it is a place where I do learn a lot right now. That is why it is important to me to stay here.'

'But do they pay you? You're not in need of anything, apart from phone money I mean? Do you have a place of your own?'

'Assistants like me are getting a small allowance, once it is decided that they will stay. But we don't pay rent, and everything else is free. It's not like a boarding house. You could think about it as a large family home.' Ouch! It had slipped out before he knew it. He hadn't meant it to be cruel to his mother, but it was, and she noticed it. After a moment of silence, she said,

'A family home, Jonathan?'

'Sorry, mother, I didn't mean it that way. It was just to explain the financial arrangement to you, since that was what you were asking about.' Jonathan was honest enough to hear the cleverness of his father in this response.

'When are you planning to come back?'

'I have no plans to come back any time soon, mother. I have been invited to stay for two weeks' time, which ends a week from today. When I decide not to leave, I can stay for another month. Then I will have an interview to see whether they want to have me, and whether I want to stay longer, six months perhaps, or a year. This means I will be here at least for five more weeks, and if all goes well, it will be longer.'

'So, you've set your mind on staying there, then?'

'Yes, I have.'

'What about your future in the company? You know your father will be very disappointed, not to speak of his anger. He will say that you've let him down.'

This was the sore spot in his soul, as his mother could, and should have known. He responded quietly but very seriously, 'I don't think that I've ever let my father down, mother.'

He could hear his mother was crying. Perhaps she was crying about her oldest son drifting away from her, perhaps about her unhappy marriage, perhaps about the wound in her own soul. She was well aware of having failed to stand by him when he attempted to speak his own mind, irrespective of his father's opinion. She should have supported him then, as she should have defended herself when she was trying to do the same. Even though she could not make all this undone, she at least could try not to make the same mistake again. She answered him in a calm and clear voice.

'I am sorry, Jonathan. You're right. You have never let him down.'

'Goodbye, mother, I love you.'

'Bye, love you too, dear.'

As soon as he hung up the phone, Jonathan broke down and cried. The wound in his soul had been touched, and it had opened.

He sneaked away from the phone booth, not to be caught with teary eyes by the next caller, and went up to his room. Drying his eyes when he came in, he sat down to write a letter to go with his mother's birthday present. It was a beautiful vase made some time ago by Antonio that had never been taken when they were selling products from the pottery. They had boxed it together with great care.

> *Dear Mother,*
> *I am glad we just spoke on the phone the way we did. The feelings I expressed were among the reasons I had to leave. I know you'll understand this. Your birthday gift comes from the pottery where I work.*
>
> > *Love,*
> > *Your son Jonathan*

It was not the longest letter he ever wrote, but surely the most important. His mother would understand, which was why she would not show it to his father. He decided to enclose it in the box, and not send it separately. On Saturday he would go to the post office in Sanlúcar.

15.

A New Idea

The object that Sofia and Jonathan had produced together with Lucie had been a modest success. The result was a nice looking paperwork that had grown in artistic quality because Sofia had it painted white. The backdrop for Jonathan was that Lucie only had produced three of the twelve paper balls that it consisted of. This was not only less than the number he had assigned to her, it was also a disappointing achievement in view of the fact that if she was making them just for herself, she did the same quantity in about five minutes. Of all the people in the workshop, she was the least interested in the end result.

Jonathan had been thinking about this during the weekend. 'The problem is she has no conception of what she is doing. Paper balls on a piece of board paper, it doesn't mean anything to her,' he said to himself. He didn't ask himself the question what it meant to him other than that it was the first result of his project.

To solve the problem he came up with a new idea, something he hoped Lucie could relate to. Instead of just producing paper balls and sticking them on a sheet of board paper, he wanted to see whether Lucie was interested in a bracelet. Having seen how she reacted to beads, it might be worthwhile trying to let her have a whole jar of them, and then let her pick out whichever she liked, and stick them on a needle with a cord. When it worked, the result would be a bracelet. Eventually the beads could be made from clay, and fired in the kiln, glazed and coloured. Antonio might even be pleased with a new item to be produced by the pottery.

It didn't strike Jonathan as odd in working with a person like Lucie to change a plan if it didn't work out the first time he tried it. Had he only reminded himself of what Sofia had suggested about how to understand the girl, he might have thought twice about his new idea. He might have thought about trying to follow instead of taking the lead. Among the examples of effective behaviour that Jonathan had seen in his lifetime, however, 'follow' was an unknown specimen. He had simply nothing to relate it to.

Since he planned to go to the post office in the village of Sanlúcar to send his mother's birthday present, he thought to stop by the little craft shop that he knew was there. Since he had no car, it provided him with the opportunity to walk the distance from Benacazón to Sanlúcar. It was supposed to be a good three miles' walk, he had been told, and so it would take him a good deal of the afternoon.

The village of Benacazón was a sleepy country village. Apart from a bakery, a grocery and a small stationery store, there were not many businesses. In fact Bethany's pottery was one of only very few craft workshops. The house was located out in the fields west of the village, with the pottery on the same property. The dirt road that took him to the railroad track was bordered by big oak trees. In the orchard behind the pottery there were fruit trees, oranges, lemon, plums and almonds. It was an extraordinary rich climate to grow things here. 'What doesn't grow in Andalusia doesn't grow anywhere,' he had heard people say.

After a few minutes the road turned left and he saw the railway station in front of him. A local train that stopped in Benacazón used the track. It was the distinguishing feature of the village: it had its own railway station, which the much more industrial village of Sanlúcar didn't have.

Given the time of day the road was pretty hot. In Seville Jonathan had learned that most of Spain closes between two and five in the afternoon, which was *siesta* time. Walking a hot country road at that time was not a sensible thing to do, according to local custom. Soon after he had crossed the highway by a little bridge, he arrived at the first houses of Sanlúcar. In the garden attached to one of them an elderly lady with a large brimmed straw hat sat under an oak tree in the shade. He greeted her in his best Spanish, '*Buenos tardes.*' Her response was a silent nod with a face that expressed contempt for someone crazy enough to be walking at this hour of the day.

Thinking about his errand to the crafts shop, he was elated about his idea. He was under the impression that Antonio liked his initiative to try and develop new things for the pottery. What he didn't realize was that the way he approached Lucie's 'lack of meaningful activity' strongly resembled the road he was walking on right now: straight as an arrow, that's how he went for the target he had set. His colleagues at Bethany could have told him that he was repeating the same mistake he made with regard to the paper balls. To relate 'beads' to bracelets and allowed little consideration for what Lucie was about. Just like her little paper balls were not related to objects of paper art, beads were not related to jewelry. Had Mrs Recuenco on that fateful afternoon worn a necklace with beads, she might as well have been choked instead of having her dress torn apart.

The crafts shop was a nice little store with supplies for painting, drawing, and other things people do in their spare time. It also had a large selection of beads in different shapes, colours, and sizes. Jonathan noticed a little box with a sticker on it that said it came from a pottery in Seville. He looked at the lady in the shop and made a gesture asking, 'Can I open it?'

'*Si, si!*'

When he opened it, he saw just what he had been thinking about earlier that morning: beads from a pottery, round and shiny because of the colourful glaze. 'Ah, look at that!' He picked a dozen of the beads from the box. Two hundred pesetas apiece, the box said. He could afford the modest sum to obtain this precious discovery. If the plan succeeded to produce a bracelet with these beads, Antonio would be stunned! Jonathan forgot to ask himself whether Lucie would be stunned too. That remained to be seen.

16.

An Unfinished Necklace

On Monday morning's early coffee-time it was customary for the pottery to spend some time on exchanges about whatever adventures the weekend had brought. It was Jonathan Harrison's third week in the pottery. He was anxious to tell them of his visit to the craft shop where he found the beads, but he had to wait.

'What have you been up to, Alfredo?' Antonio wanted to know. 'Roaming the streets of Benacazón?' Alfredo knew the potter well enough not to feel abused by this way of addressing him.

'Kind of,' he said boldly. 'Pascal and I took Philippe for a beer, we went to Carlos's.' He made it sound as if he was a regular in the cantina. Antonio appreciated the gag.

'One of the regular bums, aren't you?' They kidded one another till the artist changed the tone. He reminded Alfredo not to use the wheel until there was a solution to his back problem. 'Till then, we can use some fresh ideas.' Antonio had said. Jonathan felt it was not his turn yet to jump in, but he hardly managed to keep quiet. His boss went around the table to who was next.

'Sofia, tell us, what exciting things did you do during the weekend?' Antonio said cheerfully. He had seen her nervous look and expected trouble.

'I went to visit my mother,' Sofia said in a weak voice.

'How was it?'

'Not so good. She was still very angry about the dress. I tried to say that we did our best, but that made it worse. She said I was an ungrateful child, defending those stupid people of the workshop. I couldn't help myself and started to cry. That made her even angrier. "Stop feeling sorry for yourself!" she shouted at me. Then she was sorry about being mad at me, and she started to cry too, and then she kissed and hugged me all the time, calling me her little angel. I felt so bad.'

Antonio laid his arm around her shoulder when she started sobbing. Her account of her mother's conduct was exactly what Antonio had described when Jonathan had asked about her. 'I am so sorry to hear this, dear. I do not know what to say, except that we will do our best and make sure we have a great day together.'

'Maybe I have something that can help us out.' Jonathan saw a chance to generate even greater enthusiasm for his new idea, and seized the moment. 'I have an idea that might just be what we need.' He explained what he had been thinking, and how he had been to the crafts shop to find wooden beads. 'But what I found was even better. I will show it to you,' he added and got a little paper bag from his pocket in which he kept the beads he had bought. He spread them out on the table. 'They are made of clay!' he said. 'Look how beautiful they are glazed and coloured. Perhaps Alfredo and Pascal can try and produce a few like them, then Sofia can assist Lucie in making a chain like a bracelet or necklace.'

While Jonathan was talking with great enthusiasm, Antonio's face grew darker. 'Wait a minute, wait minute, not so fast! We have regular work to do, and if we want to start a new kind of product, it needs some time to think it through.' Both Pascal and Sofia had listened to Jonathan with beaming eyes, but it seemed Antonio was going to spoil the fun. They looked disappointed.

'Can I not start working with Lucie when she comes?' Sofia asked in her sweetest voice. Seeing another opportunity for working together with Jonathan, she wanted to be part of his next project. 'We can find out whether she likes making a chain of beads.' Pascal added, 'We do not have to make new ones yet, because we can use the ones that Jonathan bought.'

'All right, all right,' Antonio conceded, 'that will probably do no harm.' It was not so much that he disliked the idea. Only that

Jonathan had behaved like a kid, throwing new things on the table before even mentioning them. When Maria had her meeting with the young man later that week, she needed to straighten him out on a few points.

Lucie came in later that morning. She was assigned to work with Sofia, after her morning coffee, of course, without which any plan would be doomed to failure. Sofia was in her best of moods. In that regard Jonathan's initiative was a happy coincidence. The success of the paperwork she and Jonathan made with Lucie's assistance in the week before shone on her too. This was just another opportunity to please the young man, as was her heart's desire.

Jonathan had suggested to Antonio to leave the two girls to themselves, and see how it would go. 'That's fine,' was the brief response. The fact that Antonio had given in did not mean he was pleased with the new experiment. While Jonathan kept himself at a distance from the girls, he gestured to Sofia to go ahead. She pulled her wheelchair to the same table in the corner that they had been working on before.

'Come, Lucie, will you sit with me?' Lucie had her usual blank face, but sat down beside her, which was a more than welcome response.

'Look here what I have got for you,' Sofia said. She had put the beads in a bowl to make sure they would not be all over the table and then fall to pieces on the ground. Lucie was all eyes focused on the beads that were truly beautiful. Sofia took her hand, opened and put one of the beads in its palm. 'See, just like your little balls?' she said. Lucie's face produced a smile, and her voice squeaked an eerie sound, which she occasionally did when she was excited. Then she started to roll one of the beads in her hand in the same way she did with her paper balls.

Jonathan was stunned by Sofia's wit in going about her task, and in the corner of his eyes he noticed Antonio's surprised look. The latter had mostly regarded the two girls as potential rivals for his attention, but now he had to acknowledge that a talent for working together seemed to have been wasted.

Lucie picked a second bead and put that in her hand too. Sofia did not stop her, and let her also take a third one. Seeing them all three together rolling in the palm of her hand made her very happy, as was visible from the intense look of her eyes.

'You like to play this game, don't you dear?' Sofia said as if talking to a younger sister. She was not at all inclined to interrupt Lucie, and sat perfectly content and patient with one hand in her lap and the other on the bowl, just in case.

Usually the little paper balls ended up somewhere on the floor of the workshop. Therefore, when Lucie stopped Sofia gently but swiftly took her hand and put the beads back in the bowl. 'Do you want to try another one?' Lucie didn't react, and was about to get up from the table. Instead of stopping her, Sofia let her go. Seeing Jonathan's face she made a sign that it was all right. Lucie started one of her flittering movements through the room, seemingly paying no attention to anything. In the meantime Sofia had taken a needle with a cord, and made a knot at the end. Then she started to stick the beads on the needle one by one to produce a chain. It appeared that Lucie had been watching her somehow, for as soon as the third bead went down she was back at the table, and sat down again.

'You like this chain, don't you?' Sofia said with a smile, 'Why don't you help me? Here take this bead and put it on the needle.' Since the holes in the beads were sizable, they allowed a big needle. The point was not sharp. Lucie picked up the bead in front of her and pushed it on the needle's point.

'There you go!' Sofia said again in her big sister tone. 'What about this one?' Within a few minutes all the beads were on the cord. The two girls cooperated in a way that made Jonathan smiling at Antonio, who could not help himself looking happily surprised. Just when Sofia turned her head towards the men with a triumphant glance, however, Lucie's 'impulse' got the better of her. Before Sofia could hold her back, she pulled the chain from her hands and ripped it apart. The twelve beads went everywhere, some of them smashing to pieces.

'So much for the necklace,' Antonio said dryly. He went over to comfort Sofia who was about to break down in tears. 'Don't worry dear, that was a wonderful job you did with her. *Muchas, muchas gracias!*' he said and then bowed for her, taking off his imaginary hat. Antonio's sense of humor always worked to produce one of her nervous giggles, as it did now.

Jonathan was very much taken aback by what had just happened. He could think of nothing other than getting down on the ground to pick up the beads, or what was left of them. Lucie was on her feet again, flittering around the room and paying no particular attention to anyone, as if nothing unusual had happened.

17.

Interesting Observations

There could have been a better moment for Jonathan's second meeting with Maria. It was supposedly scheduled after his first two weeks, but it was actually a week later when it took place because she had been away for a few days. It so happened that he was to see her the day after the incident with the unfinished necklace. He vividly remembered the first conversation; it was not the best of his memories.

In the three weeks since he had learned a lot, and he even would have looked forward to speaking with her, had not his idea about ceramic jewelry been shipwrecked on the cliff of Lucie's unpredictable behaviour. Despite its negative result he was not tempted to give up, but even so he could not but admit that 'changing her impulse' was easier said than done.

The conversation Maria was to have with him concerned the question of whether he wanted to stay another month. If he said 'yes' there would be no objections at this point on their part, she had concluded from what Antonio had told her. Occasionally new assistants were so little at ease that they didn't want to stay, but she did not have the impression that Jonathan would be one of them.

So their conversation would be about the prospect of the next three weeks, and what there might be that required special attention. Maria meant to bring up things she had heard from Antonio about his work in the pottery. Their policy was to try and keep the two responsibilities separated. One was in charge of recruiting and supervising new assistants; the other was in charge of the workshop. Antonio's role in this was only to provide Maria with information about what he had observed about Jonathan's work. This made Jonathan slightly more nervous than he thought he would have been.

'Please sit down, Jonathan.'

'Thanks.'

'So your first two weeks are past.' She said it with a pleasant smile on her face. 'How has it been for you?'

'I had not expected that a pottery could be such an interesting place, given the people who are my colleagues there. Once I had heard their stories and became aware of the difficulties they have had to face, my respect for them grew deeper. And I also should say that Antonio has been a big help. He can be a grumpy old man, of course, but that's not the real man as I have learned. There were a couple of incidents – you have heard something about it, I guess – that turned up his gentle side. I really feel I have been accepted.'

'That's good to hear. I take it, then, that you haven't been so unhappy that you want to leave us right away?'

'Oh no, not at all. I definitely want to stay for another three weeks.' He almost had added 'at least' but he did not want to sound too eager.

'I am happy about that, really. This means we can use this conversation to look ahead and see whether there are any specific things that you might want to put your attention to in the coming weeks.'

'Yes, I expected that.'

'How come, are there things that are troubling you?' Maria was a smart woman. He gave her an opportunity to throw the ball in his court and she immediately seized it. Now it was up to him to say what he wanted to talk about.

He did not immediately respond. Then he said, 'I don't know. From the beginning I have been taken with Lucie. She is an intriguing character, at least to me. I am not sure how to put it. Her appearance is a curious mixture of presence and absence. She is there but also not there, and right at the point where you think she doesn't notice anything, she will surprise you by showing that she does.'

'Interesting observations. I see what Antonio meant when he said about you "He knows how to use his eyes!" You do indeed.'

'Oh thank you, that is very kind of you to say. So I have been thinking about Lucie quite a bit, and brought up some ideas that Antonio thought were worth exploring.'

'Good. What were they?'

'I am trying to think about a way to extend what she does impulsively, and develop it into an activity.' He mentioned the example of the paper balls, and how he had been exploring that together with Sofia.

'Yes, I've heard a little about that. Antonio said that the way you got Sofia involved in working together with Lucie was just great.'

'Is that what he said? Nothing else?' Jonathan replied, turning the tables again.

'No, that's not all he said. He also said that you are pushing your idea a bit too strongly in his opinion, at least for Lucie. As if you want to change something about her behaviour instead of letting her just be herself.'

'But you see, Maria, that's what I don't understand. As a human person you are not just "being". You're meant to do something, to have a purpose. It made me wonder how Lucie's being could be developed into an activity. That's how I came up with the idea of beads made of clay that we could use to make a necklace, or something.'

'A very creative idea I must say. I heard about the somewhat disappointing result as far as the end product was concerned. But otherwise I would say: continue to explore, but don't run ahead of everyone else. That won't work in exploring new ideas.

'Yes, I know what you mean.'

'Good, that's agreed then, because there is another thing that troubles me more.

'What is it?'

'Frankly, it's about you yourself. Let me put it this way. It seems you know a lot more about your friends in the workshop than all of them together know about you. From what Antonio told me, he has not heard more about you in the past three weeks than I heard in the first conversation we had, which lasted about twenty minutes. You told me you're here because you want to find your own way.'

Jonathan felt again the way he felt the first time they spoke, when she was seeing right through him. Then he had gotten away with a bold answer, but he sensed this time that would not do. Maria wanted to hear more about him, and he would have to respond.

'So my question to you is very simple. What are you finding out about yourself?'

He immediately saw that he couldn't say 'nothing' without getting in trouble, so he had to say something. 'I, uh ...., ' then he stopped, thinking about the phone call with his mother.

'You don't have to say anything you don't want to say right now.'

'Well, it was difficult that my mother...' He paused. 'That my mother had her fiftieth birthday last week, while I had left home without saying goodbye.' There was a sigh of relief after this sentence, Maria noticed. Apparently, the silence had been broken. 'Careful now,' she said to herself.

'Did you get to congratulate her at all?'

'Yes, yes, I phoned her. That was good.'

'Very good! What did she say; was she upset?'

'Yes, but she tried to hide it, not to make me feel too bad about myself.'

'For not being home.'

'Hmmm. Then she asked about the future, and I told her that if the community wanted me to stay, I might stay for a longer time. I think that was unexpected.'

'Did she say she wanted you to come home?'

'She mentioned my future as the head of my father's company.'

'What did she say about it?'

'She said my father would feel that I am letting him down if I don't.'

Maria understood that he was getting close now. She had seen quite a number of young people at her desk fighting the same problem: not wanting to be what their parents expected them to be. Or at least they wanted to get some time to find out. Since this young man had felt he had to run, he seemed to have had a narrow escape. She waited, and said nothing in response.

'That was hard,' Jonathan continued. 'I said that it wouldn't change my mind. But there were no hard feelings left when we said goodbye.'

'You must have felt very lonely.'

Jonathan only nodded, knowing that he was about to start crying again if he were to say another word.

'Well, for the time being, you have a couple of people waiting for you in the pottery.' She had laid her hand upon his when she said it. 'That might help,' she added with a comforting smile.

He nodded again.

'Thanks for sharing this with me. I hope the coming month will be good for you, not only as our assistant, but also as Jonathan.'

'Thank you.' He uttered it barely audibly, with a hoarse voice. Fortunately he had until after lunchtime before Antonio expected him in the workshop. Not being prepared to face other conversations he decided to take a walk.

18.

Antonio's Story

'I heard you decided to stay and bear us out for another month,' Antonio said when they came in together after lunch. Jonathan took the irony in his voice as friendly and decided to join the game.

'You did?' Jonathan surmised Maria had briefed him. 'Did she not tell you I added a condition?' Using Antonio's own sense of humor would probably be a good way to find his poise again. The potter was completely taken by surprise, and for a moment did not know what to say.

'A condition?'

'Hmmm,' Jonathan nodded. 'The condition is that you tell me your story with Mrs Recuenco.'

'What?'

'You heard me.'

'Who gave you the idea that I have a story with her?'

'You did when you said it was something for another time.'

'And now that you decided to stay for another month, you think that time has arrived.'

'You got me!'

Antonio raised his brows and took a deep breath. 'So it's losing a secret or losing an assistant.' He sighed, but the dimples in his cheeks betrayed him.

'You know what? Even the thought of having to talk about her makes me thirsty already. When we're done here this afternoon, you and I will go to Carlos's for a beer. Then I will tell you.'

'I can't wait.' Jonathan responded with twinkling eyes.

Antonio walked to his office but then turned around in a way that Jonathan by now was familiar with. Now he would get the real message.

'Thanks for staying,' his boss said, and offered a handshake, which the young man took with gratitude.

At four thirty in the afternoon they left together for the village. Bethany and its pottery were on the fringe of the village, and walking to Carlos's cantina took them about twenty-five minutes. It was a small bar on the corner of two quiet streets with virtually no businesses. Antonio was the one in Bethany's community who liked to hang out with the locals, so that when he came in with the young American there was a noisy welcome from the owner. Jonathan's Spanish, let alone his knowledge of the Andalusian dialect, was too poor to understand the jokes that were passed between the two men.

'Carlos says you look far too clever for a dumb *ceramista* like me,' Antonio said, 'so he wants to know what you're doing here.'

'I am having a beer with my boss who owes me a story,' Jonathan responded in a bold voice. 'I bet he won't understand English; you can tell him anything you want.'

Antonio turned to the man, and spoke rapidly. Jonathan didn't understand a single word. 'I told him you're a lost soul,' he said with a straight face.

'I bet you did. What about yours? Soul, I mean.'

Antonio laughed; he could not help liking the boy. They sat at a table in the corner of the cantina where it was much cooler than outside. Then he started to talk.

The story was that Carina, Mrs Recuenco, came from Seville years ago with her daughter Sofia, who was then four years old. She was a gorgeous woman at the time. Anybody who saw her loved her at first sight. Apart from being beautiful, she was friendly and witty. Everyone liked her. Sofia came to live in Bethany when she was sixteen. From that time onwards her mother became a very frequent visitor, almost to the point where she was a member of the community.

'You were in charge of the pottery already?' Jonathan asked.

'Yes. I came a few months before. I had been working in one of the factories in Seville. As a potter, a studio of my own was my dream, but you know a career as an artist in this business is only for the happy few. I came to Andalusia because of its famous tradition in pottery. I am originally from Galicia, from a small village in the North West. One day I met Ramón who incidentally dropped by our store. When I visited Bethany we started to talk and before I knew I was going to be the head of the workshop. That was good enough for me, so I accepted.

'Did you know much about the community that it was part of?'

'Nothing at all, to tell you the truth. When they mentioned that I would be working with handicapped people, I bluffed a little.'

'You bluffed a little?'

'I said I didn't know what that word meant. Claire who did the hiring interview looked surprised.'

'You don't?' she asked me.

'Look,' I said, 'Juanito, my youngest brother, has Down's syndrome. I looked after him most of my youth. He was just Juanito to me.'

Antonio told it with a grin, but Jonathan knew by now how his boss liked to hide the truth behind a grin.

'The thing about my brother was true enough, but I took a gamble putting it in a way that was in tune with what I took to be their view. So I got hired as the head of the pottery. I think they were happy. An artist from one of Seville's ceramic factories, on top of which came someone who was experienced in assisting a brother with Down's syndrome. What more could they want? I know for sure I was happy! I got my own studio with people I knew how to work with.'

'Then there was Sofia with her mother.'

'To be honest, that's not exactly how it went. I already knew her a year before Sofia came here. As a matter of fact, Carina was looking for a place for her daughter after her husband died a few years ago.

I suggested that she might ask the community in Benacazón and see whether they had a place for her.'

'How did you meet?'

'On a lonely night in Triana in a flamenco bar, across the river. I will never forget that night. I was on my own, and about to drown my melancholy in red wine and gypsy music, when there was this radiant beauty at the bar. She was in everything the opposite of the very impressive lady singer of the band: blonde, tall, and with a kind of serenity that would place her more adequately in a chapel than in a bar. My God, she was stunning.'

Antonio's eyes were beaming again as he recalled the scene. Jonathan thought there was little doubt that he would be on his knees for Carina Recuenco if she walked into Carlos's cantina that very moment.

'You fell in love with her?'

'Instantly. What I didn't know – couldn't know – was that the woman had her own attention deficit disorder; she never had enough of it. I had to find that out the hard way. Seeing her sitting there like a Madonna, I approached her for a drink, with my usual charm,' Antonio winked when he said this. 'She accepted, and we chatted the night away. The next day she was on the phone to tell me she had loved the evening, and asking me if I would take her to some of the galleries in the city.'

'You said "yes", and that's how it started.'

'More or less. We loved strolling through the city when I went to see her. We were a couple that people turned their heads for to take another look. She in colourful dresses, I with my broad brimmed straw hat, and leather boots. But when we had been together for longer, we were fighting most of the time. Don't ask me why and about what. It was just awful.'

'How long did it last?'

'Much too long. Fortunately I wasn't stupid enough to marry her, which she wanted very much. That would have made for a complete disaster.'

'When did you break up?'

'Three years later, right before Christmas. There was a huge event of the ceramic industry. Exhibitions, workshops, parties, you know, the best occasion to meet people working in the business. Most of the people I knew were there, including old friends from Galicia. I bumped into a few of them at a reception in one of the factories. We talked and had a few good laughs; I think I must have been away no longer than about twenty minutes, leaving Carina to the people she was talking to when I met my old buddies. When she came over, she was furious. I should not have left her alone; I was a selfish bastard, and so on. She started to make a scene on the spot. She was very good at that.'

'A nice way to introduce herself to your friends.'

'She didn't give a damn about my friends. She was never pleased with my happiness unless she herself was the source of it.'

'Some people would call that jealousy.'

'When I said so, she exploded. Jealousy was for mean spirited people, and of course that was far beneath Carina Recuenco's noble character. Now that I think of it, most of the fights we had started that way. It was always about her complaining that I was paying too little attention to her.'

'When she visited the workshop, I noticed that she was very effective in drawing all attention to herself,' Jonathan interrupted.

'What can I tell you? She used to say, "I am just like a flower, give me a little water every day, and I will blossom." I tried and tried, but it was never enough. Man, I swear, with all the water she needed you could drown the desert. I always wondered about the water supply of her late husband.' Jonathan laughed. Antonio had his sense of humour working for him again.

'What did people in Bethany say when she came asking a place for her daughter. Did they know you were seeing each other?'

'Yes, I told Claire before they met. It was no big deal, she thought. But when I told her a few months later that I had ended our affair, she looked me in the face and said, "How could you ever think you would be happy with that woman?" I did not know what to say. It was one of my biggest mistakes.'

'One last question,' Jonathan said.

'You're taking this interview very seriously, aren't you?' Antonio said with a grin on his face.

'Why are you telling me this?'

'Well you've got a nerve, young man, I must say. First you take over my interview with you and start to ask me questions, whereas I am supposed to be your boss, mind you, and then you threaten to leave the workshop unless I tell you this story, and now you're asking me why I am telling you? What are you thinking?'

Jonathan could not help smiling. 'No, seriously …'

'I probably have had this much too long on my chest. Apart from Claire, and now you, only very few people know anything about it,' Antonio responded. 'Oh, and of course, because I would hate to see you leave.' He said it with a straight face, as if it didn't matter too much, but needed to be said anyway.

19.

Another Incident

Everyone agreed that the beads experiment had been too promising to be given up after the first time. Sofia's contribution in getting Lucie involved had been an important consideration in arriving at this conclusion.

'You did a great job in how you caught her attention,' Jonathan said. 'I never knew you two could work together so well,' Antonio added.

'There are lots of things that you don't know,' said Alfredo, winking to Jonathan. He was working with Pascal to prepare the fire for the kiln.

'Are there now?' Antonio retorted. 'How lucky am I to have you in this place to tell me about them.'

Alfredo grinned, but remained silent.

'Catching Lucie's attention was not so hard,' Sofia said, 'I didn't try to make her do things. Just invited her to look at what I was doing.' Jonathan was reminded of his own manner of pushing Lucie in the paper ball project without any success. In this mood the evaluation of the beads project arrived at a positive conclusion, the only question remaining was when it would be continued.

It was to be Tuesday afternoon a week later. There would be another attempt to work with Lucie on a necklace made of clay beads, and bring it to a good end. The first attempt had resulted in the loss of half of Jonathan's collection, so at the weekend he had revisited the craft shop and got himself another dozen from the same box.

The plan was to go about it in the same way as the first time; after lunch Sofia was to start as she had done before. She sat down at the table in the corner of the room, and emptied the little paper bag with the beads in the same bowl. Then she took one of the beads from the bowl and let it roll in the palm of her hand. Everybody was expecting to see the girls engaging in Lucie's game and then to witness how Sofia would be leading her away from it.

Unfortunately Lucie was not in a cooperative mood. Since there were no clear signals that she wasn't, nobody was prepared for what was about to happen.

When Sofia took the first bead in the palm of her hand, Lucie was in no time at her side. But instead of taking a chair at the table, she bent over to fetch the bowl. 'No dear,' Sofia began, but before she could continue, Lucie let go of the bowl and walked away. 'Will you come and sit with me?' Sofia asked her. At that point Lucie was about four or five steps behind her. She had a tense expression on her face, and was breathing very fast. Suddenly she was beside Sophia, and raising her clenched fist she hit her with a heavy blow on her back. Sofia was taken by surprise and, terrified and in pain, she screamed and cowered away from Lucie.

In a split second Jonathan was at her side, while Antonio held Lucie. 'What are you doing? Are you crazy?' he yelled at her. 'You don't hit people! Sit down!' When Lucie didn't respond immediately, the potter pulled out a chair and pushed her on it. Then he took her face between his hands, and looking into her eyes from a very short distance, he shouted, 'You don't do that again, you hear me?' Lucie remained seated quietly on the chair. From the blank expression on her face one could not tell whether she had any notion of what she was told.

In the meantime Jonathan was comforting Sofia as well as he could. She was sobbing from misery and pain, but mostly from the injustice done to her good intentions. Jonathan was stroking her back softly. He was completely shocked by this totally unexpected violent impulse from Lucie. 'I am sorry, I didn't see this coming,' he said.

'She has done this before,' Antonio tried to set him at ease. 'Don't be sorry, there are no signs to see this coming. She has even hit her father this way, coming at him from behind with a heavy blow on his back for no reason at all. We don't understand why, or what brings it on.' Then he gestured to move over to his office.

'As a rule we try not to speak about people in their presence. I suggest you and I try to keep things quiet for the rest of the afternoon.' Jonathan nodded to confirm he understood his task. 'You try to get Sofia back in shape. Let go of the beads project, at least for now, and see whether you can get her to drawing a sketch for another bowl. I want her to leave without tears this afternoon.'

The incident clearly had upset everybody present in the room. Even the peaceful Fernando seemed agitated. His buddy Joaquin held up his head so as to gather from the voices what had been going on. Seeing his unrest, Pascal went over, laid his hand on his arm and said, 'It's me, Joaquin.' In a few words he explained what had just happened. Joaquin nodded to say he understood. Then he said, directing his words to no one in particular, 'Lucie does not intend to hurt people. She has no clue.'

Pascal did not respond. 'I am going back now to what I was doing,' he said and returned to the kiln. Alfredo had not moved at all. He just sat on his chair, looking intensely saddened. 'Are you okay?' Pascal said when he saw his face. Alfredo silently nodded.

Everybody in the workshop felt the same about the incident. The girl whose behaviour nobody really understood had blown to pieces what seemed to be a promising start for new and exciting work.

The rest of the afternoon was quiet, just like Antonio wanted it to be. Lucie had been sitting on her chair for about fifteen minutes, which for her restless, wandering soul was quite an achievement. Antonio watched her closely, as she was sitting there, moving slowly back and forth on her chair. She appeared peaceful. Since he had some urgent business in running the workshop, he went over to Pascal.

'Could you do me a favour and take Lucie out for a walk?'

'Of course,' Pascal responded in his usual quiet manner. 'How long do you want me to walk with her?'

'Try to make it thirty minutes. Then I will be done with the most urgent things, and I can take over.'

'I can do that.'

When they left, Antonio looked through the window to see how Pascal guided the girl out of the pottery and into the orchard. He saw them walking towards the chapel where they sat down on a bench in the shade. He always wondered where the boy got his inner strenght from. When he heard for the first time what had brought Pascal to Bethany, he had asked himself just how screwed up people must be to mistreat a child to become so depressed that it almost got him killed.

Meanwhile Jonathan succeeded in helping Sofia to overcome her upsetting experience earlier that afternoon. The unexpected blow she had received would have scared anyone but for someone like Sofia it was even more painful. More than anything else, her pain was caused by disappointment, feeling that she was the last person to deserve such a treatment. But apart from the injustice, Sofia was sorry because it ruined the first tangible result in Jonathan's ceramic jewelry project in which she had been shining. That hurt the most.

The young American was sensitive enough to understand this. Contrary to Antonio's instruction he decided not to let go of the beads project. He surmised, correctly, that his boss had meant to say no to the beads project that included Lucie's cooperation. But this didn't rule out Sofia from producing a piece of ceramic jewelry. That's what he decided to do, and when Antonio saw it, he understood it was the best way 'to get Sofia back into shape' as he himself had put it.

Jonathan's plan had been a great hit, of course. Sofia was the queen of the afternoon for having produced the pottery's first necklace, even when the beads were bought instead of made. As soon as she had finished it, she showed it to Antonio, with reddened cheeks. He sent her a broad smile from the office as a sign of approval. 'Where do you want me to put it?' she asked him.

At this point Jonathan intervened with one of his typical moments of good sense. 'Excuse me,' he said, 'I think I am entitled to answer that question.' Without awaiting anyone's permission he took the chain of beads from Sofia's hands, and with a gracious smile he put it around her neck, 'Do you allow me, my lady?'

When Antonio saw this he gave Sofia thumbs up, accompanied with another big smile. For a brief moment an image of his little brother Juanito passed his mind, full of pride showing him his first work of pottery, and he realized that he was very happy to have the young American as his new assistant.

Despite the painful incident earlier that afternoon, in the end everyone seemed to have settled in, again, including Lucie. When Pascal came back with her, she looked elated, no longer the over-excited, unpredictable character she appeared before, but the introvert flittering bird – with 'a broken wing' as Sofia had put it – that everybody in the workshop was familiar with.

Shortly before they finished the day's work and had started to clear their tables, Lucie was again wandering around when she approached Joaquin's table. Before anyone knew what was happening Fernando had seized her hand.

In reconstructing later what had happened the conclusive story was that she must have seen a scrap of paper on the floor under Joaquin's table and was moving a chair to pick it up. Fernando was never at ease when Lucie came too near, but especially after what had happened earlier, he got very agitated when he saw her coming. At the point where she was about to dive underneath Joaquin's table, Fernando's loyal mind flipped. Quicker than anyone would think he could move, he went down on his knees, grabbing Lucie's hand and squeezing it till she nearly fainted.

'Fernando!' Antonio called from a distance. A split second later Jonathan was beside Fernando. 'Let her go,' he said in an alarmed voice. Then, in a flash, he appealed to Joaquin to intervene. Unsure about what was going on the blind man had no clue what was going on, but when he heard Jonathan's voice he said, 'Fernando, it's okay, it's okay buddy, please stop.' The big guy immediately responded and let go Lucie's hand.

The poor girl had no idea what had happened to her, or why. Nor did she scream, like Sofia had done before. Neither did she start to sob. She just sat there, on a chair, looking nowhere, playing with her fingers. When Jonathan saw her sitting there, the flittering bird with the broken wing, he couldn't stop the tears streaming down his face.

20.

After Six Weeks

Another three weeks had gone by in the pottery since that dreadful day. They organised it so that Lucie stayed in her apartment for a few days, and she was placed under Maria's guidance, in which task Sylvia assisted her. Antonio decided to keep the work low key. Not only because he thought it wise not to make demands, but also because he needed time to recover the quiet atmosphere that had been so important in this place.

It was then that Antonio started to do something he had not often done before. When in the evening he wanted to be on his own, he began to go to the chapel. The walk through the orchard in the moonlight calmed his busy mind. He just wanted to be quiet for a while.

One evening when he entered to sit on one of the benches in the back, it turned out he wasn't the only late visitor. Claire had found her way to the sanctuary too, largely for the same reason. She needed to somehow get the busy day out of her system, not to be conquered completely by every day's fullness.

'I have been thinking about the workshop since the arrival of the young American,' he said to her after they had left the chapel together. 'The place has certainly been busier.'

For all his acting out as the rough customer from the North, Antonio was in his own way an amiable and wise man. He was pretty certain that Jonathan's energy to do his own thing had much more to do with the life he had left, than with the life he was looking for. What he shared with Claire, however, was not about the young American. It was about whether he himself had been too lenient.

'I allowed him to work with the girl without telling him about my own failures. You know we've been trying very hard to have Lucie taking part in the workshop, but it has been a disaster. She has been constantly disturbing the others and even managed to ruin their work occasionally. Seeing the interest Jonathan took in the girl, I decided not to be too restrictive in what he could or could not do. Looking back, I see I should have told him more about our own experience than in fact I have.'

'Perhaps, but I am not sure about that,' Claire responded. 'There is something to say as well for not burdening new assistants with stories of our own experiences with the members. It leaves everybody the space for a fresh look at things.'

In the meantime Jonathan was also reflecting on his time in the pottery since his interview with Maria, but for a quite different reason. The following day he would meet with Ramón Jimenez for his six weeks interview, a prospect that made him nervous.

After both incidents with Lucie on that Tuesday afternoon a few weeks ago, he had abandoned his project. Whether it had been the result of him giving up was hard to tell, but the place had been much quieter afterwards, including the girl herself. In spite of the peace that had returned, Jonathan could not get rid of the feeling of having failed.

'You will have your interview with Ramón tomorrow, I believe?' Antonio said it in a tone that was meant to be reassuring. He had noticed that the young man looked tense.

'Yes.'

'Are you looking forward to it?'

'I am troubled by what happened with Lucie, it bothers me. I am not looking forward to telling him that story. But perhaps it's a good opportunity to get it off my chest.' Jonathan tried to speak with equanimity, in which he didn't really succeed.

'Get it off your chest? I would not worry too much about that. You need to get your head around what has happened with you since your arrival here. That's what he will be interested in. Not your project, but your own self.'

Jonathan knew his boss was probably right. But also in this regard there were clearly things that bothered him; the phone call on his mother's birthday, and the letter she wrote him afterwards. All this had been on his mind quite a bit, but these thoughts usually came late in the evening when he was alone in his room.

'Do you know what time he will be here?' Antonio wanted to know.

'He said at lunch time. Why?'

'Claire wanted to see me about something. It wouldn't take too long, she said. Can I leave the workshop to you for around half an hour after lunch?'

'I guess you can. If Ramón is in a hurry, I can ask Pascal to go and get you.'

'Ramón in a hurry? That is not very likely. He would rather sit down and have a chat with somebody.'

'All right, then,' Jonathan said.

The next morning Antonio was assisting Sofia and Joaquin who were working on a piece of pottery. Pascal and Alfredo were busy rearranging things in their storage room, where they lacked sufficient space to keep all their materials and finished products. Jonathan would be keeping an eye on Lucie.

Just as he saw her move in the direction of the shelved pottery that was ready to be baked in the kiln, there was a knock on the door. Ramón entered greeting Alfredo and Pascal, embracing Sofia, shaking hands with Joaquin and Fernando. He was not alone. Alonso followed his entrance, and jumped for joy as soon as he spotted Lucie near the shelved bowls.

'Wuz! Wuz!' Looking at Ramón he pointed his finger to her.

When she turned around towards the boy, Lucie's face grinned in a way Jonathan had seldom seen before. Ramón stepped aside just in time to witness Alonso jump upon the girl and hug her. From the corner of his eye Jonathan he saw Lucie dangerously close to a few bowls on the lowest shelf. To prevent them from sweeping a bowl from the shelf he tried to stop them. 'Enough, enough of this!' he said with a loud voice. 'Lucie watch yourself, or you will be ruining a day's work.' Alonso backed off, and turned his head to see who was talking. Ramón raised his brows. Then he turned to the young man.

'Jonathan, how are you?' he said, taking both his hands. Jonathan had rehearsed a greeting, but the way he had imagined it did not come close to the actual scene.

'Fine, I am doing fine … most of the time.' He intended a smile that would make the comment to sound relaxed, but he didn't succeed; he sounded anxious. While he was speaking Ramón held both his hands in a way that almost felt like an act of friendship. Somehow Jonathan felt embraced. He had been quite nervous about the interview, like he would be taking an exam. That feeling was gone now that he looked into the man's face.

'You know this fine fellow here is very fond of Lucie, as you can see.' Alonso's face was a smile from ear to ear. 'Where do you want us to sit?'

'I suggested to Antonio we would sit outside, so we would not be disturbing anybody. But I need a few minutes, because Antonio is not here right now. He is talking to Claire but will be back very soon.'

'Oh, I'd almost forgotten. We met him on the way from the house, and he said he would be here shortly. Let me sit down here till he is in, and then we can sit outside.'

A few minutes later when Antonio arrived, Jonathan and Ramón went out. There was a set of garden chairs and a table placed under the big walnut tree in the orchard, close to the chapel. Jonathan pulled out a chair and offered it to Ramón. He seated himself opposite him at the other side of the table. Not knowing what to say, he waited.

'You know we speak with all new assistants after six weeks,' Ramón began, 'the goal of which is to see whether they want to stay, and whether we want them to stay. The goal is to arrive at a kind of mutual understanding. So, will you tell me a bit about your experience thus far? How has it been for you to be here?'

Jonathan told him about his work in the pottery, and how he learned about the people and their stories. How he had to get used to Antonio, but that the two of them got along quite well. Much of what he told Ramón was more or less the same as what he had told Antonio after a few days, and Maria after two weeks. He added a brief account of the two incidents that Lucie was involved in, but deliberately left out everything that was related to home. The reason was that he didn't want to talk about it, if it could be avoided at all. In this he soon was proven to be wrong.

'I see, I see. Well I am glad that you seem to get along with everybody. That's good. But I would like to know a little bit more about you. Where you're from? What did you leave behind? Why did you come to this place? It is important that we understand each other. That is only going to happen when we know a bit about who you are.'

Jonathan told him about how he had come to leave home, more or less to escape a future designed by his parents, particularly his father, and that he had called on his mother's birthday to inform them of his whereabouts. He even mentioned the letter he wrote to his mother afterwards, explaining that he probably wouldn't come home for some time. But all these things were not all that important now that he was working here in the pottery. 'Home does not worry me so much,' he said, not very honestly.

'What does?'

'The incidents Lucie was involved in.'

'Why?'

'It troubles me that she was so restless.'

'What troubles you about it? She is quite often restless, as you call it. It's just part of who she is, I guess.'

Jonathan was silent. He felt safe enough to speak his own mind, but he wasn't sure how to put it. The question was what his project had to do with her restlessness. 'I keep asking myself what it had to do with the fact that I was trying to get her involved in the work,' he said. 'I am afraid I have been pushing her.' He spoke his mind directly before second thoughts kicked in.

'How would you have been pushing her?'

Jonathan said that he had wanted to work with Lucie, how he had discussed it with Antonio, who had given him a chance to figure it out. He also told what his plan had been, which in the beginning seemed to work quite well, but then went wrong.

'What were you thinking about Lucie?'

'My impression was that she is only acting from impulse, and that we might be able to include her in the workshop by changing her impulse into a meaningful activity.' Then he mentioned the rolling of her paper balls in the palm of her hands as example.

'I have seen her doing that, yes,' Ramón said. 'To me it seemed like an innocent game, something she liked doing.'

'Sofia said exactly the same.'

'Sofia?'

'Yes.' Jonathan told him how Sofia got involved and that she too had suggested looking at Lucie's rolling of paper balls in her hands as a game. As Jonathan spoke Ramón nodded, ready to interrupt him.

'It's important to understand why you didn't listen to her.'

'Oh, but I did! From that very moment Sofia got involved; it became our project together with Lucie.'

'That's not what I mean. You did not seriously listen what Sofia was telling you, namely the possibility that you were about to change something that was important to Lucie.'

'But it is impulsive behaviour, something she doesn't control. Sometimes it looks like an obsession. She sees nothing else but these small paper balls in her hand.'

'People get lost in their games, that is true,' Ramón admitted. He was in fact rehearsing his own experience with the girl from the days that trying to be her assistant had almost broken his back.

Jonathan did not know this, but the reasoning behind his project had been exactly what had caused a crisis for Ramon. He had also meant to be recreating Lucie to become a human being by changing her impulsive behaviour into meaningful activity. But he kept this part of their history together to himself, at least for the moment. Instead he pushed the young American to rethink what he had been trying to do.

'Jonathan, tell me this. Can you imagine learning from Lucie?'

Jonathan fell silent, not knowing what to say. Where was he going? 'To be honest, I don't see what you're driving at. It seems to me that Lucie doesn't do anything, so what is there to learn from her?'

Ramón looked him kindly in the eyes, but was very serious when he spoke. 'Perhaps. But what if she is just trying very hard to live being Lucie. Can you imagine what that must be like? Not being able to speak your mind, probably not even being able to make up your own mind, and nonetheless trying to respond to what people want from you every single day. When we look at her this way, can I again ask you whether you can imagine learning anything from her?'

Jonathan sensed he was asked to enter unexplored territory, a mental space where he had not been before. 'I would like to respond but you have to help me out.'

'I will try,' Ramón said softly. 'Have you realized that for Lucie, as for Sofia, or Joaquin, or the others you work with, there is no way but to give themselves in the hands of others. They're out in the world depending on who ever is there to assist them. They cannot hide whatever their problem is but nonetheless they are gentle and loving people, most of the time at least.'

At this point Ramón stopped. He could have continued, but he didn't. Nor did he need to. Jonathan took a deep breath, and was silent, feeling closer to himself than he had been for a long time.

Then he said, 'I think I see your point. You're asking me what the problem is that I am trying to hide, aren't you?'

Ramón smiled at him. 'I am not asking what your problem is. You may tell me if you want, but that is not the point. The point is for you to find out what it is, so that you can solve it. Or when that is impossible to accept it and be in peace with yourself. I hope you will. You're an honest person. I would very much like you to stay with us. But you have to think about the question regarding Lucie.'

Jonathan knew that the man was right. What would it be to live being Jonathan? To be at peace with himself and have nothing to hide? Not trying to succeed in being his father's son, and not trying to run from being that either? Ramón looked at him, nodding his head in silence as he saw Jonathan's pensive look. When Jonathan looked into these kind eyes, he felt having his soul touched in an unfamiliar way; it moved him deeply.

Ramón stood up from his chair, as did the young man, and laid his hand upon his shoulder. When they went inside the pottery he said, 'How about a cup of tea, or whatever it is you people drink here at this hour of the day?'

21.

I Want My Son

Approaching the end of his first six months in Bethany in December 1982, Jonathan Harrison had no plans to leave, nor did anyone in the community intend asking him to go. He was firmly attached to its people, and they were firmly attached to him. Unfortunately, this was only half of the story. The other half of the story was the difficult connection with his family.

During his six weeks interview, Ramón had asked him why he had come to Bethany and what he had left behind. Jonathan had not told him very much, except that he was trying to get away from the future his father had in store for him. 'Home does not worry me so much,' he had added, which he knew was not true. It worried him quite a bit. Nonetheless, in the months since he arrived he had been happy in Bethany. Living in a community surely had its ups and downs, but the perks outweighed the downside. His fascination for Lucie Miles, Antonio's friendship, and particularly the artist's sense of humour made working with him in the pottery a delight.

Then there were the men, Alfredo, Joaquin, Fernando, and Alonso, not to forget Pascal, although he was still a boy; with each of them he had found a connection. And then of course they had Sofia. Her desire to be his favourite sometimes troubled him, at which moments he deliberately kept her at a distance. On the whole he felt his presence was appreciated. The limited space for privacy, beyond the privacy of his own room, was something he had learned to take for granted.

The feeling he had of being loved had made it easier not to be worried too much about his family. It also allowed him not to be occupied by the future of his father's firm and his own role in it. He made his regular phone calls, usually with his mother, sometimes with his brother, and rarely with his father. Most of the time these calls were filled with the exchange of stories about his life in Bethany, and theirs in San Francisco. From both sides it was understood that one question had to be avoided to keep their phone calls agreeable. This was the question of when he was planning to come home. The truth of the matter was he wasn't planning anything of the sort at all.

The *status quo* around this question was suddenly interrupted when in early December Ramón asked the young man to see him the next day. Something had come up that he wanted to talk about, but he could not make it that evening. The truth was that Ramón had received a phone call from Jonathan's father, and he needed some time to think about what had been a most awkward conversation.

Mr Harrison had asked whether Ramón could tell him when his son planned to come home. Ramón had answered with some reservation.

'I understand your concern Mr Harrison, but with all due respect, Sir, it seems to me that this is a question for your son to answer.'

'Jonathan deliberately avoids talking about the subject,' the man said.

'Did you actually ask him?' Ramón tried not to make it sound too impertinent. The response left Ramón flabbergasted.

'That is what I want you to do.' Mr Harrison was a man used to being in charge of his conversations.

'I am sorry, Mr Harrison, but I don't see any reason for doing so. I certainly do not want to give your son the impression that I want him to go.' Ramón expected this response would be taken as offensive, about which he was proven right. Mr Harrison was a man not to be trifled with, which he wanted to be absolutely clear about.

'You should not have given him a job in the first place, if you can call it a job. The boy is needed here to be my successor in the firm, a career for which I want him to be prepared. Being in Spain and living with these people is certainly not going to work for him!' The man apparently could no longer control the anger that had been building up in his soul since his son had left. Ramón was at the point of retaliating to the attack, but just in time he managed to control himself.

'I suspect by "these people" you mean the people living in our community here, including myself. If you do not hold us in your esteem, Sir, why would you expect me to be the one to guide your son in returning home?'

Mr Harrison felt he had overshot his mark, and backed off. 'I did not mean it personally,' he said by way of apology. Ramón was convinced he had meant it very personally, but he kept quiet.

'My son does not belong in your community, Mr....'

'Jimenez.'

'... Mr Jimenez. The simple truth is, I want my son back. He belongs in California where I raised him.'

What an impossible character, Ramón thought, knowing that Jonathan was beholden to his mother who had done much more to raise him than his father. The moment he let his response out of his mouth he regretted it:

'Maybe Jonathan has a very good reason not to come back to you.'

This was a big mistake, Ramón instantly knew, because he was not helping the young man at all by fuelling his father's wrath.

There was a moment of silence. Mr Harrison's response was as clear and brief as it could be. 'Beep, beep, beep...' And the phone died. Without any further comment the man had hung up on him.

When Jonathan stepped into Ramón's office the next morning he had no idea what was coming. Ramón decided to tell him straight away.

'Good morning, Jonathan,' Ramón greeted him. 'The reason I wanted to see you is to tell you that I received a phone call… ' after a moment's hesitation, he added '…from your father.' Jonathan's face grew pale. Even though Ramón was careful not to show any sign of approval or disapproval in telling him about the conversation with his father, the young man was very upset.

'He just can't understand that this bossy attitude towards other people, his own family to begin with, is exactly the reason why I left home,' Jonathan said. 'I don't want my life to be a copy of his, and I certainly do not want him to be in control.'

Not knowing what else there was to say, Ramón told him not to let this phone call throw him off-track.

'You came to this place to figure out something for yourself. When the time has come you will know the answer.'

Jonathan nodded, but said nothing. When he was about to leave, Ramón tried to make sure the young man was at least clear about their intention.

'If you want this community to be part of your future, you're most welcome. I am sure everybody here will agree. But you cannot answer your father's question by looking the other way. You know that. Whatever part Bethany will play in your future, your family will always remain your family.'

When Jonathan left him he realized it was the same question Ramón had put in his six weeks interview. That question was still unanswered. He did not want to be the son his father wanted him to be, but so far the only way for him to deal with it had been not to think about it.

Following these events, the holiday season started for both men in a most unusual way. Ramón understood that Mr Harrison regarded himself as a man of consequence whose orders were not lightly ignored, which was what Jonathan already had learned a long time ago. Even though both were aware of this, neither Ramón nor Jonathan could have imagined that Mr Harrison would show up at their doorstep in person. But this was exactly what happened.

It was the week before Christmas when early in the morning a taxi rolled into the grounds of Bethany. When Sylvia answered the knock on the door, the man in front of her introduced himself as Mr Harrison.

'Claire, there is a gentleman at the door,' she said when she had found Claire in her office. 'He said his name is Harrison,'

'Oh my,' Claire exclaimed, intuitively foreseeing trouble. Ramón hadn't informed her nor Antonio about his clash with Mr Harrison. Since supervising assistants was Maria's responsibility, only she knew about it. 'Why don't you go upstairs and tell Ramón. Tell him I will receive the gentleman here.'

When they had welcomed the man he told them the purpose of his unexpected visit. He had come to persuade his son to come home. 'I still count on your assistance in this, for the boy's own good,' he added, looking Ramón straight in the eye.

Ramón politely repeated what he had already told Mr Harrison on the phone: that it was his son's call to decide what to do. To underline this response he sent for Jonathan who was in the pottery, and asked him to come immediately to Claire's office.

The conversation that took place while they were waiting for the young man was not at all constructive. The father told Ramón that he was confusing his son, who was too weak to know his own direction. Clearly Mr Harrison was not used to seeing his authority over his subordinates break down. Now that it had happened, he decided it must have been because of someone else's bad influence. Had it been in his power to 'shut down' the House of Bethany he would not have hesitated to do so. Ramón was furious, but fortunately he had asked Claire to stay. She signaled him to keep quiet, which he barely managed to do.

When Jonathan saw his father in the office he could not muster any of the politeness he had been taught by his mother.

'What are you doing here?'

'Is this the way to welcome your father?'

'Sure it is, after my father bullied a man I hold in high esteem, and whom I am allowed to call my friend and mentor, Dr Ramón

Jimenez.' Mr Harrison was not stupid. He immediately sensed that Jonathan knew about the phone call and that he had to back off if he wanted to have any success with this son of his.

'I am sorry to have offended either you or Dr Jimenez,' he said.

'What do you want?' the young man wanted to know.

'I want you to celebrate Christmas with your own family, as most people do.' Jonathan was not at all impressed. He knew all too well his father didn't care one bit about how his family celebrated Christmas. Instead of responding the young man fired back at him right away.

'Are you here on your own?'

For a brief second his father looked confused. 'Your mother is also here. Why?'

'I don't see her here,' Jonathan said dryly, not willing to grant his father one inch of unearned sympathy.

'She is at the hotel in Seville.'

'I refuse to discuss the issue of coming home unless mother is present,' Jonathan said. Had he been able to read his father's mind, he would have noticed the state of alarm his response created. The truth of the matter was that the man had opposed his wife when she announced she would be joining him, but Hannah Harrison had insisted.

'You have pushed our son away from us, and now you are going to make things worse by bossing him around among his friends,' she had said.

'Friends? He doesn't even know who his real friends are!' Jonathan's mother had been at the point of exploding, but had managed to hold herself together. Perhaps it was the calm and collected manner in which she had replied that made her husband give in.

'You can go to Spain alone. But if you do, you will regret it for the rest of your life.' Recalling this argument with his wife, Mr Harrison was not at all willing to have mother and son reunited before the homecoming had been settled.

'Your mother wasn't feeling too well after the long flight, so she decided to stay in the hotel.'

Jonathan felt no inclination to believe a word his father spoke.

'My mother will soon feel much better when she can embrace her oldest son.' It was said with such confidence that his father understood he was losing his ground.

'If that's what you want,' he said, barely able to hide his irritation.

'Yes, that's what I want.'

22.

A Shocking Discovery

After the meeting in Claire's office, Jonathan had told his father to wait for him because he had to see his boss in the pottery. His sudden absence for the rest of the day and perhaps also part of the following day would at least require an explanation. When Jonathan told him what had happened, Antonio gave him a hug and wished him all the strength of heart and mind he would need. He said he hoped he would come back in peace. 'If not with your father, then at least with yourself,' he had added.

After the exchange in Claire's office, the taxi ride from Bethany to the hotel in Seville was anything but pleasant. Mr Harrison attempted conversation, but instead of asking his son about his months in the community, he started to talk about his firm, hoping to awaken his son's interest in it. He could not have made a bigger mistake. Jonathan said nothing but looked out of the window at the suburban areas of the city they were approaching.

As cold as the meeting with his father had been, as emotional was the reunion with his mother. She was weeping when he embraced her, and Jonathan could not keep his eyes dry either.

'Oh, Jonathan, how wonderful you are coming to see me!' she said brushing the tears from her face. 'How are you? You must tell me everything!' Within a few moments they were engaged in a conversation in which the husband and father had no part. The warmth it radiated made Mr Harrison jealous of his wife's success where he had failed. Having exhausted the little patience he had, he interrupted them.

'I hope we can have a conversation about when you are planning to come home, son,' he said with a grave look on his face.

Jonathan looked at his mother to decide whether to overlook the interruption, but she gestured with her eyes he would do better to respond; not completely without self-interest, of course.

'I have no plans in that direction,' he said flatly.

'But how do you think you will get prepared for your role in the firm?' his father wanted to know.

'I don't see for myself any role in your firm.' The young man knew that this response meant that the battle was on.

'What's that supposed to mean? You are going to be my successor as director and owner of the firm,' his father said in the dismissive tone his son hated.

'Who says so?'

'You did! We discussed it in my office before you left.' The man was about to lose his temper once again and move himself to a position where he did not want to be.

'You mean you addressed me by saying that one day the firm would be mine. But you never asked for my opinion. The whole idea of me being your successor is entirely your idea, not mine. I suppose this is news for you, but I am not going to work in that firm of yours.'

All this time Hannah Harrison was listening anxiously to where this was going. She was afraid of losing her son, but this fear was not as strong as her resolve not to forsake him once more in his struggle to be his own man. If it meant opposing her husband, so be it. As soon as Mr Harrison had called to tell her that he was on his way back to the hotel and that he had Jonathan with him, she had anticipated the battle she now saw playing out before her eyes.

'This time I will not let him down again,' she said to herself. If she were to take sides, which she expected her husband would force her to do, she would speak on her son's behalf. She knew Jonathan would never put her in that position, but she would be at his side.

When his son squarely opposed him, clearly not intending to give in, the father felt that he could not push further without risking defeat, so he made the move his wife had foreseen.

'Hannah, you talk some sense in that boy!' The man apparently failed to see that rather than giving orders, posing questions might be a more intelligent way of negotiating.

'Sense or not,' she said bravely, 'for once in your life you had better ask your son what he wants to do with his life.'

'So you're with him then, in this nonsense?'

'Is it so impossible for you to at least try and listen what people are trying to say to you? You have been treating your son as if he were a marionette. Well, he isn't, nor does he want to be, as he has found out in the last six months, and if you had any sense in you, you would be happy about it! It wouldn't do the firm any good were it to be directed by a man who was his father's puppet.'

Jonathan looked at her, hardly trying to conceal his surprise. This was not the appeasing mother he knew. She seemed strong, and was consciously seeking to stand by him. Strengthened by this unexpected support he looked his father straight in the eye to see where his next move would take him.

'Do I understand you have known this all the way?' the man asked his wife. Now that his suspicion was added to his anger, Mr Harrison lost control. He turned into a loose canon that was about to do much more harm than just lose one battle.

'What do you mean?' his wife said defiantly.

'What have the two of you been talking about in these endearing phone calls you had? I should have known, how stupid, I should have known!'

'Should have known what?'

Much to her own surprise Mrs Harrison felt lighter than she had in a very long time, awful as the cause might be. Holding ground with her son, she felt herself losing the weight of self-contempt that had lulled her into submission all these years. That was about to end now.

'That you could not be trusted in this matter! That you would fall for his talk about that wonderful community he has been wasting his time with!'

'Wasting his time? For the first time Jonathan has experienced a life where he is his own man and is respected for it! Can't you see what this means to him?'

'Respected? Bullshit! He has been running from the real world, that's what he has been doing. Respected! By whom, I may ask? By these morons that he is assisting in that house in the middle of nowhere?'

'Morons? How do you even dare to insult him like that?' His wife was furious. 'They love him in a way that you never have loved him. You wouldn't even know how!' The audacity of her resolve to stand against her husband was invigorating, but it had made Hannah Harrison forget what her husband was capable of when he was facing the naked truth of resistance. His eyes grew dark and cold as steel, and then he lashed out with acid sarcasm.

'And of course *you* do! Of course *you* know how loving these handicapped people can be. That was why you decided to reject the one we had coming!'

Jonathan's mother flinched. Both her hands went up to cover her face, which had turned pure white. 'Oh... no... no... Peter, please... don't. Don't!'

'Excuse me? You are throwing everything you have at *me*, and now you ask *me* to stop? Tell him, woman, tell him he would have had an idiot for a younger brother if you had not made it go away before it even was born.'

The man's fury unleashed a cruelty in him that knew no bounds. Alarmed by what he was witnessing Jonathan jumped from his chair to hold his mother who was crying bitterly. All her courage was gone, and what was left was a miserable creature sobbing and grieving over the wound in her soul that had been torn open again.

Jonathan repeated very slowly what he had just heard.

'I had a brother coming who would have been disabled?' He spoke softly, but without any anger or bitterness in his voice. His mother's sobbing shook her body, now that she knew her son was witness to her crime. While she was testifying her guilt with her tears, she feared the truth would alienate him from her, and held onto his arms so as to make sure he would not turn away from her.

But instead of turning away from her, Jonathan caressed her gently, a grown-up man now, comforting his weeping mother. Then he looked at his father's face, very quietly, without contempt, with a serenity that confused the man completely.

'I don't think there is anything more to say, father. I am your oldest son, and I love you. I know you have set your heart and mind upon having me as your successor in the firm so that you would be proud of me. I am sorry, but as much as I love you, this is not going to happen.' Then, looking at his mother who was calming down slowly as he spoke, he continued.

'I think you better go now.'

Perhaps it was her anxiety about losing him that had made Hannah Harrison fail to see that in some respects Jonathan was very much like his father. Not his son's words, but the way they were spoken, moved Mr Harrison to pick up his jacket and his coat, and instantly leave the room.

When the two of them were alone, mother and son sat quietly together for a long time in the hotel room. She was finally telling him about her aborted pregnancy that had taken place three years after he had been born. It was discovered that the child would be born with Down's syndrome. Her husband had been worried about what it would take in terms of energy, money, and time, to raise a child like that.

'But your father never urged or pushed for an abortion. That was my decision. I swear it had nothing to do with the disability, you must believe me!'

'I do believe you,' her son said.

'I doubted strongly that your father would be capable of loving such a child, that's why I did it.' Again she broke down in tears. When Jonathan stroked her hair, and kissed her she calmed down a bit, and continued.

'In my heart of hearts I knew what I never dared to face, that at that point my marriage was over. One cannot think such a thing about one's husband and assume that all will be well somehow.' She rested her head against her son's shoulder.

It was a moment Jonathan would not forget for the rest of his life. The times were changed, and the tables were turned. From here onwards his mother would lean on him instead of the other way around.

Being his father's son Jonathan Harrison immediately knew what to do, but unlike his father he first consulted his mother about it. His intention was to take her with him to Bethany to stay there for Christmas. He was sure she would be welcome. He would tackle all the practical details with Claire.

'I can't leave Josh alone with dad in San Francisco, not at Christmas time,' his mother said.

'No, you can't,' Jonathan replied, 'so we have no other choice but to bring Josh to Bethany too.'

'You cannot invite two people on your own, can you?'

'No. But I can take you to Bethany for the night, and talk to Ramón and Claire about what happened. I will be sober in my account, I promise. I will ask them if you and my brother are welcome to celebrate Christmas in Bethany.'

So it happened. Ramón was as gentle as he could be in welcoming Mrs Harrison, and Claire was delighted to have his family members for Christmas. It was announced at the dinner table that same night. All were thrilled to have Jonathan's mother and younger brother as their guests. When this was settled, Jonathan agreed to call his brother Josh, and tell him what had happened. His brother was confused and upset, but he understood how much his mother dearly hoped to have both her sons to be with her.

23.

A Walk in the Orchard

'You're very welcome, Mrs Harrison, it's our pleasure to have you here,' said Ramón to Jonathan's mother when she thanked him for being her host for Christmas. It was the day after. Claire and Maria were preparing a dinner of leftovers in the kitchen; Sylvia spending the day with family in Seville; while Antonio had volunteered to spend the afternoon with Lucie in her apartment. Jonathan was taking time to catch up with his brother Josh.

'Would you perhaps care for a walk with me?' Ramón asked their mother.

'I would, and I would be very pleased if you would call me Hannah,' Mrs Harrison responded. 'That is, if you don't mind.'

Ramón was not necessarily given to familiarity with people he hardly knew, but this time he did not hesitate. Jonathan had given both him and Maria a sober account of what had happened in the hotel room, while leaving the discovery of his mother's abortion out. It had made their feeling for the young man more intense, and including his mother in this feeling was no effort. 'No, I don't mind … Hannah. It's Ramón.'

'Thank you, Ramón.'

They were strolling into the orchard, where the clear sky of early winter created long shadows of a fading sun. The air felt crisp. Very soon the evening temperature would drop, and they would return to the house because of the cold.

'Your oldest son is a special young man,' Ramón said.

'I cannot tell you how happy it makes me that he is loved by his friends here at Bethany. I know it means a lot to him. Therefore it means a lot to me.'

'Oh yes, everybody in the house is fond of him. He is a sensitive character, and truly understands what Bethany is about. He needed some time to adjust, but that was only for a short period. Particularly Antonio, the head of the pottery, was soon pleased with him.'

'How did he need time to adjust?'

When she raised the question, Ramón recognized the way Jonathan would ask questions. The young man had a talent for assisting their members to speak their minds by asking them the right questions. Ramón understood this talent to be his mother's influence.

'In the first six weeks, which is the time we take to see whether we would like a new assistant to stay, he had to find out that our goal is living together without taking control over people's lives. They need assistance, guidance sometimes, like we all do, but we try not to take over.'

'Jonathan was inclined to do so? That's not like him.'

'He was friendly, and very polite. But soon he had his own ideas about what people might do in the pottery, too soon one would say, in view of the fact that he had been there only for a short time.'

'Really?' It was the first time Hannah Harrison heard her oldest son described in a way she didn't know him, but she recognized the trait. 'Perhaps, he is more his father's son than I have cared to notice.'

Ramón smiled, but said nothing. 'The wonderful thing about your son is his ability to pay attention to people, and learn quickly. And, I should add, Antonio is a great coach. He taught Jonathan to use his eyes and listen, and then try to follow instead of trying to push. Your son responded very quickly. I think the two of them are quite happy working together.'

'I know for sure Jonathan is; talking on the phone with him I learned much about the pottery, and particularly about his boss.'

'He called Antonio his "boss"?'

'Not without explaining that he was not acting like a boss at all. In fact, he was always trying to explain that nothing in Bethany was what one would expect it to be.'

Now Ramón raised his brows. 'How so?'

'Most of what he told me had to do with Bethany not being about caring for people with special needs. "They don't focus on people's shortcomings". That was what I heard him say all the time.' When Ramón did not respond, she continued.

'Now that I am here and see the place and its people, I understand that this comment tells as much about Jonathan's experience as a child in our home, as it tells about your community.'

'Well, you shouldn't do yourself an injustice,' Ramón said, 'He must have learned his sensitivity somewhere.'

'That is very kind of you to say, Ramón.'

They were silent for a few moments. Mrs Harrison understood quite well that her son had run away from a home where 'shortcomings' meant the failure to meet his father's standards. Now that she saw the impact it had on him being away from that, she was no longer troubled about Bethany as his new home. It was clear that Jonathan was happy. What he experienced here was new to him, and Mrs Harrison began to see what it was.

'Would you mind telling me why this house is called Bethany?' Since Ramón did not know what she had been thinking, the question came somewhat unexpected.

'It will be my pleasure to tell you, but may I ask what prompts the question?'

'You may. I was just thinking that I would like to understand what my son has found here. Clearly, Bethany has become very important to him. Therefore I would like to know as much about the place as I can. I noticed that wonderful tableau on the front of the chapel, and then realized I have never heard him speak about its name.'

'I see. The tableau you're alluding to is called a *mural de azulejos*. You'll find many of them in Andalusia, especially in Seville. The one on the chapel tells a story taken from the New Testament.

Bethany is the name of a village in Palestine in the days the gospels were written. Actually, it appears in the Gospel of John as a small village where people were very poor. Some of them had been expelled from the city; they were lepers. They were insignificant, little people. I suspect the powers that be in those days hardly knew they existed. It was probably not by accident that Jesus and his friends were acquainted with Bethany's inhabitants. From the beatitudes we learn they were pretty much the same people.'

'The beatitudes?'

'Oh, I am sorry, that is probably a very Catholic expression. It refers to Jesus' Sermon on the Mount, where he speaks to his followers as people from the lower ranks of society. He repeatedly addresses them with the phrase "blessed are they, who" and then he names different kinds of people in the margins of their society, and reassures them they are special in the eyes of God.'

'I see,' Mrs Harrison responded. 'So the house did not have its name when you bought it? You gave it this name, correct?'

'Yes, that is true.'

'So the name explains how you see its inhabitants?'

Ramón did not see where Mrs Harrison was going, but he felt uneasy about being quizzed in this way. Hesitant to answer her directly, he decided to turn the tables.

'Are you a religious person, Hannah?'

'I think I am, but why do you ask?'

'The question why I chose the name "Bethany" makes me aware of the fact that I find it hard to explain what this place is about without seeing its inhabitants as being special in the eyes of God.'

When he said it, a conversation with Claire came into his mind many years ago, when he wanted to build a chapel. It was about whether Bethany was a religious community. He had realized then that making sense of it in terms of his faith was dear to him. After a few moments of silence, he spoke again.

'I think what I am trying to say is that I am more at ease with a religious account of Bethany than with any other. It is therefore important for me to know how what I say will be heard.'

'Try me.'

There was again a directness about Mrs Harrison's manner of speech that Ramón did not quite like. Was it American culture? Was it the need of being close to the people her son was close to? Her tone was one of confidentiality as if they had known another for a long time. In situations like this, particularly when they involved women, Ramón was a not a man of the world. He was cautious. Not knowing what to think of a person he was talking to usually put him on guard. So it did now. It made him answer Hannah Harrison with a question.

'What do you make of people like Alonso who have a disability, Hannah?'

Of course, since Jonathan had not told him anything about his discovery in the hotel room, Ramón could not possibly have known that this question would hit her right between the eyes. When he saw her face turn pale he was worried about where this conversation was going.

Mrs Harrison was in shock. It couldn't be that Jonathan had told him of her abortion, could it? He had promised her to keep his account of why his mother had to stay in Spain 'sober', as he had put it. She had understood this to mean that he would keep to himself what had happened in their hotel room. But then, the discovery he had made might have upset him in a way that he needed to share it with someone, particular in this place.

'Are you not well, Hannah?' Ramón asked her.

Mrs Harrison saw a chance for a narrow escape, and she took it. 'I think so, I felt a brief spell of dizziness coming over me. Perhaps it is fatigue, the last week has not been relaxing, as you can imagine.'

'It might perhaps be better to go inside then, and lie down before we have our dinner,' Ramón said kindly, and without waiting for a response he took her gently by the arm and moved to turn around towards the house.

Mrs. Harrison was happy to have him leading her as they went inside. Ramón noticed that she did not look well at all when Claire took her to her room, leaving him behind in the hall. While he was not unhappy that their conversation had been interrupted, he decided to go back to the orchard, and sit down for a while in the chapel.

Part III

The House of Bethany

24.

A Farmer's Daughter

The House of Bethany was an old farm. It had been a bodega, like so many other Andalusian farms. This was before an alien parasite had been accidentally imported from America that had destroyed their vineyards early in the twentieth century. The family who owned the house had not made it in the production of olive oil; that came after the wine industry in the region. For generations they had barely survived on a small herd of sheep, some goats, and a luscious orchard full of fruit trees. Wool, goats cheese, and almonds had been the main source of their income until a few decades ago when the agricultural industry sealed the fate of small local farming.

The house itself was very spacious, which was why Ramón Jimenez had cast his eyes upon it in the first place. It could easily accommodate two families instead of one. The fact that Bethany nonetheless had survived partly as a farm was not his doing. Ramón had no clue about farming of any kind. He had no idea of what could be done with the property he had just bought. The reason for buying it was the house; not the land attached to it. That the land had turned out to be very useful for the production of fruit and vegetables was entirely due to his first assistant, Claire Gomez Moreno.

Ramón knew that living together with his friends would be hard without providing them with an occupation. It would be difficult to save them from boredom unless they had something useful to do. Even though he was aware of the problem, the solution had not been his, but Claire's achievement.

When she arrived at Bethany, she immediately saw the possibilities of a rich vegetable garden. 'Leave the farming to me,' she had told him. He had been more than happy to obey. After all, she was a farmer's daughter.

Claire had told him that her ancestry was from the South where she grew up on her father's farm. It was situated at the fringes of the Jerez region where the British had dominated the wine industry for centuries. When she was young, the owners of Pedro Domecq and other houses continued to live like British nobility. Not only did they live like barons, they also behaved that way. The bailiffs who managed their estates were bullies. They had treated her father like dirt after he had refused to sell his bodega. Her family had produced excellent wines, but their powerful neighbours had succeeded in making life hard for them.

Claire had left home in the summer when she was twenty-two years old. She wanted to get away from the permanent state of war existing around the farm. A few weeks before she had decided to go, her father was involved in a violent conflict with the neighbour whose land enclosed most of his own property. There was always the threat of denying him right of way. That spring the rain had been poor. The water level in the little river flanking their property was so low that it became difficult to pump it up into their irrigation system. Since her father's property was further upstream, he had the best of the water supply. When he pumped up the water he needed, his neighbour was infuriated and closed the gate that enabled her father to go to town for supplies.

The conflict escalated in a most irresponsible way. Her father was beside himself. One night he had been drinking, and in his drunken rage he had set fire to his neighbour's vineyards. A few days later one of his own men was shot in the open field. That was the moment that Claire knew she had to go. Her father's bitterness had been very hard upon her. 'You're leaving because you're a coward. You just don't want to fight for your own land.' She had said nothing in return, except: 'Goodbye, father.'

The year that followed had been tough. She went north to Madrid to find a job to enable her to pay for her education. Her dream was to become a teacher. It didn't work out that way. Despite her objection to her family's belligerent attitude, Claire remained a girl from the South. She could not bear the arrogance of the Castilians towards southerners, whom they treated like illiterate gypsies. After the first year she returned to Andalusia, and made Seville – the city of the gypsies – her hometown. 'If that's where people think I belong, that's where I will go,' she said to herself, and left Madrid. Whatever her virtues were, and they were many, Claire Gomez was not the fighting type.

In Seville she found work in a tapas bar. It was not long before she saw that her future as a teacher was not coming any closer. So she started to look around for another job but without much luck. Just when she was about to give up she had met Ramón Jimenez in a backstreet in the old inner city. It was October 1974.

She bumped into a gentleman who came up to her from across the street asking for directions. He was looking for a small street in the centre of town that he couldn't find. Since she didn't know exactly where this street was located, she asked him where he needed to be in that street. Was it a company, or a firm, or a shop, perhaps? If she was familiar with the name, she might be able to assist him.

'You probably do not know this place,' he said, 'it's a building of the Catholic Mission.' He was right; she didn't know it.

'Are you a priest?' He did not exactly look like one, but who else would need to go to the Catholic Mission?

He smiled. 'Me? No, I am not a priest, but I surely need one. Preferably one with a lot of money to give away!' She must have looked surprised because he continued, 'Excuse me for speaking in riddles. I am on a mission to find funding for a house that I am trying to buy.'

'What kind of house?' she asked.

'A house where I can live with a few friends who have had a rough life. They need assistance because on their own they will barely manage to survive. So where better to go than to the Catholic Church, and see what they can do to help?' With this last remark there was a grin on his face, as if he had been joking. But he hadn't, he was quite serious about it.

Before she knew it, they were talking as if they had known one another for a long time. Claire did not yet have a sense that this might be her chance at a different future, but she liked the way he spoke about his project.

'It started out of the blue some years ago,' he said, 'but I want it to grow. I have seen institutions where people are living in horrible circumstances. They are fed, and to some extent their personal hygiene is looked after. But that's all. The sadness in their eyes I found unbearable. I believed there had to be a better way. So here I am, begging for funds. Any rich uncles?' He said it with a charming smile.

'Unfortunately not,' she said laughingly, 'but perhaps shaking out rich uncles is not your vocation.' She had no clue where this came from, but the man had looked at her with curiosity. After a few seconds of silence, he spoke again.

'Maybe you should pay us a visit some time.'

'Maybe I should.'

'Let me introduce myself,' he said stretching out his hand. 'Ramón. Ramón Jimenez'

'Hi, Ramón. I am Claire Gomez Moreno,' she said shaking his hand.

'I am pleased to meet you, Claire.'

That's how they got started. Before they went in different directions, he gave her a phone number. Then he said goodbye.

'I have still not found my street, but maybe I have found something much more important.' He crossed the street. Once at the other side, he turned around. 'I hope to see you again.' Then he was gone, leaving her behind in confusion.

25.

The Garden

When Claire arrived at the railway station in Benacazón, a village west of Seville she had never heard of, it was a pleasant day early in spring the following year. Glad to be out of the city, she took a deep breath to enjoy the fresh air. It was all the more enjoyable because the station was located outside the village. When she found the stationmaster, she asked directions to get to the House of Bethany. He told her that it wasn't hard. 'Just follow the road alongside of the railway track in that direction, and then follow the dirt road under the oak trees, it takes you straight to Bethany. It will not take you much longer than ten minutes.' She thanked him and went in the direction he had told her. The verges of the dirt road had their first flowers; behind them on the right there was a field with olive trees. On the left there was an orchard with orange and lemon trees. Walking through them Claire felt that she had not been in the countryside for far too long. After a few minutes a large farmhouse appeared along the road that the stationmaster had pointed out.

Bethany was what in Spanish is called a *cortijo*, a whitewashed Andalusian farmhouse with wooden shutters. The house immediately struck her as friendly. It had a major two-storey part of about fifteen yards in length, and extended to its right in a lower part of about half this size. It had a garden in front of the main entrance with magnificent oleanders. The road she came from passed the house on its left; behind it was a spacious backyard. A second building stretched from its right for about twenty-five to thirty yards. 'Probably the barn,' Claire said to herself. A wide corridor separated the two buildings, giving access to the back entrance of the house. 'A substantial property indeed,' the farmer's daughter noticed.

She decided to go for the back entrance. When she had passed the corridor she entered the patio that was surrounded by what in better days might have been a large garden but now was more like an overgrown wilderness. It was located right behind the house. To its right, adjacent to the other building there was a big orchard, in which she noticed a number of fruit trees that from the richness of their blossom appeared to do quite well.

When she approached the door, it was opened and the man she had met in Seville stretched out both his hands and welcomed her. 'Claire! How good to see you!'

'Ramón! You should have told me about your orchard! The fruit trees blossoming! The scent!' He saw the sparkling light in her eyes, and could not help himself feeling happy about seeing her.

'And I thought you came to visit me!' he said joking.

'That's why I am here, isn't it?' He had not meant to upset her, but there was a moment of confusion in her voice.

'Oh, yes, sure, no. I was just kidding.'

When in later years they were revisiting this moment he would say he behaved like a boy nervous about his first date. To tease him Claire would respond with saying, 'What was there to be nervous about?'

'Well, after all you were the first woman to visit us.'

'I see, I see,' she would then say, 'you would have been just as nervous had I been your sister.' Even after all these years, she was still able to confuse him, being the lovely woman she was.

'No, Claire, you know that!'

'I do, dear, I do.' Even though Ramón was almost twenty years older, she still could not resist this girlish play to make him blush. They had been together for so long, and Claire had come to understand what he really was about. She had been in love with him for sure, but she had learned to accept that this was not why he needed her. The new house was much bigger than the one he came from, and he would not be able to run the place on his own.

When he started his journey, he had found a small house in the village of Olivares, also close to Seville. He had lived there with the two men he had virtually saved from spiritual death in a mental hospital: Philippe Bousquet and Eduardo Villanova. Both of them had been in a terrible state when he found them, but once they came to life again they turned out to be very different people.

Philippe Bousquet was a man of extrovert character who would say anything to anybody at any time without any sense of propriety. Having been institutionalized in his childhood, Philippe had no conception of intimacy whatsoever. He could approach complete strangers as if they were close relatives. Claire learned this the very moment he laid his eyes upon her.

'I like your dress,' was the very first thing he said to her. 'Ramón told me you might come to live with us. I like having a woman in the house, and not only this grumpy old bear.' When Claire did not respond, he continued.

'Are you married? I want to get married some day. We might make a nice couple, don't you think?' Claire had not known what to say, but Ramón had come to rescue her from this unexpected proposal.

'What about introducing yourself, say your name, trying to be polite?' he said to Philippe, who immediately started mumbling apologies.

'Uh… hmmm… sorry, miss. I meant it to be friendly, miss. No offense, miss. Philippe, my name is Philippe. Sorry, miss.' As if to underline his apology he offered her his hand, but he stuck it out much too high, as if he were a lady offering her hand to be kissed. Instead of shaking she patted his hand, making it a muddled gesture, and felt uncomfortable about it.

Eduardo Villanova was a completely opposite character. Very shy, he didn't say anything beyond his own name, and that only after Ramón had encouraged him.

'My name is Eduardo,' he whispered hardly audible. She felt clumsy for not hearing what he said.

'Excuse me, what is your name again?'

'His name is Eduardo.' Philippe was quick to be up front again.

'Thank you, Philippe, but I think Eduardo can speak for himself,' she responded. 'Right, Eduardo?' He raised his eyes, looked into hers very briefly before casting them down again. It was just enough to notice a bleak sign of gratitude that his presence was recognized, but he remained silent. Ramón had said nothing. He just had looked at her with observing eyes, as if to see how she handled meeting his two companions.

In the years since, Claire had learned that these first moments at Bethany had been a pretty accurate forecast of what it was like to live there. There was a friendly familiarity, but Bethany could be your home and you could still be missing the special feeling that usually comes with having a place of one's own.

After her introduction Ramón had shown her the premises. She had told him right away what she thought about the garden. 'I bet this is rich soil, which, if it is done right, can bring at least two, and perhaps three crops a year,' she said. 'That would supply your household with much of the fresh vegetables and fruits you need. Perhaps you might even be able to sell some of it. There will be a lot of work to do,' she continued, 'and there will always be some extra hands needed.'

'Oh, but I am not much of a garden type of guy.' He said it in such a clumsy way he made her laugh.

'I didn't mean you. I meant your friends. I am sure Philippe wouldn't mind!'

'I am sure he wouldn't.'

After this visit to Benacazón they had talked on the phone. At some point when Claire intimated that she might want to be part of his community, Ramón suggested that as soon as he would have two other persons coming to live with him, he would call upon her and ask her to come. In April he had called her. Two more people had joined him and his two friends: Alfredo, a crooked youngster, sixteen years of age, with a horrible family story, and Fernando, a boy of nine. He was a big kid, too big for his age anyway. His father had more or less dumped him because he was supposedly incapable of learning.

It had been quite a spectacle: three and a half men and a schoolboy assembled under one roof. But at age twenty-four an energetic young woman like herself didn't mind the challenge. She liked Ramón, she needed a job, and she saw that for now this was probably as close as she would get to being a schoolteacher. Not exactly the kind of teacher she had anticipated, but a teacher nonetheless.

Claire kept her promise and came in May, seven months after they had met in the streets of Seville. Being his first assistant, she intuitively decided that the garden would be her territory. She would take care of what she knew best, which was to look after flowers, plants, and trees. 'If you know how to look after plants, looking after people cannot be all that difficult,' she told herself. In the years to come she would learn that she couldn't have been more wrong about this. Yet at the time her youthful optimism had been exactly what was needed in Bethany. But all of that was hindsight, of course.

The first thing Claire did was to clear the garden and let it rest for a while before she planted new vegetables that could be both consumed or sold, produce like tomatoes, beans, melons, and peppers. The garden flourished in no time, and it wasn't long before Claire had Philippe as her assistant.

The two of them worked day and night in the garden and got along together very well. Claire didn't notice that it was the male chauvinism she had witnessed during her childhood that had taught her how to deal with intrusive characters like Philippe Bousquet. Ramón was pleased to see how their gardening contributed not only to the household, but how it also brought a rhythm in the house. Living with one another under the same roof was not always easy, but having regular work proved to be very salutary, especially for Philippe. There were always practical gardening tasks that required attending to, and so it helped them to structure how they spent their days.

Following the time of the season entailed a kind of wisdom that Ramón was not familiar with, being a person of the mind. Claire was the one to teach him. She brought a kind of natural rhythm to their lives that served them well.

'When all is said and done,' she would say, 'there are still plants that need to be looked after. Not because they solve anyone's problem, but simply because the season tells you it is time to do so.'

26.

Alfredo's Mother

Of the four members of their incipient community, Claire had a special connection with Alfredo Garcia, the teenager whose spine was so crooked that he could only with great difficulty lift his head. After Ramón had told her the story, she caught herself seeking to find the boy's eyes, something she rarely managed to do with an occasional exception at the dinner table. There was an almost unbearable melancholy in those eyes.

'How did you find him?' she wanted to know.

'His mother came to ask me if he could live with us. It was an awful family tragedy.'

'Why?'

'Her son's condition of a crooked spine ran through her family. His father abused him mentally by holding him responsible for the effect of his disease. To avoid being despised by his father the boy tried to keep his head up, which was not only painful but also exhausting. So he had to lie down for a while in the middle of the day. When his father would find him he would scorn him for being lazy. His mother is weak. She was too much humiliated to do anything but cry about her miserable fate. The poor woman had no heart to protect her son against his father.'

'Why would she not leave him?'

'A woman in her position, with no income? What do you think? All the shame and guilt that she went through; she believed it to be her fault.' Claire had known women like that. They would abuse themselves for anything rather than confront their fathers or husbands. She had seen it in her own family, the family she had left behind without a child to take care of, but also without a fight. Perhaps it was because she knew the world Alfredo came from that she felt she had to make up for his loss whenever she could.

One of the nicest things in the House of Bethany was a luxurious bathroom upstairs. Claire found out that taking a bath was one of the best remedies to soothe Alfredo's aching body. So she made sure he was bathing at least twice a week. One evening, after a rough day for the boy, she prepared a bath for him, and asked if he would mind her sitting with him. He said he wouldn't. She took a chair and looked at his peaceful face, as he was lying there with his eyes closed.

'Boys your age usually hate to have a woman around in a situation like this,' she said, implying the intimacy of his naked body.

'Boys my age usually don't have bodies like mine. They don't need assistance in situations like this,' he aptly retorted. She smiled.

'You were used to having your mother around, I guess.'

He nodded. Then after a few seconds, he continued. 'Actually they were the very moments both she and I would be safe from my father's rebuke. That meant a lot to me.'

'You must miss her then.' Claire knew he had not seen his family since he had come to Bethany, and she imagined that the melancholy in his eyes had much to do with this. Alfredo didn't respond.

'How long is it now that you've been here?'

'About a year. I came only shortly before you.'

'Oh yes, of course.' She was silent for a moment and then, with some hesitation she began. 'I was wondering, Alfredo, how it would be to invite your mother to visit us.' The boy was silent, and didn't look at her. Just when Claire thought she had overstepped a line, he spoke softly.

'She wouldn't dare.'

'Is it okay with you for me to try?' Now he opened his sad eyes, and looked at her.

'Only tell me when she will come.'

'I will. Promise.'

Obviously Alfredo didn't need another disappointment in his young life. He had had enough of those; a surprise he could use, however. Claire told Ramón about their conversation in the bathroom, which made him raise his brows, but he agreed that it would be good for the boy not to lose his family altogether.

'What am I going to say to her so that she will accept?' she wondered.

'What about if I called his father?' Ramón suggested. She quickly perceived his point. Men like Alfredo's father were like rulers who do not tolerate insubordination on their own territory. So they agreed that Ramón would call him. Two days later he came back to her with a twinkle in his eyes.

'She will come.' Claire did not understand. 'Alfredo's mother! She will come.'

'Really? How did you manage to arrange that?' He pulled up his nose so as to look down upon her. 'I talked to the man as a gentleman.'

'No, seriously.'

'I lied to him.'

'You what?' it sounded almost indignant. 'What did you say?'

'I told him we had a doctor here who was looking after Alfredo, and who wanted to have more information about the family history. He asked me what for. I told him that medical knowledge about hereditary diseases is advancing, and that information about family histories like theirs will be very helpful. All of which is true by the way.'

'Did he buy it?'

'He wanted to know if his son could be cured, of course. I said that would be impossible, but understanding the disease would be good for next generations. That he bought. Yesterday I had him on the phone for the second time. He said he had told his wife to visit us, a week from today.'

'So now we need a doctor,' Claire said taking a deep breath. Ramón's unorthodox manner of dealing with the man almost made her forget to be glad for the boy who was to see his mother again. Ramón told her not to worry about it and leave that to him.

'Can I tell Alfredo then?'

'Sure.'

After lunch she asked him if he had a minute. She laid a hand on his shoulder when he stood before her and said, 'She will come.' It was as if she felt an untapped source of energy running up his spine when he lifted his head. She saw his eyes. No more words were needed.

When Mrs Garcia arrived at Bethany, Ramón received her together with the local doctor, Henrique Solares. The doctor had been a good friend for some time. He had agreed to interview her about her family. He would aim to draw up a tree of family connections in order to see how the disease had affected which part of her family. Of course, the interview did not take more than an hour or so.

'Can I perhaps see my son Alfredo?' she asked anxiously when the doctor told her he had all the information he needed.

'I will ask Ramón,' the doctor answered, quasi-officially.

Afterwards Claire had told Ramón about the reunion of mother and son. 'It was heartbreaking,' she said, 'you should have seen it. The sight of his mother alone already straightened his back by at least an inch. I have never seen that much energy in his body. How that boy must have suffered from having been sent away.' It had been a most happy afternoon, she told him, with Alfredo and his mother walking together in the orchard and sitting outside in the garden. Before she had left late in the afternoon, Mrs Garcia found Claire in her office to thank her. Alfredo had told her everything about the house, and how much he loved being with them. It had eased her pain, she said, seeing him happy.

'Then she started fidgeting with her handkerchief,' Claire said, 'and looked at me as if with a heavy heart. I asked her if something was troubling her, expecting something about her husband. But it turned to be something entirely different.'

'What was it?' Ramón wanted to know.

'Hold your breath.'

'What?'

'Remember that she was informed about Bethany by her cousin? She said she had been so grateful that he had helped her to find this place for Alfredo, and now this cousin was in trouble.'

'What kind of trouble?'

'She said that about ten years ago the cousin's wife had given birth to a child with Down's syndrome. He had told her they couldn't manage their son anymore, and were looking for a place where he could stay. She said since he had helped her she now wanted to try and help him.'

'My God, Claire. What did you say?'

'I said to tell the cousin that he could bring his son. It was a woman to woman conversation, you know.' Ramón didn't notice she was mimicking his own act.

'You said what?' He almost exploded.

'Of course I didn't, you silly man.'

27.

Alonso Calderon

What made the parents of Alonso Calderon think they could no longer manage to take care of their boy? The question had been on Claire's mind the very first moment she had laid her eyes upon him. Alonso was a very likeable child in the same way most of the children of his age were likeable. Ordinarily he was lovable and amusing, sometimes he was annoying, and occasionally you would rather lock him away. He was a little short for his age, a bit too heavy, with blond hair and blue eyes, and most of all, a charming smile from ear to ear, at least most of the time.

What Claire didn't realize, or didn't understand, was that his parents wanted to find a place for their son to stay *because* they loved him. He was one of those creatures whose life people either thought to be very precious or deplorable. For some, children like Alonso were a burden that didn't come for no reason. Parents of these children must have been at fault. God does not send punishment randomly. For others, they were precious. Children like Alonso were called 'little angels,' or 'God's innocent' because of their presumed purity. Either way, they had a slim chance of growing up like their siblings and peers.

In Alonso's case a bit of both was true. His mother adored him for his blond curls, and his father loved the little games they played together. But they suffered the stares in their neighbourhood, not to mention the offensive comments within their own families. Most of all, however, they suffered from the boy's pain when he came running inside after being rejected or ridiculed by the children in their street.

His parents were not at all abusive, like Alfredo's father had been, but they were sensible people, too sensible perhaps. They anticipated his future life in the city and believed it would be very hard for him. If they couldn't prevent the disappointments and sorrows, they at least could try to find a better place for him to grow up.

'It's not that they don't want him at home any longer,' Claire said to Ramón, 'it's just that they are afraid their son will not be happy while growing into a young man in their own neighbourhood. But how many parents would send their kids away for that reason?'

Ramón disagreed. 'Seeing their child suffer from abuse is more than most parents can bear,' he said, refusing to put any blame on Alonso's parents. The truth of the matter was, however, that Ramón had been attached to the boy as soon as he got to know him a little, in the same way that Claire had been drawn to Alfredo.

The very first weekend Alonso spent at Bethany they celebrated Philippe's fortieth birthday. They had *tapas* for dinner, for which occasion Claire had worked hard to make Bethany's dining hall look like a Sevillian restaurant. Afterwards there was singing and dancing, the finale to which was Ramón jumping around the room like a horse with Alonso on his back. That was how their special bond started. Claire had been thrilled to see Ramón so happy. It was a year and four months since she had arrived. Coming to Bethany she had no idea what to expect. Now she had to admit that it had surprised her in every possible way.

The next day, early on Sunday morning, Ramón was wandering through the orchard, not for any particular reason other than to be by himself, when all of a sudden he was called.

'Hamon, Hamon!' Running as fast as his little feet could carry him Alonso arrived at his side. Before Ramón had been able to say anything the boy put his arms around his waist, and laid his head against him.

'Hey cowboy, you're up early,' Ramón said, stroking his blond curls affectionately. 'Claire didn't want you in the kitchen, I bet.' The boy raised his head and looked up to him with his adorable smile. 'So now you're my responsibility, apparently.'

They wandered around among the trees, when Ramón stopped him, and bent his knees to be able to hold the boy's face between his hands. 'What if you and I would surprise Claire with a nice bowl of blackberries? What do you say? Wouldn't it be fun to surprise her?' At this point Ramón learned something about Alonso that took him in for good. Having no clue what was said to him, the boy just spread his arms and laughed as if he just heard the best of jokes he had heard in years. Alonso didn't respond to words, Ramón realized, he responded to emotions.

Close to the stables they found an old jar that would just about do, and then they started berry picking at the other end of the orchard. When Ramón told Claire about it later, his eyes were still beaming.

'I never knew picking blackberries was this kind of adventure. Most of the berries he found went into his mouth right away, but every time I put a handful of berries in the pot he would clap his hands and roar as if Spain had scored a goal. I tell you, if you ever need an encouraging audience, put Alonso in the front row, and you're safe.'

The fall season arrived, which made sunny Andalusia a much more pleasant place to be than in the heat of summer with its hazy skies. The sky turned to a deep dark blue that people from the north could only dream of. With the first occasional rain showers the fields turned green again, after a long sunburnt summer. The countryside was bustling with the sounds and sights of harvesting farmers, and so in its own modest way was the community of Bethany. The house and its people radiated new energy, but alas not everyone did. The habitual happy appearance of Alonso Calderon was gone. He fell ill.

About six weeks after he had arrived, the boy lost his usual happy demeanor. He had almost stopped eating. His eyes lost their liveliness, and his face grew pale. Most of the day he would lie on the sofa in the living room, without an appetite for anything. His condition deteriorated. Claire decided to call the Doctor Solares for a visit, but when he came and examined the boy, he found nothing.

Ramón spoke with the doctor about the boy suffering from some unknown medical condition. After due deliberation they decided to call Alonso's parents. May be there was a history they were familiar with.

'Señor Calderon, good afternoon, it is Ramón Jimenez.'

'Ramón! How are you doing? How is Alonso?

'That's why I am calling. Alonso is sick. We called the local doctor who came to see him, but couldn't find anything wrong. Claire and I are worried. I wondered whether you could help us. Did Alonso have such periods of infirmity when he was with you?'

'Does he have a fever?'

'No. We have checked that, he doesn't.'

'Kids with his condition are known for heart failure. My wife and I were always worried about this when he developed a fever. But if he didn't, as you say, I wouldn't know.'

'It's really unexpected, given how happy he seemed since he came to us.'

'You know what, let me consult my wife for a few minutes. Then I will call you back.' Ramón thanked him for understanding.

When Alonso's father called him back he told Ramón that his wife had no clue either of what might be wrong. If Ramón agreed, however, she would come tomorrow to visit their son. Not that they suspected something was wrong with his treatment at Bethany, but she just wanted to see him. Ramón agreed, and informed Claire about it.

'Alonso's mother will come to visit him tomorrow.'

'No cause for alarm, I hope?'

'No, I don't think so. She just wants to see him. I didn't see any harm in it.'

'That's fine.'

When Mrs Calderon arrived the next day, the boy was still on the sofa. Claire had made him some fresh fruit juice, but he didn't seem to care for it. This changed rapidly, however, when his mother entered the room.

'Mommy!' She sat down with him, and held him close.

Ramón had been away that day. In the evening, when he came home, there was no Alonso on the sofa. He looked alarmed at Claire.

'Where is he?'

'Upstairs in his bed sleeping,' she said. 'Ramón, you won't believe this. The moment his mother came in the room, his energy started to flow, and in no time he was his own self again, smiling his beautiful smile. His mother put him to bed before she went home.'

'This boy being taken away from his mother got homesick. How stupid we haven't seen this coming!'

'Don't blame yourself.' Claire wanted to comfort him. 'You and I are amateurs, remember? We're just trying to assist people by being gentle to them. That's all we have.'

Ramón was grateful for Claire always having her feet firmly on the ground. They agreed that it would be wise to ask Alonso's parents to visit him once every week. When they did ask them, they were more than happy to cooperate. Alonso became the first and the only member of Bethany to be frequently visited by his closest relatives.

28.

The Chapel

In the spring of 1977 the House of Bethany entered into its third year as a community of seven. Ramón was aware of the fact that this was not the end of it. More people would show up at their gate. Looking back it struck him that from the time he invited Philippe Bousquet and Eduardo Villanova into his house he never had done much planning. He was not even sure when he had been able to buy Bethany that he had had a plan other than having a bigger house. The immediate need for a bigger house came from the inconvenience of the small place where he had lived with the two men. There had been hardly any space in that house where he could be on his own, which at times he desperately needed. Then he found Bethany. It clearly had enough space for many more people than their party of three. It was only then that he contemplated the possibility of enabling their party of three to grow into a larger community.

Though Ramón knew he was not a planner, he certainly was a reflective mind. Looking at how their community developed, he began to see it as a possible response to a society that was struggling, but had no clue what to do with its marginal people. There were many people who had difficulties with living on their own, like his two friends, but they did not belong in mental hospitals or institutions. They just needed family and friends to assist them. Most of all they needed to be loved. But in the lives of Philippe and Eduardo he had seen that the caretakers in the hospital where he found them simply could not respond to this most crucial need.

It was far from a man like Ramón Jimenez to doubt the dedication of the people working in such places. But the regime of a service system did not seem to leave much energy to be attached to the folks they were supposed to care about. How were human beings supposed to live like this, having their need to be loved remaining unfulfilled? When he thought about it, he did not apprehend this need in a sentimental, but rather in a spiritual sense. Loving people he believed, is trying to be attentive to their souls. Looking at Bethany from this angle he developed the notion of a spiritual community.

If anything was alien to Ramón Jimenez, it was to fail to act on ideas that he thought were important. When years ago in that mental hospital he had noticed the question in his friends' eyes, and understood they were longing for friendship, it had to be turned into something practical. Now that the notion of a spiritual community was in his mind, he needed to do something with that too.

'Claire, I would like to make an addition to the house,' he said one evening when she was showing him around in the garden.

'What do you want to add?'

'I have set my heart on building a chapel,' he said. 'It has been on my mind for some time now, and I believe now the time has come to do it.'

'A chapel?'

'Yes, a chapel.'

'I always knew you had something of a priest in you,' she said remembering their first conversation in the streets of Seville.

Ramón didn't like her remark. It felt awkward, but he said nothing. Claire was not responding to what he wanted to share with her. When she noticed her mistake she regretted it and started anew.

'What do you want to do with it?'

'I want it to be a place of silence, and meditation. And a place of worship too.'

'I see.' She tried to sympathize with him, but really didn't know how. Being from the Andalusian South, where religion was mostly an affair for pious women, Claire was not familiar at all with speaking about the subject with a man. As a matter of fact she felt like she didn't have anything useful to say.

Now that she came to think of it, what was her idea of religion? When she asked herself the question, which she would never have asked had she not been living with this man, there was nothing like a clear answer. In her year in Seville she had witnessed the processions during *Semana Santa* but the devotion of the people had not really touched her heart.

'I am afraid I am not much of a religious person myself,' she said with some hesitation.

He looked at her with a frown. 'Is that what you think I am asking of you?'

'You're not asking me anything.'

'Then I will. Do you agree that we spend money to build a Chapel?' He said it with a sober voice, which could not hide his disappointment.

'No Ramón, that's not how you and I want to work together, do we? As if this chapel is going to be your thing, for which you only need my consent regarding the money. I know you want to share your thoughts about this idea, but I am not much of a spiritual soul, you know that, so you have to guide me here.'

He turned to her and took her hands in his.

'Thank you dear, thank you for saying this.' Claire noticed Ramón was really moved in speaking to her as he did. 'For a moment I felt indeed like it would be 'my' chapel, rather than the chapel of the House of Bethany, which would be a dreadful thing. I don't want you to become a religious person, nor anyone else for that matter, but we, that means I, need a place where I can be in touch with my soul. Living together with our friends is draining our energy. Assisting them with gentleness is hard work. You know that.'

'A place to re-energize, is that what you mean?'

'Well, not exactly,' he said with a faint smile. 'Let me put it this way. When I look back at my life as it has developed since I came to live with these guys, and since you and I started here in Bethany, it is clear to me that we have been blessed. To me Bethany is a community of grace. We could have failed in so many ways, but so far it hasn't happened. I see that as a blessing, and I simply want to have a place and a ritual to say 'Thank you.' Besides, since there is no guarantee we will not fail as yet, I also want it to be a place to speak the fears and worries of my heart and assume they will be heard.'

He laid his hand upon her shoulder. 'Let's get in, it's getting chilly.' Claire looked up to him, not knowing what to say. They walked out of the garden into the house.

A few days later Claire decided to come back to the subject herself. She wanted to surprise him. 'I have been thinking about your idea of a chapel,' she said with a pleasant smile. 'What would you say if we put it in the far end of the orchard? The little walk that it will take to get there is just enough to prepare oneself for entering it as a sanctuary.'

Ramón was very surprised indeed. 'I love that idea! I hadn't thought about it that way. Thank you for setting your mind to it, that means a lot to me.'

'There is only one thing,' she continued. 'I would hate it to be one of these ugly modern things that do not fit into their surroundings whatsoever, so you would make me very happy if it can be a building that really fits in with the house. Would you allow me to come up with a plan?'

Ramón had been more than happy to oblige her on the chapel's architecture, and when he saw the result, he could not but admire her for her taste. Claire had remembered how small farmers in her childhood added new barns to their property even though they were mostly short of money. They went around in the neighbouring villages to look for properties that had fallen to ruin, and then bargained with their owners for building materials they could use: brick stones, wooden beams, roof tiles, and so on. This way they collected what they found here and there, loaded it on their trucks, and built with it whatever needed to be built. She had seen farmhouses expanding in ways that after some years made it difficult to recognize their original plan.

'That is how I would like the chapel to be built,' she had told Ramón. He was very much taken in, and asked her if she would like to arrange everything that was needed for it.

'What about the interior?' she said.

'Nothing special, I would say. Make sure the windows let in enough light, but can keep the heat out. You would do me a favour if there would be a special place for an altar in the form of a robust table opposite the entrance.'

'You mean that part of the floor needs to be elevated a little like a podium?'

'Yes, but just about four or five inches.'

'Good, I will make sure that it is rightly done. I will give that builder in the village a call, and see what he can do for us.'

Three months later, at the beginning of the summer, the community of Bethany inaugurated its new chapel. It was a rectangular space with the door in the middle of its longer side so that the altar opposite the door was only eight yards away. The two parts of the building left and right of the entrance were facing west and east. The chapel didn't feel like a church at all, which had been one of Claire's concerns.

From the outside it looked just like Claire had intended. Built from old brick stones and beams, painted white, it resembled the house so much that it could have been part of the property for a long time. She had made the final plan with the builder from Benacazón who had been very cooperative. Not only had he taken care of the technical details of the building plan, he had also made sure they obtained the necessary permission from the local authorities to add a building on Bethany's premises. Claire had been very pleased when the builder informed her that he had found a ruin in the fields north of Sanlúcar la Mayor. There had been just enough to build the entire outside wall to cover the building blocks they had used for construction.

The opening ceremony was on a Sunday morning when Ramón had asked Father Gilberto, the priest from Sanlúcar they had befriended, to say mass. Ramón had invited a few people from Seville who had helped him buying Bethany. They came, together with people from the village, among them the mayor of Benacazón, who had been generous in her support. Mr and Mrs Calderon, Alonso's parents, were also there. For this special occasion Alfredo's parents had also been invited, without telling their son, but that did not work out.

When at the opening of service the bell was rung, the priest entered followed by Alfredo and Alonso who had been prepared by Ramón and Claire to assist him. It had been a sober but moving service due to the solemnity with which the young man and the boy had observed their task.

Afterwards they had coffee and apple and cherry pie in the orchard, for which they had prepared a kind of terrace under the fruit trees. Ramón looked very pleased with the chapel's inauguration.

'You seem very pleased, Mr Jimenez,' the mayor had said to Ramón.

'I am, your honour, I am. It feels like the House of Bethany really got started today.'

29.

An Artist from the North

As Ramón Jimenez saw it, the House of Bethany was still not complete. The garden had provided its members with some opportunities to work, but it was mainly Philippe who spent most of his days in the garden with Claire. Alfredo would love to help out, but with his back the way it was he couldn't do much. Working in the garden was a rather painful exercise for his crooked body. Eduardo also was not a strong man. Fernando was very strong, but he ruined more than he knew, so he was not much help either. The lack of being able to provide all of them with a useful occupation kept Ramón brooding about the possibility of some kind of workshop. When one night at the dinner table he started to talk about it, only Alfredo had some idea of what he would like to do.

'I loved drawing, as a child,' he said. 'I usually was with my mother when I was drawing. Sitting at the kitchen table, she with some needlework, and me with a sheet of white paper. They were the most peaceful hours in our house.'

'What did you draw?' Claire wanted to know.

'Mostly what they call still life, for example, I would put a bottle of wine, and glass in front of me and start drawing.'

'Did your mother like your drawings?' Philippe wanted to know.

'Yes, she did. Actually, now that you ask, I had almost forgotten she kept the ones we thought were good in a map that she hid in her cupboard.'

'She hid it? What for?' Philippe asked.

'From whom, you'd rather ask; from my father. Drawing was for lazy people he thought, like painting, or art in general.'

Ramón said nothing and just listened, but what Alfredo had told them made him think about the idea of some kind of art workshop. That was what Bethany needed.

'You might have told us this before, Alfredo,' Claire said. 'We will make sure we get some paper and pencils in the house, so that you can have these peaceful hours again. We do have a kitchen table, as you might have noticed.'

'Claire can do the needlework!' Philippe's comment was not intended to be funny, but it did cause much laughter. In their opinion Claire was not the sewing type.

It was some weeks later that Ramón had to be in town where he had to speak with some people of the archdiocese of Seville about money. It was the same place that he had been looking for the day he had met Claire. After he had finished his business there, he had taken the opportunity to visit some of the Andalusian ceramic art studios across the river. He also wanted to see some of the tableaux that the city was famous for. The one he was especially fond of depicted one of his classical heroes, *Don Quixote de la Mancha*.

Turning right after the bridge, he entered the first studio he could find, where he was greeted by a man who, given his outfit seemed to be one of the *ceramistas*. Ramón asked his question. The man had responded with pointing out where to go and how to get there, and commented that it was very interesting, particularly if he was a fan of Cervantes' story.

'I am,' Ramón had answered.

'Then you must see it. It shows Don Quixote on his horse Dulcinea with a spear in his hand, and Sancho Panza on his mule, while they are looking at a windmill in the distance. The way they are depicted displays his heroic clumsiness in a sublime way.'

'You're a connoisseur, then?'

'As you can see,' the man said, pointing at his apron, 'I am a potter myself, so at least I know what it takes to make such a piece. Magnificent craftsmanship.'

'Thank you for the information, very helpful. Oh …eh my name is Ramón Jimenez, from Benacazón, a small village west of the city.'

'Antonio Ardiles,' the man responded. 'I am an artist, I am from the North, Galicia.' They shook hands, and when the man accompanied Ramón to the door, they said goodbye. Standing on the doorstep, Ramón turned around and said:

'We are looking for an artist who would consider coming to assist us setting up a pottery workshop.'

One of the great gifts of Ramón Jimenez was his ability to see the miracle of the present moment. Many people know how to use their eyes, of course, but not many are inclined to look at what presents itself to them as a possible sign. Ramón was always open to that possibility. Standing on that doorstep of a famous ceramic studio in Seville, he saw the possibility that the *ceramista* in front of him might just be the man he needed. He turned out to be right. Three months later Antonio Ardiles came to Bethany just before it was entering its fourth year.

Antonio did not come alone, however. Only shortly after he had arrived, he went to speak with Ramón and Claire. It turned out he had a fiancée who was looking for a place for her daughter Sofia for some time. Carina Recuenco was a widow whom the potter had met not long before he came to Bethany. She was worried about the girl's future. As a preschooler her 'little darling' had fallen ill. A strange infectious disease had affected her central nervous system. She lost the control over her feet, and her speech had not developed well since then; it was a little slurred. At school it turned out that her learning difficulties were significant. The advice to the mother had been to take Sofia from school and find her a place where she could be happy.

'When I told her I was working here in Benacazón, she wanted to know why I would do such a thing, and leave the studio in Triana. After hearing about Bethany she was convinced that this should be the place to give a home to Sofia.'

Carina Recuenco had not anticipated the advice of taking her daughter from school, let alone being ready to devote her life to a daughter in a wheelchair. A very attractive woman herself, she had little affinity with imperfection when it came to looks. Her daughter had a kind heart, but her appearance was not that of a 'pretty' girl. In the presence of her mother she became a teenager who was full of anxiety; not the usual anxiety of girls her age who were enjoying giggling and gossiping about friends and new relationships. Confined to her wheelchair, Sofia's anxiety was directed at pleasing her mother when it was expected from her, which could be at any given moment. The result of living with the fear of her mother's disapproval was that at the age of sixteen the girl was a nervous wreck.

Ramón and Claire had accepted that Carina should come with her daughter and visit Bethany to see what the place was like. It happened to be after her third visit that Ramón spoke afterwards with Claire.

'I am worried about what we're getting ourselves into, Claire.'

'Why is that?'

'I am not happy with having the daughter of Antonio's fiancée. I don't trust the woman to begin with. But more importantly, it might affect the other members. We will have that woman in the house every other day, and she will start to try to command us as she does her daughter,' he muttered. Claire had assured him Antonio would not let that happen.

'I am sure he will not want to have her around in the pottery all the time,' she said with her usual foresight. Antonio had indeed managed to limit his fiancée's visits to Bethany, which was a relief to his friends.

Sofia arrived in September, six months after Antonio had started the pottery. Within a few weeks it was clear that Claire's tasks had become too heavy. Apart from the girl's wheelchair, being the first female member meant that her personal care largely fell on Claire's shoulders. Seeing that she needed help, they hired Sylvia, a young woman from Benacazón. She came to work with Claire for three days a week, which meant that Claire was relieved of much of the kitchen work.

After a while Sofia was settling in, and the men were adjusting to having another woman in the house. Ramón was surprised about how life was evolving. He had never anticipated living with a traditional division of family roles, but as it happened he was not unhappy with it.

30.

The Project of Expansion

Being a man of letters it was only a matter of time before Ramón Jimenez wrote about their experiences in Bethany. When his first book came out, its main theme was the presence of people in society whose lives did not count for much, people who were considered *'minos validos'*. He argued that if people are measured by their usefulness to society many will appear indeed as of minor value. Ramón explained why in Bethany they never used that kind of language. Rather than looking at what was missing, they preferred to look at what each of their members had to contribute, in particular with regard to what he called the 'qualities of the heart'. Referring to human beings like Alonso as 'handicapped' said nothing that was interesting to know about him, which was that in Bethany everyone thought about him as the most joyful and loving person in the house.

The publication of the book received positive responses. People who read it were inspired by its vision, and wanted to learn more about the project. Invitations to give talks came in from all over the country. Ramón was acutely aware of the fact that Bethany would be seen as a critical response to the world of institutionalized care. It was no accident that when Bethany came to be more widely known, the requests from parents for a place for their child grew in numbers.

'It will not be long before we will have to consider a second house,' he said one evening to Claire and Antonio. 'Seeing the number of requests we get for admission, there is clearly a great need for homes that are like family homes.'

'Is that what you consider Bethany to be?' Antonio asked him with a frown.

'No, not exactly, but that's how people see it when they approach us with the question of whether we can have their child.'

'Do you already have something in mind?' Claire knew by now that Ramón seldom opened a conversation about a topic without having some sort of idea of where to go with it.

'There is a property for sale in Sanlúcar. I noticed it when I was visiting Father Gilberto the other day. I haven't made any inquiries, but it might be what we want.'

'If we want something,' Antonio added, not yet quite convinced.

'You don't think expanding with a second house is a good idea?' Claire asked him.

'I am not sure, but I don't have a feeling we have used all of Bethany's capacity. There is still unused space upstairs.'

'Yes, there is,' Ramón agreed, 'but I wouldn't want to wait till we have used it. Instead I would rather have new people build a new community, and not only stay focused on Benacazón. We could at best have two more members in this house, and the need is far greater than that. Wouldn't you want to take a look at the one that is for sale?'

Two weeks later the two men went to Sanlúcar to see the house Ramón had been looking at. It was a spacious mansion that could be renovated into a community home for about seven people. It would take a lot of financial resources to be able to buy it, but Ramón hoped that the local authorities would be interested in supporting the project.

What followed was a busy time of inquiring, consulting and negotiating, before any final decisions could be made. Ramón's hopes of official interest in the project turned out not to be in vain. They had invited the mayor of Sanlúcar to Bethany and he was quite impressed with what he saw. Particularly the apparent peacefulness of the house was in marked contrast with what he had seen in mental health institutions in the region. It had been entirely because of Claire's ingenuity that they concocted a plan to persuade him.

'You want the man to leave enraptured with Bethany? Make Alonso your ambassador!' she said.

'What do you want him to do?'

'Nothing in particular. Just make sure he is around, and he will do whatever is needed. You will see, you told me so yourself.'

When the mayor came at the set date and time, Ramón was there to welcome him with Alonso at his side.

'Welcome to Bethany, your honour.'

'Thank you, Mr Jimenez, I am happy to be here and to have found…' Before he had finished his sentence, someone was pulling his sleeve. A little put off, the man turned around and looked at Alonso's broad smile.

'Com … com … !'

The mayor was not the first to be unable to resist the boy's happy face, and he gave way. 'And who is this friendly young man?' he said. Before Ramón could answer him Alonso was pointing in the direction of the garden, and took the man's hand in his.

'It seems like Alonso has a surprise for you, your honour. Alonso, where do you want to go … into the garden?'

'Fowes,' Alonso responded, nodding at Ramón's question.

The boy turned around to lead the party into the garden where a wealth of flowers welcomed them: showers of pink mimosa and purple bougainvillea were catching the eye, orchids and daisies in front of them, while in the back the quinces and pear trees were blooming in the orchard, which completed the exquisite scenery. Alonso held the mayor's hand and led him to a little patio in the garden with a table and some chairs waiting to be used. On the table there was a vase filled with early spring flowers. The boy took the vase from the table, and with the broadest smile he could muster he put it in the hands of the mayor.

'Fo you,' he said.

'Are these for me?' the man asked him looking very surprised. The boy nodded. The mayor looked up to Ramón only to notice that his host was as surprised as he was. It made the gift even more special.

Ramón saw an opportunity for a most pleasant start of the mayor's visit, and he took it. 'Why don't we sit here outside, your honour? I am sure Claire will want to bring our coffee outside. I take it that you want to share a coffee with us, that is?' The mayor said he would love to, upon which Ramón turned to Alonso.

'Alonso, will you go and get Claire for me?' he asked him pointing in the direction of the back door.

The boy went in, but he had hardly reached the doorstep before Claire appeared with a tray with coffee and cake. She had put on a white blouse and colourful skirt that matched the wealth of flowers in every respect.

'Good morning Mr Mayor,' she said with a radiant smile, 'I assumed you would like your coffee in the morning sun.'

'Oh, how nice, what a splendid idea.'

'May I introduce Claire Gomez Moreno to you,' Ramón said, 'Claire has been with us from the start; she runs the garden. And a lot of other things, I should add.'

'What a wonderful garden it is,' said the mayor.

'Thank you, your honour,' Claire smiled.

She put the tray on the table, and when she saw Ramón was casting a curious look upon her, she put on an innocent face as if to say 'What are you looking at?' In the meantime Alonso had taken the chair beside the mayor and was watching him intensely with his big blue eyes. If the plan had been to make a positive impression on the man, then the mission was accomplished.

After he had seen Antonio's workshop and was ready to return to Sanlúcar, the mayor said to Ramón that he already heard quite a bit about Bethany, but what he had seen and heard had by far surpassed his expectations.

When Ramón came back into the house and saw Claire, he said, 'Was that your idea with the vase?'

'Why? I told you Alonso would be your best ambassador!' When Ramón looked at her, she just gave him the same innocent face again. He laughed. 'Very well done!'

A busy time followed in which Ramón was occupied with talks and presentations to attract new interest in Bethany from people who might be able to contribute funds to the expansion of their project. Somehow he had managed to convince Claire and Antonio that the second house was only a matter of time, and that it would be wise to start to work on increasing the number of people and organizations ready to support them.

31.

The Blessing of an Unanswered Prayer

It was on one of these occasions that Ramón met a man by the name of Jorge Lopez Diaz. He had read Ramón's book and had been captured by its message, and was deeply moved by Ramón's stories about Bethany's members. He was the son of a well to do businessman from Malaga, and had a sister with a child with Down's syndrome. His father was committed to make sure that his grandchild would have a happy life, which led Jorge to think about the possibility of starting a house like Bethany in his hometown, a small village to the northeast of Malaga.

When Jorge learned that Ramón Jimenez would be speaking at a meeting in the city, he knew he had to be there, and he had not been disappointed. Ramón's talk impressed him deeply, and only invigorated his idea, so that afterwards when there was time for some questions and answers, he raised his hand, and the moderator allowed him to speak.

'Dr Jimenez would you encourage people to start a house like yours in order to extend the possibility of sharing their lives with handicapped persons? In other words, is it one of your hopes to see the project grow and lead to similar houses in other places?'

'Thank you for this very important question,' Ramón began, but then he paused for a moment, indicating that the answer did not come easy. 'Whether or not I would encourage them would depend on their understanding of what living in a community is like. It is not always a blessing. It is also hard work, both spiritually and mentally. My friends in Bethany have things I like about them, and things I don't like. Of course the reverse is also true. But we cannot pick and choose whatever we like about the other members, and reject what we don't. People are what they are, and they are not always what we would like them to be. I know for a fact that my friends at Bethany think the same about me.'

He added the last comment with a smile. Then he continued. 'The other day I heard a song on the radio. Its title was 'The Blessing of an Unanswered Prayer'. There is much wisdom in that title. People often pray for what they would like to be or have, indicating they want some things in their lives to change. Unanswered prayers refer to things that don't change even though one would want them to; they remain as they are.

'The wisdom in the title of that song is that when things do not go our way, we may find an opportunity for growth. Our task in life is learning to live in peace with the people that we are given. When we are willing to learn this, a house like Bethany will certainly create the opportunity to live that way.'

After Ramón's presentation was finished, Jorge came over to approach him, which was not unexpected. When he had told him what was on his mind, Ramón said,

'I had a feeling already that the question was more personal than you phrased it. What is your connection with handicapped people?'

In response Jorge told him about his sister, and about his grandfather's intention. He also told him that he had worked in Malaga as a student of psychiatry for a number of years in a mental hospital called *San Francisco Asís*. There he had seen that part of the problem of his patients had not much to do with psychiatry. They lacked the intimacy of friendship; there simply was no one who loved them, not even someone who liked them. The nurses of the hospital saw them as 'inmates' who needed to be looked after. Since many of these patients had lost contact with their families, they were suffering from a life without affection.

'I wanted to do something about it, but didn't know how. Then I heard about your project in Bethany, and I read your book. When I had finished it, I knew what I wanted to do. Your talk tonight only strengthened me in it. I want to start a house like Bethany for people with a chronic condition of mental illness.'

Ramón looked him in the eye when he replied, 'Of course there is much more to say about your question than is appropriate here and now. If you are serious in pursuing this, we should have a longer conversation sometime.'

'What will convince you that I am serious?'

Ramón was a bit taken aback by the directness of this question, but then decided to respond in the same way, 'When you are willing to travel to Seville, and visit us for a day or two in Benacazón. Then I will assume that you're serious.'

'Fair enough. Let me know when Bethany will have me, and I will be on your doorstep.'

Traveling back from Malaga to Benacazón Ramón was rewinding his meeting with Jorge Diaz. He had been impressed by his determination and thought the young man was quite an efficient character. For a moment he had even considered the option of inviting him to Bethany on the spot, but just in time he had called upon himself to slow down. It needed at least some further discussion before things could get going. Instead he had departed from the young man with the promise to call him as soon as he had discussed a visit to Bethany with his friends. With this promise in his pocket, Jorge had said goodbye.

A few days later Ramón called the young man from Malaga, but only after he had consulted with Claire and Antonio. He suggested inviting him for a stay of two days at the end of the week. That would allow him to see both the house and the pottery while they were at work.

'What kind of guy is he?' Antonio wanted to know.

'He used to work in a mental hospital in the city of Malaga, but he was discontented with what they did there. Their patients

lived lives without affection, he said, which in his eyes made their
condition worse than it otherwise could have been.'

'That point has been proven,' Antonio commented dryly. 'What
did you make of him? How would he be to work with?'

'That I don't know, of course. But there was a kind of
determination in the way he spoke that struck me.'

'How did it strike you?' Claire wanted to know.

'Well, when you and I started, we just did what we believed
needed to be done. We had no plan, no blueprint of what it
should be like. Whoever starts a new community under the name
of Bethany will have an example, which makes it a much more
daunting task because there is a standard. The man struck me as
someone with the determination not to shy away from it. I think
I liked him.'

'That leaves only the question of whether he possesses all the
rest of what it takes, apart from determination, I mean.' Antonio
said with grin, 'But don't worry, I won't tell him.'

When Jorge Lopez accepted the invitation, Ramón announced
his visit at the dinner table. As soon as they heard a guest would be
coming, there were questions about the purpose of his visit.

'What is he coming for?' Philippe wanted to know. 'Is he coming
to live with us?'

'No, I don't think so. He told me he would like to start a house
like ours in his own town. He is from Malaga.'

'Does he have friends like us?' Sofia asked.

'That is a very good question, Sofia. I don't know what the
answer is. Perhaps you should ask him this while he is here. That is
of course if you do not object to his visit.'

'No, I don't,' she said, 'I like visitors.'

With the preparations for a new house in Sanlúcar la Major
and the visit of Jorge Lopez Diaz, the community of Bethany had
entered a new phase. Their first house in Benacazón had not yet
been used to its full potential, but the way it had developed in
the four years since it had started proved that it was sustainable.
They had faced difficult moments to be sure. Mostly the biggest

of Ramón's worries were concerned with raising sufficient funds to keep things going, but there had been difficult decisions to be made too. These were about whether to accept new members, like the one that Alfredo's mother had asked on behalf of Alonso's parents. They had allowed them to bring their son and had never regretted it, not for a single moment, because his presence had been a delight in every way. Nonetheless Ramón foresaw that in times to come the burden of accepting new members would be heavier on their shoulders than it had been so far. So with more of these questions coming their way, he was quite certain that they would become harder to accommodate.

That Ramón was right in this respect, more than he possibly could have known, was still hidden in Bethany's future. Their first challenge came when they were asked to help out in an emergency concerning a little boy who was battered from the wounds of an unsafe home. The worries they had about accepting this child were almost trivial, however, when compared to what they would face at the time when Lucie Miles came along. She would rock the foundations of Bethany's community to the point where it nearly collapsed.

32.

An Emergency

When the boy named Pascal Marais came to Bethany he was only seven years old. It had been an emergency. A psychologist from Madrid who knew Ramón from one of his trips to the capital, called him for help.

'Ramón it's Jacques,' the psychologist had said. After friendly inquiries had been exchanged, he came up with the reason for his phone call.

'I have a deeply depressed child, Ramón, a boy that I need to get out of the hands of his completely hysterical mother. Here in Madrid the only option I have is to take him to a ward in a psychiatric hospital. But if I put him there, he is not going to recover. The only thing that will heal this child, if anything can, is a home. Otherwise he just might turn inward for good. I know what you're trying to do in Bethany, so I can think of no other place where the boy has a chance of healing.' Then there was silence.

'Are you still there, Ramón?'

'Yes ... Yes, I am still here.'

'Can you help? If only for the time being? It's urgent. Not for my sake. Thus far this boy has had no chance in hell to a normal childhood.'

Ramón took a deep breath. 'What does 'only for the time being' mean? Will you take him back as soon as he is doing fine, if that were come to pass?' Ramón was not usually given to sarcasm, but here he felt himself trapped and he didn't like it. He knew very well that when Alonso Calderon appeared on the scene they had allowed themselves to be persuaded into accepting him, and he was fun to have around, at least most of the time. But they should not go down the same road again. From what Jacques was telling him Ramón felt this child was an entirely different story, and he did not want to be lured into saying 'yes' by a vague promise that it was only temporary.

Now it was his friend's turn to remain silent. He knew Ramón was right. He could not take the boy back without putting him in the same situation from which he had just saved him.

'To be honest? No, Ramón, you're right. I cannot send him back home.'

'That much is clear then.' Ramón said it matter-of-factly, without any emotion, which didn't raise his friend's hope.

'Ramón, the boy is seven! Taking him to a psychiatric hospital will be very traumatic. You have seen those places. He will most likely be a wreck for the rest of his youth, if not for his entirely life.'

No immediate response came from the other side of the line, and Jacques was just about to launch an emotional argument, when he could hear Ramón taking a deep breath again before he spoke.

'You need at least to give me some time. I cannot make this kind of decision on my own; you know that. It is a child, so the task of nursing and looking after him will largely be Claire's job. I cannot say yes without at least consulting her.'

Since the psychologist had never met the woman, the proposition made him very uneasy. The more discussion in these situations took place, experience had taught him, the lesser the chance of a quick decision. Had he known Claire Gomez Moreno, he might have been more confident about her advice.

'Can you not just decide and tell her it's your decision?'

'That would be very unwise. Claire is not my maid or anything, if that's what you're thinking. She is the rock on which Bethany survives. Wait till you meet her and you'll see for yourself.'

'I can bring him then?' his friend tried again, jumping on the suggestion that he would meet Claire in connection with the boy.

'Don't push me, Jacques. For God's sake! You heard what I said. And by the way, doesn't the boy have to go to school?' The question sounded almost unfriendly and was far from reassuring.

'Not in his present condition.'

'Afterwards?'

'We will find a way to organize his education.'

'Hmmm.' Ramón thought of Claire's dream of being a teacher, but said nothing. 'I will call you back as soon as I can.'

'Today?'

'Yes, today.'

When he went to find Claire to inform her of this phone call, Ramón was hoping that her vocation as a teacher would assist him. He felt that he was preparing to face her opposition, which made him realize that he himself was inclined to accept the boy. His concern about her opinion turned out to be unnecessary, however. The decision went smoothly. There was no argument between them whatsoever. Within five minutes they were agreed that the boy should come. Ramón was not even sure he liked the way Claire seemed determined to have this child in her house.

No doubt Claire was happy, even though it felt a bit strange, because it was about giving help to an endangered child. She had been working on the education of the members, which was fun to do with Alfredo and Sofia, but then they had been to school as a child. Teaching Fernando was a different matter. It turned out to be very hard, not to say impossible, to get even the most basic principles of reading into his head. Obviously the opportunity to have her talent probed by raising a boy of seven was strongly appealing, even when accepting him meant she had to deal with his condition. It did not bother her, at least not for the moment.

'Tell your friend we are willing to take the boy, on one condition,' she said.

'What's that?' Ramón wanted to know.

'He needs to be available for advice, for the first three weeks, on a daily basis. We are amateurs, you know, and have no idea of this child's condition. If he is a good psychologist, he will understand this.'

Claire did not for a moment doubt Ramón's view that the problem of the members of Bethany was a wounded soul because of the lack of loving-kindness that had dominated their lives. The problem of this child would not be different, to be sure. But she nonetheless wanted to have professional assistance at hand immediately when it was needed.

'You think we can do it?' Ramón asked her.

'I know you can, when I assist you.'

He smiled because of her ingenuity. 'All right then. I will call Jacques and tell him we can have the boy the day after tomorrow. We at least need the time to prepare a room for him.'

When his friend in Madrid heard of their resolute decision he was thoroughly relieved. His worries about the boy were serious, and he had in no way exaggerated his diagnosis of an acute danger to his mental health. The timing was all right. He first needed to get a legal permission to put the child in foster care as an emergency. This he would do the next day. The day after he would take the boy with him and drive straight from Madrid to Seville and then to Bethany. Since they probably would not arrive before late afternoon, Ramón and Claire would have a day and a half to prepare for the boy's arrival.

'The eyes of a wounded deer,' was what came to Claire's mind when she first laid her eyes upon Pascal Marais. He looked very withdrawn and scared, and avoided looking her in the face. When Jacques had left to speak with Ramón, Claire remained with the boy.

'I am glad to see you safe after such a long drive,' she said gently. 'Come, sit with me here on the sofa. You must be thirsty. I made us some lemonade; do you want some?' The boy nodded, but didn't say a word.

She gave him a glass of lemonade. When he took it his eyes very quickly looked up to her and then went down again.

'What is your name?' she wanted to know.

The answer was hardly more than a whisper, 'Pascal.'

'Pascal? That's funny. When I was a girl I knew a boy whose name was Pascal. We played together. He used to be my best friend.' Her aim was to make him feel that everything about him was exactly as it should be, to begin with his name.

The boy said nothing, but briefly raised his eyes to see her face.

'When I left my home town, I lost touch with him.'

She looked at him while he was sipping from his lemonade, and saw the slightest change in his face. No doubt 'loss' was a subject to be dealt with very carefully.

'Sometimes, I still miss him,' she said quietly. She waited a moment and then she continued. 'But you know, one can always make new friends, don't you think?' The boy said 'yes' with his head without speaking. Claire decided not to push him, and switched the subject.

'It will be dinner time soon. Are you hungry?' There was no response. 'Perhaps I should show you the dining room, so that you can see where we eat.' Again no response. She got up from the sofa and stretched out her hand. 'Come,' she said. He slid from the sofa too and took her hand in silence. It was a small and much too cold hand. She held it gently, and led him into the dining hall.

The hall held a large dinner table where more than a dozen persons could easily be seated, and a large cupboard at the side, opposite the window with a view onto the garden.

'We usually eat with ten people, but since you are here tonight together with Señor Jacques we have laid the table for twelve. Shall I show you where you will be seated?' A silent gesture told Claire he would like to know.

'At the head of the table sits Sofia, she is in a wheelchair so she needs more space. Have you seen someone in a wheelchair?'

The boy nodded 'yes'.

'Next to her are Ramón and Alonso. Here is the seat of Ramón. He is a kind man; everybody loves him. Opposite him is Alonso. He is funny; he always smiles. Next to him is Philippe. Philippe talks a lot, but never mind; he is a good man. Opposite to Philippe is

Eduardo, who is very shy; he doesn't say very much and that's okay. Next to Eduardo is Fernando. Fernando doesn't speak at all'

She pointed with a stretched arm to everyone's chair, not expecting the boy would take it all in, but she wanted to make him feel safe about his own seat as much as she could.

'Over there is Alfredo, who is a friendly man but he cannot sit straight and look you in the face. It's because of his back; it is bent, you will see. The next seat is the seat of Antonio. He is an artist and works in the pottery. Opposite Antonio is Sylvia, but she's not here tonight. We will ask Señor Jacques to take her seat. Then comes your seat that is beside him, and I will sit opposite you.'

'Why doesn't he speak?' Speaking was apparently a sensitive issue, Claire noticed.

'Who? Fernando?' The response was again a silent nod. 'I do not know. Perhaps he doesn't know how to speak. Or perhaps he doesn't want to. Some people cannot speak because they want to be silent. When someone doesn't want to say anything, that's fine.'

They left the room to go and look for Señor Jacques. Claire noticed that the boy took her hand. Apparently she had been moving in the right direction, so far so good. No doubt the psychologist would tell Ramón the details about the boy's story. From what she had seen of him so far, Claire knew she was right in insisting that Jacques would be available for advice when needed. She was certain they would need it.

'But for now, just being kind and attentive will not harm him,' she thought.

33.

The Little Gardener

It was fair to say that once in Bethany, which was in May 1979, Pascal recovered in the garden. That was his place of healing. At the dinner table he hardly spoke at all, but in the garden he came to life. For a child of his age who was used to an entirely unreliable parent, plants turned to be a blessing. They didn't speak nor move, while he could speak to them and move around as much as he liked. His first thing to do in the morning after breakfast was a round trip through his plants. Everyone at Bethany could see his eyes lighting up. Occasionally a smile appeared on his face.

All of this had been Claire's doing, no doubt, although Jacques had been a great help. In the beginning he had her on the phone every night for at least half an hour. After a few weeks Jacques had commented that a good teacher was lost in her.

She had assigned a small part of the large garden to the boy. 'This part is yours,' she said, pointing out the perimeter of his lot. It was about twenty square meters. To make sure this would not be a source of envy for her first assistant, Philippe, she had given him the same, but at the other end of the garden. Claire knew him well enough to anticipate that rivalry with a boy of seven was not beyond him. Philippe had been used to receiving all her attention when they were together in the garden. It would not surprise her if jealousy were Philippe's response when the boy was receiving much of what previously had been only his.

Philippe Bousquet was a man who was utterly insecure about whether the world could be trusted. He needed reassurance every day that everything was all right. When Claire arrived at Bethany getting her attention had from day one been his main goal. When some time later it was suggested he would assist her with the garden, Philippe felt he would be getting what he wanted. Working together with her was his daily treat, and he certainly knew how to make use of his privilege. Constantly trying to keep her attention focused upon himself, he would not allow even a minute of silence between them when they were at work.

'We are having a great day, isn't it Claire.'

'Yes, we do Philippe.'

'I am a great help to you, ain't I Claire?'

'Yes, you are.'

'I take good care of the garden, don't I?'

'Hmmm.'

Philippe could easily repeat this train of questions a dozen times a day, which was his ritual to make sure he was not forgotten. Claire never found the man at ease with himself or his surroundings. He was never at peace with whatever he did, whatever he had, or wherever he was. Somehow he reminded her of a drug addict, always attuned to finding the next fix. When Claire was busy pulling out weeds and given to her own thoughts, he would be worried not to have her attention.

'You are not mad at me, Claire, are you?'

'No, of course not.'

'We are friends, then.'

'Yes, we are.'

'We make quite a team in looking after the garden.'

'Sure we do.'

Obviously this was not the kind of conversation Claire wanted the boy to be exposed to, so she placed them in opposite corners of the garden to keep them at a distance from one another. In this way Philippe was less likely to discover that the boy was another possible source of attention.

Providing Pascal with a spot of his own turned out to be a brilliant move. She could have thought of nothing more effective.

It gave him the secure space he so desperately needed. On the very first day, he was at once ready to do what needed to be done. The last time this part of the garden had been used it had been for a bed of onions. It was not difficult to pull out the withering plants and clear the field from what had been left behind.

'Wonderful,' she said when he had worked his way through it. 'Now, here is a question for my new assistant,' she said with a smile. 'If you were a plant to be put in the soil, what kind of soil would you like?'

'One that feels good?' he said, making his answer sound like a question.

'Very good. What we need to do then is to work the soil so that it makes the plants feel good. Do you know what this is?' She showed him a hoe. He shook his head. 'This is a hoe. One uses it to loosen up the top layer of the soil where the plant goes in. You use it like this.' She took the hoe, one hand at its top end, the other half way down the pole, and started loosening up the soil. 'You see? Now you try it.'

The boy took the hoe at the top and tried to copy what he had seen. Because the pole was much too long for his height, the hoe's blade peeped up above ground with every push. He looked at her somewhat disappointed, but didn't say anything.

'I am sorry Pascal, I am a bad teacher. That pole is too long for you, I should have thought of that. Try to hold it like this.' She put one hand a foot below the pole's top end, and the other a foot below half way. When he tried it, the hoe was adjusted to his height and it worked.

'You see? Now it works! This was lesson number one. When you push the hoe, make sure it stays underground just about an inch. Now lesson number two. Look what happens when I hold the hoe in exactly the way you just did.' She placed her hands on the pole where he had them, and started to work. Now the blade got in too steep, and she got stuck in the soil with every move. 'You see what happens?'

'You get stuck.'

'Why?'

'Because now it is too short.'

'Very smart. But there is something even more important. I will do it again; watch my back.' To use the shortened hoe Claire had to bend her back. 'Now I will repeat how I did it the first time.' She straightened her back and adjusted her grip on the hoe's pole to her own height. 'Once again.' She demonstrated the first, and then the second move. Then she asked him what he had seen.

'When you use the short pole, you bend your back.'

'Wow, you are very clever,' she said with admiration. 'Lesson number two is this. When using the hoe: never bend your back, because it will begin to hurt very soon. This is very important. Just make sure you keep your back straight and you will automatically have your hands on the pole right where they should be. The important point about hoeing is your back. If you watch that, the rest is easy.'

For the first six months of his stay, Pascal worked in the garden with Claire every morning, for at least half an hour. To make sure she wasn't interrupted, she arranged that Philippe would take his daily turn in the kitchen service at the same time, and not come outside to join them before she was finished.

Learning how to use his garden tools was only one of many things she taught the boy. Each day she had a single topic. When to water your plants? How do you get rid of weeds? Which plants do you put together? Which do you keep separate? During her lessons Pascal was all ears, frequently surprising her with his quick mind. Withdrawn as he was in the house, he was opening up in the garden.

Claire soon realized that these thirty minutes with the boy in the garden had become her favourite part of the day. She was happy for him, of course, but also because she had found her destiny as a teacher. Most of all she enjoyed her glimpses of the boy on his own, talking to himself, or to his plants, and looking upward more and more each day to face the world. Pascal Marais was healing from the wounds inflicted upon him in his home in Madrid.

34.

Pascal's Dream

His enthusiasm for gardening notwithstanding, however, Pascal discovered that it was not his vocation. Or, rather, he discovered that in spite of his love for the garden, he was even more attracted to something else.

After his first night at the dinner table he had been given the seat next to Antonio. Each night he would listen to the potter talking to Claire about what they were doing in the workshop. Antonio often spoke with her about new ideas he was working on. The boy loved to listen, and imagined what it would be like to make a pot or a vase with his own hands. Without being aware of it Pascal had found his dream.

Even though he had become much more lively since he had arrived, no one in Bethany was used to hearing him speak unsolicited. Unless someone asked him a direct question, Pascal would hardly say anything, till one night when he had once again been listening to Antonio talking about the pottery.

'Could I perhaps come and visit you?' he asked with a timid voice. Claire looked at him with surprise. Antonio, who never lost his irony, not even in front of the boy, fell silent. Then he responded.

'Claire, did I just hear someone whispering a question about visiting me?'

'I am not sure, who could have been asking?' She noticed a faint smile on the boy's face. These little games no longer threatened or confused him.

'Well, let's see, could it have been the gentleman at my left?' Antonio said, turning his head toward the boy. 'Did you say you want to visit me in the pottery?'

The boy nodded.

'What do you want to see?'

'I would like to see how you make a bowl or a vase.'

'Ahhh! You want a peek in the artist's sanctuary,' Antonio said. Claire laughed and shook her head. 'What?' He shrugged his shoulders. She kept silent and didn't say anything.

'When would you like to come? Tomorrow?'

Claire noticed a glimmer of light shining from the boy's eyes she didn't remember having seen before. She sensed a change was about to occur in their relationship. Since she was very beholden to him, she could not be happier than in seeing him spread his wings. If it had to be outside the garden, so be it. She would be thrilled to see him fly.

'Can I?'

'Yes, Sir, you can.'

Pascal's eyes sparkled with joy, but then his face changed, as if something just occurred to him. He looked up in Claire's face to see how she reacted. She smiled at him, and blinked.

'Go ahead. Your plants will have to get used to less attention from their gardener.' Pascal looked at her in a way that touched Antonio's heart even more than it touched hers. His eyes told how much he loved her, how safe he had felt having her at his side all these weeks, and how much he trusted her with the trust he had found in her garden.

Antonio got his handkerchief out to blow his nose. 'Tomorrow morning it will be!' he said. Claire was amused by the flippant tone with which he was trying to hide his emotion.

The next morning at a quarter past nine the pottery's door was opened, and Pascal appeared on its doorstep; his little hand in Claire's.

'I bring you a visitor,' she said.

Antonio got up from his chair at the table where his crew was having morning coffee. He took the boy over from Claire who waved him goodbye, and left for the garden.

'My lady, gentlemen.' Antonio quasi-formally addressed Sofia and the men, who together made up their company. 'We have a guest this morning. It's our friend Pascal. He has asked me whether he could have a peek at the work we do to produce all the wonderful things we make here.'

As if it were rehearsed in advance, Sofia and Alonso cheered the arrival of their guest together, while clapping their hands. Alfredo pulled out a chair for him, and even the subdued Eduardo got up, and shook hands with the boy, smiling, so as to leave no room for doubt whether he was welcome. Pascal's face was glowing because of this happy surprise.

'You must know,' Antonio started, 'that before we go to work each day we have a cup of coffee together. We take a few minutes to talk about what we did last night, whether we have been sleeping well. So, the first question is: can I pour you a glass of milk, or a cup of tea?'

The boy said he would like a glass of milk.

'Good choice,' Sofia said.

'You're very right, Sofia,' Antonio responded. 'To be a potter your body must be in good shape.' As soon as he said it, he noticed a faint shade on her face.

'Brilliant remark, really brilliant,' the artist commended himself. Then he continued.

'But not only the body, also the spirit must be okay. Bad spirit makes bad pottery. Look at our friend Alfredo here, his body is not in good shape as we all know, but his spirit is. He is already a great potter, but he will even get better. And Sofia's legs don't walk, but she has a good heart. That's very important too for being a great potter, as she will become.'

Notwithstanding the pretense of casualness in these remarks, Antonio Ardiles would never miss an opportunity to embalm the soul of his people, battered as they were by their respective pasts.

'Did you ever work with clay before?'

Pascal shook his head without speaking.

'Let me tell you about it, then.' The artist told him about different kinds, and why you would choose this kind rather than that, depending on what you wanted to do with it. The boy sat silent behind his glass of milk, but he listened intently to what he was told. And while Antonio's words were not directed at the members of his crew, they were listening too with glowing faces, even Alonso. Even when he did not get the potter's words, he certainly felt the energy they generated. When Antonio was finished speaking, Alonso got up from his chair, and with his broad smile he hugged his boss.

'All right then,' Antonio said laughing, 'so much for your first lesson. On to work! Pascal, I want you to do two things this morning. First you will go and sit with Alfredo, and see how he draws a bowl. He is our master drawer. Alfredo, you will draw a simple bowl, round in shape, widening its circle from the bottom to the rim. You know what I mean.'

'Yes, I do,' said Alfredo, pleased with this assignment.

'Good. You will teach Pascal how to draw a bowl,' Antonio continued, turning to the boy, 'in this way you will learn how to get a clear picture in your head of what you will be making. When it is finished you will take your drawing to Sofia, who will show you how to make the bowl that you have been drawing.'

'Sofia, you know how to do this, don't you?'

'Yes, Antonio, I do.' Sofia was proud of her assignment. To show she understood it to be a very special moment she spoke almost solemnly. 'I will do my best to show you, Pascal,' she said.

'Very well, you will assist our friend here in making his first piece of pottery.' Apart from being good at his trade, Antonio was also a great teacher. He insisted upon his students taking the art of pottery utterly seriously. He made them feel that 'making a decent pot', as he put it, was something very different from giving them a chunk of clay to keep them busy and let them do whatever they liked. So they were used to being told exactly what to do, but he always gave his instructions in a way that made sure everyone would be up to the task. Looking at the faces of Alfredo and Sofia, he saw he had succeeded.

Alfredo went into Antonio's office where he got two sheets of paper from the filing cabinet, and a box of pencils. He sat down together with the boy at one side of a table, when the artist brought them an exemplar of the bowl he wanted them to draw.

'Alfredo, show Pascal how to draw such a thing.'

Alfredo started drawing while the boy was watching. Since they were looking at it from the same angle, Pascal could see how he built up the image. He tried to copy what he saw Alfredo doing, and after a few minutes the first sketch of the bowl was ready.

'What do you think?' Alfredo asked.

'I want to do it again.'

They were busy drawing, while Antonio was watching them from a distance. He had chosen to treat the boy as an apprentice because he wanted him to feel that his visit to the pottery did not mean to spend an hour among the grown-ups just to see what they were doing.

When a few drawings were produced, Pascal picked the one he liked best and went over to Sofia, who immediately started with explaining how to proceed.

'First you start with moulding the clay to make it soft. Here, let me show you.' She showed him how to prepare the chunk of clay that was already on the table. Then she began to make strings, the shape and size of a little finger, each string a couple of inches long.

'You need to get them into the same size,' she said, 'then your bowl will come out also in a regular shape.' Then she showed the boy how to connect the strings in circles like a spiral.

'You see?'

'Hmmm.' He nodded.

Their work was progressing when Antonio came to have a look. 'This is really going quite well, isn't it?'

Sofia agreed with shining eyes, and was as proud of the result as the boy himself.

'This is only a start,' Antonio said, 'but you need to make a number of these simple bowls so you will learn what a chunk of clay allows you to do with it. When you have learned that, we will turn to the potter's wheel. But for today, you have done very well.'

The artist could not have done the boy a greater favour than treating him in the way he did, just like Claire had done when she started to work with him in the garden.

About two months after Pascal had arrived at the House of Bethany he started his career as an apprentice in the pottery. The time of healing was over; the time of growth was about to begin.

Part IV

Lucie Miles

35.

What Are We About?

Things had changed for the people of Bethany on the day Lucie Miles arrived to live with them. It all started with an invitation to speak at the University of Salamanca. Two months before Ramón had given a talk in Valencia the subject of which had been social responsibility. A professor who had been in the audience had considered it a very relevant talk given the uncertain situation of the nation after Franco's death, and so he had invited the speaker to his university, which happened to be in Salamanca.

In his talk Ramón he had argued that social responsibility could not be only a matter of public policy; it also had to be a matter of personal engagement. 'Every one of us is needed because we all need one another,' he had said. Given the deep divisions in Spain this was by no means received opinion. Naturally the substance of his claim was rooted in the experience of living in Bethany. That his talk would start a chain of events that would end with having Lucie Miles on their doorstep was hard to imagine, but so it happened. 'There is no such thing as chance,' Ramón would say when he thought about this episode later in his life. It was early in the summer, a few months after Bethany had celebrated its fourth anniversary.

Ramón Jimenez knew how to choose his words in order to capture an audience. On such occasions he was like a fish in the water. Never inclined to speak as an academic, he preferred to be a storyteller because that was how people usually enjoyed listening to him.

The meeting in Salamanca had not been different. The audience was mesmerized by his talk. After time for questions and answers the chair of the meeting called it 'very challenging'. Ramón knew this meant that his views were taken to be too demanding. Most people admired Ramón for the project he was engaged in, but then they thought such a demanding life could not be expected from 'ordinary' people. He accepted the comment in a friendly manner, even though he did not see either himself or his friends in Bethany as extraordinary people. At any rate, they surely did not appear as moral heroes to each other.

After he had finished his talk there was a short break, and Ramón was about to get himself a cup of coffee, when a tall, but lean man approached him.

'Thank you for your talk, Sir. Can I ask you a question about it?'

'Certainly.'

'What you told us has a background in personal experience, I understood. You said something about two men, a Philippe and a…'

'Eduardo,' Ramón said.

'Yes … Eduardo. Thank you. What you said about their lives in the place where you found them struck me like a hammer. You see … I have a daughter… Lucie. She has been living in a number of these places. She still is …' He fell silent for a moment. 'I could not help sending her there after my wife died … now five years ago …' The man was clearly struggling. Deep lines of sorrow marked his face.

'I understand,' Ramón said gently, 'If there had been a choice you wouldn't have sent her there.'

The man nodded, but could not speak, his eyes filled with grief.

'What is your question?' Ramón did not at all want it to sound rude, but after his talk he was desperate for a cup of coffee. A quick glance showed the man felt put off.

'… No, let's get a coffee first, shall we?' Ramón said quickly to correct himself.

'Oh, I am sorry, I should not have kept you from it.' Stepping back, the man seemed to give up on the speaker. 'Perhaps another time.'

'Not at all, señor…'

'Miles, my name is Juan Miles.'

Being impeccably dressed in a dark grey suite Juan Miles had the appearance of a corporate businessman. His lean figure made him look even taller than he was. His head was nearly bald with a small corona of short white hair. His thin moustache and hawkish nose would have made him look sharp, had not his sad eyes betrayed him. At any rate, he was far too polite to continue an apparently unwanted intrusion.

'Not at all señor Miles, by all means, you are most welcome,' Ramón insisted. He saw the man noticed a touch of politeness in his response, and hesitated whether to move on.

Ramón regretted his impatience. He looked at the man with friendly eyes and laid his hand upon his arm when he said, 'Is there something I can do for you?' He could be very direct in addressing people and speak to them as if he was reading their hearts, as he seemed to be doing now.

When he saw the man's face change, he knew there was something. He ventured a guess:

'You want to know whether we have a place for your daughter in our community, is that what you wanted to ask me?' The question was out before he knew; it was his way of showing that he was listening to the person before him.

'I wouldn't dare to ask,' the man said, almost in a whisper. When he fell silent, Ramón saw the lines of sorrow returning in his face. Recovering, he spoke again.

'Lucie is a lovely girl, but she is far from easy to handle.'

'How is she far from easy?'

'Basically because she behaves like a toddler, that's how her psychologist puts it, even though she is fourteen now. She cannot talk, but she walks. My late wife had a good sense of humor. When it was very difficult she would say to our daughter, 'how about trading you for someone who cannot walk but does talk.'

Ramón smiled. When in later days he remembered this moment he could not help thinking what an idiot he had been! He realized very well what had happened that day. Truthfulness had obliged him not to turn the man down, even when he had no clue of what he was getting himself into. It had been one of those moments.

So he said 'yes'. Not exactly 'yes,' thinking of Claire, Antonio, and the others, but then he didn't say 'no' either, which for the gentleman in front of him amounted to virtually the same.

'You'll understand that I do not make such important decisions on my own. Give me a few days when I get back home. You can call me a week from now.'

'Oh thank you… thank you, Doctor Jimenez, thank you so much. I will, I will call you!' There was not a shadow of a doubt in Ramón's mind that he would.

When he got back to Benacazón he had two questions on his mind: 'Can we do this?' and 'How to tell Claire and Antonio?' The first occasion to mention the subject after his return to Bethany was at dinnertime.

'How was your conference in Salamanca?' Claire asked him.

'Any great ideas from the scientists there?' Antonio asked with his usual open-mindedness when it came to the world of academic learning.

'That is exactly what I wanted to talk to you both about, but not now.' Ramón had snapped, which in a strange way sounded alarming to both of them. 'Can we meet in the chapel at ten tonight?'

'Any idea what's coming?' Antonio asked Claire in passing by when they were clearing the dinner table. She shrugged her shoulders and gestured she didn't know.

'To be honest, no. I haven't seen him before dinner, so I don't have the slightest idea. But if he wants us in the chapel, it will be something important.'

When they met in the chapel at the designated hour Ramón told them about his talk in Salamanca and the encounter with Señor Miles during the coffee break. He also told them how the man had described his daughter Lucie.

'Why did he tell you all this?' Claire asked.

'He asked me whether we would have a place for her.' Ramón said timidly, anticipating her response to that question.

'What did you answer him?'

'That I would consult both of you, and that he should call me in a week from yesterday.'

Claire had not been happy with him. 'Ramón, you cannot be serious.' All of a sudden it struck him how tired she looked.

'You better be ready for this, my dear,' Antonio joked. 'I am pretty sure our friend here is quite serious. Okay, boss, let's have it.'

Ramón looked very serious indeed when he said, 'I didn't say yes but I simply couldn't say no.' He paused, not at all content with himself. 'I couldn't. In my speech I had been talking about the kind of institutions where Philippe and Eduardo lived before they came to live with me, and about how here in Bethany we are trying to do things differently. The man's daughter had been living in such places, still lived in one, so he rightly saw that what I was saying held true for his daughter. He took his chance to find out whether we might be able to do something for her too.' Antonio's face produced a grin, gesturing to Claire with his hands 'What did I tell you?'

Claire was exasperated. 'Ramón, please, no, how could you? Look at us. We're only three, three-and-a half when we count Sylvia in, and apart from Philippe and Eduardo we already have Alfredo, Fernando, and Sofia on our hands, not to mention Alonso and the boy. We cannot possibly handle a girl like that!'

She had always admired her friend for his vision, but when she decided to assist him in Bethany she instinctively knew that 'vision' requires a lot of practical sense to get off the ground. Ramón looked very unhappy, as he knew she was right. It would just be too much, as it sometimes already was. He was about to admit his fault, when Antonio stepped in.

'Now wait a minute! What is it that we supposedly cannot handle? Have we even seen this girl? Claire, my dear, you know I love you, but sometimes your practical mind drives me up the wall. Ramón answered a man because he saw a consequence of what he had been saying, so he voted for truthfulness. What else could he have said without betraying what he had been talking about?'

Claire was not at all convinced and certainly not ready to give in. 'According to what her father said, the girl has a mental age of not even two years. She is totally dependent in every respect of her life.'

'Mental age? Give me a break! What's that supposed to mean?' Antonio was all fired up by her objection. 'For God's sake, Claire, she is an adolescent girl, she most likely has her periods!'

'That's just biology,' Claire retorted.

Here she found Ramón in opposition too. 'No Claire, she's not a baby. She has fourteen years of lived experience weighing on her soul.'

The choice of words indicated that Ramón harbored no illusions about the girl. Yet he could not accept her diminished abilities as a reason that would set her apart from the rest of humanity.

'I won't allow it.' Claire said firmly, 'And by the way, why did you bring us here in the chapel to discuss this?' When Ramón raised his eyebrows at her irritated tone, she looked at him defiantly, clearly intending to stand her ground.

'Antonio is right. I strongly feel that this is about truthfulness, but as I share your doubts, I find myself in a difficult position. The question is what we think Bethany is about. Forgive me for thinking that this kind of ultimate question would be properly addressed in the chapel. At least I hoped we could share reflecting upon such a question with one another.'

His forbearing response somewhat softened her opposition. 'I am sorry Ramón, but I will not concede to accepting Lucie Miles into our community, at least not without new assistants, otherwise we will break our back. If the three of us are worn out, it won't do the others any good.' On this point she insisted. By bringing in a condition she opened the space for negotiation, unintentionally, and the two men immediately started deliberating on how it could be fulfilled. The result was that Lucie Miles would be invited to come to Bethany.

When Claire was alone in her room later that night she felt very tired. She was still annoyed by the fact that Ramón had wanted their meeting to take place in the chapel, as if the urgency of the question would more adequately felt in a sanctuary. As usual, Antonio didn't seem to care, which she also hated.

Thinking about their conversation she thought it had something to do with men. 'It's a male thing,' she said to herself. 'They get these ideas in their heads about how to live, and before you know they start living their ideas instead of living their lives.' Whether she really believed this, she didn't know. But one thing was very clear. Ramón and Antonio must be out of their minds in thinking they could have this girl in Bethany!

36.

Lucie and the Others

One of Claire Gomez' many virtues was her lack of resentment. When someone acted against her better judgment and the result was as bad as she had foreseen, she would never say 'Didn't I tell you this would happen?' As can be imagined, Philippe Bousquet frequently found himself in that position, but Claire never made him feel like he had failed her. In his case the results of neglecting her advice were usually moderate. At any rate, they were in no measure to the consequences of Ramón's refusal to listen to her and tell Señor Miles his daughter couldn't come.

Four weeks after Ramón had returned from Salamanca, the girl came to Bethany with her father. It was the summer of 1979. Very soon Lucie's presence was casting dark shadows on what was to come. It was simply horrible. Within two days it was clear they could not have chosen a bigger challenge than taking this girl into their home. The peace and quiet of Bethany's community was gone. It was about to lose precisely what for its members had made it 'home' to begin with.

There was not a single object in the room where Lucie Miles was flittering around that was safe for her. She moved through the house, picking up things, looking at them, and then throwing them down. The difference with an infant was mainly that she didn't crawl on all fours, but walked on her two legs, which meant she was actually even more destructive than a toddler.

It affected everybody's way of being in the house that up to this time had been their own. When entering a room, they would immediately begin to scan it for any object that the girl could lay her hands on. It took a while, of course, before they developed that skill. In the meantime there were frequently tears and fits of anger about what she had broken, or torn apart.

It could not be denied that Lucie was indeed an infant in the body of a teenager. The main difference was that she lacked the innocence of an infant. Among the members Eduardo and Alfredo clearly were afraid of her. Even Fernando was running away from her in spite of the fact that he was much bigger than the girl. Apparently, his physical supremacy didn't feel like natural protection.

Although Lucie did not mean to hurt anybody, she nonetheless could do nasty things, like pulling someone's hair, or pinching their arm. She did not seem to understand what she was doing, or why she was doing it. To be safe from her unanticipated attacks both Eduardo and Alfredo would never enter a room when they saw that Lucie was there without someone else at her side. The two men instinctively knew she could hurt them in ways that would make them very uncomfortable.

Claire had foreseen that Sofia would be the one for whom Lucie's presence was most threatening, and here she had been right too. To begin with, Sofia could not move around quickly in her wheelchair. At least she could not move fast enough to stop Lucie from doing whatever needed to be stopped.

Yet Sofia was not afraid of the girl in the way that Eduardo and Fernando were, but she was too delicate a character to know how to deal with Lucie's lack of empathy. Throughout her life Sofia's main concern had been to tune in to her mother's moods in order to be able to please her. It had shaped her way of relating to people, which meant she was always looking for a way to please them.

With Lucie Miles she could not find one. She simply did not understand why the girl did the things she did. Since there was not much to understand, at least most of the time, she had a hard time relating to her.

'Oh no... Lucie... You wouldn't... Lucie!!' This was how most of her conversations with the girl would go. Consequently, as soon as Lucie was around, Sofia would start to display the red spots around her neck indicating her emotional state of being.

Even though Philippe managed not to be bothered by the girl, there were three people in Bethany who knew how to handle her without apparent effort: Pascal, Antonio and Alonso. Without knowing it Philippe had developed his own strategy, which was to deal with her as he dealt with everybody else. As soon as he spotted her he would start to talk to her, which had the effect that Lucie usually was distracted by Philippe rather than the other way around.

During the first week of the 'Lucie experience' Claire had noticed that the boy was a miracle of self-possession in the girl's presence. He simply would neither be alarmed, nor distracted or concerned with what she did, or did not do. Even Ramón, with all his wisdom and good sense, could not handle her with the same equanimity as Pascal did. Ramón had objected to the notion of her 'mental age,' but now that he had to share his home with her, he could not and would not deny that in many respects she was like a toddler.

Somehow the boy didn't seem to notice, or he didn't care. There was an amazing matter of factness about his way of responding to her. For example, Lucie had the habit of picking up a newspaper, a magazine or a book, and when she found one she would tear off a little piece from the top corner of its cover, or the front page. Every time he saw her doing this, Pascal would comment dryly: 'Torn by Lucie Miles' as if there was nothing more to say.

Claire saw how he got along with the girl and wondered what was going on between them. At home Pascal had been tormented in trying to understand the motives of a hysterical mother. It had almost driven him to the point of self-destruction. Bonds of emotion being absent he wasn't trying to make sense of what was essentially senseless. He simply dealt with the girl by not trying to understand whether there was any motive in what she was doing.

Alonso negotiated Lucie's presence in his own irresistible way, which was to hug her as soon as he saw her. After a few seconds she would push him away. Even though she was not the hugging type, most of the time there was a faint smile on her face when he came up to her, which was almost every day. As a result Lucie never bothered Alonso like she did the others.

Most of all, however, Claire was amazed about Antonio. In no time he knew how to handle the girl, partly because he followed the same rule as Pascal: if there is no point in trying to make sense of what she does, stop trying! But Claire saw that this was not all. It occurred to her that Lucie's 'impossible' behaviour spoke to the potter's bohemian mindset. Antonio was not the kind of man to be impressed by rules of propriety. 'Who cares what the neighbours think?' was more like his attitude. Nobody had to tell him that Lucie's conduct had nothing to do with lack of inhibition, and yet he responded to her as if her persistent acting from impulse was an expression of freedom. Of course he knew this was nonsense, but it was nonetheless how he came to admire Lucie for her courage to live her limited life every day.

Among the people in Bethany then, Antonio, Alonso and Pascal were the only ones who found a way not to be constantly annoyed by the girl. All the others were very much troubled by her behaviour, and this included Ramón and Claire.

Lucie got on Claire's nerves more than she liked to admit. The same was true of her friend who was irritable and nervous, way beyond how she had ever seen him. A month went by and Ramón seemed to become more anxious every day. He seemed very unhappy. Finally he asked Claire and Antonio for a meeting about Lucie. Since Claire had not appreciated being asked to the chapel to speak about the issue, he refrained from doing so again.

'All right,' she said when he asked her for a meeting, 'Where do you want to meet? In the chapel?' Seeing he did not know what to say, she continued, 'Look Ramón, if it has a special meaning for you, I am happy to oblige.'

Ramón tried to smile, but he looked sad. 'I had hoped you would feel the same about it as I do, and that we could share the experience of being on a journey that is taking us beyond ourselves. But I don't want to put any pressure on you; meeting in your office is fine.'

Claire was not the woman to be patronized in this manner, of course. Looking defiantly in his face she said, 'Accepting the girl in our house has certainly taken us beyond the life we used to have, if that is what you mean. I understand that in thinking about our responsibility towards her we need a strong spirit helping us to overcome our anxieties. If the chapel is for you the place where that spirit is more appropriately found, I am happy to join you. I may not be a religious person, but I do understand the concept of reaching beyond my own powers.'

Seeing she was speaking earnestly, Ramón nodded and said he would ask Antonio to meet in the chapel again at ten. When they sat on the front bench, Ramón began to talk, not in high spirits, that much was clear from the worn out look on his face.

'I have to admit that Claire was right and we were wrong,' he said, turning to Antonio. 'You both know I strongly believe in the communal life that we are trying to live here, but it useless to deny that this is more than we can handle.'

While he spoke Antonio's face grew darker, but he said nothing.

'It's not only useless, it is harmful as well,' Ramón continued. 'We cannot offer the others a home like we did before, and have Lucie under the same roof at the same time. I want to call her father.'

Antonio interrupted Ramón. 'Excuse me? It's getting tough and now you want to quit?' Sometimes the artist could be rude in a way that he himself mistook for honesty. It made him say things that, even when he was right, were said in an unnecessarily offensive tone. This was one of those moments. Claire saw Ramón flinch under this rebuke.

'Antonio!' she warned him.

'What? I want to say what I have to say,' he barked at her.

'You can, but leave your biting sarcasm out, please.'

Antonio was always shocked when he noticed he had been hurting people, even though he could have foreseen that his 'honesty' would be painful. Seeing the misery in Ramón's face he softened his tone. 'Sorry, I didn't mean to be rude,' he said, wanting to explain what he did mean. The question was not only whether Lucie could stay, he said, but also what it would mean to send her back.

'We must understand, Ramón, that we can never speak about the spiritual vision of this community and not be haunted by the fact that we have sent the girl away. It's going to remain a wound in the heart of our life together.'

It was starkly put, but Antonio clearly had a point. That he had used 'we' instead of 'you' was a brilliant move. It took away the sting of accusing Ramón of betraying his own views. Ramón nodded in silence. The artist was right; he knew that.

'What do you suggest we should do?'

'Seeing the struggle to come to terms with Lucie's presence, I have been thinking of a possible solution, as no doubt you have been doing too. Perhaps I have found a way out that is worth trying,' Antonio responded.

'What is it?'

'We have turned the old stables into a pottery that is quite spacious. I have more space than I need. If you agree that the group of people working in the pottery will not be expanded, I suggest that we use part of it for building a separate apartment for Lucie. She will work in the pottery, she will have meals with us in the house, and join us for celebrations and events as best as she can, but otherwise she will live in her own place.'

Both Claire and Ramón immediately saw that this idea was worth thinking about. Building an apartment as the artist had suggested would not be too difficult, technically speaking, so it would not take a lot of their resources. It might be much more convenient for Lucie as well.

'It does mean that we will need at least one extra assistant,' Claire said, 'or better perhaps, two. There will always be someone needed to assist Lucie, and with two we can organize shifts to avoid their becoming worn out.' The two men agreed. The last thing they wanted was a worn out assistant in Lucie's apartment. It would be a recipe for irritation, or worse.

'What do we communicate to Señor Miles?' Ramón wanted to know.

'Let's tell him about our plan,' Antonio suggested, 'and explain the crucial factor that we need to find at least two new assistants. Then we add that if this doesn't work within two months, we are going to need his help. We don't have to explain to Señor Miles that his daughter is high maintenance; he knows that. But instead of sending the message that she might have to go, we get him involved in finding a solution.'

Antonio's occasional rudeness was only one side of his character. Ramón looked at him in silence. Then he said, 'You are a graceful man, Antonio. This week I was at the point of breaking down about the girl, but you have lifted me up.' Claire didn't say a word but her eyes were moist, betraying her emotion. Instead she got up from her chair and gave the potter a hug that he wouldn't forget for a long time.

'What's this supposed to mean?' he commented with his usual ironic demeanor. 'Did you finally decide that you love me?' Ramón smiled, noticing how Antonio was trying to cover his feelings by making a joke, as was his wont. By now Claire had learned how to play the artist, and she proved it with gusto. Without even looking at him she answered in a most careless manner, 'Silly man! You know I have always loved you!'

When they left, Ramón was the last to turn out the light and close the door. Before he did he turned around, and looked into the silent space, his heart filled with peace, for the first time in weeks.

37.

Eduardo's Funeral

Eduardo Villanova had never been a strong man. During the years he had lived with Ramón and Philippe, he had been ill several times. Unexpectedly, while the House of Bethany was struggling with Lucie, he came down with a serious illness. It began with a slight fever, which was something he was familiar with due to a chronic condition. Usually he would get over it in a few days, but this time it didn't go away Claire decided to keep him in the house not to expose him to the heat of mid-August. The day after this Eduardo's fever increased, and after lunch his temperature was higher still. 'We need to call Solares at once,' Claire had said to Ramón.

When Doctor Henrique Solares examined him, he couldn't find any other symptoms except a positive response by Eduardo on the question of whether he was in pain. He didn't speak but pointed to his chest.

'Does this hurt?' Doctor Solares had asked when he pressed his ribs a little. The patient's face showed that it did. After the usual checks of auscultation, heart rate, and blood pressure, the doctor was not sure what was wrong with him.

'Perhaps it is an infection in his chest. I will prescribe antibiotics; that's all we can do right now.' He took a notebook from his bag, and wrote a prescription. 'Start this right away,' he ordered, 'and call me tonight at nine o'clock sharp about his temperature.'

The medication was given to the patient as soon as Sylvia had picked it up from the local pharmacy. When Claire called the doctor at nine, Eduardo had already taken his second dose. 'He took his medicine at four, and then again at eight, but so far his fever is not going down.'

'That is a bit too early. What is his temperature?'

'40.2 degrees,' she said, 'the poor man is terribly ill.'

'Hmmm.'

'What are we going to do?'

'Do you think you can keep an eye on him during the night? Otherwise we need to take him to the hospital right now.'

'Eduardo would be scared to death,' Claire responded.

'That would not be very helpful,' Solares responded dryly.

'I will make sure I will check him every hour, you can rely on me.'

'Good, let's keep him there for the night, then, and watch closely how his fever is developing. If there is no change in the morning, we need to bring him in . In the meantime, call me immediately if his temperature rises above 40.5.'

Claire promised to do so, and reported the result of her phone call to Ramón.

'I need you and Antonio to step in and look after Philippe, Alonso and Fernando in the morning for their personal care. I will ask Sylvia to look after Lucie and Sofia. The two of you also need to have breakfast with them. Maybe Sylvia can come a little earlier tomorrow morning. The others will eventually take care of themselves.' Knowing she would be up all night at Eduardo's bedside, Ramón took her orders without further questions.

Shortly after midnight the patient's condition got worse. He was restless, and was clearly in pain. He seemed to be breathing with increasing difficulty. Claire checked his temperature and found it was past the critical level of 40.5 degrees that the doctor had set. She called him immediately.

'I am on my way,' was his only comment. 'You will see me within ten minutes.'

Claire had been very worried at this point. The moment Doctor Solares came in the room and saw the patient, he said, 'He needs to go to the hospital at once. I will call for an ambulance.'

The ambulance had to come from Seville, which they heard afterwards when everything was over. The local ones had been busy. 'Rough night,' had been the doctor's terse comment. 'I am very sorry; tough luck for the poor man.'

'Would he otherwise have made it?' Claire wanted to know.

'I cannot possibly say. He was nearly gone already before the ambulance arrived, so his chances would have been slim anyway.'

Eduardo Villanova died on August 19 in the summer that Lucie Miles came to live with them. It would be the first funeral in their house. Claire sat together with Ramón and Antonio and told them what she planned to do. 'We will clear the front room next to the hall, and ask the undertaker to prepare Eduardo's body there, and then bring him to the chapel in his coffin, so that we can visit him there. Is there any family that we must inform?'

Ramón said that there was not. They would bury Eduardo from the chapel, and bring him to the graveyard of Benacazón.

'Let me think about the funeral,' Ramón said.

Claire had expected a lot of anxiety in the house the next day, particularly with Lucie and Sofia. The former because she would not have a clue about what had happened, the latter because she would be in tears for most of the day. In Claire's opinion, where the one had little empathy, the other had far too much. It turned out she was wrong about both.

There was a serenity in the House of Bethany that made having Eduardo's body in their midst an extraordinary experience. By noon the undertaker had completed his work and brought Eduardo into the chapel. The site where the coffin was placed was covered with velvet material of a deep blue colour and decorated with candles and white flowers, lilies and freesias. The man had done an excellent job. Eduardo's face looked peaceful without any sign of his struggle to breathe in the last few hours of his life. 'We need to bury him tomorrow because of the heat,' the man said. 'Please, make sure there are no candles left burning, we want to keep the chapel as cool as we possibly can.' Claire had promised to look after it.

At lunchtime Antonio came into the house with the crew from the pottery. 'Dear friends, let's eat in silence, and think about our friend Eduardo,' Ramón had said. 'After lunch we will go to the chapel and visit him together. We will light a candle that we will pass on from one person to the next, and we all will say how we want to remember him.' There was nothing of the usual jokes and laughter that filled the dining hall that day, but there were no tears either. The house was solemnly quiet in a way it had never been before.

When she noticed that everybody had finished lunch, Claire gave a sign that it was time to visit Eduardo. She said they would go in couples. Antonio would take Lucie at his side. 'Fernando, you will take Sofia through the orchard, following Antonio and Lucie.' She spoke softly. 'Philippe you go with me. Alfredo you follow with Pascal. Ramón will have Alonso at his side, followed by Sylvia.

They proceeded to the chapel just as Claire had instructed. When everyone was standing around the coffin, Sylvia closed the door. Claire took a candle, and lit it. Then with her clear voice, she was the first to speak.

'I will remember you, Eduardo, because of your quiet and peaceful presence in our house.' She stood still for a few seconds before she passed on the candle to Sofia, who was beside her.

Sofia took the candle, and without a trace of her usual nervousness she said gently, 'Eduardo, I will remember you because you always made me feel safe.' Then she passed on the candle to Pascal. Though only a boy he spoke confidently, saying that he would remember Eduardo as he always sat beside him at the coffee table in the pottery.

Next, Antonio took over the candle from the boy and put it in Lucie's hand, while holding her.

'Dear Eduardo, Lucie will remember you because you were never mean to her. And I will remember you for making the first vase in our pottery.'

Alfredo followed, and spoke for Fernando in the way Antonio had spoken for the girl. Ramón did the same for Alonso. When Ramón spoke, and mentioned his name, Alonso stepped forward to the coffin, and delicately stroked Eduardo's hair, which brought a smile to their faces.

And so it happened that of all the members, Eduardo's buddy Philippe came last. He took the candle, and stood in silence looking at his friend. He sighed, took a deep breath, sighed again, and then he spoke.

'You and I have been best friends together with Ramón, haven't we, Eduardo? If I have been bad to you, you must forgive me. I didn't mean to. You will forgive me, won't you? You have been lonely sometimes, Eduardo, without family I mean. I know that. But you also have been happy with us. That I know too. Where you are now, I don't know. Nobody does, not even Ramón. But you will not be lonely ever again because I will always miss you.'

Philippe had spoken from his heart and in a more composed manner than anyone had ever heard him speak. While he held the candle, they stood there together in silence for a couple of minutes. The chapel felt as if it were filled with peace. Standing close to Antonio even Lucie seemed at ease. After Claire gestured to Philippe to quench the flame of the candle they formed a queue in pairs of two, and then solemnly left the chapel.

Early the next day, they went to bury Eduardo Villanova in the graveyard. The funeral was brief and sober. When the coffin had been let into the ground, Ramón said a prayer in which he thanked God for Eduardo's life. Just as they were about to turn away from the grave, Pascal pointed his finger in the air and said, 'Look!' They all looked up in the sky. From the top of the tree above them a white stork spread its wings and flew upward into the fresh morning air.

38.

A Bad Samaritan

Unfortunately the people of Bethany were not granted the time to mourn the death of one of their own. The day after the funeral there was a terrible incident with Lucie in the house. She had dealt Alfredo one of her 'out of the blue' punches on the back, as if to say that she wanted them to pay attention to the fact that she was still around. Being in the solemn state of mind of the day before, the poor fellow had forgotten to stick to his rule never to be on his own in a room where Lucie was present.

Sylvia had found him, hanging in his chair, apparently in great pain. Not knowing what had happened she called for Claire. When she came hurrying from the kitchen, Claire found Lucie standing in the corner from where she was looking at Alfredo.

'What did you do to him Lucie? Did you hit him on his back?' Claire said in a stern voice. She took Lucie's arm and said it was the meanest thing she could have done to Alfredo. Lucie's face turned pale, and she was very quiet as if she sensed that something was seriously wrong.

Alfredo sat on his chair, unable to move because of his aching spine. Claire knew that in this condition there was only one thing to make him comfortable. 'Do you want to take a bath, Alfredo, so that your back can rest a little?' Still not able to utter a word, he nodded 'yes'. Claire laid her hand on his shoulder, and could feel the misery not only of his aching back but also of his soul. When she went down on her knees to find his eyes, she saw his desponding look, still in mourning, not only over Eduardo's death but also over Bethany's peacefulness.

'Dear, oh dear,' she said with a teary voice, 'I will prepare a bath for you, but I think you ought to lie down for a moment.' Alfredo was relieved that Claire saw what he needed. 'Just give me a minute so that I can take Lucie to Antonio. He will look after her. Then we will not be disturbed.'

After this incident the need to carry out Antonio's plan to build a separate apartment for the girl was weighing heavily on their minds again. But this was only the material part. Claire had insisted on finding new assistants, which was the other part. This second part created an even bigger challenge. Who would want to come to be Lucie Miles' assistant?

'Perhaps I know how to go about this,' Ramón had said to them. He had been making phone calls to a religious order in Seville that he knew, the Convent *de las Hermanas de la Cruz*. He had asked the head of the Convent, Mother Chiara, whether there was someone she could send to help out for a couple of weeks. When she had asked what the job would entail, he had given a brief description of Lucie. Mother Chiara had promised to see what she could do. She would call him back as soon as possible.

When she did call him back later that same day, it was to bring the message that one of her nuns, whose name was Maria, would arrive in Bethany the next day. She proposed that Maria would commute from Seville starting in Bethany at noon and returning after dinner there at eight.

'Maria is a dedicated woman,' Mother Chiara said. If it worked out well, she might come and stay at Bethany as an intern till they had found someone to replace her. Ramón had expressed his gratitude to the Convent, and said he hoped that Sister Maria would feel welcome in their community.

'I hope so too,' Mother Chiara answered, 'please let me know in a few days from now, how things are developing.'

When he told Claire the result she was only partly relieved. 'You know we will need two of them,' she said. 'How in heaven's name do we find assistants who will stay?'

'I don't know, but there will be an answer to that question, there always is.'

Over the years Ramón had learned not to despair. This time the answer he was hoping for came to them through his elder sister who had spent a lifelong career in higher education.

'There are professional schools that have internships as part of their training program,' Imelda told her brother. 'Produce a flyer about Bethany, in which you describe what you are trying to do there. Tell the story of one of your people; and also brag about Andalusia and the ancient city of Seville. You can send it around to schools with that kind of program and ask for students who may be interested. Oh… and don't forget to offer free lodging and meals. That will help.'

'How do I find these schools?'

'I will make sure you get a list. You make sure you get that flyer done.'

'You're an angel!'

'Consider it my contribution to your project,' she said. He wanted to comment that it was by no means his project any longer, but instead he thanked her, also in the name of Claire and Antonio.

Sister Maria was the first of their new assistants; she arrived from Seville on a hot afternoon in late August. Since Lucie would spend most of her time in the pottery, it fell upon Antonio to coach Maria.

'Sister Maria is the prototype of a worldly nun,' Antonio said when later that night Claire asked him what she was like. Claire chuckled.

'What for heaven's sake is a worldly nun?' she wanted to know.

'No habit,' he answered, 'jeans and a sweater; and of course no "Sister," just "Maria." Apparently she does not want to be recognized as a nun.' Claire was not at all sure whether he regarded this as a recommendation of the woman.

'Did she meet Lucie?' Claire wanted to know.

'Yes she did. She spent the afternoon in the workshop. Lucie was also there.'

'How was it?'

'Honestly? I don't think she has it in her. She clearly came to be good to the girl, who doesn't want to have anything of that, of course. This afternoon when she offered her a glass of lemonade, she wanted Lucie to sit down first and then have her lemonade. But Lucie had no patience for such manners. She grabbed the glass from her, and then spilled most of the lemonade on Maria's sweater. I think she only just stopped herself from barking at the girl, but it was a narrow escape. We will see, it's no simple task.'

'Do you think she will take your advice?'

'Perhaps, although I suspect I am probably not the kind of guy whose manners Sister Maria will hold in high esteem.'

'Now, why am I not surprised to hear that?' Claire laughed.

'Maybe because there is something of a nun in you too?' retorted Antonio with a grin on his face.

'Pooh!' Claire responded, as if she were offended by his joke.

The truth of the matter was that sooner or later Maria's good intentions were bound to run up against the wall of Lucie's lack of empathy. She struggled to keep up her friendly face in the face of behaviour that she thought was quite impossible. When Antonio saw her struggling he made a suggestion to her.

'Don't try to educate her in your manners. Let Lucie be Lucie, so you can hope to get in touch with her.' Maria looked at him as if he had spoken Chinese.

'Let her be Lucie?'

'That's what I said, yes.'

'But how can you be serious? Look at her behaviour!'

At lunch Antonio noticed she had insisted that Lucie would use a napkin in order not to spoil her T-shirt while eating. 'Now I ask you,' he later complained to Claire, 'who is being impossible here? With a bit of luck Sister Good Manners will be teaching the entire pottery how to behave properly.'

'Which in some cases would not be a bad idea at all!' Claire could not let go the opportunity of getting even with him for calling her a nun.

'Yeah, yeah,' he said in a dismissive way, but then he became more serious. 'I doubt she is capable of liking the girl.'

'Give her time. I only ask you to be nice to her. Even if she is not perfect we cannot afford to lose her. Not now when everybody is stressed.' Antonio promised to try but again expressed his doubts. Maria was a nun with high aspirations to moral virtue. Loving her neighbours was apparently her daily occupation.

In this respect Antonio was certainly right. Maria was devoted to the tasks that her vows as a nun entailed. But she was also a woman convinced of her principles. When the next neighbour that God sent her to love happened to be Lucie Miles, she would not hesitate for a minute, but not without asking herself whether 'loving' meant condoning all kinds of obnoxious behaviour.

'That cannot be,' she decided. 'The fact that God loves the sinner doesn't mean he condones his sins,' an insight Maria saw as a reason to try and love Lucie but not for what she did. What she failed to see was that the equation she just made placed her on the moral high ground. Sister Maria could not possibly imagine that eventually she might be proven wrong in judging the girl's behaviour.

Antonio sensed that something like this was going on when one afternoon he said to her, 'Try to like her instead of constantly judging her, Maria.'

'I do like her, but I don't like what she does. When we believe that God loves sinners we don't mean that He loves their sins.'

'Nice equation,' was all that the artist had said in response.

That same afternoon Maria asked Antonio to excuse her because she had to see Claire about something. She would be back within ten minutes.

'Of course, go ahead. Take your time, I will look after the girl.' He had observed that Lucie was restless, so he had to keep an extra eye on her. To see whether he could get her attention to do something, he placed a basket with scraps of paper before her on a table. First it seemed to distract her, but after tearing a few of them apart, she got off her chair, and moved in the direction where Sofia was sitting in her wheelchair.

'Don't, Lucie,' he heard Sofia saying even before the girl had stuck out a finger to touch her. When he looked a second time, he saw Sofia in tears. At that moment sister Maria came in. Seeing Sofia cry she went over and grabbed Lucie's arm to reproach her for hurting Sofia, without having asked any question.

'You should not hurt other people, Lucie,' she said with an angry voice.

Had the girl been able to talk she would have cried, 'I didn't do anything!' She looked aghast. There was more to come, however.

'Now you sit here on this chair while I help Sofia.' Maria had not loosened her grip on the girl's arm, and wanted to pull her on a chair. Lucie's face turned pale. Clearly not intending to comply, she tried to get away from Maria who wouldn't let go of her. But somehow she lost her grip, and Lucie fell against the chair, and then to the ground.

Antonio, who from his office had watched the entire scene unfold, moved over quickly to find Lucie lying on the ground in a convulsion. She was trembling over her whole body, while white foam came out of her mouth.

'Lucie … girl … it's okay … come back now,' he said gently, stroking her face. After a few seconds, Lucie awoke from her stupor. Her watery eyes were a physical reaction, as was the fact that she had wet herself. Antonio helped her up onto the chair that Maria had wanted her to sit on, and sat beside her.

'Good girl,' he said softly, 'good girl.'

It was perhaps not the wisest thing he could have done, but in his anger about what had happened, he turned to Sister Maria.

'What's gotten into you?' he barked at her in front of everybody, 'grabbing the girl without asking anything?'

Turning to Sofia, he wanted to know, 'Sofia, did Lucie touch you at all?'

'No,' she said softly, 'I didn't have the brakes on my wheelchair and got my hand squeezed between the wheel and the table.'

Poor Maria, who had probably never seen an epileptic convulsion in her life, was lost. She hardly knew what to do or say.

'But ... I thought...'

'Thinking is exactly what you didn't do!' Antonio shouted. His eyes betrayed his fury. This was more than Maria could take. Instead of apologizing for her mistake, she started to defend herself.

'You cannot in front of all these people...'

'Oh yes, I can, and I will in front of *all these people*,' he shouted at her, making the last words sound as awful as he could. 'I tell you what Sister! If you would just stop making her comply with your rules, and for one second, for one second only, would try to imagine living the life of this girl, you would stop giving a damn about those rules.'

Sister Maria's face turned white with indignation. She didn't say anything, took her bag, and left the workshop, running away from this awful man with his awful girl. It had been Claire's job to calm her down. She decided to send her home for the rest of the day.

'I asked you to be nice to her!' she scorned Antonio after dinner.

'Not when she starts getting mean to Lucie. Being good to her, my foot! A Samaritan, that's what she is, but one of the worst kind!'

39.

'We are Hiring!'

'I want you to have a look at this,' Claire waved a sheet of paper in front of Ramón. She had produced the text for a flyer to be approved by him. The plan was that Antonio would illustrate it to make it look attractive.

'A text for the flyer? Ah, let me see what you've got.' His eyes scanned quickly over the words she had written, but he wasn't going to make any substantial comment even though he saw a few things that could have been better. Ramón knew how to work with his companions.

'It looks pretty good to me. Why don't you take it to Antonio and the two of you see how his ideas for illustrating it fit in?' he suggested, leaving the first comments to Antonio who probably would speak his mind about anything he didn't like. Claire had expected a bit more from him but said nothing to that effect.

'Okay, if that's what you want, I will.'

'Sit together with him, and when your draft is final, the three of us will look at it.'

'All right.' Claire wasn't really happy foreseeing Antonio's criticism in the same way Ramón did. She asked him when he could talk about it.

'I will be doing something in the workshop tonight,' he said. 'Why don't you come over and grab me there, say at nine?'

When she came in that night she found Antonio working on a piece of pottery.

'What are you making?' she wanted to know.

'I am trying a new glazing technique,' he said, 'but I will stop now. What have you got?' He wiped off the paint from his hands on his apron, and took the sheet she handed him.

'Please, sit down. Oh, do you care for a glass of wine? I have some good bottles from Malaga.'

'Hidden treasures for lonely hours?' she said smiling, 'I would love to.' He went to his office and picked one of the bottles he kept in a drawer with two glasses.

'Let me do that while you read,' Claire offered. She opened the bottle when she noticed the grin on his face.

'What are you grinning at?' He looked at her with twinkling eyes, and then read aloud what she had written.

'You will be able to work with Antonio Ardiles, an artist who worked in the famous tradition of Andalusian pottery and made his career in Seville where all the great ceramic studios are.'

Claire shifted nervously on her chair.

'Boy if that were true, I probably would not have come here!'

'Well, an intern will spend most of her time with you.'

'Yes, but they're not supposed to come as students interested in pottery. But thanks for the compliment anyway.' He read again the whole text, which ran as follows:

We are Hiring!
The House of Bethany is a spiritual community in Benacazón, a village a few miles west of Seville, in Andalusia, Spain. We are a community of nine people among whom there are six of us with special needs. Bethany is a large house located outside the village in the midst of olive trees, and has a large garden and orchard. Adjacent to the house is a pottery workshop. There you will be able to work with Antonio Ardiles, an artist who works in the famous tradition of Andalusian pottery and made his career in Seville where all the great ceramic studios are.
Your work will be to assist our core members with their daily activities. Each of them has lived a difficult life that we are trying to

*transform by being a community of peace. The members are working
either in the garden or in the workshop. Our goal is to live together
while valuing one another for who we are.*

*We are looking for students who want to do an internship at
Bethany as a practical training for learning to assist people with
special needs who are not valued in society because they need assistance in living their own lives.*

*Travel connections with the outside world are good. Benacazón has
a railway station, and is less than an hour away from the inner city
of Seville.*

*You will live with us in our spacious home, and have a comfortable
room of your own. Lodging and meals are free of charge. On top of
this you will receive a modest monthly allowance. We will assist you
in getting a visa that includes a working permit and the permission
to travel throughout Spain for six months.*

'What do you think?'

'A marketing agent could hardly have done it better.'

'Don't make fun of me!'

'No, seriously, I think it's pretty good. I would take out the
recommendation for the pottery, even though I am flattered!
Cheers!' He took a sip from his wine and looked really happy.

'Well thank you, I had expected a bit more opposition, to be
honest.'

'Opposition to what?' Antonio could be a shrewd customer. He
had Claire raise questions about her own draft without having said
anything critical.

'I am not happy with the "special needs"' terminology.'

'Hmmm. Anything else?'

'The explanation of our goal as a spiritual community is a bit
thin, I think, but all my attempts of making it thicker made it worse.'

'Explain what you mean. Which sentence, for example?'

She took the sheet and read: 'Our goal is to live together valuing
one another for who we are.' After a brief pause, she continued. 'I
had another version of that; it read, 'Our goal is to live together

celebrating the lives that God has given us to live'. I don't know.'
She didn't look content.

'How is this second sentence making things worse?'

'It makes us a religious community.'

'That bothers you?'

'It doesn't bother you?'

'No, as long as Sister Maria is not in charge,' he said laughing.
'But perhaps this is a point to discuss with Ramón. He will know
what to say about it.' Claire agreed to put the question about being
a 'spiritual community' to Ramón. The artist could be a bully and a
far too blunt, but he could also be very constructive. She was quite
pleased with how their conversation was going.

'Care for another glass?' he asked lifting up the bottle.

'Yes, please. It is very good wine.'

'Let's look at what we want to do with illustrations. Any ideas?'
Antonio asked. She explained what she had in mind about a picture
of the house, the garden and the pottery. They agreed that Antonio
would take some polaroid shots just to be able to design the layout
of the flyer. Then they would take the result to Ramón to finalize
it.

Two days later the designing part of the job was done. They sat
together with Ramón later that evening. Apart from the technical
quality, the photos were beautiful shots. The house taken from the
road to the railway station made it look very large and very rural.
The orchard with the almond trees looked lovely. Above all, Alfredo
with his bent back at the potter's wheel was a stroke of genius!

'Thanks for the flowers,' Antonio said. 'I will take my camera
and take the same shots, they will come out much better in colour
and in detail.'

'Good,' Ramón said. 'Let's get to the text then.' He had noticed
that the passage about the pottery had been removed, which had
been one of the things he thought needed to be deleted.

'Any points you want to discuss?'

'Are you satisfied?' Claire wanted to know.

He hesitated just long enough to be noticed.

'I am not sure,' he said.

'Of what?' Antonio wanted to know.

'I am not sure I understand how it describes a spiritual community.' Claire looked at Antonio.

'We have been discussing the same thing,' she said. 'Antonio did like another version much better.'

'Another version? What did it say?' Ramón wanted to know.

Claire pointed to the sentence about valuing one another and quoted the alternative sentence from her earlier draft. *'Our goal is to live together celebrating the lives that God has given us to live.'*

Ramón repeated it slowly, probing the words in his mouth as if he were trying a new wine. He paused. He had that intense look in his eyes that Claire loved about him.

'That is a beautiful sentence, Claire. Really beautiful.'

'But it depicts us as a religious community,' Claire said.

'Does it? Because it mentions God?' Ramón asked. 'I must say I like it very much. With all the difficulties our people have faced in the past, and will be facing in the future, 'celebrating our lives together' aptly describes a spiritual community. At any rate it reflects how Bethany hopes to be different from other places.'

40.

Moral Character

After this conversation, the work on the flyer was done quickly. There had been a brief discussion about the use of 'special needs' language. None of them had any stake in it. 'When it comes to celebrating life I don't think Lucie's needs are any more special than yours or mine,' Antonio had said.

'I don't think she likes wine.' Claire had commented. Ramón chuckled, and then he suggested, 'Let's keep "special needs" in. It is the language that is familiar to most of the people who are supposed to read our flyer, whether we like it or not.'

To get things moving with recruiting another assistant for Lucie, Ramón would find out from his sister where to send the flyer. Claire encouraged Antonio to make peace with Sister Maria, which also meant that Ramón should send a note to Mother Chiara, head of the Convent *de las Hermanas de la Cruz*. Ramón suggested he should call her. Her support for Bethany was something they could not do without, he said, even though he knew her as a generous person.

'If she has any questions, I will try and answer them right away. Calling her is much more direct than writing a note.'

Claire agreed, and Ramón decided to call her immediately.

'Mother Chiara, it's Ramón from Bethany,' he said.

'*Olá Ramón*,' she responded joyfully, 'teaching my sister Maria a tough lesson, are you?' Surprised at this jovial reception of his call, Ramón was not entirely sure how to take this.

'Well … There was an unfortunate incident that….'

'What did he say to her, that artist of yours? "Try liking her, instead of judging her." What a brilliant number!'

'You're not upset, then, Reverend Mother?'

'Well, I hate to see one of my most dedicated nuns come back in tears from a job I sent her out to do, that's for sure. But other than that, my dear fellow, Maria's account of what happened was heavenly music to my ears; Mozart, nothing less.'

'How's that?' Ramón said, having no idea what she meant. He did not yet know Mother Chiara well enough to understand how she saw Sister Maria's experience as an opportunity to learn something about herself she had not yet discovered.

'Well, what we nuns are supposed to do is a hell of a job, I can tell you. Being present in the world, accepting it for what it is with all its ugliness, and nonetheless love it instead of condemning it! The Good Lord could have assigned us a much easier task, I swear. What Maria is facing in your community is apparently a challenge of the same kind. Learning to like a girl whose behaviour she dislikes. Not a piece of cake from what I heard! But what am I complaining about to you, of all people? Keep up your spirits Ramón; this world needs you. I will patch up Maria, so she can go back to Bethany. Tell that ruffian artist of yours to send her a note apologizing for something, but not for what he taught her. Brilliant!'

Ramón had been flabbergasted by this phone call. 'Maybe we are doing something right after all,' he said to himself. When he saw Claire he told her about it, and asked her to remind Antonio to send Maria a note.

'Tell him what the head of the Convent said. He may apologize for yelling at her in front of everyone, but not for what he said about Lucie.'

Antonio did as he was asked. When Sister Maria received the note she was honest enough to see its fairness. After all she had made a terrible mistake. Two days later she returned to Bethany to be received by Claire. Maria was quick to point out that she was glad to be back, and that she was hoping to see Antonio and Lucie in the workshop.

'Antonio will be there, but it's almost time for their lunch break.' Since Claire had nothing further to discuss, she suggested to Maria to go to the pottery, and bid her goodbye. Then she moved quickly to the living room were Ramón took his turn in looking after Lucie.

'Ramón, take Lucie in a few minutes to the pottery where you will find Maria with Antonio. The others will have left, which is a good moment for them to be reunited.'

In the meantime it happened that when Maria was walking past the garden she was stopped by Pascal, or rather by his cheerful way of greeting her.

'*Olá, Maria!*'

'Hi, Pascal. What are you doing in the garden?' She walked over to the boy, and brushed her hand through his hair. He looked at her with bright blue eyes.

'Didn't I tell you? This is my own! Claire gave me a small lot in the garden for myself!'

'How nice of her. What are you growing?'

'Right now? My peppers are doing pretty good. Onions, potatoes, and a few melons.'

'I'm impressed. You are a gardener, then?'

'Claire taught me everything.'

'She must be a wonderful teacher,' Maria said with admiration.

'Claire? None better than she.'

'But you're also in Antonio's workshop.'

'Yes. I want to be a potter like him.'

'What is it you like about pottery?'

'I like making things with my hands.'

'What do you like about getting your hands covered with mud?' Maria asked with a smile.

He laughed. 'That doesn't matter. I love the skill. You cannot just do everything you want with clay. You have to look carefully and feel what it allows you to do. If you don't, you'll mess up, and your pot or vase will come to nothing.'

The boy had no idea of what he had just said meant to Maria. She smiled at him with a graceful smile, 'Thank you, Pascal, I will go and meet Antonio.'

When she walked into the workshop, she said to herself, 'Substitute "Lucie" for "clay" Maria, and you will know what to do.'

The pottery crew came out of the door to go to lunch, but without their boss. She went inside to find Antonio who was standing in the corner where the pots were shelved to dry before being baked in the kiln.

'Hello.' She greeted him, a bit shy, sounding like a young girl.

'Maria! Hello. You found your way back into the lion's den.' It was not a very reassuring line, of course, but he said it in a friendly way with laughing eyes. When she noticed this, Maria had courage enough to return the compliment.

'I accept that description only when you are supposed to be the lion,' she said it with a smile that caught him by surprise.

'Actually I meant ... I was just kidding,' he started. 'It's good to have you back. I should not have barked at you the way I did,' he continued, repeating what his note to her had said. She nodded but said nothing.

'No hard feelings, I hope?'

'I am not sure how to say this, because what you said went deep.'

'You mean about not using your brains?'

'Oh no, had I been using my brains this would not have happened. No, what you said about Lucie, trying to imagine living her life. That really hit me.'

'But ...'

'You were entirely right,' she said.

At that moment Lucie came in, accompanied by Ramón, and went past them as if they weren't there. She wandered through the workshop, but Antonio saw that she had noticed Maria. Then she came over again without looking at anyone in particular. Passing Maria she very briefly touched her sweater.

'Hello, Lucie,' Maria said with a sober voice, 'thank you for not being mad at me.'

To everybody's surprise the girl responded with a little high-pitched squeak, which she very rarely did.

'You only do that when you're happy about something, don't you Lucie?' Antonio said, more to Maria and Ramón than to the girl. Lucie moved again away from them.

'I am very glad to hear that,' Maria said with a trembling voice. Ramón laid his hand on her shoulder.

'Thank you for coming back, Sister, it really means a lot to us all to have you here. I will leave Lucie now with you people because I have things to do.' Maria responded with a grateful smile.

When Ramón had left the workshop, she turned to Antonio. 'I suppose letting Lucie be Lucie leaves me with some free time,' she said laughing. 'So you might as well teach me some pottery, or would you rather have me flittering around here too?' Pleasantly surprised that she had wrapped her head around what he had said, he responded.

'Teach you some pottery, by all means. Um… Let's see. Why not start right away?'

'What about your lunch?'

'And waste the opportunity of a private lesson with a new female student?' Maria did not know him in this way; otherwise she would have known he was back to his usual irony. Now he was amused to see her blush a little. He went to the shelves where the clay was stored, and cut about the third of a loaf, which he put before her on the table.

'Lesson one: you got to learn what you can do with clay. So I am going to give you some, and ask you to make a bowl for me by using the oldest technique in the world. You make strings of clay about the size of your little finger. Here, let me show you.'

He sat down at the table and took a chunk of clay, which he moulded till it was soft and supple. Then he rolled it back and forth on the table till a string appeared of a couple of inches.

'You see? The more regular the shape of this string comes out, the nicer your bowl will be. You will get a bowl by connecting the strings layer after layer on top of each other, like a spiral. Like this,' he said, showing her what he had explained. 'As I said, people in prehistoric times made bowls in this way, so…'

'You mean if they could do it, I should also be able to?' He smiled but didn't say anything further, and walked into his office. Maria started to work. When she was just about to turn the first string in circles as he had demonstrated, Antonio noticed Lucie was coming at her. Curious to see what would happen, he took his chair and pretended to be looking in some papers on his desk.

'Hi dear, you are coming to assist me?' Maria asked her. To Antonio's surprise Lucie pulled out a chair and sat beside her at the same table. She stuck out her finger slowly and touched the bowl that was appearing from under Maria's hands.

'You think it is any good?' Maria asked her without looking at her. Watching the two of them, Antonio saw a grin on the girl's face. Then Lucie got up, and left the new student alone. Maria looked at her when she was wandering around again in her own way and smiled. The principle of 'let Lucie be Lucie' had begun to do its work.

41.

A Letter from Birmingham

'Ramón, look. There is a letter from England, a college in Birmingham; it's sent from the Department of Social Studies.' Claire held out an envelope and gave it to him. 'It's addressed to you.' Ramón raised his brows, and opened the letter. Going over it quickly, his face brightened.

'It seems we have a candidate for an internship. A student from this department writes he is interested in coming to work as an assistant for three months. The school has approved of it, but he asks me to contact his supervisor. There are some questions that they like to have answered before a final decision is made.'

'Are you going to contact that person?'

'Of course. I have a few questions too.'

Since matters concerning assisting Lucie weren't getting easier, Ramón resolved to call the very next day. When the phone was picked up the man at the other end of the line made himself known as professor Williamson.

'Good morning, professor, this is Ramón Jimenez calling from Andalusia in Spain.'

'Yes?'

'I am calling you on behalf of a student of yours, Peter Entwistle, who wrote me a letter about the possibility of an internship in our community, the House of Bethany in Benacazón.'

'Ah, Mr Jimenez, yes, I know whom you are referring to. Peter. Yes.'

'We are interested in his application. He wrote there are a few questions at your end that need to be answered before you can give your final consent.'

'Yes, there are.'

'Hopefully I can answer them for you. What is it you need to know?'

'The main point is academic. When our students do an internship, there is supposed to be someone in the organization where they go, who is responsible for their training. Now this may sound heavier than it actually is. Students need to submit a report about their experience and reflect upon what they have learned from it. Running this program has taught us the results are much better when there is someone on site who guides them in the process.'

'I see. Well, there are three people here who can take on this responsibility. But do they need academic qualifications for it?'

'No, that's not necessary, because they have no responsibility for the program as such, just for guiding the student. Usually local mentors are people with a senior position in the organization.'

'That should not be a problem, I think. I can do it myself.'

'Wonderful.'

'Are there other questions I can answer for you?'

'Well, yes, there is one in particular. Two of my colleagues heard your address at a conference in Salamanca last May and were highly impressed. My question is actually a request. Would you consider talking about your project in a guest lecture in our department?'

'I hope the decision about the internship does not depend on my answer.' Ramón meant this to be a joke, but the professor took it seriously.

'No, no, it won't. That would be unfair to the student.'

'It would. Let me think about your request. It's going to take me away from Bethany for a couple of days, and things can be pretty tight over here. Did you have a date in mind?'

'It's not finalized yet, but we were thinking about the second week of December. We would be really grateful if you would come.'

When Ramón didn't respond immediately, the professor became a bit worried that his invitation was about to be declined.

'Perhaps I may suggest to you,' he said, 'that using our college as a platform might help you in the future to attract a wider audience for your project, which I personally think would be very important. It might also mean more students would regard it as an excellent opportunity for their internship.'

'You make it sound like it would be a mistake not to accept,' Ramón said with some irony. The professor laughed. Then he said, 'If you accept the college will make a donation to Bethany, and of course we will cover all your expenses.'

Ramón felt he could not decline this generous offer, and of course the man was right about the opportunity of having a wider audience. 'Ah, but you should have mentioned the money first,' he said.

'Uhh…'

'Excuse me, professor, I was just kidding. I will gladly accept your generous invitation and come to Birmingham in the second week of December.'

'Oh, that's really terrific. My department will be honoured to have you as a guest.'

'Any more questions that I can answer?'

'No, thank you, not at this point.'

'Then I have one for you, if you don't mind.'

'Not at all, go ahead.'

'Could you ask your student for a resume? I only have the address of the college. It would also be very helpful if you could add a letter of recommendation for him, and tell us what you think his gifts are.'

'Certainly. I will be glad to look after both these things,' the professor promised.

'That was all on our part.'

'All right. Thank you for calling. I wish you a good day.'

'Thank you, Sir. I wish you the same.'

When Ramón had put down the phone, and went into the kitchen, he bumped into Claire who was just making some fresh coffee.

'Ah, fresh coffee, just what I need,' he said.

'What was that all about?' Claire wanted to know.

'If we want to have this student as an intern, we need to appoint someone as his mentor. They want to make sure, their students work on their report in time, I guess.'

'A report? What needs reporting?'

'Oh, their experience working as an intern, and their personal reflections on what they have learned from it.'

'That sounds pretty wise. It might be useful for us too,' the teacher in Claire observed. Ramón agreed. He suggested taking on this responsibility himself. Both she and Antonio had enough on their plate right now. Claire happily agreed.

'There was another thing,' Ramón continued while she was pouring him a cup of coffee. 'They invited me for a guest lecture on our project.'

'That's wonderful, Ramón! Oh, really!'

'You think so?'

'Of course! Think about what it might do. Opportunities like this will be important for our future. More people will know about Bethany. That cannot hurt us when it comes to attracting new assistants. I am pretty sure we will need them.'

'That's what professor Williamson … the guy from the college on the phone, also said to persuade me to accept.'

'You needed to be persuaded? What a strange fellow you can be sometimes! It's your calling Ramón, in case you didn't know.'

It would be an understatement to say that compared to her enthusiasm, Ramón felt slightly more sceptical. He knew he had a talent with words, but he was not keen on travelling abroad. Besides, speaking to an academic audience was not his favourite thing to do.

'"My calling?" I am not under the impression that Bethany is "my" thing, so can it be "our" calling, please?' he responded to Claire's comment.

'All right, all right, if you say so.' She turned away from him to get back to her work, muttering 'He gets an invitation to speak about his life project and needs to be persuaded to accept the opportunity to do so!'

Part V

The Crisis

42.

The Foreign Intern

When Peter Entwistle arrived in Bethany, everyone was curious to see what it would be like to have a foreign intern in the house.

'From England?' Sofia wondered when she heard the news at the dinner table. 'They don't speak Spanish there, do they? How can I even understand him then?'

'When you want to welcome him and do not know how to say that in English,' Antonio advised her, 'you just welcome him with a kiss, it means the same in all languages.'

'Oh, Antonio!' Nervous giggles indicated Sofia's feeling about this frivolous idea.

The language issue did not pose a serious problem, however. Proficiency in Spanish was not likely to be the most urgent qualification to be able to assist Lucie Miles. But the student from Birmingham spoke the language fluently. The resume that he had sent upon Ramón's request to professor Williamson indicated that he had been raised bilingually. His father was English but his mother was originally from Spain. He knew the country well; throughout the years of his childhood they had visited his mother's family in Barcelona more than a dozen times.

'If his mother is Spanish, he is not really a foreigner,' Claire had ended the discussion. At this point Antonio interrupted her.

'Folks from Barcelona?'

'Dear Antonio,' she had pestered him, 'when we have accepted someone from Galicia we might as well accept someone whose mother comes from Cataluña.' General laughter suggested that the artist had lost the point.

Much more important was the question of whether the new assistant would know how to work with Lucie. Afterwards, when they were together in her office, Antonio and Claire discussed the matter in a much less playful manner than they had at the dinner table.

The student's resume indicated that he had no experience in this respect, which was no surprise. That had been true of everyone at Bethany. It seemed wise to have him at least supervised by Antonio for two weeks before he would start to assist Lucie together with Maria.

'When will he come?' Antonio wanted to know.

'He will arrive later this week and start his internship officially on the first of October.'

'How long will he stay?'

'Till the week before Christmas, then he returns to England.'

When the foreigner arrived he instantly conquered everyone in Bethany with his appearance. He could have walked out of a painting by Diego Velazquez, which made it unlikely someone would take him for an Englishman. He was a handsome young man with bright dark eyes, and the thick black curls falling on his collar made it hard to see him as an ordinary person from the English Midlands. His looks more likely descended from Spanish nobility.

'*Buenos dias los todos,*' he greeted them. Claire was the first to get up from her chair and offered him her hand. 'Welcome to the House of Bethany,' she said with a lovely smile, 'You must be Peter. I am Claire, Claire Gomez Moreno.

'Pleased to meet you, Claire.' The young man bowed his head a little as he took her hand. 'Shall we all say hello to Peter, please?' She invited the others to stand up and welcome him too. As he went around the table from one person to the next he made a pleasant impression on everyone. 'What an agreeable young man,' Claire said to herself. Then he arrived at Lucie's chair. Lucie had not responded to her invitation to stand, of course, and remained seated, being much more interested in her food than in the newcomer.

'I am Peter,' he said. Lucie paid no attention. Not knowing what to do, the young man repeated, 'Hello I am Peter…' The girl did not even turn her head. Seeing he didn't know what to do Claire was about to step up when Antonio, who was standing next to Lucie's chair, interrupted him.

'Excuse me, young man.' Peter Entwistle looked at him. 'May I introduce you to Ms Lucie Miles who would be very pleased to meet you, but is otherwise occupied at the moment, as you can see.' Claire saw that the quasi-formal tone confused the young man.

'Never mind Peter, we're all glad you're here.' She found the young man far too delicate to be subjected to Antonio's irony. Before Antonio could make his next move, Claire got the better of him.

'Let me in turn introduce this gentleman to you. This is Mr Antonio Ardiles. He is as hard to understand as the country he comes from.' Then as if she was taking him into confidence, she added softly, 'He is from Galicia.' Remembering the earlier comments on Peter Entwistle's Spanish family, there were a few grinning faces around the table. Then in her normal voice, 'but more importantly, he is the head of the pottery, that is our workshop.'

'Hello, Sir,' Peter said and shook hands with the potter. Claire took the young man by the arm and gestured to him to sit and have dinner with them.

'Why must you always be so obnoxious?' She asked Antonio later when they were clearing the dinner table.

'I was obnoxious?'

'Yes, you were. We need these people to help us out, so you might as well make an effort to make them feel welcome, like we all do. Instead your greatest joy seems to be to confuse them. Do you plan to make this one run away also after two days?' This attack on him was more than unfair. Antonio enjoyed confusing people; that much was true, but he was not mean spirited.

'Claire, give me a break! You know that's rubbish.'

'What are you two fighting about?' Ramón walked into the kitchen after returning from a meeting. 'Has the new assistant arrived?'

'That's what we were fighting about, as you put it,' Claire responded. 'This gentleman here was deliberately confusing him instead of helping me to make him feel at ease.' Ramón did not say anything. He knew Antonio's sense of humour, which he appreciated most of the time. But he also knew his timing in using it wasn't always perfect.

'I will see him tomorrow. We did set a time for an appointment. That will be the moment for his official welcome, I think,' he said abstaining from any further comment. Turning to Claire he asked, 'Tell me about your first impression.'

'An agreeable young man,' she said, 'very delicate in the way he introduced himself to everyone. Much too delicate to be played with.'

'I wasn't playing,' Antonio protested, 'I just assisted Lucie in introducing herself.'

'Pffff... You were annoying.'

'Okay children, are we done?' Ramón apparently had no appetite for their squabble. Turning to the artist, he asked, 'What did you think of him?'

'Me?' Antonio asked surprised. 'He might become a very good assistant for Lucie if he learns how to handle her lack of empathy.'

'Hmmm. We'll see. I will be in my room. If I don't see you again this evening, good night.' Not used to this kind of abruptness from their friend Antonio and Claire looked at one another. It made them feel childish that he caught them quarreling.

When the next morning the young Englishman stepped out of his room Ramón might have noticed what he had missed the night before. Claire had been charmed by his 'agreeable' appearance, as she had called it, and felt she had to protect this 'delicate' creature against the potter who she thought was playing with him. But her comment had failed to interest Ramón. What mattered to him was affection rather than infatuation. His interest was primarily with people's souls rather then their hearts. Whereas Antonio only needed the slightest hint to see what was going on in a woman's heart, in this respect Ramón found himself largely on unfamiliar territory.

'Good morning, you must be Peter,' he said as he approached the young man on his way downstairs. 'I am Ramón Jimenez, the one you sent your letter to.'

'Oh, good morning, Sir, I am very pleased to meet you in person,' the young man responded with a slightly reddening face.

'We will meet later this morning, right?'

'Yes. Your letter said I am to meet you at ten.'

'Good. You'll find me in the kitchen at that time, having a coffee. So, why don't we meet there at ten and then see if we can find a place to talk.'

When they met later that morning, Ramón proposed to sit outside in the shade as the day was warming up already.

'I received a very promising letter from your supervisor in Birmingham. He wrote that you're a young man of many talents.'

'That's very kind of him,' the Englishman answered. 'I hope he did not raise your expectations too high. I have not been an assistant before, so I have to learn everything.'

'Can you tell me what attracted you about this place to apply for an internship?'

'My mother had a younger sister who used to live with us for a number of years when I was little. My father spoke of her as "retarded". I believe there had been a problem of insufficient oxygen when she was born. She and I were very fond of each other. She was a very gentle character. Perhaps that experience was what made Bethany seem attractive to me.'

'Tell me a bit about your aunt.' The young man told how she had played with him when he was a toddler, and had walked him to school every day when he later went to kindergarten. He had spent most of his days with her until he went to high school. When she had to leave their house, he had missed her terribly, he said.

'Searching times gone by,' Ramón said kindly, 'most of what attracts us is what we have learned to love earlier in our lives.' Because he did not really understand what he was talking about, the young Englishman politely remained silent. An agreeable person, Ramón thought, but apparently not a reflective character. He paused for a moment. When there was no response coming, he asked whether he had already been introduced to Lucie.

'She was introduced to me, yes.'

'What was your first impression of her?'

'She did not seem to pay attention to her surroundings, that's what struck me.'

'At least she didn't show it,' Ramón added. 'You can imagine that she needs assistance during most of her daily activities.' Peter Entwistle nodded but did not say anything. 'We have decided to build an apartment for her so that she will have a space of her own to be herself. But this can only be effected when we have people especially assigned to assist her.'

'Permanently?'

'During most of the day. This can be a demanding task, as you will understand, so we planned to organize her assistance in alternating shorts shifts between meals. We hoped to find two new assistants for this task, and it appears we now have found them. One is Maria, whom you will meet this afternoon. The other is you.'

The face in front of him was blank. Ramón could not detect any emotion. Since the young man did not respond, Ramón asked him. 'Do you think you are up to the task of assisting the girl?'

'I hope so.'

'I hope so too.' Ramón said it kindly to make sure the young man would not take his response for doubt. In the silence of his heart, however, Ramón was worried.

43.

Lucie's Apartment

With the arrival of the new assistant Claire's condition for letting Lucie Miles stay in Bethany had been met, and the plan of building an apartment for the girl came much closer. Peter Entwistle's task would be to assist Lucie together with Maria. Her apartment was to be ready for use within a fortnight after his arrival. That was the plan. Lucie's father was informed about it as soon as the new assistant had arrived. Ramón called to tell him the news. Señor Miles was clearly overwhelmed.

'Ramón, I cannot tell you what it means to Lucie and me that you and your people in Bethany are making this effort.'

'I am pleased to hear that our plan has your approval, Sir.'

'Oh, much more than that! My wife always used to say that if we had a separate place for Lucie next to our home, she might never have to leave us. She would have been so happy!'

It occurred to Ramón how completely lost the man must have been after his wife died; so much the better that Antonio had convinced Claire and himself not to send the girl away. Ramón did not want to think about what would have happened had they persisted.

'Can I ask you a question, Ramón?'

'Sure señor Miles; shoot.'

'I would like to make a contribution to the project. There are still a number of things from Lucie here that would help to make the apartment her own. Would it be all right to have them shipped to Bethany?'

'Will you take them yourselves or hire some transport firm?' It was a polite question that would give them some idea of what señor Miles had in mind exactly.

'No I will have them shipped. There is some furniture, and some other things, like linen, clothes, and toys of course.'

'I don't see any objections to bringing Lucie's things. On the contrary, it will make her feel the apartment is her own place. I am sure Claire will be happy to discuss the practicalities with you. We have to realize that assisting Lucie will be increasingly difficult when the apartment is stuffed with things that can be broken or torn apart.'

Even before he was finished Ramón realized what a stupid remark this was. Señor Miles corrected him discretely.

'I know my daughter, Ramón.'

'Of course you do, that was a clumsy thing to say. My apology, Señor Miles.' Why hadn't he left this phone call to Claire, Ramón thought, she was so much better in these matters.

'No offense, Ramón.' As if to back up this response he continued, 'Apart from Lucie's stuff I also wanted to make a financial contribution. I am donating a million pesetas to the House of Bethany.'

'That's wonderful!' Ramón exclaimed. 'We will be extremely grateful for such a donation, Sir, but I think that the costs of our plans for Lucie will not even take half of that amount of money.' It was really not his day because now he had seriously offended the man.

'I meant to donate it to the house, not merely to pay for the extra expenses you are making for my daughter.'

Not to pay further attention to this second mistake, Ramón ignored the man's response. He had a better idea. 'Would you be so kind, Sir, and come and visit Bethany as soon as the apartment is ready? We would appreciate very much if you would come to officially open it.'

Fortunately Mr Miles didn't mind his diversion. 'I would be very pleased to do so. Of course, yes, it would be my delight! I would also see Lucie again.'

'You would. Lucie will love to see you again too.'

It was agreed that her father would arrive two weeks later and stay till the next day, unless he would be notified that the opening had to be postponed. He also would have the opportunity to meet Lucie's new assistants.

Ramón was happy to bring the good news of the donation to Claire and Antonio. They went through the building plan once again, and having agreed on the budget, Claire was commissioned to talk to a local contractor. Her negotiations went smoothly. The contractor promised his men would be able to start very soon. As the project was not complicated, there would be enough time to have Lucie's apartment opened two weeks later, as planned.

A new wall was to separate the apartment from the pottery, and a second wall was to split it in two. In one of both spaces a bathroom had to be built. This was all the construction work that needed to be done. Installing a toilet and a shower in the bathroom would follow next. This might be a bit more work, the man said. Fortunately water and electricity were already available.

'So we will see you the day after tomorrow to get started,' Claire said when she shook hands with the contractor to seal their agreement.

'Yes you will, Ma'am. I'm sure the men will be ready on time; I will keep an eye on it myself.'

'Thank you, Sir, that's good to know.'

Exciting times followed for Bethany's inhabitants. The presence of construction workers proved to be a genuine source of delight. The very first morning they came to work Alonso had hugged each of the man with his biggest smile, before anyone knew what was happening. And of course Philippe was best friends with them within an hour after their arrival. As for Pascal, he would sneak away from the pottery whenever he saw an opportunity to watch what the builders were doing and ask them questions about it.

Even Sofia had a part in the general excitement. Her lack of mobility made access to the construction site more difficult, but her moment of fame came with every coffee break, when she would make a fresh pot of coffee for the men. It was the best coffee they had ever had, of course, which compliment was sufficient to elicit some of her most charming giggles and a reddened face.

The contractor proved to be a reliable partner. His workers finished their job within the amount of time he had said it would take, and Lucie's apartment was ready for use two days before her father was due to arrive. It had a spacious living room with a kitchen dresser opposite to the door to the pottery beneath the windows on the short side that looked upon Bethany's backyard. There was a big sofa against the wall on the left with a little table in front. On the right the bedroom was separated from the living room with sliding doors. The bedroom had windows looking out over the flowerbeds in the garden. Access to the apartment could be had from two entrances, one through the pottery and the other through the bedroom. The door to the pottery was exceptionally wide, which made the apartment accessible to a wheelchair. Sofia had been elated because it meant that she could visit Lucie's apartment too.

The apartment not only seemed quite spacious but it was also full of light. When Claire saw the result she was very pleased with it. She realized that other members of the community might envy Lucie for having her own place, if it were not for the fact that the House of Bethany would regain its peace and quiet. Lucie's presence would no longer be a constant source of unrest. All in all everybody had reason to be happy and excited about the change.

What about Lucie herself? In fact, nobody knew. Antonio had the good sense to leave the door to her new apartment permanently open so that she could get used to it. Since her rooms were spacious, she could wander in and out as much as she wanted. Her father had informed them that a professional mover would bring her things from Zaragoza to Benacazón the day before he arrived.

The next day a huge truck came slowly down the little road along the railway track to bend towards Bethany. It was another moment of great excitement. The mover's crew was taking furniture and boxes into the apartment. Peter Entwistle was to look after Lucie so that Claire and Maria could unpack the boxes with linen, clothes and toys and put everything in drawers. Philippe and Pascal were there to help them. Sofia and Alonso were present to share in the general excitement.

In the afternoon Ramón came over from the house to see how things were going. 'This looks terrific,' he said just when Lucie came in through the entrance from the pottery. 'What do you think, Lucie?' When she passed him she briefly touched his arm and moved on to her new bedroom.

'If you ask me, Lucie is very happy to see her own toys,' Peter Entwistle said.

'How so?'

'Claire unpacked a box that was loaded with dolls and stuffed animals. As soon as Lucie saw them, she was all over them. It was obvious she recognized them as her own.' The new assistant was satisfied that he had been able to answer Ramón's question.

'Wonderful!' Ramón said. 'It will help to make her feel that this is her place!' Then he noticed Sofia in the bedroom, where Maria was unpacking linen and towels. 'Hello Sofia. You are busy too, I see. What do you think of the apartment?'

'Hi, Ramón. It's looking great.' Then she turned her face towards him, much more serious than expected.

'When I first heard about the plan, I was jealous. "Who gets to have their own apartment?" I said to myself. "Lucie! Of all people!" But when I saw her being happy with her dolls just now, it changed my mind. Look at all the things I can do that she cannot.'

'That is a very generous thought, Sofia.'

'You know what Antonio says about her. Lucie is like a flittering bird. Well, you know, flittering birds need space.' Ramón was moved. He went over to her, and gently touched her cheek.

'You have a very kind heart, my dear,' he said in a way that made her blush.

When Señor Miles arrived the next day, everything was ready for the opening of his daughter's apartment. Claire had asked Sylvia to bring as many flowers from the village as she could carry. There were half a dozen bouquets in all colours. Antonio had sent for a few bottles from a wine shop in Sanlúcar to celebrate.

With everybody in the best of spirits, all of them came together in front of the house, Lucie's father towering above them all because of his height. He would open the apartment with the key for the front entrance. The man had prepared a speech but when the moment had come to deliver it, he almost broke down and couldn't say a word. Just in time Antonio was at his side and laid his hand on his shoulder.

'We are so happy today that Lucie and her father are part of our community, aren't we?' Everybody cheered. Now in tears, the man turned to Claire and hugged her, and then he embraced Antonio. Claire started to applaud, as if he had indeed spoken, and soon everybody joined her. When the applause faded, Ramón stepped forward to announce the finale of the ceremony. He held a key in his hand that he handed over to Lucie's father.

'Señor Miles, may I invite you to unlock the door to Lucie's apartment?'

44.

Alonso Is Very Upset

Peter Entwistle's handsome appearance had enchanted Claire more than she was ready to admit. As soon as he appeared in the dining hall, which was the place where they were most likely to meet, she couldn't keep her eyes off him.

There was something about the young Englishman that appealed to her and made him appear a precious gift, something to keep wrapped up in silk paper, and definitely not to be smudged by sticky hands, or by sarcastic jokes, for that matter. His presence made Claire aware of something that had not much troubled her before. This was not the right time however, and definitely not the right place to get involved, but deep down inside she had an unfulfilled heart.

In the meantime Bethany had found its peacefulness again, except for the hustle and bustle at mealtimes, but that was okay. Especially in the evenings, mealtimes did not only mean food, although that was important, but also stories, laughter, songs, and, occasionally even dancing. Lucie seemed to thrive on the general merriment, simply because she didn't draw the negative attention she was used to before, when everybody found her annoying.

This change was definitely the work of Maria and of Peter Entwistle. They succeeded in making the girl keep her seat and not start roaming around in the dining hall. When this nonetheless happened, as it sometimes did, she would be taken outside for a brief walk. Within a few weeks, her two assistants succeeded more and more in having her attention during mealtimes. They learned that being connected to her within a few minutes was crucial. Once she was at ease on her chair and focused on her meal, she was okay.

Her two assistants switched off and on between breakfast, lunch and dinner, just as they did in her apartment and the pottery. This meant that whenever it was their turn to take over, they started with new energy, just as Claire had anticipated when she brought up the idea of short, alternating shifts. This was very important. Assisting Lucie without lots of energy was not possible; that they had learned the hard way.

Peter and Maria arranged between them to have Lucie in a corner seat at the dinner table, so that she had the one in front, and the other beside her. It was not before long that this arrangement was interrupted. Frequently another person had taken the seat in front of her, and turned out to be an unexpected ally in assisting Lucie during mealtimes. It was Alonso.

The two were clearly attached to one another. Alonso always made funny faces at the girl, which was something he couldn't help doing. When she had a hand on the table, he would put his out to play with her fingers. 'Wuz,' as he called her, was 'thweet.' This he would repeat whenever Peter or Maria would compliment her with a spoon that went in her mouth instead of on her t-shirt, 'Wuz thweet.'

After some time, his affection for the girl took him to the next level of their intimate friendship. When he had taken his preferred seat in the dining hall, which was opposite hers, and Lucie arrived, he would get off his chair and move over to her side of the table, declare that she was sweet, and then give her a kiss on her cheek. At first Lucie would push him away, apparently not in favour of being kissed every mealtime.

Alonso didn't seem to mind her rejection at all. After some time, when she saw him coming, a grin appeared on her face, and she pulled up her shoulders as if he was tickling her. Alonso saw his affection rewarded and so it turned into a ritual. In view of her usual demeanour of not paying attention to anyone addressing her,

Lucie's assistants were quite surprised to see that as soon as Alonso came up to her, she would hold up her cheek so as to welcome his kiss, and receive his affection.

The bond that had been growing between them impacted not only on Lucie's assistants, but also on how the others responded to Alonso. It changed their view of him. So far he had been the cuddle bear of Bethany, someone who could make everybody feel happy, very pleasant to have around, but otherwise not of great help. For example, the fact that he didn't do much in the pottery even though he spent most of his days there, didn't seem to matter to anyone. Alonso was fun to have around. That was all.

But thanks to how he handled Lucie this view changed. Whenever they got stuck with assisting Lucie, Antonio would say, 'Go, get Alonso, he will know what to do.' After a while, this response became habitual. When her own assistants needed some help, as occasionally happened, Alonso was called upon to step into Lucie's apartment, which he always did.

The notion of Alonso helping out was in a sense curious because he himself had no idea what it was he did with Lucie. So in fact Antonio's advice that Alonso would know what to do was a bit strange. The boy didn't do anything other than just being Alonso and this, apparently, was all that was needed.

Perhaps it was because of his promotion to the ranks of those who knew how to handle Lucie, that it came as a shock to find him in the bedroom of her apartment one day, very obstinate and aggressive. It was at the end of November about seven weeks after Lucie's father had opened it.

Nobody knew what exactly had happened in there. Lucie had walked into the workshop, and Antonio noticed she was crying. He immediately went to her apartment to see what was going on. Entering her living room he saw Peter Entwistle sitting on the sofa reading a magazine, apparently oblivious to the fact that something was wrong. When Antonio stepped into Lucie's bedroom he found Alonso sitting on her bed.

'Alonso what's wrong?' he asked. No response but an angry face.

'What happened?' Antonio wanted to know and laid his hand on the young man's shoulder. Instead of answering him, Alonso pushed his hand away.

'Gow!' he barked, 'gow!' All this was very disturbing. Antonio turned away to the living room again.

'Peter what happened in there?'

'I don't know, why?'

'Lucie is crying and Alonso seems to be very upset about something!'

'I don't know.' The assistant said it with an apparent lack of interest that Antonio didn't like at all.

'Excuse me? Lucie walks into the workshop crying, Alonso has lost his temper and appears quite disturbed and angry, and you are sitting here, reading a magazine and telling me you don't know? I will talk to you later, young man!' He left the apartment to find Lucie in the workshop, where Sofia seemed to have taken over. In her wheelchair she had Lucie sitting beside her on a chair. The girl's tears were drying on her face, but she looked hurt.

'I comforted her,' Sofia said gently. 'I think she must have been hurt by someone. See how sad she looks?' Antonio nodded. If she were only able to speak, he thought. He very rarely had this thought about her, except when she got hurt.

'You're an angel,' he said to Sofia.

During the rest of the afternoon Lucie found her own self again, and no longer seemed disturbed by whatever had happened. Antonio told Peter to stay with her. As Maria was away, this meant that the two of them spent most of the afternoon in the pottery. Alonso was not seen for quite some time.

It was just shortly before dinnertime that he came out of Lucie's apartment. There was something unusual about him, Antonio noticed; he was withdrawn, no smiles, not even a response when Antonio said hello. This unusual behaviour continued in the dining hall. He didn't greet Lucie as he always did. No kiss, no smile. Apparently Lucie was not sweet any more.

When dinner was over Antonio told Claire about the afternoon and asked her to speak with Peter Entwistle that same evening. Since Maria was absent Claire agreed to do as she was asked, but in her heart of hearts she felt quite uneasy about a private meeting with a young man for whom her feelings were not neutral.

'Hello, Peter,' she welcomed him, 'please take a chair.' She looked at his black curls, then at his dark eyes, and gave him a smile to make him feel at ease. 'Antonio told me what happened this afternoon with Alonso and Lucie, and asked me to speak with you about it.' She spoke kindly to him, but there was no response. She waited a moment and noticed his face was blank.

'What do you think happened?'

'I don't know, I didn't see anything.'

Claire looked at him in silence. There are people who are capable of lying without provoking any doubt, but Peter Entwistle was not one of them. She noticed that his words were spoken carelessly, as if he was annoyed by her question. There was a deliberate disinterestedness in his demeanour that Claire didn't buy. She decided to confront him.

'You sound as if you don't care what happened in that bedroom.'

There was a quick response from his eyes when he looked at her a split second, as if to check something, and then his eyes went down again. 'What does she know?' the eyes were asking. His look convinced her that he was hiding what he knew. She waited for a response, but he remained silent.

'Is that why you were reading that magazine this afternoon?' she asked sharply. His eyes showed she was confusing him. 'To make Antonio believe you didn't think much had happened?' Again the same look.

Claire sensed that she was right. 'You were in that bedroom too, weren't you?' she said.

This was a bold guess. If he denied it, she had no grounds to contradict him, even though she wouldn't believe him. But if he admitted, what would he tell her?

'Yes, I was,' he said, still without looking openly in her face.

'What happened?'

'I was washing a coffee mug, when I heard Alonso yell at Lucie. He wanted her to go. I went into the bedroom to see what had happened and saw them on her bed. Lucie was all over him.' The response had come far too quickly. Claire looked at him and felt he was not speaking the truth.

'Did she really?' Claire answered him as if she was amazed that the girl would do something like that. He nodded but didn't say more.

'When she came into the workshop she was crying.'

'I pulled her off him but she resisted and then fell from the bed against her drawer, unfortunately she hurt herself. It was clumsy. I'm sorry,' he said. He didn't feel sorry at all, Claire thought. She felt that he was confessing a clumsy intervention that had not taken place.

'Why did you lie to Antonio?'

'Lucie is his favourite. He always gets angry when something happens to her. He scares me.' He spoke with a timid voice that made Claire think it was the first thing he said that was true.

'Hmmm.'

'Will you tell him?'

'Of course I will. We don't lie here about the things we find difficult to confess,' she said looking him straight in his eyes. Again the same quick look before his eyes went down. He has not told me what really happened, Claire thought. She decided to play her final trick to check if she was right.

'You better go now.' She made sure there was no trace of irony in her voice when she said 'I want to thank you for being honest with me.' This time he did not look her in the face, not even quickly. Claire was certain he had not told her the truth.

The next day she spoke to Ramón and Antonio about the affair. 'I have no idea what really happened, but I am sure it is not what he told me.'

'Why would he lie if not to hide something that in his eyes is worse than what he told you?' Antonio wondered.

'Or something that he thinks is much worse in our eyes!' Ramón replied. He was aware of having had doubts about this young man right from the start, even though he did not know exactly why.

45.

The Lecture

Peter Entwistle's assignment to assist the girl had worked well until the awkward incident about a month before he was due to leave Bethany. Neither Ramón, nor Claire nor Antonio believed the story told by the intern that Lucie had harassed Alonso, since this seemed a highly implausible account of what had happened. Being unable to find out the truth, they were glad the young Englishman was soon to return home.

It was in the second week of December that Ramón was to deliver the lecture in the Department of Social Studies of a college in Birmingham. Had they enclosed Peter Entwistle in their hearts, as they had done with Maria, Ramón might have been more at ease with travelling to England to fulfil his obligation. Under present circumstances he was not. Somehow the mixed feelings he had about the intern spilled over to the school, and particularly to the supervisor who had sent him.

Two weeks before his trip to Birmingham Ramón had received a phone call from professor Williamson. The call was expected, because the professor was to ask for a title and summary of the lecture he planned to deliver.

'Mr Jimenez, this is Williamson from Birmingham. How are you?'

'Fine, we're doing fine.'

'That's good to hear. We are looking forward to having you as our guest in a couple of weeks.'

'So am I, professor,' Ramón responded politely. Had the professor seen his face he may have doubted the sincerity of the response, because Ramón looked far from happy.

'Good, it will be our pleasure.' The professor was very friendly. 'To make sure we get the crowd that your presence deserves, we want to announce it big. Can I ask you for a title and a brief summary of your talk?'

'I should be able to do so,' Ramón responded firmly. Since Williamson had lured him into this lecture with the prospect of a donation, he definitely wanted to try to make as much money out of it for Bethany as he possibly could.

'I would be very grateful. Send it directly to me by express mail if you don't mind. I don't want to bother you with delayed mail within the college mail system.' He gave Ramón his home address, and said he was looking forward to their meeting.

'Oh, and before I forget, the lecture begins at 4.00pm.'

'Splendid, then I can travel the same day, and return on the next.'

'Good, we will arrange for a hotel after your talk. I hope to see you in a couple of weeks then.'

'Thank you. Likewise, professor,' Ramón replied, putting down the phone with a big sigh.

'Pfffff. What am I going to tell these people?'

'What are you going to tell which people?' Claire had just heard his exasperation as she stepped into his room.

'That was Williamson from Birmingham about the lecture I am to give there in two weeks' time.'

'About which you are very excited, I can tell,' she said a bit too sarcastically to his taste. He didn't want to be made fun of about this.

'Why don't you go and deliver that talk, if you think it's funny?'

'Come on, Ramón, you've done this before, and you know you are good at it. Speak straight from the heart; that always impresses people. Tell about them about the men, or about Lucie and Alonso.' Ramón knew she was right. Let that lecture take care of itself.

When he arrived in Birmingham, professor Williamson came to pick him up from the airport. He appeared to be an upper-class Englishman, and was very correct in every respect.

'Welcome to Birmingham Metropolitan College, or 'BMet' as it is called by the locals. We will go to Sutton Coldfield, the campus where my department has its offices. The lecture hall is also on that campus. We will have some time left when we get there, would you like something, refreshments, coffee perhaps?'

Ramón said he could use a coffee, and a visit to the restroom to freshen up. He realized the incident in Lucie's apartment was on his mind constantly. The question now was how to arrange a conversation with Williamson about his student Peter Entwistle. But the professor solved this for him while they were having their coffee.

'How is our intern doing?' the professor started.

'Ups and downs, I should say,' Ramón responded. 'He is a friendly young man, very polite, but not always as sensitive as one would like him to be.' Ramón chose his words deliberately not to upset the student's supervisor.

'They can be blunt, can't they?' Williamson responded with a dry smile.

'Yes, they can.' Then he paused for a brief moment. 'Professor can I ask you a personal question about him?'

'Certainly.'

'It is with some hesitation that I am asking you this, but do you have any information on whether Peter Entwistle has ever been accused of sexual harassment?'

The professor looked at him with a darkened face, apparently not too keen on having a conversation on the topic. 'Why do you ask me this question?' he responded.

'There was an incident with two members of our community, a girl and a young boy. Peter was there, but we don't believe he told us the truth about what happened. He suggested the girl had sexually harassed the boy, and that he had found them. If you knew the girl you would see why this is hardly credible. But we haven't been able to find out the truth.'

'You think he himself was involved?'

'I don't know, but it might be useful for us to know whether he has a history in this respect.' Ramón tried to put it as delicately as he could, but the professor was nonetheless not amused.

'Unfortunately, the answer is "yes", he replied bluntly. 'Peter Entwistle was accused by another student. But nothing was proved.'

There was an abrupt ending to this uneasy conversation when Williamson looked at his watch and said, 'I am sorry, but it is time to go to the lecture hall.'

Ramón took a deep breath when they entered the hall where a sizable crowd of about two hundred people was gathered. He asked the professor about their background.

'I think mostly students in social work,' Williamson said. Then, as if reminding himself, he said, 'Oh, I almost forgot to ask you. How do you want to be introduced?'

'My name, and perhaps the House of Bethany.'

'No title?'

'No title. It's such a long time ago that I hardly ever think about it. I have a doctorate in social studies.' The professor looked at him wondering how that could be something to forget.

'Dr Ramón Jimenez, initiator of the House of Bethany, a house for handicapped people. Do you think that will do?' Ramón never used the word 'handicapped' with regard to the members of Bethany, but he let it pass and did not correct the professor. 'Yes, that's fine.' After having been introduced, he took the floor.

'Good afternoon, Ladies and Gentlemen,' Ramón began, 'it's my pleasure to be here this afternoon, and I am grateful for the invitation to speak to you about an important topic, especially since many of you are studying at this college to be a social worker, as I understood from professor Williamson. "Social work", I take it, means you will be working mostly with people who in one way or another are at the margins of society. If I am correct in making these assumptions, then I have a most important question for you.' He looked at the faces before him, and noticed their curiosity.

'The question is this. What is it that makes people valuable? This is the question I want us to think about this afternoon.' Looking around the hall, Ramón repeated the question, mainly to feel if the audience was with him. Then he continued.

'We all know how our society answers this question. People are valued because of what they achieve in their lives. It's on every billboard, and we find it confirmed in the media every day. The lives advertised in our society are the lives of successful, happy people. But most of the people you will be working with as a social worker do not belong in this category. Many of them are perceived as "losers", rather than "winners". They need support because they cannot make it on their own. That's why they come to you, ultimately.

'So the answer to our question cannot be what society tells us it is, unless you agree, that is, that the people you will be working with are indeed 'losers'. Assuming that you don't agree, the answer cannot be that people are valuable because of what they achieve. That would make "underachievers" into people of lesser value. But this is not what you believe. Otherwise you wouldn't be here. Correct?'

Here Ramón paused and looked again around the hall to see many of the students in front of him nodding. Satisfied that this argument seemed to work, he continued.

'I therefore want to suggest a different answer. People are valuable because they belong. This is what I ask you to think about. Why is belonging crucial for human beings? And why is it crucial for you as social workers to understand this?'

Ramón noticed that the students in his audience were listening, but they were not yet on the edge of their seats. It was time to throw in some of his stories to capture their hearts.

'Let me tell you about my friend Alfredo, who lives with us in the House of Bethany, which is in Andalusia close to the city of Seville.' He told them the story of Alfredo's childhood. When he saw its effect upon their faces, he made his point. 'Ultimately his father drove him out of his house. "Who does not work shall not eat from my table." The message to his unfortunate son was, then: "You don't belong here." That's why Alfredo had to go.'

The atmosphere in the hall had changed by now. Human interest had kicked in, and the students in front of him were all ears. 'A similar story is true of another member of our small community, Pascal, who as a small boy was in deep depression because of his hysterical mother. No one knows what might have happened had the doctors not taken him out of her hands, but his home was an extremely dangerous place for this child.' From the faces in front of him – some of them looking sad, others pained – Ramón could see that some of these students had stories to tell that might not be all that different from the ones they had just heard.

'These stories show human beings who do not belong, sometimes not even in their own homes. Usually it is because they are seen as a burden. That is, for example, when they are called "handicapped". I do not like that word. It names people who are not going to make it, but who are excused because they can't help it. Their families are ashamed, or feel guilty about them, as in the case of Alfredo's mother.' To illustrate the point he told them the story about Alonso's parents who had sent their boy to Bethany because of family pressure.

'The important thing is this. The message "you don't belong here" leaves the person behind with a deep wound. Basically people tend to feel that they are not wanted. I assume that many of the people you will be working with have received that message. They are wounded people. It will be your task as a social worker to recognize this, and to help and find out how they can be healed. You cannot heal them yourself, but you can support them in finding out for themselves.

This is what we try to do in the community of Bethany. Its members are people with wounded souls. We try to restore in them a sense of belonging. How? Belonging means you're wanted. Somebody is glad to see you. Somebody is sad when you're gone.

Like many of the people you will be working with, our members do not make it on their own; they need assistance. The first step is that their presence is welcomed and appreciated. Every day we say to one another "We are glad you're here." To prove that we are serious about this, we provide them with a home and an occupation. And, I should add, with a lot of celebrations. This is important. When people feel welcome and appreciated there are a lot of things to celebrate.'

Rounding up his talk Ramón stated Bethany's mission. 'We want the House of Bethany to be a sign. We want it to be a sign for society to see that marginalized people are no less valuable because they need our support. I take it, then, that in fact you and I are in the same business. Our most important task is to support people in restoring their sense of belonging. I wish you all a lot of inspiration in fulfilling this task. Thank you for your attention.'

When he had spoken his last sentence, there was a moment of deep silence. The sight of all these young and committed faces had moved Ramón as he spoke, which his audience had felt. Professor Williamson was the first to get up from his chair to applaud the speaker. The crowd followed him with enthusiasm. Ramón had done well. There was some time left for questions and answers, after which professor Williamson thanked him for his inspiring talk. He also mentioned the fact that one of their fellow students was serving in Bethany as an intern right now, and that if there were people interested in an internship there too, they should contact him.

'That went very well, Dr Jimenez,' Williamson said when they left the lecture hall. 'For many of these students the world of the non-achievers you described is very much their own background here in this part of Britain. I know for sure you have inspired them. So, again, thank you very much. The university's donation will certainly come your way soon. I will make sure it's a substantial amount.'

Professor Williamson invited Ramón to his office, but he apologized for wanting to go to his hotel. It had been a long day and he was very tired. The professor excused him, and after formalities and goodbyes, a taxi took Ramón to a hotel from where he would go to the airport the next morning to fly back to Seville.

46.

A Confession ...

Ramón was back in Bethany late in the afternoon. Entering the house with his bag, he found Claire preparing for dinner in the kitchen. When he said hello she swung around.

'Ramón, you're back!' she spread her arms and hugged him. 'How was it? Did your lecture go well?'

'Yes, I think it was pretty good. Anyway they seemed to like it.'

'Are you tired? Do you want something to eat?' she asked him. He said 'yes' to both questions. Would he join them, she asked, or rather have a plate taken up to his room?

'I think I might have a bite upstairs and then lie down.' While Claire prepared his food, she told him how she informed the others about his trip to England.

'I told them about your trip, and that you had to make an important speech. They said they would all think of you. Pascal said he would keep his fingers crossed and stuck out his hand to demonstrate it. The next thing was that all were trying hard to get their fingers crossed. You should have seen Alonso trying to do the same with *his* fingers. It was very funny.'

'So that was what I felt when I was giving the talk. I had all these guardian angels sitting on my shoulder to make sure I wouldn't stumble and stutter.' They laughed. 'Are you already claimed as a guardian angel?' Ramón said playfully.

'No,' she said, 'I am available in case you have a vacancy!'

He smiled, but did not respond. Thanking her for the food she had prepared for him to take upstairs, he went off. Before leaving the kitchen he turned around. 'Before I forget, there is something that I want to see you and Antonio about tonight. Can we say at nine in your office?'

'I will make sure we will be there.'

When Ramón found the two of them in Claire's office that evening, he told about his lecture, as Antonio asked him what his message had been. 'It sounds like you did a good job,' Antonio said with true admiration in his voice. 'Bethany not as a refuge, but as a sign; I must say I like that.'

'Nice phrase,' Ramón returned the compliment. 'I wish I had put it that way. Anyhow, it went well, and we may expect a generous donation from the college, the professor said.'

'I hope it will be very generous,' Claire said. 'We need to work on the house.' They agreed the rooms upstairs needed some refurbishing, and Claire took it upon herself to make a plan. Then Ramón came to speak about what he had to tell them.

'When I met with Williamson before the lecture, he asked how his student was doing, of course. I told him we had mixed feelings about him, and briefly mentioned the incident. Then I asked him straightaway if he had any information on whether Peter Entwistle ever had been accused of sexual misconduct.'

'You did what?' Claire still was not entirely convinced but she had no alternative reading of the intern's conduct to curb their suspicions.

'There's no beating about the bush with this guy,' Antonio said grimly, 'haven't you noticed?'

Ramón ignored his remark, and before Claire could retort, he continued. 'The professor was not amused, but he was honest enough to tell me what he knew. There had been accusations from a female student about Entwistle having harassed her, but the charges were dropped because there was no proof.'

'And he sent this guy here without informing us about this?' Antonio was upset. 'What a lousy, irresponsible thing to do! What did you tell him?'

'Actually, when I was about to ask him a question in that direction, the professor interrupted the exchange because we had to go to the lecture hall. He was clearly very uneasy.'

Claire remained silent. From the first time she had met with the intern she had sensed there was something that made her uneasy about him without knowing how to name it. Now she knew that her own personal feelings had confused and blinded her.

'I must have liked him too much,' she said all of a sudden. Antonio was about to make a comment upon her female instinct, but he stopped himself just in time. There had been a delicacy in her silence. She was probably feeling ashamed.

'We all had our doubts,' Ramón said, ignoring what she just had said. 'When is Entwistle going to leave?'

'Coming Monday.'

'Today is Thursday, so that leaves only four days. Let's make sure he's not left alone with anyone from now until he leaves. I assume it will be a relief for all of us when he is gone.' Whether Ramón was deliberately insensitive was hard to tell, but Antonio looked quickly at Claire, just in time to see her eyes go down to stare at the floor. 'Poor girl,' he said to himself. 'What in the world has this guy done to her?'

Without further ado Ramón concluded the conversation. 'Before I left for the lecture, Entwistle gave me his final report about his stay at Bethany, but I have not yet read it; this I need to do early tomorrow morning. I will see him in the afternoon for his official 'exit interview', as the school requires. Maybe I will bring up the incident again, I am not sure yet. It will depend on what he has to say.'

When he had left, Antonio looked at Claire.

'Come on, Claire, you will get over this,' he said kindly.

'Oh no... Antonio. It's not Peter Entwistle himself. When he arrived that was just an infatuation. I soon felt there was something strange about him. A lack of empathy is the best way to name it, I think. No, what has gotten to me is the fact that his appearance brought feelings to the surface that I'd buried a long time ago. As long as I have been here I have never doubted for a moment that Bethany is my life, but in the last few months I have been forced to see that it comes with a price too. You and Ramón, you are wonderful friends, the best I ever had… but now I can't help thinking that I am missing something. That bothers me more than I can say.'

There was a tear running down her cheek, which underlined her last words. When he saw it, Antonio laid his arm around her shoulder. He stroked her hair, as she softly wept.

'Sssh… sssh, don't cry, it's okay.'

When she dried her tears, she looked up into his eyes and smiled. 'You're about the most sensitive heart I know.' Noticing the surprise in his eyes, she could not help adding a tease, 'At least in this place.' She laughed and kissed him on the cheek. When he stepped back and looked at her face, she saw a glimmer in his eyes that she recognized.

'Now that you mention it,' he said, 'did you really never notice how much that pretty boy looks just like me…? How odd!'

'Oh, you…!' She punched his shoulder affectionately. When Antonio in response produced his usual ironic grin, she said, 'Before you start making fun of me again, let me just say that Bethany would have been much harder to take without you.'

'Thank you, sweetheart,' he said, feeling truly grateful. Then he said goodnight, and left her office.

Claire sat alone in her office for a while, pondering the meaning of what she had confessed to Antonio. There was a natural beauty about the young Englishman that had attracted her more than she had wanted. In the spare moments that she had spoken with him, she had never found the same beauty reflected in his soul. Rather than the young man himself, it had been the strength of her own feelings that confused her. As if there was a void that had been waiting to be filled. She considered Bethany a miracle of living out what it meant to be a human being, and celebrating that. But she felt that it had never celebrated, and would not ever celebrate, what it meant to be a woman.

This feeling was confusing to Claire. Unexpectedly, it made the House of Bethany appear as second best; the next best thing she could have hoped for in her life, after she had fled the land of her father in Southern Andalusia. Sitting alone in her office that night, she silently wept again. More than ever before she felt there was a part in her that Bethany would be incapable of fulfilling.

47.

... *And Another One*

The next morning Ramón had read the intern's report, and was preparing some notes for his interview with him that afternoon. The report was as shallow as its author. His assignment had been first to provide a description of the people he was supposed to work with in the location of his internship. Next he had to list the kind of activities he had undertaken with each of these persons, and then he had to give an account what he had learned in working with each of them. The final section was required to be an overall evaluation of his time at Bethany.

When he read the section about what he had learned, Ramón could hardly believe it to be written by a college student. It had one platitude after another:

> *The House of Bethany is a place where I learned many important things. The handicapped people that live there are often quite slow in what they do. I learned that I have to be patient with the people I work with. Most of my time I worked with a severely handicapped girl of fourteen. She cannot speak so you have to find out what she wants without asking her, because she cannot answer you. She just walks around. I had to watch out that she would not hurt herself. I learned that, as a social worker I need to protect people I work with from harming themselves. Most important I learned to be friendly to people who are dependent upon my support. The people*

*from the staff in the House of Bethany were great to watch in how
they worked. I learned a lot from them.*

Ramón laid the report aside and took a deep breath. 'What a
deep learning experience!' he said to himself. Being particularly
interested in what the student had to say about Lucie, he read the
following observations.

*The name of this person is Lucie Miles. It was my task to work
with her in short shifts of about one hour. Then I would switch with
my colleague Maria, and do something for myself in the pottery, or
in the garden. Lucie is capable of walking, but she has the mind of
a toddler, and cannot think straight. Therefore she cannot focus her
attention. Most of her time she just wanders around without doing
anything. I had to make sure she did no harm to the others, and
did not harm herself. Lucie is toilet trained, but sometimes I had to
assist her. She takes her meals with the other people in the dining
hall. We had only to look after her in between. Two times a day we
served coffee or tea. The short shift system was very good, because
looking after someone who is doing nothing basically can nonetheless be very tiresome.*

Reading the students' prose Ramón felt almost ashamed that
they had exposed the girl to someone with an apparent lack of
talent for making observations, who on top of that could only see
what she did or could not do. He wondered how Entwistle's study
results so far had been, and considered himself lucky that he did
not have to grade his final report. He only had to sign the pages of
the student's report to prove that he had seen them. Ramón could
not say he was looking forward to the conversation, except for the
fact that he might perhaps find out more about the incident with
Lucie and Alonso.

When Peter Entwistle stepped into his room, Ramón
immediately saw that he was not very comfortable.

'Hello, Peter, please sit down.'

'Thank you ... Sir.' His voice was insecure, and the hesitant formal address indicated his level of uneasiness. It was not what one would expect from a student facing an evaluation by his mentor, particularly when that mentor was Ramón Jimenez. 'He expects me to ask him about the incident, well let's have it then,' Ramón thought.

'I have read your report, and I have seen that you fulfilled your requirements in it, so I will sign it before you leave.'

The average student would have relaxed after this kind of message right at the start of an interview, but not so Peter Entwistle. His eyes were restless, and never stayed with Ramón for longer than a split second. Ramón was by now certain that the young man had a troubled conscience. He decided not to take on the role of a policeman, and started on a friendly note.

'Tell me, Peter, how has your time with us been for you?'

'Very rewarding, Sir.'

'Has it? That's good to hear. So did it bring you what you hoped it would? I do recall that you told me something about your aunt who was 'retarded' I think you named it, and that you were very fond of her. Wasn't your memory of that experience the reason why you were attracted to Bethany?'

'Yes, it was.'

'And, did we fulfil your expectations? Or was it very different from how you remembered spending time with your aunt?' Ramón continued. It seemed a rather stupid question, but after having read Peter Entwistle's prose, he thought it just might do. Expecting that the young man would relax a bit, Ramón was quite astonished to see that his face reddened.

'Uhh... it was... different ... Sir,' Peter Entwistle stumbled.

'Of course, how naïve of me. Your aunt was a grown up woman, and you were still a little boy. You spent a lot of time with her, I think you told me.'

'Yes ... yes, I did.'

'Why is this guy so nervous,' Ramón was asking himself, 'when I am asking him these harmless questions? What's going on in his mind?'

'I think you also told me you missed her terribly when she had to leave your home. So, will you miss Lucie as well, even though it has been a much shorter time?' Having no idea where to go with this interview, Ramón was just trying to get a conversation started.

'I am not sure that she even liked me,' the intern said.

'Hmmm. I am pretty sure many of us often have that same feeling. By the way, why did your aunt have to leave your home?'

Before he even had finished the question, Peter Entwistle's face lost all its colour. Ramón had so far said nothing unfriendly, but the young man looked very alarmed. When he tried to speak, he just stammered.

'I … I don't know… really… I was only little.'

Had he looked at Ramón's face, he would have seen a startled gaze. A wild guess struck him like lightning. 'He was abused as a child.' When the word came into his mind, he knew he was right. 'Good God, the boy was sexually abused by his aunt, that's why she was sent away! That is what he is not telling me.'

He looked gravely at the young man before him and took a deep breath. Then he spoke.

'Peter, look at me.'

The young man was very pale when he raised his eyes and looked Ramón in the face.

'Your aunt was sent away because your parents found out she had abused you?'

Peter was trembling. His entire body bespoke his anguish, but he could not speak. Ramón was now absolutely certain of his conjecture.

'What happened? Did it start when you were still very young?'

The young man was on the verge of breaking down. He said nothing, but barely noticeably he nodded his head.

'What an awful, awful experience, Peter, it must have made you a very lonely child.' Ramón spoke from his heart, like he always did in such situations. Had he intended to break Peter Entwistle's secret, he could not have asked a better question. Looking no more than a shadow of the agreeable, good-looking young man who came to Bethany three months ago, he broke down, and sobbed.

'After your parents found out, and your aunt was sent away, it was not openly spoken about with you, I presume?'

'No.' It was a whisper from a cracking voice.

'So you have carried it with you in your soul alone, all these years,' Ramón said, now deliberately seeking to break down Entwistle's defences because he was sure there was more to come. The young man was wretched. Like a lonely boy grieving, he lost control completely. Ramón could almost feel the pain.

'Do you want to tell me what happened? It's none of my business, but it might be a relief to finally tell someone.' Ramón got up to leave him alone for a moment and came back with a glass of water. 'Take your time,' he said as he handed it over. The young man took it, and when he was a bit recovered, he began.

'It started when I was a toddler, I think … It must have. Aunt Suzie was baby-sitting me, when my mum was at work. My family was poor, so my parents needed every penny. They could not afford daycare, and Aunt Suzie was not terribly handicapped. Later she would take me to school on her own… I probably was her real life doll, whom she loved to play with… She wouldn't hurt a fly. Later when I was in kindergarten … she took me with her under the shower … That went on till I was already a schoolboy. Then one day my mum caught us under the shower … and Aunt Suzie was touching me.'

'You said your mother caught "us". Did you feel caught too? Were you punished by your parents?'

'Yes. When my father heard about it, he beat me up.'

'How terrible, Peter, how terrible.'

Silent tears came running down the young man's face. The pain they revealed made clear he was going through it again. Ramón began to see the picture. Aunt Suzie had been a safe haven. The boy never experienced abuse in the relationship with his aunt.

'Am I right that you truly missed your aunt when she was sent away?'

'Yes, I missed her very much.'

'At that point you did not understand the impropriety of her relationship with a schoolboy, I guess.'

'No, I never knew otherwise than that sweet Aunt Suzie was playing with me. When my father cursed her as a "dirty cow" it hurt infinitely more than her behaviour towards me ever did.'

Ramón nodded, but said nothing. He remained silent for a few moments to let the young man find himself again. Then he continued.

'Peter, you know I have to ask you this. I think what happened in Lucie's bedroom has everything to do with the story you just told me. Were you playing with her in the way your Aunt Suzie was playing with you?' Leaving out harsher terms to describe the scene Ramón received the response he was looking for.

'Yes ... I was.' It was a confession barely audible. Ramón noticed this time the young man looked him in the face. The truth was out, finally.

'I assume Alonso found the two of you, and you scared him off. Is that true?'

'Yes, or ...' He paused a moment, looking confused. 'No, I didn't ... Lucie did.' Peter looked ashamed when he said it, understanding he was pointing away from himself, but this time Ramón believed him.

'Alonso did not have a clue what we were doing... I had my hands on Lucie's body... but we had our clothes on. So he thought we were cuddling and wanted to join us. Then Lucie pushed him away. When he didn't understand and came back she pushed him even harder the second time.'

'What happened then?'

'I was scared to be caught; I left the bedroom, and picked up a magazine. That's how Antonio found me five minutes later.'

'You left the two of them together in that bedroom?'

The young man nodded. 'I know that was the act of a coward.'

'It was,' Ramón responded with knitted brows. 'Do you know what happened when you were gone?'

'Not for certain, but I think Lucie fell, because I heard her banging against her drawer. Perhaps Alonso wanted to be friends again, but she turned away, and fell.'

Ramón was very serious when he responded.

'I am glad you told me this. In a sense I am grateful that you did, because you could have tried to save your skin for a few more days. But you are aware I cannot pretend not to know the truth. What is more, I spoke with your supervisor when I was in Birmingham, a week ago. He told me that there had been accusations of sexual misconduct.'

Peter Entwistle's face changed from grief to fear. He looked terrified. 'Why did he tell you that? The charges were dropped.'

'He told me because I asked him. My hunch was that you had been sexually harassing either Lucie, or Alonso, or both, that I couldn't say. I have now learned that I was right in my suspicion.'

The young man was devastated. Apart from his name in Bethany, now was his career as a student was also in ruins. Ramón noticed him shivering. 'What are you going to do?' he asked in a timid voice.

'That I don't know yet. I will think about what you have told me, and about how to act. Tomorrow is Saturday. I want to see you in the afternoon at four.'

48.

Replacing the Intern

After dinner that night, Ramón managed to have a quick word with his two companions. 'I found out the truth about the incident in Lucie's bedroom,' he said. 'I had the exit interview with Peter, and found out he did not tell Claire what really happened, as we already suspected. His future as a student is at stake. Can you join me tomorrow morning at ten?' Claire and Antonio looked at one another, greatly alarmed by this brief report, and promised to be there.

When the next morning they met, Ramón told them what had happened, but the first thing they wanted to know was how he found out. When he had told them the whole story, Claire felt relief. She finally understood her feelings when speaking with the young man. He was shielding himself from people who were trying to find out who he was.

'How was he?' she wanted to know. 'Did he at all feel guilty about what he did?'

'I am not sure about the sexual misconduct. The way he talked about what his aunt did to him suggested to me that he doesn't understand the boundaries of physical intimacy. But he clearly saw that leaving the girl alone with Alonso in her bedroom, in order not to be caught by Antonio, was very wrong. I did not contradict him.'

'When you mentioned his future as a student,' Antonio said, 'what did you mean?'

'Well that's what we need to talk about now. I told him what I had learned from his supervisor when I was in Birmingham about accusations of sexual misconduct. He was devastated. I told him I could not pretend not to know the truth, and sent him away saying that I didn't yet know what we would do. So that's where we are right now.'

'We must inform Lucie's father.' Antonio said it in a way that left no room for dispute. 'He has a right to know.'

'Do you think we should?' Apparently Claire was in doubt. 'Within a few days Peter will be gone!'

'I don't see what that has to do with anything,' Antonio said. 'The reason for telling him has nothing to do with Peter but with the fact that Lucie is his daughter.'

Seeing her head go down, Ramón jumped in. 'I am afraid Antonio is right, dear. I will call Señor Miles right away when this meeting is over.'

When he had Lucie's father on the phone, the man was very concerned. 'Can you tell me exactly what happened?'

'Yes, Sir, I can.' Ramón told him everything he knew about what happened in Lucie's bedroom, including the fall out between Lucie and Alonso.

'I think the fact of letting that happen between them is the worst part, if you don't mind my saying so.' Ramón was relieved to note that the man was staying calm.

'I told him it was the act of a coward,' he said, which was not entirely true, of course, but he wanted to strengthen Señor Miles in the impression that they shared his concern.

'What are you going to do?'

'Well, now that we found out, the first thing is to ask you if you want to officially accuse the student of sexual harassment and press charges against him.'

'I appreciate you're asking this question, as you should. But I don't think I will. The guy will be gone in just two days, and pressing charges against him will neither do Lucie nor Bethany any good.'

'Are you sure? You know you have every right to do so.'

'Yes, I know. Again, I appreciate you're taking this seriously, but I won't go to the police.'

Ramón could not deny that he was relieved at his decision, foreseeing the trouble of having a court case at their hands, but he didn't say anything.

'So the question remains what you plan to do, Ramón.'

'You're right, and we have been speaking about it this morning. I want to suggest the following. Bethany will make officially known to his supervisor what we have found out about the incident. Going directly to the school's administration would end his career as a student.'

'And that should not happen?' there was a sting in Mr Miles voice when he said it. Ramón hesitated for a moment, but then told him about the story of Peter Entwistle's childhood. He stressed that being a victim of child abuse himself did not excuse what he did, but it could perhaps be accepted to justify a degree of clemency in the measures to be taken against him.

'What measures?' Señor Miles wanted to know.

'I suggest we write an official letter to inform his supervisor, and ask him to send us documentation proving that his student gets professional counseling to deal with his problem.' Señor Miles had a few questions before he gave his consent, which he was clearly reluctant to do. 'No offense, Ramón, I think you handled this well, but you understand my concern. The thought that this guy would ever be in the position to do this again makes me shudder.'

'I understand, Sir, I do. I promise I will make sure we are kept informed about his counseling. I will tell them that if we are not satisfied with the steps they take, we will take it further ourselves.' With this promise Mr Miles agreed with what had been proposed and thanked him for his phone call.

Ramón communicated their decision to the young Englishman when he came to see him later that same afternoon. 'Since you are leaving Bethany in two days there is no reason to expel you,' Ramón said, 'but we cannot and will not refrain from informing your supervisor professor Williamson, about what we found out. I will write him a letter in private, which informs him of your involvement in the incident here at Bethany in the light of your own history. I will add that we need official documentation that you will get professional counseling to deal with your problem. If we don't there will as yet be legal charges against you as their student. That is all that I can and that I am willing to do.'

The intern thanked Ramón for his consideration, and said he hoped they would be able to find better assistants than he himself had been. Ramón was relieved to see that he was apparently capable of understanding what he had done. He promised the young man that his last dinner before he left would be a regular farewell dinner. After their conversation Ramón briefed Claire and Antonio about it, and that concluded their business with Peter Entwistle.

When he left Bethany two days later, there was no immediate replacement, which created a big problem. While Maria was continuously working with Lucie, they knew she needed to be relieved every now and then in order not to be worn out. It would be very bad for Lucie, as well as for Maria herself and the entire community, should she be unable to go on.

The question of how to support her was resolved by looking at who could step in until they could find someone to replace the intern. Antonio suggested that he and Pascal could take over some time in Lucie's apartment during the working hours of the pottery.

'Pascal? The boy is only eight years old!' Ramón objected.

'I won't leave him alone with her,' Antonio assured him. 'I will keep a close eye and instruct him to keep the bedroom closed. In that way I can hear most of the time what's happening, since the door to the apartment is mostly open. I will make sure it is permanently so, when the boy is with Lucie.'

When Ramón accepted this suggestion, Claire added that she could ask Sylvia to come an hour earlier, then she herself could start the morning shift with getting Lucie through her morning routine. 'In this way we can offer Maria the opportunity of commuting, which might help her to relax.'

'I will take the first hour in the pottery with the boy,' Antonio added, 'which means Maria would only start at ten in the morning.' Within a few minutes, the schedule for supporting Sister Maria was completed. Ramón would step in at the end of the afternoon, and Claire would put the girl to bed, so that Maria could return to Seville for the night.

Thus it came to pass that after his lecture in Birmingham, Ramón had to spend an hour each day with Lucie taking turns with Maria, which was more than he had ever done before.

Part VI

A Blind Potter

49.

___

The Orphan from Seville

The autumn season had been dry. There had not been much rain, which left the road towards the House of Bethany dustier than it already was now that the harvest of olives had started. Trucks and wagons went off and on in taking their produce to the factory in Sanlúcar. Hundreds of olive trees would be shaken out of their grey-green marbles in the weeks to come. The days were still mild, but soon the temperature would drop, and it would become much colder.

When Ramón and his two companions left Bethany's premises, the last workers were leaving the orchards. He had asked them to come for a walk, which they knew meant he was brooding over something that was bothering him. 'There is something we need to talk about. Can you make it at seven?'

Claire had answered she would ask Sylvia to stay a bit longer and take care of the coffee. 'Maria needs to go to catch her train, which means we can't be longer than half an hour.'

'That will do,' Ramón had responded, 'see you at seven in front of the house.'

They took the dirt road that after half a mile went into the bush behind the olive groves. In the yellow light of the disappearing sun, Claire was looking lovely. She wore a red sweater hanging loose on her shoulders with a white blouse above her light blue jeans, and looked fresh, even after a busy day. Ramón didn't notice she had changed for their walk, but the artist in their company enjoyed the sight of her.

When Ramón began to speak there was a gravity to his voice that Claire found alarming. 'I received a phone call from Seville today. Mother Chiara from the Convent *de las Hermanas de la Cruz*.'

'What did she want?'

'She wants help. One of her nuns came home about two weeks ago with a boy. He was blind. She had found him in the streets of Seville begging for money to buy food. Being somewhat suspicious the nun asked him where his family lived. He said he had no family. She figured that if he was lying, he certainly would not go with her to the Convent. So she asked him to come with her for a meal, which, to her surprise, he did.'

'Oh my, I can smell where this is going!' Antonio took a deep breath. Then he said with an ironic look on his face, 'And the question is?'

Ramón ignored him, and continued. 'They gave him a meal, and a bath. Since he apparently had no place to go, they also gave him a bed for the night. The next morning Mother Chiara spoke with the boy, together with the nun who had found him, to find out why he was on the street on his own. They learned he was only fourteen years old and had a gruesome life behind him. After his stepfather had abused both him and his mother, she took him and ran away, leaving home without any money, or help. A few months followed of moving here and there for shelter and food and it took a heavy toll. His mother got very sick. When she was finally taken to the hospital it was much too late. The poor woman had died within a few days.'

'Hail the great city of Seville!' Antonio could not help commenting.

'It is an awful story. To tell you the truth, when I had Mother Chiara on the phone she was in tears, which is about the last thing you might expect from her.'

'What does she want from us?' Claire asked, a question to which the answer was quite obvious, but she needed time to adjust her mind to what was inevitably coming.

'That is the question I asked her too.'

'What did she say?'

'That the Convent is not the place for a boy,' Ramón answered her. 'She was very worried about what putting him in an orphanage might do to him. I could not deny that he may indeed have a rough time there, which is the last thing you would want, knowing what he has been through already.'

'So you accepted to take him?'

'No, not without consulting the two of you.'

'What do you suggest we should do?'

'I suggest we propose Mother Chiara a deal.'

'A deal…? As in a business deal?' Antonio wanted to know.

'Something similar, yes.' Antonio raised his brows at the very thought of Ramón coming out as a man of business.

'What kind of a deal do you have in mind?'

'We will explain what rough times we ourselves have been going through, such that with our current strength we cannot possibly take the responsibility for a battered child, who is blind on top of it. If we are going to accept the child anyway, which I am willing to consider, we need additional support from the Convent.'

'What kind of support?' Claire wanted to know.

'Someone who helps out. I have been thinking about our experience with the intern. We will need some kind of assistance if this community is to survive, but then we need to screen people applying for it. And we need to support and coach those who are accepted.'

'So we need someone to supervise new assistants that are coming in?'

'That's my suggestion. Someone who supervises and runs a support programme.'

Obviously, after the incident with Peter Entwistle, they had come to realize that bringing new people into the lives of Bethany's members needed much more careful preparation. Ramón's suggestion seemed to be a sound way of getting this organized. But none of them had any experience in this kind of work.

'What kind of person are we looking for?' Claire wanted to know. 'Any candidates?' Ramón shook his head.

'We certainly cannot afford to hire someone for an official job.'

'I might know a person we could ask,' Antonio said pensively. His two friends looked at each other with surprise when he continued. 'What about Maria?'

Maria? After a moment of consideration Claire was the first to respond. 'Why not Maria? After her unfortunate start she has been really doing well, and in the time she has been Lucie's assistant, she has come to be appreciated by the entire community.'

'That's true,' Ramón stepped in, 'she has experience as an assistant, both in how they can go wrong, and how they can change. She is used to a spiritual life. She knows what it takes. We could hardly get a person with more experience.'

They concluded that Ramón would go and visit the Convent in Seville to talk to Mother Chiara. The condition for taking up the boy in their community would be that he could not come before the beginning of spring. Furthermore, Bethany would request that Maria would remain attached to the house permanently. Since there was no point in postponing the visit, Ramón would go to Seville in person as soon as possible.

50.

A Successful Visit

Arriving at the gate of the Convent *de las Hermanas de la Cruz*, he was welcomed by Mother Chiara herself. 'Ramón, what a pleasure to see you!' she said heartily. 'You must have something important to tell me, if the message needs to be carried in person.' When he had made the appointment with her, Ramón had said that he wanted to speak with her about the boy face to face rather than on the phone.

'I do have an important message, Reverend Mother.'

'First let's get you out of your coat.' Before they stepped into her office she called the novice who was assisting her, and asked her to bring coffee. 'You will take a coffee with me, Ramón, won't you?'

'Oh yes, Reverend Mother, please.' When the coffee was brought in, and all the informal chatting was done, she asked to know what he had to say to her. Ramón started to describe the state of affairs in Bethany, leaving out what was the direct cause behind the request he was about to make.

'Since Maria became our first assistant to work with Lucie we have realized that we will need a fairly constant flow of new assistants as not many of them will stay for a longer period of time. We have learned the hard way that we must put more effort in coaching them, to support them with their difficult task. But we are too busy running the place.'

'Don't tell me. It's a constant hassle that I am supposed to be a mother to my nuns, while I am also their managing director. I find myself struggling with it every day. The spiritual life is difficult to maintain if one is running a place like this. Bethany won't be any different in this respect, I bet.' Ramón nodded, and continued to get to his point.

'So we came to the conclusion that we need a support program for our assistants in order to guide them in their work.'

'What a wonderful idea,' Mother Chiara said. 'But what has this to do with my request about Joaquin ... the blind boy, I mean?'

'You may guess now what my question is, since you already expect one is coming.' Ramón played on his charm that he knew she was receptive to, as he had learned on previous occasions.

'Go on.'

'I have come to you in person to propose a deal. We will eventually accept the boy as a member of our community, if you are willing to help us out. A support program for new assistants needs someone to run it.'

Mother Chiara looked at him with a frown.

'What does eventually mean?'

'It means he cannot come before February. We are barely hanging on at the moment.'

'What deal do you propose? Am I to lose another of my nuns to your project?'

'Well, yes and no,' Ramón said.

'What's the "no" part?'

'You're not going to lose another of your nuns.'

'How so?'

'I have come to ask you, Mother, whether Sister Maria can be the head of our assistants program. Claire, and Antonio and I think she is the best person we could find for that task, and we love her.'

'My Maria? Good Lord! I must admit I didn't see that one coming. What a surprise! No! What an honour!' The woman never failed to amaze Ramón with the agility of her decision-making mind. If she already had decided how to respond to his request, he hoped it would not be regardless of what Maria herself had to say about it.

'I think you will agree that this must be a voluntary mission,' Ramón said with some delicacy. 'Would you mind if I asked her myself?'

'No not at all.' Mother Chiara said, but with a stern face she added: 'I have to say I would be surprised should she say 'no'.'

'You're not afraid she might be reluctant in any way?' When she raised her brows, Ramón understood that in view of decisions regarding her nuns, the Reverend Mother was not a negotiating type.

'Perhaps it would be better that I see the boy first.' Ramón had no clue why that would be better, but he just wanted to slow down a bit not to rush things over.

'See the boy?'

'Yes, to make his acquaintance, and ask him a few things.'

'You're not thinking of measuring him up to see if he fits into Bethany, are you?'

Now Mother Chiara was doing him an injustice, which she sensed the moment she watched his face. Before he could say anything she had already seen her mistake, and was quick to correct it.

'That was not a sensible thing to say, Ramón, I am sorry. It's just that I hope you will take him in Bethany because I am absolutely sure that is where he belongs. He's such a gentle creature.'

Ramón found his charm again to conquer her. 'And you were trying to keep from me the sight of this gentle creature?'

She laughed heartily. 'You are quite something!' The tone of voice in which she said it made Ramón aware that he would receive what he asked in return for taking the boy. But he might need his charm even more to convince Sister Maria. The head of the Convent sent the novice to find her, and ask her to come to her office. Five minutes later, there was a knock on the door.

'Maria, my child, come in, come in!' The nun stepped in, looking surprised to find Ramón in the office. She turned to her superior to pay her respects, and then turned to the unexpected visitor.

'Ramón! How good to see you. What…? Excuse me, Reverend Mother.'

'Sit down my child, sit down.'

'Thank you, Reverend Mother. You asked for me?'

'Yes I did. The gentleman here has a question for you.'

'Ramón?'

Mother Chiara made a gesture that he should go ahead. Ramón told Maria basically the same he had told her. Then he came to the final point.

'Claire and Antonio and I have been thinking about who we should like to see added to our team for this new task, and we decided it should be you, and that's what I am here to ask.'

Maria was startled by what he was asking her. She was clearly moved. 'Me? But…'

'But what?' Mother Chiara wanted to know. As with all people, her virtues had their shady side as well. Her decision-making mind was quick as lightning, but patience was not her greatest gift. 'You're not worried about your start with the girl, are you?' Ramón almost felt sorry for poor Maria. In an attempt to give her some space, he took over. Mother Chiara feigned not to notice, and didn't say anything.

'Tell us what's worrying you about my question, Maria.'

'It was entirely Antonio's doing that I survived in Bethany,' she said softly, 'I tried, but … I am not sure, Ramón.' Then she turned to her superior.

'Would I have your permission, Reverend Mother, if I said "yes"?' she asked.

'It would be given wholeheartedly dear. Ramón is a very wise man to ask you.' Seeing Maria's questioning eyes, she continued. 'What better coach can one have than someone who knows what it is to fail the task, and who is then able to turn around and learn?' Ramón nodded to show he fully agreed.

They saw the woman's face change. First she smiled, and then her eyes beamed. 'You know Reverend Mother, were I to leave Bethany in a few weeks' time, as originally planned, I would terribly miss it. They're such wonderful people!' Turning to Ramón, she said: 'Yes, Ramón, oh yes, I would love to work with the assistants.'

The head of the Convent looked at him with a self-contented smile that said, 'See? Why waste another minute when you can do business straight away?' She gave Maria her blessing before she left the room.

'That part of the deal is done, then.' She called her novice in again, and asked her to bring Joaquin for there was someone to see him. A few moments later she came back with a skinny child, leading him by her hand. It was hard to see how this child could be a boy of fourteen. The novice told him they were in the office of the Reverend Mother and that there was a gentleman coming to see him.

'Hello,' Ramón said kindly, 'It's Joaquin, isn't it?'

The boy nodded slowly, but didn't say anything.

'Joaquin,' Mother Chiara said, 'this is Dr Ramón Jimenez from the House of Bethany. He wants to ask you something.'

'Yes I do, Joaquin.' Ramón replied. 'I live in a place where we have a few teenagers your age that you may like. They can no longer be at home either, just like you, and they would like to meet you.'

The boy listened attentively, but didn't respond. Ramón continued.

'We would like to invite you to come and visit us for a while. If you don't like it, you can always come back here. I am sure Mother Chiara will agree.'

Mother Chiara did not look amused by this proposition, but Ramón took the liberty of silencing her before she could say anything. He gestured her to wait for the boy's response.

'Would you like to come and see what Bethany is like?' The question was raised in as gentle way as Ramón was capable of, just to convince the boy that nothing would happen if he declined the invitation.

He stood there, silently, and then slowly nodded. Ramón looked at Mother Chiara and winked. Now it was his turn to claim victory. 'See?' His eyes said to her.

When the boy had been led away, she turned to Ramón. 'What was that all about, telling him he may come back here if he doesn't like Bethany?'

'Why, Reverend Mother?' Ramón responded, putting up an innocent smile. 'Don't you trust your own judgment? If it is true, as you said, that he absolutely belongs in Bethany, how could he not like it there?'

'You're a scoundrel! You know that, don't you?' she said with a broad smile. 'Come here, you.'

When Ramón got up, she hugged him, which made him blush like a boy. It was agreed that the boy would remain at the Convent until February, as Ramón had convinced Mother Chiara that it would be irresponsible to have him before that time. Organising the assistance of Lucie Miles put more than enough strain on Bethany already.

A few minutes after he said goodbye to the head of the Convent he passed the gate. The sun was just breaking through after a rain shower. The air was fresh on this winter's day. He drew his coat together, and felt lighter than he had for some time. Soon Bethany would have two new people in its community: Joaquin, the orphan from the streets of Seville, and Sister Maria, coach of their new assistants.

———

51

'I Can See With My Hands'

When Joaquin entered the pottery for the first time, Antonio had no idea what to do with a blind boy. But his practical instincts would help him. As an artist, he had a great talent looking at things from a different angle. It proved to be a valuable skill, also this time.

'Hello, son,' he said, taking Joaquin's hand in his for a jovial handshake. 'Welcome to our workshop where we make pots, and bowls and vases.' Interrupting himself for a second to see if there was any response, he saw the boy was listening, but remained silent.

'I hope you don't mind but I am going to need a lot of help from you, Joaquin. I know what a pottery looks like, but I have no clue what it is like when you cannot see anything. The same is true of my crew here. So you need to teach us what it is to be blind. When you do, I promise we will teach you how to make a decent pot. Do we have a deal?'

Joaquin's face showed the beginning of a smile, and when Antonio again took his hand in his own, and asked, 'Do we?' the smile got bigger, and he nodded, 'Yes, we do.'

'Very good! Now you need to tell me this. How do I show you what is in the workshop? How does that work?' The message Antonio sent to the boy could not be clearer: 'You're not the problem, I have a problem, and I need your help to solve it.' The response came with a barely audible question.

'Where is everyone?' Indeed his new colleagues were so taken in by his entrance, even though they had met at the dinner table the night before, that they had been very quiet.

'Perfect point; hey everybody, make some noise, Joaquin wants to be able to locate where you are!' Philippe was the first to start slapping his hands on the table in front of him 'I am here!' and was followed by Alonso, within a second everybody was slapping a table, clapping in their hands, and shouting out loud.

'Ho… Ho… All right folks, that was not bad for a start, but now we do it one by one. Philippe tell Joaquin your name. Say: I am Philippe and I am here.' Philippe did exactly as he was told, and everybody who could speak, followed. Then Antonio went over to Fernando, 'Joaquin I am calling for Fernando. Fernando doesn't speak, but he is here!'

'Did this work for you?' he asked the blind boy. The response was again a nod with his head. 'We work at tables, so everyone you just heard has a table in front of them. I think I know a perfect place for you,' Antonio said, and took his hand to bring him to Fernando's table.

'Can our friend sit here with you, Fernando?' he asked gently. Fernando's face reddened a bit, as if he was ashamed of something. Then he pulled out a chair from under the table, which Antonio took as a welcoming gesture. 'Thank you, Fernando,' he said. 'Fernando is pulling out a chair for you Joaquin, you can sit here.'

The boy nodded with a smile on his face as if to thank Fernando for his gesture. Antonio took his hand to place it on the table, and the boy went around trying to catch the chair that he had heard being moved. He inadvertently touched Fernando's shoulder. 'Oh, excuse me. Hi, Fernando.' The words were again softly spoken, and when he stuck out his hand, Fernando took it. Then he looked at Antonio, apparently surprised.

'All right,' said the artist, 'now that the two of you have met, we may as well start doing some work. Or no, perhaps first you want me to show you where everything is. Do you?'

Joaquin was getting acquainted with the idea that a lot of questions were coming his way, and that Antonio had meant what he said, when he had asked for help. He had found the chair that Fernando had pulled out for him, and sat down. Antonio noticed that for a brief moment the boy's shoulders were slightly shivering, as if they wanted to get rid of something that had been weighing upon them for too long.

'I would like to see the things that you are making,' he said, still speaking softly. Antonio did not miss the peculiarity of his phrasing, and made a point of it. 'Hey friends, did you hear what Joaquin just said?'

'He said that he would like to see, but he cannot see.' Pascal's bright eyes looked truly puzzled at the blind boy.

'You're way too smart for your age, but we knew that already. Okay people, let us ask Joaquin what he means by saying that he wants *to see* what we make in the pottery.' Turning towards Joaquin he asked him, 'How do you see, Joaquin, if not with your eyes?'

'With my hands, I can see with my hands.'

'Can you show us?'

'Hmmm.'

'Pascal, fetch one of the finished things from the shelf over there. Pay attention people, Joaquin is going to teach us something.' Pascal went over and came back with a delicate bowl that Alfredo had made. He put it carefully on the table in front of Joaquin. Then the artist invited him: 'Please tell us what you see, Joaquin.'

Feeling the object with his fingers, he went around it, touched the rim, went down inside the bowl, and made out the depth of its bottom. Then he looked up with shining eyes. 'It's a bowl.'

'There you go,' Antonio said to Pascal, and saw the little boy's admiration. 'This is how Joaquin sees – with his hands!'

'I wish I could do something like that with my feet,' Sofia said wistfully.

'How is that?' Antonio wanted to know while approaching her wheelchair.

'Joaquin knows how to use his hands to do what his eyes cannot do. I wish I knew how to do what my feet cannot do.'

'Oh, sweetie, you are perfect as you are,' Antonio comforted her by gently touching her arm. But there were more creative responses.

'Why, you can always walk on your hands!' Philippe commented with the distinct idea that what he said was funny. And indeed, it took an effort for Antonio to keep his face straight, because he didn't want to hurt Sofia's feelings.

But she took it lightly, he was happy to see. 'No doubt you could teach me how to do that!' she said dryly.

'Of course, I can, let me show you.'

'Ho, ho, mister. Don't get carried away by your own swagger!'

And so Joaquin's introduction to the workshop and its crew ended on a merry note: the boy felt that it had been a successful start, and that he would be shown step by step how to find his way in the workshop. Antonio also thought it had been a good beginning. For the rest of the morning, Joaquin would receive his first lesson in pottery, which the artist set up in a such a way that Fernando was supporting his new friend by getting whatever he needed.

It came as no surprise, then, that when lunchtime had come, Joaquin asked Fernando whether he could take him there. 'Just take my hand if you want to,' he added. Without hesitation, Fernando took it, and so they left for the dining hall in the house.

As the days went by, the community of Bethany learned more about the two newly found buddies. Joaquin was guiding Fernando's mind in a most subtle and gentle way, without ever raising his voice, or scorning him for his slowness. Likewise Fernando was guiding the blind boy's feet so that he always arrived where he needed to be. His life on the streets of Seville had of course made a lasting impact on the boy, but it rarely became apparent within the walls of Bethany. Once outside, he showed much more caution, as if he felt he were back on the street again. Gradually his traumatic experience seemed to disappear behind a recovering trust in people, but it still needed very little for the fear be reawakened.

It was an unfortunate encounter in the fields behind the House of Bethany that made Antonio and the others aware of the deep wound in the boy's soul. It was early in the evening before sunset that Joaquin asked Fernando to go for a walk. As was his habit, Fernando just took his hand to indicate that he would like to come. They turned away from the house to the west in the direction of the olive groves. When they arrived at the small bridge where the dirt road began, there was a stranger hanging over the railing.

When he noticed that his friend had become a little restless, Joaquin asked him, 'What is it, Fernando?' Of course there came no answer, but the blind boy sensed there was trouble ahead.

'Who's there?' His voice sounded insecure, and his hand fastened its grip on Fernando's arm.

'What are you shouting at me? What business do I have with you?'

The response sounded ugly, which made Joaquin stop. He had been living too long on the street not to recognize the sound of a drunkard. He trembled when he heard the man's feet dragging over to where they stood awaiting him.

'Hey, who are you? Something wrong with your eyes, isn't it? I could use a big fellow like this one here to get me home safely.' The man sounded unpleasant, even though Joaquin did not feel he was intent on harming him.

Unfortunately the drunkard made a move on his unsteady legs that almost caused him to stumble against the railing where they were standing. In order not to fall down, the man grabbed the boy's arm. This time Fernando made a move too, quick as lightning, a move that would make the drunkard regret his carelessness for a long time after. Without making a sound, he placed himself before Joaquin, and grabbed the man's fist, and then squeezed it like he once had done with poor Lucie.

The man screamed with pain so loud that it was heard inside the house, a few hundred yards from the bridge, and he went down on his knees. Not knowing what had happened, Joaquin wanted to get away, and with a voice full of anxiety begged him, 'Come

Fernando, let's go home!' His friend finally let go of the man's hand, and left him moaning on the road. Then he turned around, took Joaquin's hand and laid it on his own arm. From that day onwards, the two buddies were inseparable.

52.

Finding New Assistants

Having secured Maria permanently to supervise new assistants, the most urgent task had been to find them. Various possibilities came up, among which was Claire's suggestion to ask Jacques Mendoza, the psychologist from Madrid. They had helped him immensely by reacting positively to his emergency call about Pascal, whom they had accepted in their community shortly before his eighth birthday. Now Jacques could do something in return.

'Maybe,' Ramón said. 'He works in a clinic, and also teaches at the university, so he might know a few young people with a potential interest in what we are trying to do.' They agreed it might be a good place to start. Ramón promised to call the psychologist the next day.

The psychologist's response was immediately sympathetic, and Ramón hardly had to emphasize the urgency of the matter. 'You don't have to explain "emergency" to me, Ramón, we face them most every week. So, no, I absolutely see what you are asking. I will call you back by the end of the week.'

Jacques Mendoza kept his promise. Not only did he call back quickly, but he also had a candidate. A student in psychology at the university was looking for a place to spend a sabbatical. Since the community of Bethany represented the kind of project that he wanted to study, he was willing to consider working without a regular salary.

Ramón thanked Jacques for his support, but when he told his friends about the result, they were concerned. There was also a hesitation felt by Ramón himself.

'Why does he want to come?' Claire wanted to know.

'How long will he stay?' Antonio added.

'If we want him to, a year, starting this month.'

'Well, to find out whether we want him is exactly why we have a supervisor for new assistants,' Antonio said, looking at Maria. 'There is work for you, Sister.'

'I suggest we invite him for an interview. I will prepare the questions I want to discuss with him, and report you after I have seen him. I will inform him that decisions about hiring new assistants are subject to a strict procedure.'

'What procedure?'

'Here is my plan. If he passes the interview, he is welcome for a short period of two weeks. If he wants to stay, and we want it also, he can stay for another four weeks. Then he will have a six weeks evaluation, which I propose should be done by Ramón. If he passes, he can stay as long as he wants, but it must be for a minimum of six months.'

The others were pleasantly surprised about the clarity and determination of Maria's proposal. Claire and Ramón responded positively and accepted her plan without any amendments. Antonio had his own way of congratulating Maria, of course.

'Gee, I was bloody lucky that you were not here to guard the gate of Saint Peter when I came to Bethany, for I am not sure I would have passed.'

Maria, who was getting better and better in handling the potter's sense of humor, retorted with unexpected wit. Speaking with an austere voice and without blinking an eye she said:

'You certainly would not have passed had I heard you swearing like that, and I might even consider suspending you now that I have.'

Antonio fell completely silent, which they all found quite amusing.

'Wow!' Claire looked impressed.

Maria watched Antonio's perplexity. Then her face softened up with a giggle, and her austere look changed into a defiant smile. 'Got you there, didn't I?'

There was a moment of silence, and then they all burst out laughing, including Antonio. One of the reasons why his friends could handle his jokes was that he had no problem whatsoever with being made fun of himself.

Enrique Valdez, the student that Jacques Mendoza had found for them, was invited to come to Bethany for an interview. Since he would be coming all the way from Madrid, she offered him an overnight stay in their guestroom.

Naturally the experience with Peter Entwistle had made them cautious, so Maria was not inclined to take lightly her task of 'measuring up' the new guy. But she noticed very quickly that he was a totally different character than the Englishman had been.

'He appears to have a kind and gentle nature, and at the same time he made a very solid impression,' she said when she reported to her friends about the interview. 'He was interested in projects where people with support needs were included as part of a communal life, and when Jacques informed him about Bethany, he was immediately interested to see what it was like.'

'Jacques said he would take a sabbatical; what does that mean?' Antonio wanted to know. 'Are we to be his guinea pigs who will later appear in his doctoral work?'

'That's not my impression. On the contrary, it sounded quite convincing. He had been working very hard for a number of years to get into the university, and then again had studied conscientiously, and now would take a year off away from books and libraries. The fact that Bethany is the kind of community he is interested in was a no more than a happy coincidence. When I informed him about the procedure, he showed to be very sensitive to the fact that we were not taking our responsibility lightly.'

'What about work without a salary?' Ramón wanted to know.

'He had saved some money, and with the small allowance we pay combined with free meals and lodging, that was fine with him. All in all, I think he is a well-balanced character. Besides, we have the two weeks and the six weeks interview to evaluate him, and on both occasions we can tell him we do not want him to stay.'

'How did he respond?' Claire asked.

'As I said, he found that procedure only fair to the members, given their histories, of which I had told him very briefly in the beginning of the interview.'

'What is your advice?' Ramón wanted Maria to understand that her role in this was taken very seriously.

'My advice? Ask him to come.'

When Enrique Valdez came to Bethany Maria was happy to find her intuitions about him rewarded. Enrique was in every respect a good man, and within a few weeks after his arrival most of the members already felt like he had been there for years. But even with him on board Maria noticed that assisting Lucie was taking a heavy toll. Apart from Enrique, the task of stepping in fell upon Ramón and herself. Having young Pascal in that same spot, as Antonio had suggested, was clearly not a good idea, at least not in the long run. Ramón in paricular was struggling, even when he took only a one hour shift each day. Claire noticed he was very unhappy with himself.

One night she sat down with Maria to share her concern. 'Why don't we do what we agreed with Señor Miles when Lucie's apartment was opened,' she said.

'What was that?' Maria wanted to know.

'When we came up with the plan of an apartment for his daughter, we told him that we might have to call upon him if we got stuck with insufficient people to support Lucie. He accepted and insisted that we should call him if that came to pass, and it seems to me that's where we are right now.'

'Perhaps you should call him then.'

'Let me do that' Claire said. 'I will ask him whether he can help us out. If not with another person, then with supplying us with the resources to hire someone. We don't necessarily need a new assistant for his daughter. We would also be relieved if we could hire someone for the household work. Sylvia could take over my role, with a new maid for the kitchen. I would be free to take shifts with Maria and Enrique, and work in the garden with Philippe and Pascal. I could also assist Antonio in the workshop, when needed.'

'I'd rather not hire a professional nurse as Lucie's assistant,' Maria commented.

'Neither would I,' Claire responded. 'That's why I am primarily thinking about staffing the house, so that the rest of us can focus on supporting our members without too much stress.'

They agreed that Claire would proceed in this way. When she called Señor Miles the next day, and explained the situation, she found him more than willing to help out.

'We still need someone for Lucie's apartment. Now that we have also Joaquin we need an extra person to make sure your daughter receives proper attention.'

'I get the picture, Señora Gomez, and I am glad that you are calling,' he said politely. 'I will do whatever I can.'

Claire told him about their idea of finding either another assistant or the resources to hire someone to assist in the household. 'I see,' he said, 'but I don't see why it should be one or the other. Why not do both at the same time? When my wife was still alive and Lucie was living with us in Zaragoza, we got help from a young woman from the neighbourhood, Patricia Nuñez de Castro. She was actually quite good with Lucie. I will ask whether she is still around, and if so, whether she would be willing to help us out. For how long, you said? Six months? I will pay for her expenses, and also for the allowance you pay your assistants. Apart from this I will also pay for the costs of hiring a cook or a maid until, what shall we say, this time next year? What do you think?'

'Thank you so much, Señor Miles. That is more than generous, Sir, thank you for helping us out.'

'*De nada*, Señora Gomez, *de nada*.' The man was truly delighted that he could do what was urgently needed. 'If you only knew how much I appreciate what Ramón and you together with Señor Ardiles and Sister Maria have been doing since Lucie came to Bethany.'

It was not very likely that the young woman from Zaragoza he had been referring to would be available, Claire suspected, apart from the fact that she would not be young any more. 'It must have been more than six years since she assisted Lucie's mother,' she said when reporting to Maria the result of her phone call.

'Let's hope for the best,' Maria said. 'You know what Ramón would say.'

'What would he say?' Claire wanted to know.

'That there is always a solution when you don't expect one.'

The call from Lucie's father two days later did in fact bring positive news. He had been able to trace Patricia Nuñez, the woman he had mentioned to Claire. Not only was she still single, she had also recently left her job as an elementary school teacher. She would love to see Lucie again, and was willing to work in Bethany till the end of summer. Finding another job so late in the school year wasn't going to be easy anyway, so she might as well take her time to look around for a new position. The offer that Lucie's father made her was the perfect opportunity to do so.

53.

___

Semana Santa

When both Patricia, the new assistant, and Anna, Sylvia's help in the kitchen, had arrived things were back to normal again, at least to the extent that such a condition was possible at all in Bethany. Being outside the official service system, its staff was always busy and struggling to get everything done. Except for rare incidents, the members usually did not notice much of the many concerns that needed to be taken care of. Most of the staff meetings were done in the late hours of the day, so that during the day their minds were free to be really present for the other members of their community.

Very soon after Enrique Valdez had started, everyone saw that the initial concern about him had been misplaced. Perhaps he was a little absent-minded sometimes, particularly at times when he was reading a book that had captured him, but otherwise he was very dependable. His quiet presence was a blessing for subdued characters like Joaquin and Alfredo. They simply loved him, even though they never exchanged the kind of affection that Alonso threw around so abundantly.

Enrique's major assignment was to support Lucie. As an intellectual, he did not easily connect with the girl. But he was too much of a stoic for it to bother him too much. At any rate he was not nearly as bothered by her limitations as for example Ramón was. It would be too crude to say that he didn't care, but he took her 'chaos' for granted in a way that Ramón found extremely hard to do. Perhaps it was because of his habit to distance himself emotionally from what could not be changed, so that his soul didn't suffer from things that nobody could help. Enrique Valdez's character, in other words, was dominated by his tendency to cultivate a detached state of mind.

As is true of most qualities that people exhibit, Enrique's qualities could turn into weaknesses when they went unchecked by opposing dispositions. When Lucie had one of her fits of malice and hit somebody on the back, as she sometimes still did, he would not respond in anger, like Antonio would do, but would tell her not to hurt people. It made her victims sometimes feel as if he condoned her behaviour. 'Upset' was a state of mind that Enrique Valdez rarely found himself in.

The same was true of how he deliberated on whether or not to take a particular course of action. When someone told him that what he was about to do might turn out badly, he could respond in a way that made people wonder whether he had listened to their worries at all. A more affectionate soul would have been much more prudent than Enrique was wont to be. He simply did not think that the anticipation of trouble was worth paying attention to.

Something like this was going on when one day he suggested going to visit Seville during *Semana Santa* with some of Bethany's members. It was a well-known religious spectacle that originated from age-old practices of penitence as a preparation for Easter. During Holy Week the local *cofradías* would be carrying their icon statues from their parish churches to the cathedral in the center of the old city.

For many citizens, Seville's *Semana Santa* was an intense spiritual experience, even for those who would not necessarily regard themselves as religious. Its candlelit processions and brass band music made a strong impression on everyone who had ever watched it, and Enrique believed this would be true for the members of Bethany as well. Given its mission as a spiritual community, he expected his suggestion would not fall on deaf ears.

But there were worries, mainly expressed by Maria and Claire. 'The streets will be immensely crowded, there are so many people there. Unless you're willing to stand there hours before they start you may not be able to even come close to a procession. Our people might have to wait for a very long time,' Claire objected. Like Maria, she had strong reservations about the plan, so much was clear.

'Well we have to consider who can go, of course, because not everybody will be able to,' Enrique responded.

'That doesn't sound fair to me,' Maria said, 'some of our members will be very disappointed when they're told they can't go.'

'I am not sure they will be, because they might want to decide for themselves that it would be too much. I would like to leave Bethany late in the afternoon, so that we arrive in the inner city at about six. And we should be back before midnight.'

'Who did you have in mind taking with you anyway?' Antonio wanted to know.

'I was thinking of Philippe, Fernando, Joaquin, and Sofia, but she can only join us if we also have Patricia in our party. Pascal would not be able to see much because of his height.'

'Speaking of which that raises the point of taking Joaquin, not to mention Sofia's wheelchair,' Antonio commented.

'Well, I will ask Joaquin of course, but it's not only the sight of the procession, but also the music. There is some exquisite singing by Flamenco singers from the balconies when the statues pass by in the streets. And the wailing sound of the brass bands makes one shiver. You must have heard them yourselves, since you have lived long enough in Seville to know this.'

'I used to go home to Galicia for the Holy Week,' Antonio said, 'but I once stayed and watched the processions. You're right, it is a very moving experience.'

'I am still not sure this is a wise thing to do.' Claire was not yet ready to let go. 'You could get stuck in the crowd with that wheelchair and not be able to get back to the railway station in time. I assume you planned to take the train?'

'Yes, that is part of the plan. From there we will take a taxi that can take Sofia's wheelchair. And about getting trapped, don't you think people will pay attention when they see Sofia's wheelchair, and Fernando guiding a blind boy? If I take care of her wheelchair, and Patricia looks after Philippe, we should be okay.'

'What did Patricia say?'

'I haven't spoken to her about it, because I wanted to have your approval first.'

It is hard negotiating feelings about what might go wrong with someone who does not share them, so when Antonio did not squarely oppose Enrique's plan, both Claire and Maria gave in, although with grave doubts.

The day they went into town was *Miércoles Santo*, Holy Wednesday. Looking back later at what happened on the evening of that day, Enrique Valdez could not but regret that he had been taking members of Bethany into the city of Seville. The streets were packed but this had not scared him off, as it should have done. The occasion of their trip to Seville on this day was an example of being challenged at the point where one appears to be the least vulnerable, which in Enrique's case was his stoicism. What should have been a wonderful experience, ended in horror, especially for Joaquin and Fernando, as it did for Enrique himself.

The trip started as it was planned, which was to take the train from Benacazón for a ride to *Santa Justa*, the main railway station of Seville. From there a taxi was to take them to *Plaza Nueva*, where they would look for a place to eat. Then they would try to find a spot in one of the narrow streets north of the square, and watch the procession by one of the *cofradías*. Reading about them Enrique had decided upon the *Hermandad el Baratillo*, the Brotherhood of the Marketplace, which would pass while carrying its statue from the *Capella de la Piedad* to the Cathedral.

Riding the train together had been a treat in itself. There were jokes and jests, in which Philippe was champion, there was excitement about what was to come, testified by Sofia's nervous giggles and the reddened spots on her neck, and there were memories of previous trips. The party from Bethany, in other words, was in high spirits, with the exception of Joaquin, perhaps, who may have had mixed feelings about Seville's inner city. His main reason for coming was that without him Fernando would not go either, which he thought would be a pity.

Having arrived at the railway station they soon found a taxi that could take Sofia's wheelchair, and bring them to their destination. Enrique knew a place where they could eat. It was a small tapas bar where they sat down for a light meal, another treat that was much appreciated by everyone.

While they were eating Enrique told them about the procession they were about to see. A religious group organized it. It was called *Hermandad*, a brotherhood. In the seventeenth century it had grown out of a devotional practice of praying for the dead at an iron cross located at the market of the *Arenal*, a neighbourhood that in later years would be famous for its bullfights. That's how it came to be named the 'Brotherhood of the Marketplace'.

The iron cross itself had marked the site of a mass burial that took place after an epidemic had devastated the city. In the week before Easter pious locals came to pray for mercy for the dead. The cross would be illuminated and adorned with candles and flowers. Out of this devotional practice grew the *Hermandad de la Cruz del Baratillo*, the Brotherhood of the Cross of Marketplace, founded in 1693.

'In the procession they will carry two statues,' Enrique said. 'The first of these two is very famous. It shows the Virgin Mary holding her dying son in her lap.'

'How do they carry it?' Philippe wanted to know.

'They carry it on a wooden float, covered by black curtains, and by red cloth with gold ornaments all around. It looks very beautiful. Under that float there are more than thirty men carrying the statue. Since they cannot see anything, there is a man whose task is to constantly guide their steps, the *capataz*.'

'What does Mary look like?' Sofia's eyes were shining as she was imagining the scene that Enrique was describing.

'The statue is famous for the beauty of the mother in a blue robe, also gold embroidered, who with her weeping, pale face looks inconsolably sad. It is a very moving sight. That's why people love it'

'What does the second look like?'

'It's also a statue of Mary, now called the *Virgen de la Caridad*, the virgin of charity. She stands beneath a canopy of sorrows, with tears running down her face. It has dozens of candles lighting her weeping face. There are two brass bands with very sad trumpets and horns with drums that play music as on a funeral.'

Around seven they were strolling through the bustling streets north of *Plaza Nueva*. The atmosphere was a curious mixture of excitement and solemnity. Many people were passing by, but there was no shouting or singing as would be the case if soccer fans were taking possession of the streets. Enrique decided to stay in a street named *Calle Sierpes*, where the procession would pass through.

So far he had been right in expecting that people would show some respect for Sofia's wheelchair, mainly because Philippe would make a lot of noise to warn them. Even the sight of Fernando apparently guiding a blind man was responded to by making way that they could pass. As soon as they were in the small street, however, the situation changed. Everybody was stuck in a crowd, and soon there was no going back or forth. People were packed so tightly that it would not have been difficult to walk on their heads.

Sitting in her wheelchair Sofia was becoming anxious that she would not see any of the spectacle that was about to pass by. Philippe was nervous because there were too many people around him. Instead of watching Sofia's wheelchair, he stayed as close to Patricia as he could. Joaquin was doing reasonably well, but Fernando was far from relaxed about the lack of space around him that was inevitably a part of being in a large crowd. Enrique was constantly busy to keep as much eye contact with each of them as he could.

'Even if you don't see much of the procession, just listen to the music of the band, and the songs,' he tried to reassure them. And indeed, the atmosphere was very special. There were hardly any people speaking, but nonetheless many voices were going 'sssh..., sssh...' as if to emphasize that they were witnessing a solemn moment. After fifteen minutes the first brass band was passing by, playing a wailing tune full of sounds befitting the spirit of penitence. Then the first statue followed. It was just as beautiful as Enrique had described it, and even Sofia could see it quite well.

After another ten minutes the second statue appeared, exquisitely lit by many burning candles, again just as Enrique had said. Then all of a sudden the crowd started to push back, as if the holiness of the icon came much too close. But soon it turned out that an elderly man had fallen to the ground in an apparent fit of epilepsy, kicking with his feet, while white foam came from his mouth and his eyes turned back in their sockets till they looked almost completely white. It was a gruesome sight to see.

In the chaos that followed people were pushing each other in attempting to make enough room for the poor man. They were shouting for a doctor. It turned out there was one standing close by, which again caused more shoving and pushing when people were trying to make way. Even though all this did not take much more than a few minutes, it was just enough for Enrique to lose sight of everyone, as he had to protect Sofia's wheelchair from being pushed over. Sofia had started screaming in terror when she saw the man fall, and needed to be comforted. When a few seconds later Enrique turned around to check whether they still were together, he couldn't see Fernando and Joaquin.

Patricia was a good ten yards away with Philippe. Enrique called her.

'Patricia, where are Fernando and Joaquin?' At that point the second brass band was playing at full strength right in front of them, which made the chance of being heard quite slim. 'Where are Fernando and Joaquin?' he shouted. Patricia shrugged her shoulders; she could not hear him.

Perhaps it would have been wiser to shout out loud the names of Fernando and Joaquin, assuming that they could not be far, rather than trying to find out whether Patricia had seen where they went. As it happened, Enrique started shouting their names at a point where he apparently could no longer be heard. No answer came his way. Attempting to turn around, Patricia saw a mounting fear in his eyes.

'Stay together!' Enrique called upon Patricia, 'we need to stay together!'

'Fernando and Joaquin,' she shouted back crushed by the people surrounding them. 'I can't see them!' This was too much for Sofia's frail composure. She started to cry, 'Where are they? Where are they?' Philippe was trembling with fear, and was about to lose it. A moment later Patricia noticed he had wet himself.

'We need to get out of here!' she shouted at Enrique.

54.

Back at the Convent

Unfortunately Joaquin and Fernando had been pushed forward from the sidewalk into the street as soon as the second statue had passed, which meant the procession was over. They could not go against the crowd, so the only thing left for them was to follow. It was a scary situation, Fernando without a voice to shout, Joaquin without eyes to see where they were moving. Only a few minutes had passed since it had started, but they had nonetheless been drifting away. They were still less than hundred yards away from their original spot when they turned into another street.

As soon as the pressure from the crowd was relaxing Joaquin had placed himself against the first door he could find, and stayed there. Being more streetwise than anyone in their party, the blind boy was not really scared. During his years as a homeless kid in Seville he had learned to be scared when someone came walking towards him in a deserted back ally. Crowds were not unsafe, they were just a big hassle. Being pushed and shoved around in these streets, however, Joaquin had lost his sense of direction.

Fernando was too scared to notice anything once they had been separated from the others. He was no longer capable of leading his buddy, who could do nothing but take his hand and decide for himself where to go. This he did, but without being aware of the fact he moved in exactly the opposite direction from where Enrique and the others were going. In no time they were moving again into another street.

As soon as the street got a little quieter, Joaquin began stopping people to ask them for the name of the street they were in. Unfortunately their answers did not help very much because he didn't recognize the name.

'Fernando, we need to find a place to be safe. I don't think Enrique will be able to find us.' Joaquin figured that Enrique would no doubt try to find them, but the prospect of actually finding them seemed quite hopeless, when suddenly he knew where to go: Mother Chiara of the Convent. He immediately started to stop people and ask around.

'Excuse me, do you know where we find the Convent *de las Hermanas de la Cruz*?'

Since there were a lot of tourists visiting the city during Holy Week, he was not immediately lucky. He had to try half a dozen times before finally a man answered him, saying: 'Sure, you're not all that far away. It's in the *Calle Santa Angela de la Cruz*. Follow this street about three hundred yards, then take the first right and follow that to the *Iglesia de San Pedro* and then ask again.' Assuming that giving directions to a blind boy didn't make much sense, the man was addressing Fernando even though Joaquin had asked him the question. When they started to walk in the direction the man had pointed out, Joaquin was smart enough to repeat the question about the Convent a few times to make sure they were staying on track.

'Can you tell me how to get to the Convent *de las Hermanas de la Cruz*?'

'Sure I can, boy.' Joaquin recognized a Sevillian accent in the voice of the man that answered him. Pausing for a moment while looking at Fernando, the man asked, 'What's wrong with your friend here?'

Joaquin had no idea what made him raise the question at this point, but he had other things to worry about, so he flatly responded, 'He doesn't speak, so he can't ask.'

'A blind boy and a deaf-mute lost on Holy Wednesday,' the man responded, 'It must be my lucky day. Come on boy, let me lead you to the Convent, it's only a few minutes from here.'

As soon as they arrived at the gate of the Convent, the man said goodbye. Joaquin thanked him for his kindness, and rang the bell, which he had to repeat a number of times before he finally heard someone approaching from within. The door opened. A face appeared that did not look too happy to receive visitors at this late hour. When the nun looked at him, she suddenly recognized the boy.

'Joaquin! Good Lord! What are you doing here? Who is your friend? What happened?' The boy didn't recognize the voice, so he addressed her anonymously.

'Can we come in Sister?'

'Sure you can! Come in!' When they stepped in, the nun closed the door behind them.

'Too many people in the street nowadays,' she muttered.

'Could you please take us to Mother Chiara, we need her help.'

'I will go and see her immediately, you wait here.'

A few moments later the head of the Convent appeared in the hallway. As soon as she saw the boy, she called his name and took his hand in hers, saying, 'Well, well, look who's here. It's Mother Chiara, Joaquin. What are you doing?'

When Joaquin told her the story he made sure it sounded much less frightening than she would have taken it otherwise to be.

'Lost in the crowd, were you! It was very wise of you to come to us. What a bright idea to bring you into the city on a night like this!' The scorn in her voice was an ominous sign for whoever would turn out to be responsible. That person would be in serious trouble if her opinion counted for anything. Then she looked at Fernando.

'And who's this young man? What's your name, son?'

Joaquin spoke softly as he answered her question. 'This is my buddy, Fernando, Reverend Mother. We live together at Bethany. Fernando doesn't speak.'

'Oh… eh… well, good! You're most welcome, Fernando.' She stuck out her hand to welcome him. After a moment's hesitation he took it, and bowed his head. Mother Chiara smiled gently, while looking at him.

'What's the time now?' she asked the nun who had opened the gate.

'A quarter to nine.'

'It must have been less than forty minutes that we lost them,' Joaquin estimated.

Mother Chiara suggested that the best thing to do right now was to call Bethany and tell them what had happened. She would make the call herself. It was Maria who answered the phone.

'House of Bethany, this is Maria speaking.'

'Maria, dear, it's Mother Chiara.'

'Reverend Mother! How nice to hear your voice! How are you?'

'I am all right dear, but the reason I am calling you is not. With me here are two of your people, Joaquin and Fernando. They have lost contact with the others because of the crowd.' Mother Chiara told her everything she had heard from Joaquin about what had happened. 'Not a particularly smart idea to come to the city at a time like this with your people.' She made her comment sound as if Maria had personally concocted the plan.

'I should have simply forbidden it,' Maria said. 'Claire and I were opposed, but the men were in favour. They said it would be a great experience.'

'Since when do we nuns listen to men, dear?' Maria could not see the grin on her face when she made her comment.

'I know, but they made us look like overanxious mothers protecting their babies.' As soon as she had said it, Maria regretted it. She should have been stronger in opposing Enrique's unholy plan.

'Well, we certainly do not want to appear to be overanxious mothers, do we?' Notwithstanding the serious situation, Mother Chiara could not resist the jest. Maria was wise enough not to respond, so her superior continued, 'When that young man Enrique is smart enough to give you a call, tell him to come over here. Our two friends here will stay for the night, I presume, because when eventually he gets here, there won't be an opportunity to get to Benacazón by train until tomorrow.'

While his friends arrived at the Convent, Enrique was frantically cruising the streets north of the *Plaza Nueva*. After Joaquin and Fernando were lost, he had handed train tickets and taxi money to Patricia. 'Make sure you get home with Philippe and Sofia as soon as you can. I will stay to find the other two.' He made it sound as reassuring as he could, but like Patricia he too was horrified by the idea he might not be able to find them. And frankly, the chance that he would was close to zero. After anxious embraces, Patricia went off in one direction with Sofia and Philippe; Enrique went in the other.

The crowd that had blocked his way was slowly dispersing, but now that he could move, he had no idea where to go. He became very frightened. His heart was racing, and his body was sweating all over. The student of psychology, otherwise as cool as a cucumber, was losing control over his fear.

Running around to find his lost friends, a memory from a long time ago came into his mind. It had been a sunny day when he was on the beach with his parents and his younger brother. As it was a holiday, the beach was very crowded. All of a sudden, his little brother was lost because he had wandered away from where their parents were seated. The memory of that scene almost made Enrique cry.

'Have you seen two people, a big guy and a blind boy?' he kept asking people passing by. They looked at him as if he had asked whether they had seen a needle in a haystack. Running to and fro through the streets for almost half an hour, he stopped and leaned back against a wall, wiping drops of sweat from his forehead. Having no idea what to do he was just about to panic, when his eye caught a cantina down the street. A phone call, he should make a phone call…! He went in and asked the barkeeper for a phone. As it was a noisy place, the barkeeper did not understand him.

'Can I make a phone call, please?' he said again, gesturing with his hands what he wanted. The barkeeper made an okay sign, and pointed to the back of the cantina. When he found the phone booth, Enrique dialed Bethany's number. Maria answered his call.

'Maria, it's Enrique. Something terrible has happened. We have been split. I lost Fernando and Joaquin. There were so many people; they started to push. It was terrible…'

'Enrique…'

'I couldn't do anything…'

'It's okay, Enrique, calm down, we got a phone call. It's okay, they are safe!' Maria could not recall having heard Enrique ever before in an apparent state of panic.

'They're safe?'

'Yes, Joaquin was clever enough to go to the Convent. We received a phone call from Mother Chiara. But what about the others, where are they?'

'I gave Patricia money for a taxi and the train tickets, and told her to get home as quick as she could. She has Sofia and Philippe with her. They should be home at eleven at any rate.'

'Let's hope that works out,' Maria said gravely.

'I will call you again later, to see whether they have returned safely.'

'I want you to go to the Convent as well. Mother Chiara said so. Go to them and call us from there.'

Enrique said he would. He hung up the phone, and paid the barkeeper for his phone call, and left. Being somewhat relieved by the good news, he stepped into the cool evening breeze, and took a deep breath. It was most unusual for a man like himself to be so stressed, but it was entirely his own fault. What a complete idiot he had been not to listen to Maria and Claire when they had been pointing to the risks he would be taking with this trip!

Once back in the streets he found them still very crowded. When he asked for directions to the Convent, it turned out he was only a few blocks away, so it was not before long the doorbell at the gate rang again. Since their policy was to be very careful with late visitors, Mother Chiara had warned the porter at the gate that there would be another visitor coming by the name of Enrique, and that she should let him in and bring him to her.

It was about a quarter after nine that he found himself making the acquaintance of the head of the Convent *de las Hermanas de la Cruz*. She took measure of him in a way that made him most uncomfortable.

'So you are the young man who brought them here.' The way she phrased her opening line could not have been more devastating. Enrique was close to breaking down, but managed to keep himself together. Responding to her apparent assault was out of the question, so he just bowed his head and said nothing. Seeing the poor young man was at his wit's end, Mother Chiara backed off.

'Well, you probably had more than your fair share of anxiety tonight. Would you like a coffee, or something else?'

'A coffee would be great,' he responded gratefully.

'It will take a minute. In the meantime let me take you to your friends,' she said kindly. She could not help feeling for the young man, seeing how obviously he was suffering from his mistake.

The reunion with Joaquin and Fernando was unusually emotional between them, and Enrique was so relieved he could not help crying. When later that evening the phone call to Bethany confirmed that Patricia and the other two had returned home safely, his most unfortunate plan of joining *Semana Santa* in Seville had ended without lasting consequences. But it did spawn a story that for many years to come Philippe and Sofia would be more than willing to tell at any time.

55.

A Love Affair in the Making

Whether or not it was because of their precarious adventure in Seville that Enrique Valdez and Patricia Nuñez de Castro had been drawn closer together no one could tell. But soon after that fateful evening it became apparent that the two of them had more than a working relationship.

In a place like Bethany such relationships might not seem surprising. A spiritual community was likely to foster informal ties between staff members that in official healthcare institutions would be criticized as 'unprofessional'. But also in this regard the House of Bethany was not a professional service agency, at least not in the formal sense of the word. It explicitly *aimed* at attracting people willing to share their lives with its members in 'family-like' homes, the defining characteristic of which was precisely the blessing of personal affections. When Ramón Jimenez had invited Eduardo Villanova and Philippe Bousquet into his house, it was an attempt to respond to their need of being loved. So when it came to relationships there was absolutely nothing about the House of Bethany that was not personal or affectionate.

Thus far, however, the bonds of personal affection between the 'heroes' of our story had never transcended their primary commitment to Bethany and its members as a spiritual community. There had been moments where the boundaries were shady, of course, and each of them had known their moments of infatuation. Claire's early days in Bethany was one example, Antonio's reconciliation with Maria after their clash about Lucie Miles being another. Nonetheless they had managed thus far to maintain a crucial distinction. Spiritual communion was one thing; physical attraction was something else.

The thing about the budding relationship between Enrique Valdez and Patricia Nuñez de Castro was that for the first time in Bethany's history this distinction was about to collapse. Those who cared to pay attention could have seen what was coming, but oddly enough not many of them did, with the notable exception of Antonio and Sophia, of course, who were both astute observers of amorous affections. Naturally, therefore, the first gossiping took place between the two of them.

It had been the week before *Semana Santa* when Antonio was teasing Sofia about male attraction. She was not at all indifferent to members of the opposite sex, and when Enrique was around in the workshop as one of Lucie Miles' assistants, Sofia would be constantly looking for a moment to make her presence known to him. While he would never mean to hurt Sofia, Antonio's appetite for commenting on what he saw turned out to be insatiable.

'I never knew you liked men who read a lot of books, dear,' an opening line that came out of the blue.

'Oh, Antonio, what are you saying?' Sofia replied.

'I am simply saying that Lucie's new assistant Enrique is attracting a lot of your attention.' Sofia blushed the moment he mentioned the assistant's name.

'Do you like him?' he asked her.

'He doesn't see me, he only sees Patricia.'

Her response made him regret that he had not stopped himself from teasing her. He too had observed what Sofia also had noticed; the young man was clearly attracted to the new assistant from Zaragoza. Seeing herself as the handicapped daughter of a beauty queen, Sofia anticipated she was no match for a woman who looked like a descendant of old Castilian nobility.

Patricia Nuñez had aristocratic looks; a high forehead, emphasizing dark eyes and beautifully styled black hair. It was easy to imagine her in the long black robes with high collars and long sleeves that in previous generations had distinguished Spanish *doñas*.

Patricia's demeanour was self-possessed and she was a woman who was not easily made fun of. There could be no doubt that Enrique was irresistibly attracted to the apparent aloofness of her spirit.

Even Antonio was on his guard with her, to his own surprise. One afternoon she walked into his office in the pottery. As he looked up from his papers, and saw it was she, he got up from his chair and mimed taking off his hat and bowing to her.

'Doña Nuñez de Castro, how can I serve you?'

'What makes you think I want to be served?' Although she spoke softly and smiled slightly, Antonio felt chastised.

'I… eh … only joking, I mean, what can I do for you, Patricia?'

Although there was no deliberate attempt on her part, she sometimes made people feel uneasy in their encounters with her. Enrique had this experience quite frequently, but in his case it had a lasting effect. Deep down there was something that made him feel she liked him, even though he could not have found a coherent sentence to explain why. He thought of her as a princess who scared him too much to allow him to examine his feelings. In other words, Enrique Valdez, student in psychology and self-styled stoic, was thrown off his feet.

When Enrique thought of her he often wondered whether there was anyone special in her life. He found her guarded and mysterious and this sense of mystery both attracted him and made him afraid to approach her.

Claire and Maria had also wondered about whether Patricia was close to anyone, but even they had not found a way to broach the subject. This changed when one night in Lucie's apartment Claire was assisting Patricia with getting the girl ready for the night. After she had been helping Lucie in the shower, Claire helped her into her nightgown. Once in bed, Lucie would hold her head up for a kiss, and Claire would sing a lullaby for her. This was their nightly ritual.

In the meantime, Patricia would go through the routine of cleaning up her living room, and when she had done this she would check that the security system was set. Since Lucie was alone in her apartment during the night there was a surveillance camera with an audio connection installed in her bedroom, and another one outside on her front door. The signal was received by a monitor in Maria's room on the first floor. Since the girl was a sound sleeper and never got out of her bed between nine and six, the main purpose of the security system was to make sure there were no outside intruders.

On this particular night, as Claire kissed the girl goodnight, something happened. She overheard Patricia saying to herself, 'I should have had one of these.' Claire did not understand but something in that voice told her this was no casual remark. Patricia turned around, and came over to Lucie's bed to also kiss her good night.

As they left the apartment and stepped outside, Claire asked Patricia, 'What did you mean when you said "I should have had one of these" – what was that about?'

'Oh… nothing,' Patricia said, but Claire noticed her voice waver. She saw her shiver as she said it. She waited for her to say more as they slowly walked up to the back door of the house. Then Patricia started to talk.

'Actually there was something, an incident many years ago, when I first lived on my own in a cottage in the outskirts of Zaragoza. A man came into my house and attacked me.'

'Oh no, Patricia, that's terrible! What happened? Who was he?'

Patricia turned towards her and Claire saw the early moonlight reflected in a tear that she was trying to hold back.

'Let's walk into the orchard, shall we, dear?' She took Patricia's arm, and when she felt no hesitation, she turned towards her and pulled up the zip of her jacket. It was a chilly evening. There was a light breeze bristling through the orchard where the first fruit trees were losing their blossom. It took a while before Patricia spoke again. Claire waited. A door needed to open that had not been opened very often - if it had ever been opened at all.

'I was twenty five, full of life, proud of my first job as a schoolteacher, I was immensely happy with my little house, but a novice when it came to relationships, particularly with men. Then I met this guy in a restaurant where I had dinner, usually on Friday night to celebrate the weekend. He was much older than I was, about forty, a good-looking strong guy, quite impressive. I was flattered by his attention. We started to date, which from my point of view did not mean much more than that we had dinner together.

'I was quite happy with his companionship because that was all that I wanted at the time. After a few weeks he started to become impatient, said he wanted more. What he meant was clear from the way he kissed me. I told him I was not ready for that. Things started to get awkward between us and I told him I didn't want to see him for a while.

Then one night he turned up at my doorstep. It was the first time this had happened, because I had been careful to keep him away from the house. I asked him to come in, but before I knew what was happening he forced himself upon me, saying that he was "not the kind of man I could play games with". Then he raped me.'

The matter-of-fact language she had used to tell her story had made it almost sound like a news report. Claire understood that this was her way of keeping the floodgates of her sorrow under control. Keeping her emotions to herself was probably the only way not to drown.

'Did you go to the police and file charges against him?'

'There was a female police officer at the station who was very understanding, but she warned me my case would be very hard to prove, given that he would claim we were in a relationship. It was years ago; attitudes have changed - people were less understanding back then. So I decided not to.'

'How do you feel now about that decision?'

'I didn't realise what it would do to me if I did not make it public.'

'What did it do?'

'I kept it to myself, and hardly anybody has heard the story.'

'Lonely years of grief all by yourself.' Claire said as she embraced her. Patricia allowed her tears to fall, and when Claire held her and whispered the words of comfort that no one had been able to speak to her before, Patricia broke down and sobbed.

'Dear, oh dear… How lonely you must have been!' When Patricia looked up she saw the compassion in her friend's eyes. A flood of heartbroken tears was her response.

'How sad to be robbed of your life in such a terrible way!' Claire said, and then kept silent for a while, only stroking her back with both her hands. After more sobs and tears, Patricia finally began to feel more calm.

'I could not stay in the house… The little house where I had been so happy! So I went back into the city and rented a room from a friendly landlady… I was safe there. But I stayed away from men altogether. I did not trust them any more … I had never left the landlady's house. Until Lucie's father, Mr Miles, approached me with the question that brought me here.'

'We love having you with us, my dear, and after what you have just told me, even more so. This will remain between you and me, of course, but I very much hope you will find a way to go forward with your life here.'

Had Enrique Valdez known Patricia's story he would have understood why she was not inclined to relax, particularly around a man she was beginning to like.

One of the reasons Patricia liked him was his reliability and trustworthiness. This was appreciated by all the members of Bethany, for whom it was an invaluable trait. It was important for Patricia as well, and for the same reason. Wounded souls cannot bear being in the hands of people who are playing games with them, and of wounded souls Bethany had plenty. In this regard there was not much difference between Alfredo, or Joaquin, or

Patricia. Consequently, each of them liked Enrique because he was 'rock solid' – as Alfredo once put it – and even more because he needed no signs of affection from them to prove it.

Perhaps it was because of opening up to Claire that Patricia allowed her heart to be confused by her feelings for a young man. It was a terrifying thing for her to do, and she had refused to let it happen since the time she had been so cruelly violated. For years she had shied away from any ties of affection. But as Enrique was not intrusive in seeking such ties, he created the space for Patricia's 'coming out', even though he had no clue of what was going on.

As it turned out the same practical circumstance that led to her confession to Claire also brought her together with the student from Madrid. It was again Patricia's turn to prepare Lucie for the night, but this time with Enrique. The girl had been very busy that day, which meant there was a wealth of scraps of paper, torn magazines, and toys scattered all over the place. While Patricia was cleaning, Enrique's job was to get her under the shower, brush her teeth, get her into her nightgown, and then close her evening ritual with a story. He was sitting on Lucie's bed ready to tell her what he named a 'story from no book,' meaning a bedtime story that he made up as he went along. Patricia loved his stories and she particularly loved the ways in which he made Lucie respond to them. As soon as she had finished her task, she came and sat on Lucie's bed to listen in.

'There once was a prince who was in love with a beautiful princess,' Enrique started, 'she was almost as beautiful as you,' he said, and tickled the girl's neck till she was giggling. 'The princess did not know that he loved her, however.' He again bent over and took her nose between his fingers, ' but I am sure you would have noticed, you nosy girl, wouldn't you?' Lucie loved these little gestures that had to be part of each bedtime story.

'The princess was sad because she believed the prince did not notice her. When they met he would always be speaking about important things he had on his mind. He never spoke about her.' Taking the girl's head between his hands Enrique said, 'What important things do you have on your mind?' Lucie looked at him with a sweet smile. 'Oh... I see... you won't tell me.' Then he continued.

'Now the prince did not tell the princess that it was she he had on his mind because he didn't dare tell her. He was afraid he would be rejected. So the two of them both got it all wrong.'

While he was attuned to the girl, Enrique never looked for a moment at Patricia to get a glimpse of her reaction to the story. This was not atypical of his conduct, but this time she felt blood flowing to her face, and she felt her heart beat faster. Her mind was in turmoil while her body was sending all sorts of alarming signals. In previous years she would never have allowed herself to stay in that situation, but now she found herself unable to get up from Lucie's bed.

'And of course you want to know how the princess found out about him loving her, don't you?' Enrique asked the girl. This time he touched both her ears, and said, 'If you listen very carefully, I will tell you.'

'One night the prince was so miserable, he couldn't help himself, but he had to know if she would accept him. So he made himself a promise, "If tonight there is a star above the castle, that will be a sign, then I will know she loves me." The rest of that day the prince spent dreaming about what would happen if she said yes.'

Here Enrique stopped, and after a moment of silence, he put his finger on her lips. 'To be continued,' he said and kissed her forehead. 'Dreaming is what you are going to do now too. Good night, Lucie.'

Patricia then said goodnight to Lucie giving her a kiss on her cheek. When a few moments later they left her apartment together, Enrique and Patricia went up to the house slowly, without speaking a word. But instead of heading for the backdoor, he went to the front. For a moment she hesitated before she followed him, but then she did. When she was beside him she didn't dare to look at his face. He stopped when they stood in front of the house.

'Patricia,' he said, 'There is ... I...' Then he fell silent, but he took her hands, which she allowed him to do. Slowly she looked up at him, her eyes shining like he had never seen before. He smiled and brought his face closer to hers. He spoke very quietly. 'Have you seen there is a star above the house?'

She blushed as she nodded, and said 'Yes.'

Part VII

Ramón's Problem

56.

A Senseless Human Being

When Lucie Miles had a good day, she would be quietly walking around, being her own imperturbable self. Wandering from the pottery to her apartment and from her apartment to the pottery, such days passed in a sequence of seemingly unconnected moments. Paying little visits here and there, hopping like a sparrow, from the table where Sofia was working to her room to lie on her bed, then back to join Pascal, who always found something to share with her, ending up in Antonio's office where she knew he kept a box with little sweets.

But there were other days too, when virtually all the objects in her surroundings were at risk. These 'objects' included people. During the time that Maria had been working with her, she had trained what she called her 'Lucie eyes' and had learned to anticipate where the girl's mood would take her.

Ramón did not have that experience, which most of the time meant he was too late to anticipate what was coming. He had been taking turns in assisting Lucie for some time now, but instead of getting used to her, he grew more and more frustrated about not having a connection with her. Part of the problem was his constant need to make sense of the girl. It was as if she had to be made part of his own world for him to be able to look after her. Maria wasn't at all sure that Lucie Miles would ever be part of that world, but she realized that Ramón would not accept this. Admitting there was no 'sense' in the girl would be to give up on her as a human being, and that he couldn't do.

On one occasion Ramón became extremely angry with her. It happened before Enrique Valdez had arrived. That afternoon Lucie was very agitated, which left Ramón quite desperate about what to do. Not wanting to get cross with her, he did what they mostly did in that kind of situation: she was taken for a walk in the bushes behind Bethany. While they were walking Ramón was talking to her about things he had on his mind. Even when he knew she would not have a clue what he was talking about, it was a way to get in touch with her. At least that was the idea. But Lucie destroyed it cruelly.

They were walking towards the olive groves. There was a bridge across the little river, which Lucie always was attracted to. Beyond that bridge the dirt road went into the bushes.

Before Ramón was aware of it, the girl saw the bridge and ran away from him. Being alarmed she would get in trouble he called her back. When she didn't respond he ran after her to grab her just before she sidestepped the bridge.

'No more games, you stay here with me!' Ramón ordered her. The girl's answer came quite unexpectedly. Without any warning, she turned to him and punched him on the chest with a clenched fist.

'Lucie, stop it! Stop it! You hear me!' When she stopped he grabbed her arm. 'You don't hit people, you understand?' The girl didn't want to be kept on a leash, so she tore herself loose, and ran away again, this time in the direction of the house. Again Ramón had to go after her as she approached the road where a farmer's wagon passed. Furious with her, he finally caught up with her.

'You and I are going back right now!' His grip on her arm apparently was far from gentle, and Lucie started to cry.

So it came to pass that afternoon that Ramón was back at the house with Lucie much quicker than usual. No more than ten minutes after they had left he was dragging the girl back into her apartment. It was not a pleasant sight to see that he was utterly disappointed with himself.

'It didn't work out right?' Maria asked when she saw them coming. 'Perhaps you should take her to the orchard and just let her go.' Ramón was about to explode at her suggestion, but just managed to turn his back to her in time. After what had happened he was as agitated as Lucie had been before they left. But their struggle was not over yet. Lucie had no interest in returning to her apartment, but Ramón was not offering her a choice. He pushed her inside and went straight to the workshop past Antonio who could not help feeling sorry for him.

'I can't do this, I just can't,' Ramón said. The artist thought it wise not to respond immediately.

'There is no sense in this girl,' Ramón said angrily.

'In that case it would be wiser, perhaps, to give up on trying to find one.' Antonio said it without intending to provoke his friend, but even so the effect was not what he wanted it to be.

'Are you joking?' Ramón barked at him. The man was impossible to communicate with in this state of mind, Antonio saw, and decided not to push him, and kept silent. But now that Ramón's fury was unleashed, he couldn't stop.

'You would rather give up on her, wouldn't you?'

'Now what's that supposed to mean?'

'Not minding her senseless behaviour as if she were an animal. Is that what you want?' This response not only laid bare Ramón's innermost thoughts, it also revealed a deep rift between the two men. Antonio was deeply offended.

'Keep your philosophical humbug to yourself, doctor,' he said sharply. 'People have different ways of making sense of the world even when they do not qualify for your conception of what is reasonable. They're nonetheless human beings of flesh and blood.'

'Oh please stop playing this ridiculous game of being the artist,' Ramón retorted, 'I hate it.' He walked out of the workshop and banged the door. Passing by Maria he glared at her as if it had been her fault to put him in this impossible position.

When his friend had left, Antonio felt lonely in a way he hadn't felt in a long time. He knew Ramón was a very different man from himself, but it had never hurt him the way it did now. Ramón was still too agitated to care about how he had left the pottery. Entering the house he went straight up to his room. How in the world could he ever have been so stupid to think he could handle someone like Lucie Miles!

After that day Ramón Jimenez could not get rid of a personal sense of failure. The inability to work positively with the girl made him feel like she didn't *allow* him to make a connection. She hardly ever looked him in the eye. Most of the time she would be looking just past his face, seemingly staring at something somewhere behind him. Or her eyes would be fixed upon an object before her she was about to grab. Even when he took her hand or her arm to get her attention, she would look away from him, deliberately, so it seemed.

Ramón's mistake was to take her behaviour as a sign that the girl did not like him. He was strongly convinced that he failed her, but didn't see that Lucie behaved towards him in the same absent-minded manner that she behaved towards everybody. The only thing he could see was how the others dealt with Lucie without much trouble, like Antonio, who never seemed to be bothered by her behaviour. Even Pascal knew how to handle Lucie without any difficulty.

The fact that Ramón could not manage to do the same troubled him deeply, and it caused him to raise deep questions about himself. His self-contempt made him believe that he failed where others succeeded. But what he failed to see was that no one tried to produce what he wanted from the girl. No one was trying to find her soul, like he did. Not being able to find her soul was a problem for Ramón in a way it never was for anybody else. They accepted the riddle of her absentmindedness as one of the many facts about the girl's behaviour that were just part of who she was.

Brooding over his misery, Ramón recalled how he had contradicted Claire when she said Lucie was a toddler in the body of a teenager. 'She's not a baby,' he had said. 'She has fourteen years of experience weighing on her soul.' At the time he had failed to notice what his words conveyed. He in fact saw her life as a tragedy, even though he would never have admitted it. All the members of their community had come to Bethany with a wounded soul. In this respect Lucie was no different. Perhaps some had suffered more than Lucie had before she arrived. In spite of their past, however, each of them had changed, and grown into a beautiful person. It was a delight to see Alfredo being happy in the pottery, and the same was true of Sofia, not to mention Alonso, or Pascal. For each and every one of them the gift of their lives was shining like a star. It was also clear how they had grown in being a gift for other people.

But looking at the girl, Ramón failed to feel grateful for her presence. It bothered him that he was unable to see her the same way as he saw the others. Deep inside he knew that had it been dependent on him, Lucie would have been sent back to her father a long time ago. This awareness weighed heavily on his consciousness. In his own eyes his failure to respond to the girl's behaviour betrayed him. The awful truth was that he was scared when she was around. Not physically, in the way that she scared Alfredo or Sofia. Ramón's fear was of a different kind. It was the mental confrontation with her chaos and lack of reason that was threatening. He had never learned to embrace the girl in the same way he embraced Alonso, or the boy, or even Fernando. He could not make Lucie Miles fit into his world.

57.

Ramón 'a Hypocrite'?

Living with this guilty conscience for some time, Ramón decided to speak about it with Claire. If anyone in Bethany would be capable of listening to him, it would be her, his first companion. Thinking about whether to talk also to Antonio, he decided not to. He knew Antonio truly loved Lucie Miles, for which Ramón secretly envied him, even though he didn't see how she was lovable. To be able to speak his mind freely, he needed a safer haven than Antonio's sharp wit would afford him.

A few weeks after Easter, he had asked Claire whether he could see her. They met in her office.

'What is it you wanted to see me about?'

'It is about Lucie.'

'What about her?' Since there hadn't been specific problems with Lucie recently, Claire expected that what was coming wouldn't have much to do with Lucie. She had noticed lately how Ramón was never relaxed.

'We have accepted all the people that came to Bethany without reservation,' he started. 'All of them have been doing well. Some have been doing very well.'

'I suspect you mean: all except Lucie.' Usually Ramón loved her for being sensitive to things that were difficult to say, but now he hated her for saying it out loud.

'Yes, except Lucie,' he said, irritated.

'What's your problem, Ramón?'

330

'*My* problem? Do you think I have a problem?' he barked at her, something he had never done before. Then he fell silent. Claire looked at him, feeling what she knew she couldn't say. It wouldn't do him any good anyway; she knew that too.

So she said directly, 'Tell me what's worrying you.'

'Remember when we were producing that flyer to attract new assistants, and we talked about Bethany's mission as celebrating our life together?'

'Yes, I do recall that.'

'I have to face it; I do not know how to celebrate Lucie, I am not even certain that I want to. Bethany's main intention I have deceived. I do not see what there is to celebrate in her case.'

'So that makes you a hypocrite,' Claire said, attempting to read his mind.

'If that's the word you want to use, yes.' Again there was irritation in his voice. His words were spoken by a guilty conscience, and Claire regretted that she had used such harsh a word.

It was much too a harsh word, no doubt, but it did capture the nature of his self-contempt. In fact it described exactly what troubled Ramón. He believed he held double standards with regard to the lives of the people he had committed himself to. He could appreciate only some people's lives as a gift, and Lucie was not one of them. He also knew that this fact could not remain hidden, especially not from Claire, who was much too keen an observer not to have noticed his problem.

'You know me too well not to have noticed anything,' he said.

'You're right, I have noticed it. Most of the time you seem nervous in Lucie's deranged presence, almost perplexed, as if you rather would leave the room.'

'"Deranged presence" is a good description; it's the opposite of what a human life should be.'

'You know how Antonio would respond if he heard you say this.' It was not meant as a reproach, but Ramón bristled anyway.

'Yes, of course,' he said sharply. 'He would prescribe trying to like the girl instead of judging her.' He couldn't help raising his voice,

'But that's exactly the point: I have tried and I have concluded that I don't like her.'

'You don't have to raise your voice,' Claire said gently. 'What you want me to understand is clear enough without it.' She looked him in the eye.

'You're right. I am sorry.' He looked very sad. 'I can't help it, Claire. I am done, I cannot take it any more and it makes me feel miserable.'

'What do you want to do?'

'I want to get away.' Claire's face turned pale when he said this. Her mouth opened, but she didn't know what to say.

'Ramón... We... You cannot just...'

'Of course I cannot. I am trying to think about some time off, to reflect, to get my thoughts together, re-energize. A sabbatical. I am spiritually drained, and it won't be before long that I will be getting on your nerves too.'

'Ah, so it's good for me too then when you leave,' Claire said. She could not avoid the sarcasm in her voice.

'Please don't. When I need sarcasm I will talk to Antonio. It will be good for me to go away for a while; it will be good for Bethany, and that includes you.'

'Would it help if you moved out, and create a little more distance?'

'What do you mean?'

'Perhaps you could find a room in the house of that priest you know in Sanlúcar, what's his name?' The prospect of losing him for a longer period of time was frightening, so if she could meet him halfway in his thinking instead of opposing him, perhaps his ominous plan could be forestalled.

'Father Gilberto?'

'That's the one. You would be on your own, but not so far as to be disconnected from us here. I see what you're trying to tell me, Ramón, I really do. I also know you wouldn't come to see me about this unless you were serious. But Bethany needs you. We need you.'

Listening to him Claire looked at his worn out face and saw how tired he was. They all had been working hard, very hard, but beyond Bethany's daily affairs Ramón had been constantly on the road, giving talks and retreats, trying to raise funds and find resources. For people like Antonio and herself, working with their hands was all they needed to be content, he in his pottery, she in her garden. But Ramón was different. He was a man of letters who needed time to read and write. Without it, he might lose his inspiration. She wouldn't let that happen, but the prospect of having him leave for a year, or even half a year, she was unwilling to face.

So Claire was prepared to give in because she hoped to stop a plan that she thought was much worse. She saw the need to create space for him to breathe and lighten up so that he would be able to feel grateful again for what had been achieved, even with Lucie. But her concern was not only with Ramón's feelings. Like Antonio, she was herself much too committed to their mission to let Bethany fall apart. Claire hated the idea that Ramón might lose his inspiration, not only for his own sake, but also for her own, as well as for the sake of Bethany's community.

Some days later she noticed he seemed to have recovered a bit. And she was right. The idea of moving out for a while produced an immediate response in his soul. Just the idea of finding some time to reflect and re-energize had already made him feel better.

Father Gilberto's house was situated in the middle of the village of Sanlúcar la Major. It was spacious enough for a celibate priest and a single man, both of whom were not very demanding when it came to their private quarters. It had a large family kitchen that was mainly dominated by Father Gilberto's maid Elvira, an Andalusian woman in her mid-fifties. She had been with him for a long time, but being the mother of a large family of nine with many grandchildren she was absolutely convinced that single male households were intolerable. When he announced that there would be a guest for the months to come she made no comments, but her aloof countenance left no ground to doubt her opinion.

'He is a very nice man, Ramón Jimenez.' Father Gilberto said. 'Actually he is from a very good family in Madrid.'

'If he were from a very good family, he would not be on his own!' Elvira said while she was cleaning up his breakfast table.

'Could you prepare the green room on the first floor for him, and he can also have the bathroom and the study there for himself.'

'And where will you stay, if I may ask?' The relevance of her question was underlined by the door of the cupboard being slammed shut. Usually Father Gilberto took her rugged manners lightly, and so he did now.

'I will stay downstairs. You can make the bed up in my study. That is big enough for me. Thank you Elvira.'

Ramón was more than pleased with the space with which he was provided. A single bed, a table to write, a rocking chair was all he needed. Besides, the small study held a desk, behind which he looked out over the square in the centre of the village. A nice old bookcase gave him ample space to store the books and papers he had brought in his trunk. Across from the bookcase there was a comfortable couch, inviting him to take a nap whenever he needed one.

As soon as he was settled in, he went to buy himself a few notebooks and pencils for writing down his thoughts. He found a little stationery store nearby that sold newspaper and magazines, and had a small section with the kind of things he was looking for. A smile came to his face when he found himself comparing the colour and size of their notebooks, as if these were important matters not to be trifled with. After he found what he wanted he walked back with his treasures, feeling suddenly in the best of spirits. He felt like a boy entering a new school year.

The first good effect of being on his own for Ramón was that he was able to follow a daily schedule in which each day started with the same ritual: a morning prayer and some kind of spiritual reading. It was a habit that marked the conscious beginning of the day, which he needed just like other people need to see a newspaper with their breakfast. He was always interested in the news, but it could wait. Instead he needed to take stock of what was happening in his soul. This he did in his bedroom. After taking his breakfast in the kitchen together with Father Gilberto, he would go upstairs to the study to continue with reading whatever book was on his desk. This would be followed by a light lunch, which he frequently took on his own. A *siesta* on the couch was the overture for the rest of the afternoon, which would be used for writing notes about what he had read.

As a result of this scheme his days were passing in a disciplined way, which helped to find the time to concentrate on what he needed to think about. His plan was to write a book about the nature of community, a topic for which his experience with Lucie Miles was in no small part responsible. But though he held the degree of *Philosophical Doctor*, Ramón Jimenez was not an academic scholar. He had to talk to others to discover his own thoughts, rather than getting them from the books he read. He knew this about himself, and he had been thinking about several people with whom he wanted to speak. Among them the most important was the Reverend Mother Chiara, head of the Convent *de las Hermanas de la Cruz* in Seville. He knew she would be willing to listen to what he had to tell her about his experience with Lucie. Since she had spent most of her life in the Convent's community, he hoped she would understand what he was talking about.

When he called the Convent, Mother Chiara was as pleased as ever to hear his voice. Picking up on their last meeting she immediately took off with the sense of humour that he liked so well.

'Dr Jimenez,' she opened, quasi formally, 'what a joy that you are calling me. What is it that you want from me this time? More nuns?' Ramón could almost see the twinkle in her eyes when she said it.

'No, no, Reverend Mother; no deals this time!'

'You're not going to tell me that this phone call is for free, are you?'

'I have a request to make, if that's what you mean.'

'You know very well what I mean.'

Ramón could not help laughing. 'I plead guilty, Reverend Mother.'

'Well, what's up? What do you need?'

'An evening, a friendly ear, a sharp mind, an experienced heart, and perhaps a glass of good wine.'

'Do you now? And which of these items did you have in mind when you decided to call me? The wine perhaps?'

'Frankly, I was thinking of getting all of these things from you at one and the same time.'

'Really? That's not a bit greedy?' She laughed as she said it, but sensing there was more behind this frivolous small talk, she changed her tone of voice.

'Tell me what's on your mind, Ramón.'

'I need your advice. There is an experience in Bethany that I need to get my head around, and I can think of no person more capable of listening to me than you.'

She was silent for a moment or two, and then responded. 'You're request ascribes more virtue to my character than I know I possess, but even so you are most welcome. I am looking forward to seeing you again, and to listen to whatever is weighing upon your soul.'

58.

'It's Entirely about Providence!'

A few weeks later Ramón went to Seville to visit Mother Chiara in the Convent. It was close to the *Iglesia de San Pedro*. Walking through the bustling inner city his mind went back to how at crucial times she had provided important support for Bethany, and how they had honoured her support by accepting Joaquin Morales. All this happened at a time when a further expansion of Bethany's community was the last item on their wish list. It was through this cooperation that Ramón had come to admire her, and valued her as a friend, both of Bethany as well as personally.

When he arrived at the Convent he was taken to her private rooms, where she received him warmly.

'Be welcome in my home, Ramón. It is good to see you.'

'Thank you, Reverend Mother, I... eh... I brought you a gift. It is a little book I think you might like.' When she unwrapped it, she found a collection of meditations by Teresa of Avila in her hand.

'Oh, Ramón... Oh my.... how did you know this? I love her writings, and I love the way her mind works, but I haven't seen this volume before. How thoughtful of you! Thank you so much!'

She gave him a hug, just like the last time they met, and again Ramón was blushing like a boy. Offering him a chair she called in a novice to order refreshments. As Ramón had not been specific about what he wanted to tell her, she was very anxious to get started and their conversation was well underway before their coffee arrived.

Ramón told her the story of how Lucie Miles had come to Bethany, the dispute they had about her, the apartment, the gratitude of her father, the miracle of a battered boy and a youngster with Down's syndrome who both knew exactly how to handle her, his clash with Antonio a few months ago, and, finally, his own personal sense of failure.

'That must be a painful experience for a man like you,' Mother Chiara said. Then she was silent for a moment as if pondering how to go about raising the right questions.

'Before I say anything else, first tell me this: when you were first inviting these two men into your house, many years ago, what were you thinking?'

Not seeing how her question was related to what he had just told her, Ramón was a bit confused, but he trusted her instincts and readily told her what she wanted to know.

'The decisive moment was when I realized that I saw a question in their eyes, and took it as addressed to me. I believed myself to have only two options…'

'What was the question?'

'The question, as I felt it, was "Do you want to be my friend?" I felt it as a personal call. I took their question to mean that it could only be answered by "Yes" or "No".'

'So you said "Yes".'

'Hmmm.'

'And what was true about these two men has been true, I suspect, of all the others that followed. Correct?'

'I guess so.' Ramón began to see where she was heading. He recalled discussing with his friends whether or not to accept Lucie. Also on that occasion the question that had pressed itself upon him was a choice between the same two options. For him it was a question about truthfulness.

'You see what I mean, don't you? Posing the question as a choice between "Yes" and "No" you in fact have assumed the issue is one of unconditional acceptance. And now you have discovered that there is no such thing, at least not for you. Not with regard to this girl at any rate. Right?'

With admiration Ramón saw how her mind had nailed what he felt, and why he found himself torn apart. He nodded, and said, 'I told Claire I was finding myself close to what Maria said when she started working with Lucie.'

'Help me, I don't recall. What did Maria say?'

'That she liked Lucie, but did not like her behaviour.'

'Oh, yes, my Maria,' Mother Chiara was smiling. There was sincere affection in her voice when she continued, 'Always as straight as an arrow! But tell me, how did you find yourself close to what she was saying?'

'Because I hated the girl's chaos, the complete reign of impulse governing her life. So when I was trying to be truthful about my feelings about her, I could not find anything in her behaviour that I actually appreciated.'

'Which means you're a romantic.'

Having no clue what she was talking about, Ramón raised his brows. 'A romantic? What's that got to do with anything?'

'Yes, a romantic. Your basic assumption seems to be that the essence of Bethany's community is reflected in the way you reach out to the soul of each of its members, each day, and every moment. That is romanticism. Your response must be unequivocally the same, always and to everyone, as if you were a plant that brings forth all its different parts – roots, stem, leaves, flowers, and fruits, even its colours, all from the same single seed. That seed represents your soul; it expresses itself in all your actions, at least that is how you seem to think it should be.'

'And that's wrong?' In all honesty Ramón didn't see where she was driving at.

'Well, it seems to do neither you nor the girl much good, does it? You blame yourself for not being able to express what Bethany is about in all your actions, in particular towards her. It is not wrong, but it surely is a mistake. You are not a plant, if you don't mind me saying so. A human being, let alone a community of human beings, is not like that at all. It consists of different, separate souls, each of them carrying their own stories, their own secrets, sorrows, and scars. They evoke different responses in one another, including responses that will cause trouble. To know this is one thing; to accept it willingly is quite another. That takes an effort, a painful effort, I can tell you from personal experience. In your case, given your position in Bethany, it means to accept that the community is not you, nor is it dependent on you. Let me ask you: where do you think this convent would be if it depended solely, or even primarily, on me?'

Ramón began to see where she was going. She was telling him that his problem had not so much to do with Lucie as with how he saw himself in their community. He had been their leader; and now, he of all people could not do what he expected others to do. This was his disappointment. Mother Chiara was showing him that he urgently needed to look in a mirror to find the real question. She put it right under his nose when she said:

'Did it never occur to you that whether or not Lucie is welcomed and appreciated in Bethany might not depend on you?'

'Surely that occurred to me, I have often said that Bethany is God's work, not ours. He is carrying our community in his hands.'

'Oh, Ramón, give me a break! That's just pious talk. Right now, it doesn't help a straw, even though it's true. It is true in a completely different way, though. Actually it has little to do with what I am telling you now.'

Ramón was frustrated. 'I am afraid I've lost you.'

'What does it tell you that a guy like Alonso knows how to deal with a girl like Lucie so that she is at ease at your dinner table? What does it tell you that Pascal – a kid of eight years old, mind you – knows how to assist her in the pottery so that her presence is not merely destructive?'

'I....'

'Excuse me for interrupting, but I am going to explain what it tells you.' Mother Chiara's mind was working at full speed, leaving poor Ramón hardly enough time to breathe. But there was no stopping her now.

'These people are capable of doing things that you have proven to be incapable of, and that is unacceptable to you. And the reason is that you think you need to reflect what Bethany is about in every vein and in every nerve of your body.'

'And that's wrong?' Ramón responded, not noticing he was asking the same question again.

'*No*. It's not wrong, my friend, at least not in a moral sense, but it surely is a big mistake. It puts you in the centre of the universe, the typically romantic posture I might add, which certainly is not where you belong. God has blessed you with friends who can do what you cannot do! Don't you see what that means? He wants Bethany to succeed! The good Lord has put his money on your work!' Seeing him grappling to follow her, she added playfully, 'I can tell you he wouldn't have done so, were Bethany's success only dependent upon you.'

She got up from her chair, and patted him on the shoulder. 'God knows you better than you know yourself, son, that's why he is sending you these people.' Turning away from him to a cabinet in the corner of her parlour, she said, 'How about that glass of wine now?'

Flabbergasted at her quick mind, Ramón took a deep breath. He smiled when he looked at her, and said, 'You surely do know how to administer your blessings!'

'Yeah, I know,' she said. 'First you are taught a lesson that you don't want to hear, and then you get rewarded for it with a glass of wine.'

Ramón nodded. 'I reckon what you just said reflects your own experience in this place.'

'You bet it does!'

'Can you tell me about it?'

When she responded, Mother Chiara apparently did not want to go into detail. Perhaps there were painful memories that she did not want to put into words, at least not here and now.

'Let me put it this way. This place would have ceased to be what it is long time ago, if its superiors did not catch on to what leadership of a spiritual community means.'

'What does it mean?'

'It means knowing what God is doing in sending all these people on your path. It means seeing they're there to make sure you get where you need to go, when there is no chance in heaven you could get their on your own.'

'You do agree it's about providence, then?'

'Oh boy, it's entirely about providence!' Mother Chiara was again fired up by his question, as he seemed to think she rejected his hinting at this thought before as 'pious' talk.

'No doubt about it! The only thing I was criticizing was the way you were setting up the alternatives, as if it is either God's doing or yours.'

'What are the true alternatives then?'

'Ultimately, dear friend, the question is a fairly simple one. It is not about who is the doer, God or human being. It is not whether you have created Bethany, or whether you have received it. No, the real question is a very different one.'

Ramón was listening attentively. Mother Chiara had not let him come closer to her own episodes of painful experience, but the intense way she looked at him revealed that she would allow him to enter into the intimacy of her own faith.

'You have to ask yourself how you think God is present in the people that have crossed your path.'

59.

The Heart of the Matter

Ramón Jimenez' time of spiritual reflection went well. Apart from all his reading and writing, he was evaluating the experience of more than five years. Finally he was able to step back and think about Bethany and their community without being right in the middle of it. He brought back his memories and let them pass his mind's eye, which he usually did when he was walking in the countryside, or when he was on the road for one of his talks to raise money for Bethany again.

On one of these trips he was travelling to Madrid and he decided to drop by his sister's house to visit her for her birthday. During their childhood growing up in a family of some fame and importance, Ramón and Imelda had been quite close as siblings. They enjoyed the silly little games that children play, and that get some of their attraction from being kept a secret from their parents. Somehow things that were kept secret seemed to be more important, even when there was no obvious reason for being secretive about them. Perhaps it had been because of the alleged bond of conspiracy they created, or because of the power of control they suggested, but like most children the siblings of Jimenez Cardoso loved secrets.

The awkward thing for Ramón and Imelda was that more often than not there were very good reasons indeed to be secretive about their games. Their parents were both heirs of important families, families of diplomats, military officers, and scientists. Not only were they very proud of their ancestry, they also wanted their children to be thoroughly aware of it. Educating them came with strict rules of propriety that were rigorously kept. Such rules made many of the children's innocent games appear as major crimes. Climbing trees, playing hide and seek in the park, fishing in the pond, they all were regarded as serious offenses against the rules of proper behaviour for descendants of the house of Jimenez Cardoso. Naturally these sorts of offenses were precisely the things that the two siblings loved most.

Ramón in particular had a rough time with this regime. Even though Imelda was three years his senior, whenever their father was criticizing their behaviour it was Ramón who would take most of the heat.

'If you want to be a man who is taken seriously in the world, stop behaving like a rascal,' his father would say, presuming it was the boy's greatest desire to be such a man.

The bond that Ramón had with his sister was torn apart when their parents decided his education should be continued at a boarding school, to which he was sent at the age of twelve. The boy was much too sensitive a character to thrive in a colony of other rascals that was governed by the survival of the fittest. Ramón simply hated it, and he blamed his parents, particularly his father, for sending him there.

It was years before he was reunited with Imelda, when she was able to receive him in her own house, after she married. During the time in between they had drifted apart from each other. Ramón had become interested in the world of the human soul, definitely not a subject that contributed to his status in their family. In later years only his sister knew of his life in Bethany, and even though she wondered where it would take him, she had supported her brother as much as she could.

Pondering these memories, he got off the subway in Tetuán, an upmarket borough in Madrid not far from the big football stadium, where his sister's apartment was. As he arrived unexpectedly at her doorstep early in the morning of her birthday, Imelda was overjoyed to see him. 'Ramón! Oh my... what a birthday present! You're here!'

She hugged and kissed him in a way that made him laugh.

'Wow, I'm only your brother!'

'You're my only brother, you mean!' she said. 'Come in, come in. What a happy surprise! You didn't come all the way from Sanlúcar la Mayor, did you?'

'No sis, I am afraid not. I will be attending a conference here in town before I am off to France the day after tomorrow.'

'Oh ... I see. Well, it's good to have you at this early hour of the day, since there is nobody else here, so we can at least have a chat without interruption. You must tell me everything about Bethany, and about yourself of course.'

They sat down for their morning coffee, and had lots of things to tell each other, before they finally came to talk about what he had gained by moving out from Bethany.

'I almost forgot to bring you this present from Pascal, the youngest potter in our workshop!' He proudly handed over a vase he had in his bag for her. It was very well crafted, and its deep blue colour was impressive. 'Actually, the decoration was done by Alfredo, he is their master drawer,' he added, pointing to small ornaments in white below the rim.

'It's beautiful, Ramón! Tell Pascal and Alfredo ... No, since you're away, I will send them a note myself to thank them!'

'You do that, they will be very pleased, and so will Antonio.'

'Now you must tell me everything about your sabbatical.'

Unsurprisingly, when Ramón started to tell about his move to Sanlúcar he was drawn to speak about what had driven him to this step. Perhaps it was because he was talking to this sister that he was closer to his feelings than usual. Soon he found himself confessing how hard the last year had been on him, the cause of which had been his troubles with Lucie Miles.

'I simply couldn't handle her, Imelda. I couldn't handle being with a girl whose behaviour does not serve any purpose beyond merely fulfilling her basic needs. I hate to say this, but if you would push me to explain the difference between the girl and a pet animal, I would find it hard to do so. In some respects Lucie's behaviour is even worse, because most animals are not nearly as chaotic as she can be.'

It was remarkable how strongly Ramón was drawn back to the emotional side of his experience with the girl, to see his anger, his aversion, and disappointment, all of which he had been trying to keep at bay when in Bethany. But now that he was talking to his sister, everything he had felt came back with even more force than it had before.

'How is she chaotic?' Imelda asked.

'There is nothing she actually does that has any form to it, it's all impulse. She is a nuisance for the pottery crew if you ask me. She flutters around in a room, touching this and that, throwing things on the floor, a minute here, a minute there. They actually have to protect their work from being smashed by Lucie. She's never more than two minutes on a chair, except for coffee, food, or a visit to the toilet. Her father once told me they tried to put her on a day care program, but whatever the planned activities for a whole day might entail, Lucie was through with them within half an hour.'

'What does she do in the pottery then?'

'Not much, as far as I can tell, except bothering other people.'

'You sound as if you are angry with her.'

'Do I? Hmmm… I am not angry with the girl, not really. She can't help being who she is… I am angry with myself.'

'Why should you be angry with yourself, Ramón?'

'Because… Oh, I don't know! It's so childish… I am so frustrated with that girl, as if she is doing me wrong, which is nonsense; I want her to understand me, which is even greater nonsense, of course… I don't know!'

Looking at her brother's distress, Imelda could not help but let a melancholy smile alter her face for a moment. For a brief moment she saw him standing there, the small boy in his wet trousers before his father's desk after he had been dipping in the pond, trying to save a wounded pigeon in the park in front of their house.

'I am not sure Ramón, but it seems that you feel hurt when at the same time you do not allow yourself to feel that way.'

'What are you saying?'

Now that he had opened his heart, Ramón was feeling quite unhappy. Imelda looked at him compassionately. It was sad to see him in this mood, knowing how much Bethany meant to him.

'Ramón, dear… Does it not ring a bell?' she asked him. She put the question with as much delicacy as she could.

'What bell?'

'I remember what you used to say when dad was getting at you about things you shouldn't have done. "Why does he have to be this way?" you said. "I've done nothing wrong!" You were hurt and disappointed by his rejection, which you were not allowed to feel because daddy was always right. I might be wrong, but Lucie's behaviour seems to be triggering that same response in you.'

Ramón did not like where this conversation was going, but he said nothing. He knew his sister would never say anything to deliberately hurt him. Even so, he didn't like it.

'I am not a psychologist, but it seems to me that she is touching a sore spot in your soul, dear brother, a spot that you have tried to overcome by going your own way.'

'What are you telling me?' The question was loaded with impatience. 'That my response to the girl means I am reliving unhappy feelings from my childhood?'

'I think I am telling you that.'

Seeing his face growing darker, she got up from her chair and said 'Let me get you some more coffee before you get mad at me!' Passing by his chair on her way to the kitchen, she lightly kissed his forehead with a smile.

While his sister was in the kitchen Ramón was thinking about what she had just said. He did not immediately see the connections, but he felt the same as he had during his conversation with Mother Chiara when he had asked her advice. Both women were telling him something about himself he had not realized, and that he wasn't even sure he wanted to hear. But he also noticed that his sister had managed to put him in touch with his feelings, which Mother Chiara had not managed to do. Perhaps it was because the Reverend Mother had kept her own painful experience to herself. Or perhaps it was because he was too much enchanted by her wit. She had helped him more than he could say, but she had not done for him what his sister was doing for him now.

When she returned from the kitchen Imelda picked up where she had left off. 'The thought that's coming back to me is that you feel hurt but you are not allowed to feel that way. Maybe you should put a name to that feeling. Could it be that Lucie's behaviour has made you feel vulnerable in a way that you have tried to leave behind?'

Looking out of the window he listened to what she said, and remained silent for a while. 'How old he looks,' Imelda thought to herself, seeing the wrinkles on his face. When he finally looked at her, he smiled sadly, and nodded.

'I have to think about this, sis,' he said. Then briskly changing his demeanour, brightening up as when a cloud covering the sun is drifting away, 'But not now, since I am here to celebrate your birthday!' They chatted away almost half of the morning, and Ramón only got up from his chair to leave when the first of Imelda's friends dropped by to visit her for her birthday.

'My sister is much better at gossiping than I am, so I won't be a bore and I'll leave her to you now,' he said to the lady.

'That is a pity because Imelda has told me many things about her serious brother,' the friend said with a smile.

'My serious brother?' Imelda said. 'Who would that be?'

Ramón laughed. He hugged his sister, and said goodbye to her friend. It was a lovely spring day, and he decided to take a walk. It would take him at least an hour and a half to walk to his hotel in the city centre, but it would give him plenty of time to reflect upon what Imelda had said. 'Could it be that Lucie's behaviour has made you feel vulnerable?' his sister had asked him. But was it Lucie's behaviour? Or was it what he expected from her?

It was true that he had not really given up on recreating her life for her. In fact he had behaved towards the girl as if her life had to be *made* worthy of his celebration. Even though he had rejected the idea in his mind, in his conduct towards the girl he had been trying to save her, and it clearly had not worked. But what did all that have to do with being vulnerable?

After his visit to Imelda and the conference on the next day, Ramón left Madrid in order to go to Toulouse. Earlier in the year he had been talking with a few people about the possibility of a House of Bethany in France. During their deliberations Ramón had ventured to speak about what he was struggling with, but it had not worked out the way he had hoped it would.

On the high-speed train from France back to Seville he found time to go once again over his thoughts. Enjoying the sight of the mountains in the border region, the conversation with Mother Chiara came back again. In the distance he could see the snowy peaks of the high Pyrenees, which meant the train would soon be leaving France. Looking out of the window, he remembered the advice the Reverend Mother had given him. He needed to change the question, she had said. When he had been in that mental hospital, many years ago, he had seen the despair in the eyes of Philippe Bousquet and Eduardo Villanova. He had read a question in those eyes that was directly addressed to him, and his answer had been 'Yes'. He had taken the question of Lucie's father at that meeting in Salamanca in the same way. He felt it too had been a question that could only have one answer. In this way he had put himself in the centre of his moral universe, or so Mother Chiara had pointed out. She had also said that the real question was not the one he had been asking.

While he was pondering their conversation again the train entered a tunnel, and the lights in his cabin were switched on. Ramón saw the reflection of his own face in the window. 'Look at what has happened to you.' he said to the face. His persistence in trying to save Lucie from her chaotic life had blinded him, and when he had to admit failure he had been hurt, just like he had been hurt when he failed to earn his father's praise for trying to save a lame pigeon from drowning in the pond! Then and now, he felt he had not deserved to be hurt. But who had been hurting him like his father had? Lucie? Imelda had seen what was at the heart of the matter. The penny dropped.

'I don't feel Lucie's presence as a gift!' he had said to Claire when he was utterly disappointed with himself. Now he knew that it had more to do with his own pain than with the girl's 'senselessness'. He smiled when he realized that in the dark a light had lit up his face when the train was going through a tunnel.

On that trip in the high-speed train back to Seville, Ramón Jiménez Cardoso made a discovery that would change him for the rest of his life. Figuring out how to live it would be his second calling.

His crisis had been painful but it was time well spent because of what it taught him. 'Lucie Miles as a teacher', he said to himself. 'How is that for a change?'

60.

A Time Well Spent

While Ramón was quite happy with how his 'time off' from Bethany was evolving, his companions were less content with his absence – especially, to begin with, Philippe Bousquet. For all his apparent boldness Philippe was in fact a fearful man. The sudden death of Eduardo Villanova, his buddy from the start of their life together, had clearly affected him. But its effect was not as strong as the absence of his friend Ramón. For the first time in years he felt like he was on his own again, and while much of his boldness was gone, the fear remained. His main target was, of course, Claire.

'When is Ramón coming back?'

'I don't know.'

'You can call him and ask.'

'Ramón wants to have some time for himself. He is very tired after working so hard all these years. I don't think we should push him to come back.'

'I don't want to push him; I just want to know when he will be back. That's all.'

'As I told you, I don't know. There is no date set for his return.'

'Will he be back before my birthday?'

'I am sure Ramón won't miss your birthday party. It's September 17th, right?'

'Yes, that's it. But will he stay home afterwards?'

Conversations like this could go on and on, and Claire had to muster all her patience not to lose her temper. Had she spoken her

351

mind, she would have yelled at him: 'Don't you think I miss him? Stop asking me your stupid questions! I am tired! Tired of being alone!'

Neither Philippe nor Claire was in fact alone, of course, nor was their daily life very different from what it had been when Ramón was present. But they missed him, and his resolution to get some time off from Bethany had left both of them unhappy, and more or less for the same reason. That he had wanted to get away from Bethany was okay, but why did he want to get away from them?

No doubt the other members of Bethany's community missed Ramón's presence too, but it did not leave them unsettled as it did with both Philippe and Claire. Given the special bond Ramón had with Alonso, for example, one might expect that he would be affected too, though there was actually no sign of it. Alonso seemed as happy as he usually was, throwing around hugs and smiles at whoever was ready to receive them.

What about Lucie Miles? Whether she missed Ramón's presence, or anybody else's for that matter, was hard to tell. To mention one obvious person, did she miss her father? There was in fact no way of knowing such things about her, which was one of the more difficult things in assisting her. Lucie's mind was hard to read.

One night, Antonio and Maria found themselves in a conversation about Ramón's apparent difficulties with Lucie. In the months before he had come to the conclusion that he needed a sabbatical, Maria had closely observed how the problem of reading Lucie's mind had grown to become a source of frustration for him.

'I must say I have a hard time following him in this,' Antonio said. 'I don't know what it is, but I really don't see why he should want to save Lucie from her chaotic life.'

'I know,' she retorted, 'Let Lucie be Lucie.'

'Yeah, you know what I mean.'

Antonio's rule for assisting Lucie was by no means self-evident to everybody, as not only Ramón's but also Maria's own example had shown. In the months since Ramón had moved out it was noticed that both Enrique and Patricia were soon familiar with it. Both were clear about not trying to take over her life and change it.

It was therefore quite a shock when they got word that the two of them would be leaving Bethany at the end of the summer. With regard to Patricia this was part of the arrangement with Lucie's father. Though not unexpected, it came much too early nonetheless. While Enrique could have stayed throughout the fall season, he didn't want to be separated from Patricia. And of course everyone in Bethany was glad about the young couple's happiness even though this meant saying farewell to them. Enrique Valdez and Patricia Nuñez de Castro had been engaged to spend the rest of their lives together since that night in April when they had found their star. They had been considering getting married while still living in Benacazón, but, with an eye on their respective families, decided not to do so. Their wedding would be celebrated in October in Patricia's hometown of Zaragoza.

The prospect of losing Patricia saddened Claire more than she would admit. The two of them had been especially close since Claire had found out about Patricia's story. Having her painful secret out had clearly changed the woman, even when no one except Claire, and perhaps Enrique, knew why. The others attributed the change to her happy engagement with Enrique, but that was more of a consequence than being the cause of her lighter heart.

Similarly, Maria and Antonio were very fond of Enrique, not in the least because of his skills in assisting Lucie. Along with Patricia they too had enjoyed his bedtime stories 'from no book', and his reputation as a storyteller had spread far beyond Lucie's apartment. He too would be truly missed.

In the meantime Ramón Jiménez saw the day approaching to leave his rooms in Father Gilberto's house in Sanlúcar and return to Bethany. Thus far he had kept his visits to the place to a minimum. Now that he had gained a deeper understanding of why he needed to go for a while, he felt he missed his friends. Thinking of Alonso's happy smiles, Pascal's desire to learn, or Sofia's nervous giggle, he realized that each and every one had their own special treasures, bringing lightness into his heart. Even Lucie's chaos appeared in a different light. In short, he felt he missed them all, as no doubt they all missed him too.

'How long has it been since you came here? Three or four months?' Father Gilberto asked Ramón when he told him he was thinking about moving back to the House of Bethany.

'It is about four months now. I am very grateful for your hospitality, Father, and for Elvira's cooking of course.'

Father Gilberto laughed. '*De nada*, Ramón, *de nada*. I will tell her. You know what she thinks about single males. We will see whether your compliments have softened her opinion. Do you plan to leave anytime soon?'

'No, not yet. I would like to take the manuscript I have been working on one step further.'

'So I guess your time here in Sanlúcar brought you what you wished for when you left Bethany?'

'Yes it did, very much so.'

'That's good to hear. What was the book you wanted to write about again?'

'It is about the nature of Bethany's community, but I only found what I wanted to say once I began to understand the source of my problem with the girl Lucie. That enabled me to rethink what we have been trying to do. I would like to end my time off when a large enough portion of the manuscript is done, so that I am sure it will be finished in due course.'

Looking back down the years, it struck Ramón that he had often talked about Bethany, telling his audiences that he had no blueprint of what it should be. He recalled how he had met Claire on a street in Seville, and how he had found Antonio in a ceramics studio in Triana. How Alonso came because Alfredo's mother had been advocating for the disabled son of her nephew. How meeting Lucie's father after a lecture he gave in Salamanca led to her arrival in Bethany. None of these encounters was premeditated or foreseen. Bethany had risen out of life itself.

Curiously enough he had known all this, but, as he now saw, apparently without having it entrenched in his soul. His response to Lucie had revealed that Bethany had been carried on his own shoulders, like Atlas carrying the weight of the world.

Something else occurred to him too. Their life together was only possible inasmuch as it was a life without fear – the fear of being abused, the fear of being rejected, the fear of failure, or the fear of not living up to other people's expectations. He had seen this every day, in the life of Alfredo no less than in that of Sofia, in the life of Fernando, and of the boys when they came to Bethany, Pascal and Joaquin. But he had failed to see that the same was true about his own life as well. The conversation with his sister Imelda had made him aware of this. It had taken Lucie's 'deranged presence' to make him see that he had been trying so hard because of the need to live up to what he believed was expected from him.

Reflecting on these thoughts Ramón Jiménez came to understand that the cornerstone that held Bethany's community together was its peacefulness. Its peace was the source from which all other things came, the source of what made their life together possible. Even when it was true that Lucie's life was governed by chaos, it had only turned to violence when he had been trying to change the girl into something she was not.

It was this discovery that made him conscious of his longing to return to Benacazón. His time away had enabled him to discover the truth about his encounter with Lucie Miles. Once the fear of failure could be left behind, life would flourish. It was in all sorts of ways a happy discovery.

Ramón frequently told his audiences how in facing problems in Bethany they often didn't know where to look for a solution. Most of the time, he said, they had been blessed with answers coming from unexpected quarters. All the people who had come to this place, an insignificant house, in an insignificant village, in rural Andalusia, had ventured to live by placing themselves into one another's hands. It was an amazing story, given the odds that they might have failed, and that their community would have come to nothing.

Listening to these confessions, people understood that Ramón Jiménez Cardoso was in fact a deeply religious person. His God was not a superior power whose eternal plan would conquer the world's chaos in the end. He did not doubt that there was a plan, but it worked in a different way. It had been Mother Chiara who made him see that any notion of a truly human life that had no place for Lucie Miles could not be part of what God wanted from him. He finally saw that trying to save Lucie from her chaos was dangerous because it would end in the use of force against her. The God he believed in was a God of truth and peace rather than power.

His God was sending the spirit of life to work in people, at least when they were not hiding behind the fences of their own fear. Being the cause for celebrating their lives together, this spirit could not be surpassed by anything else; that he knew for certain.

The God of Ramón Jiménez, then, was a God of surprises. For many people the point of their religion was that it would secure their world, and keep it intact as they knew it. For Ramón it wasn't about security. For him, religion was the domain of the unfulfilled desires of the human heart. All of people's hopes, all their dreams, everything they thought important, was rooted in the sacred space of a desiring heart that longed to be filled by the spirit of life. That was his faith.

61.

Picking Apples

It was the time of year that most people in sunny Andalusia were looking forward to the season of harvesting the produce of their fertile fields and trees that was about to begin. At Bethany the harvest of fruits promised to be quite rich. There was an old plum tree that had split through the middle because of its heavy burden. The almond and pear trees were loaded, and the vines looked as if they would soon be gladly relieved of their grapes. Also the cherries looked very fine, though the birds had started to steal them beforehand. Therefore Claire was assisted by Philippe and Pascal to cover the cherry tree with a net to protect its fruits against their fluttering predators.

They were just about finished when they noticed someone was walking in their direction, coming up the lane. As soon as he recognized the torn straw hat, Pascal knew their friend was visiting them.

'It's Ramón,' he said.

'Ramón?' Claire asked with surprise. To not miss the opportunity she went over to catch him as soon as he entered the orchard.

'I knew you could not bear Sanlúcar on your own, being away from us,' she jested as soon as he was within hearing distance.

'Don't get any ideas into your head!' he responded in a playfully careless manner, 'I am doing perfectly all right.'

'Come let me take you to the orchard, they are working to get the cherry tree covered,' she said and took his arm in hers leading him towards them. Philippe was especially pleased to see his old companion.

'*Olá Ramón*,' he waved his arm. 'I have potatoes for you!'

'*Olá Philippe*. Potatoes, for me? They surely look good I must say! But does Sylvia not need them for dinner?'

'I have grown them especially for you!'

'You did? You know what, I will ask Sylvia to give me some.' Philippe raised his thumb, showing he was satisfied with the compromise, but even more so with the recognition he had secured from his friend.

'Speaking of Sylvia's cooking,' Claire interrupted, 'she asked me to get her a bunch of apples.' She looked at Pascal and Philippe to see who would volunteer. 'Which of you would like to go up that tree?' Philippe saw an opportunity to make fun of her.

'I'd like to see you on a ladder with your skirt, ha, ha....'

No one paid any attention to this improper joke. Instead Ramón looked to Pascal and said, 'You're the gentleman here, aren't you?'

Philippe's face grew dark. Pascal pretended not to notice his mood change, and shrugged his shoulders in a perfunctory way, as if the question did not concern him.

'How much do we need?' he said, turning to Claire.

'Can you fill up two of those wicker baskets we have in the barn? Sylvia is making applesauce to go with a veggie stew, and she wants to make apple pie for the weekend; so she will need a lot of apples. Perhaps this good man here can help you,' she said and patted Ramón on the shoulder. Seeing the confounded look on his face, she encouraged him, 'You can earn yourself a meal!'

Claire didn't mind putting him on the spot with this assignment because she knew Ramón loved spending time alone in conversation with the boy. When he turned away towards the barn to get the two baskets and a ladder, he noticed Ramón was following him.

'It seems I just found myself the perfect apple picking assistant!' he said over his shoulder. 'I think you will need a ladder too!'

Ramón laughed. 'Perhaps it is better that I don't risk these old bones,' he said. 'Why don't you get in that tree and throw them down? I will pick them up and put them in the basket. That will be enough exercise, I think.'

When they returned from the barn they found Claire had been waiting. 'All right, guys. Shake the tree, climb it, any way you want, as long as they come down,' she said. 'Two baskets we need.'

They went to work. Pascal in his shorts up in the tree; Ramón with his straw hat standing under it. The apple tree was shady enough, so it was not too hot to be out in the sun. It was loaded with fruit this year, and they could see plenty of healthy apples. Within minutes the first of the two baskets was filling up quickly. They had been working for a while when Ramón asked,

'Do you have time for a question?'

'Only when it's not difficult!'

'You are very polite.'

The boy looked down upon him grinning. 'Shoot!' he said.

'Have you heard of a guy named Pascal?'

'Yeah, I have heard of him. I believe he is up in the apple tree right now.'

Ramón smiled. 'No, not that one. The one I mean has Pascal as his family name.'

'Who might that be?'

'He was a Frenchman who lived along time ago.'

'Have I heard of an old Frenchman by the name of Pascal? Of course I have, who hasn't?'

Ramón couldn't help thinking how much the boy had changed since he came to Bethany. No longer a quiet and somewhat subdued kid, he was growing up fast, almost too fast, as if he needed to make good the loss of his first seven years at home. 'You' are much too clever for your age,' Antonio frequently jested when the boy gave him one of his quick responses. But he was never as agile and witty as when he was alone with Ramón. Talking and teasing with his friend were the happiest moments in his life. This was why Claire had suggested Ramón should assist him.

'Blaise Pascal was his name. He was a professor. Most people who know about him have only heard of him because of one particular question he asked his students.'

'What was the question?'

'It was about figuring out whether or not God exists.'

'That was his question?'

'He took it as a question about probability.'

'What's that?'

'Something like chance. Pascal was wondering whether the chance that God does exist could be weighed against the chance that he doesn't.'

'Huh? I don't understand?'

'He asked his students: If smart people were to make a bet on whether or not God exists, what would they bet?'

Pascal shrugged his shoulders 'How was that something to take a bet on!' Ramón always asked these weird questions. Nobody he knew understood the things he was talking about.

'No, that's the very question he asked.'

'Stupid question.'

'How so?'

'When I play Parchis I always ask God to give me a six, sometimes it works, and sometimes it doesn't. There's no counting on anything. One cannot know.'

'You should have been one of his students, I am sure he would have loved that.' Looking up to the boy who was climbing higher in the tree, Ramón saw him placing his foot on a branch too thin to carry his weight. 'Be careful now, we don't want you in that basket down here, do we?'

'I will, I will, don't worry.' He stepped back to where he had been before, looking for a few big ones hanging down from twigs to his right. Looking down again at Ramón, he asked: 'Did he answer the question?'

'Hmmm,' Ramón nodded.

'What did he say?'

'He said that smart people would bet that God does exist.'

'Why?'

'Because when they win, they win more than they will lose if he doesn't.'

'Say again?'

'When they win because God exists, they win more than they will lose if he doesn't exist.'

'What does it mean?'

'Pascal assumed that people thought believing in God is about being rewarded. When you observe his commandments you will be rewarded, when you don't you will be punished. When you live an observant life you will be granted eternal life. So when you bet he exists, and you keep his commandments, you will win big! The boy looked at him with puzzled eyes.

'Too difficult for me,' he said.

'He meant to say that believing is good because you will get rewarded."

'So True believers like Sister Maria hit the jackpot? Okay! But I don't get the loss part. Why would someone lose when they bet that God doesn't exist?'

'Well, you see, that's my problem!' Ramón said emphatically.

'You have a problem?' the boy said with a playful look on his face. Ramón shook his head, and laughed.

'Observing God's commandments you cannot do everything you want. You may want to become rich, for example, and keep your money for yourself to spend it on luxury, instead of sharing it with the poor. When you keep God's commandments you will abstain from being selfish. If he does not exist however, while you keep his commandments, you will do so for nothing. There won't be any reward, which means you lose. That is why smart people bet that God exists. Their gain is much, much bigger than their loss would be.'

Whether Ramón expected the boy to understand this was unclear. He sounded like he was talking out loud to himself. When he noticed it he said, 'What am I babbling about the old Pascal who is long dead and gone, when I have a young Pascal at my side?'

To his surprise the boy was not yet done with it. 'What is your problem?' he wanted to know.

'I don't like the idea of God being like a headmaster serving out rewards for those who obey him, and punishments for those who don't. I don't believe that. I think God wants us to be happy. We are made for happiness.'

They were silent for a few moments, thinking about being happy. Seeing that the two baskets they brought were almost full, Pascal came down the ladder.

'Are you happy, Pascal?' Ramón asked him with a smile.

'Me?'

'Hmmm.'

'Uh… Let us see,' Pascal said, as if he needed to make up his mind about the question. 'For the moment, yes! The baskets are full, I didn't fall out of the tree, you have been asking me silly questions again, and Claire will be overjoyed with all these apples. I think everybody is happy.' They picked up the baskets to bring them to the kitchen, and Ramón laid his hand upon the boy's shoulder and laughed.

62.

Sky Dance

It was a sunny when Ramón was once again enjoying one of his walks. In was early in the day when he left father Gilberto's house under a deep blue sky without the haziness of hot summer weather. He went to visit his friends in Bethany. The occasion was the birthday of Joaquin Morales. The walk through the fields between the two villages was a very pleasant one. After an hour or so he arrived at the wide lane past the railway station of Benacazón that was guarded by oak trees on both sides. Soon the House of Bethany came into view. He passed the garden and went to enter the house through the backyard, and knocked on the door.

'Now look who is here!' Claire greeted him with a hug.

'Hello, Claire! Ready for the party? Where can I find the happy birthday boy?'

'He is in the orchard, enjoying the company of his musical friends.'

As it turned out, Joaquin's favourite spot was among the trees in the orchard, where he loved to sit and listen to the birds. On a quiet evening one could find him on a bench holding his head up as if he were observing something. Antonio's crew had found a nickname for this pastime. 'Joaquin the birdwatcher,' they called him. As he was not used to positive attention Joaquin enjoyed their recognition, even though 'watching' had very little to do with it. It had taken him a while to learn and enjoy the company of his birds.

In fact he didn't have much liking for them when he first came to Bethany. In Joaquin's mind birds were associated with ugliness.

The cause was a cruel memory from his youth with an abusive stepfather. When his stepfather was drunk, which he had been for most of the time, he would beat up Joaquin's mother, and occasionally he would have done the same to her son. Sobering up afterwards, he had a most twisted manner of admitting his guilt. Instead of saying he was sorry, he would look at them defiantly and say that as long he was in his own house, nobody was going to tell him what to do and not to do. Then he would end his charade by yelling at them that he was 'as free as a bird', and declared he would do whatever he wanted to his wife and to her 'miserable son'.

So as a child Joaquin never learned to associate birds with the things people usually associate them with. Even though he had only a vague notion of what they might look like, in his mind they were quite ugly creatures. To him the 'freedom' of birds meant to be brutally cruel and get away with it.

It was to his own surprise, then, that after a while his dislike of birds began to change. This happened slowly during his hours in Bethany's orchard where he went to be on his own. He chose a bench under a big pear tree to sit on after dinner. For these moments he would even leave his buddy Fernando back in the house. On his own, he would just sit there. That was when he started to notice the sound of birds around him. More and more he enjoyed listening to them, and soon he began to distinguish the ways in which they seemed to be talking to each other.

In the months since, it had turned into a fascinating occupation that taught him the sound of birdsong. If you asked him, Joaquin would tell you that singing birds are no less skilled in phrasing their notes and sounds than musicians.

Ramón's chance to share his spot under the pear tree came on this autumn day, a few months after the youngster had arrived in Benacazón. At the time Ramón had been preparing for his move to Sanlúcar. Hence the two of them had not seen much of one another, apart from the fact that the boy was not a big talker anyway.

This was why Ramón had set his mind especially on a conversation with him, not for any particular purpose other than just to get to know him better. From what he had been told, the friendship of Joaquin with Fernando was a special thing for Bethany. Besides Antonio had mentioned several times that Joaquin was a smart boy whose future might have great potential. Having these things in mind when they met, Ramón said he would love to join him in the orchard if he wanted to go there. Joaquin had quietly agreed.

'You spend a lot of your time sitting here, I have heard,' Ramón said when they passed the fence separating the orchard from the garden. 'Is there a favourite spot you would like to share with me?'

'There is. I will show you.' Ramón observed how the boy picked up a stick when passing the fence, and effortlessly reached the bench under the big pear tree. Even though birdsong was not at its peak in the afternoon, it was sufficiently lively to draw their attention.

'You must have a lot to listen to in this spot right here,' Ramón said.

'I call this my music hall,' Joaquin responded with a smile.

'Do you? What's on the programme today?' The boy's response was an even bigger smile.

'Birds are always singing to each other. The best time is right before sunset. I think they are actually talking to each other. When you listen carefully you can hear a first call, after two or three second followed by a response from another bird in one of the trees over there.' He pointed in the direction of the trees behind the pottery.

'So how does it sound like music then?'

'If you listen to them long enough you learn how they are varying their tone. The other day I heard two violins playing together on the radio, I was struck how much it sounded like my bird music, a melody by one violin, a response from the other, the same line again, but sounding slightly different, followed by similar changes in response. Birds do this all the time. I think they are enjoying it.'

'Do they all sound the same?'

'Oh no, not at all. Some don't sing at all, they're just twittering out loud.'

'Do you know what they're called?'

'No I don't, but I have given them names myself. There are two kinds. The ones I love best I call the "sunset singers". The others I call the "hullabaloos". They don't sing; they just make noise. Last week there were a lot of them in a tree over there.' Joaquin pointed in the direction of the big cherry tree.

'It sounds like you are studying them very closely.'

'I am just bird watching, I guess. The hullabaloo is a strange kind of a bird.'

Ramón was surprised by the casual way in which the boy called himself a birdwatcher, as if it were the most natural thing in the world.

'Why is that?'

'I cannot figure out what they're doing. They're twittering in that tree over there with a deafening noise that makes me believe there must be lots of them. The next moment the noise is almost gone, and I hear a buzzing kind of sound, which probably means they are flying. It sounds like they are moving swiftly through the air, back and forth. After a few minutes they are back in the trees again, making their terrible noise.'

'What strikes you as strange about that?'

'The sound of their flight. It is constantly changing, from left to right, back and forth, first nearby, then further away, and then coming close again. I think they must be flying in great harmony, which is a contrast with the noise they make in the trees when it sounds more like a market place.'

Antonio was right. Joaquin's was a bright mind; his speech was lively and spirited. Demonstrating how he heard the birds flying, his arms and hands went up and down, making loops, turning inside out, spreading wide and then coming together again.

'It must have been a very curious sight to see, so many birds flying as a crowd that is constantly changing in shape and size.'

Ramón responded deliberately phrasing his comment as he did, but the boy did not care to comment.

'Have you seen them before?' he asked him.

'From what you tell me they remind me of starlings. I once saw a whole bunch of them flying the way you just described. One moment they were assembled twittering in a tree, the next they were up in the air. Hundreds of them, no more than a few inches from one another; flying together, turning back and forth, spreading out one moment in the air and coming together again the next, exactly as you said. It was a mesmerizing sight! Their flight was a perfect harmony that looked like a sky dance.'

'How big are they? Do they have colours?'

'The ones that I saw are called spotless starlings because they are entirely black without the little grey spots on their necks and wings that you see on a brown starling. They are only 5 or 6 inches long.'

'Could they be the same as my hullabaloo birds?' the boy wanted to know.

'They might be.'

They sat silent for a minute or two, enjoying the shade, the air filled with the sounds of the few birds above their heads. Then Joaquin turned his head towards Ramón and said, 'I have heard people talk about being as free as a bird. But I wonder if people could be free and still have something like a sky dance together.'

'What do you mean?' Ramón asked him, sensing that something deep inside his soul was coming to the surface.

'It was my stepfather's favourite saying. 'I am as free as a bird in the sky!' he often said to my mother. 'But what they had together was far from a sky dance.'

'He was a violent man, wasn't he?' Ramón asked him gently.

'Hmmm … Especially when he was drunk, which was most of time.'

'That must have been horrible, hearing him do that to your mother.'

The boy did not respond, drawing loops in the sand with his improvised cane. It would take a while, Ramón thought, to understand that feeling no inhibition about beating someone up doesn't have anything to do with freedom.

'I am glad you said "yes" when I asked you whether you wanted to come and see the House of Bethany,' he said laying his hand on the boy's shoulder.

'I am too,' Joaquin spoke softly. 'I am not afraid any more, even when I cannot hide from the other people in the house.'

What terrible wounds this boy must have had inflicted upon him, Ramón thought, to see the presence of others primarily as a reason to hide oneself from them. Noticing how Joaquin turned up his head towards him again, Ramón's saw to his surprise he was smiling.

'In Bethany we are a bit like my noisy birds. We are living no more than a few inches from one another. We spread out one moment and come together again in the next, without getting into trouble.' Then he laughed. 'Free as the birds for a sky dance.'

Ramón Jimenez was a much too contemplative mind not to appreciate the beauty of the young man's confession of how his battered soul was redeemed by watching his birds, despite the horrible origin of its wounds. Life never failed to amaze Ramón in its unexpected ways of lifting up broken people. He took it as a sign that the universe was more than just things being 'out there'. The spirit of life had rekindled the battered soul of this young boy. Its amazing strength was hard to grasp. But Ramón knew for certain it was this spirit that against all odds kept the heart of people like Joaquin Morales alive.

Part VIII

A Door of Hope

63.

Fire! Fire!

It was soon after Joaquin's birthday that Andalusia's dry season reached its peak and the House of Bethany in Benacazón faced a terrible disaster. The weather was hot, and for weeks there had been not a single drop of rain. Claire and Pascal managed to water the garden from the tank, but the grass and weeds in the orchard had turned yellow and brown. In recent years shortage of water had become a serious issue in northern Andalusia, and this year was no exception.

'We need to be very careful with the distribution of water; without rain the water tank will eventually run dry and the well will be our only source,' Claire had instructed the young man. 'Perhaps you could put together a schedule of how to spread the hours that we will be watering various parts of the garden.'

The very next day he showed her a table he had made, dividing the garden in different lots with an estimated time of watering needed for the plants in each of them. When Claire complimented him on his work Philippe came over to ask her about watering his plants.

'There has been no rain; we need to be careful with the water, Philippe.'

'Yes, I know that.'

'I asked Pascal to make a plan when to water each part of the garden so that we will not spill any.'

Philippe's face darkened. He didn't like the way Claire always turned towards Pascal, and referring him to Pascal's watering plan was just another occasion to feel as if he was second-rate. At moments he had this feeling, he could be very cross.

When she addressed the subject to Antonio, he blamed Philippe's unfriendly behaviour on the absence of Ramón. They had noticed before that when he was gone Philippe had a difficult time. Now that his old companion had moved out, the times that Philippe was not his usual cheerful self but rather bad tempered became more frequent. It affected the atmosphere in the garden quite a bit.

Discussing the watering plan turned out to be one of the times when he really got angry. Claire had told him to do some weeding in the bed of potatoes before watering his lot, but for some reason he had it in his head that this was Pascal's job. If his watering plan was such a terrific thing he could also do the weeding!

'I am not going to do his job for him,' Philippe shouted at Claire pointing his finger at Pascal. Apparently his position as the oldest member of Bethany's community was at stake, and he behaved so as to make sure that the others would pay him the respect that was his due.

'Pascal is already weeding,' Claire responded with mounting impatience in her voice, 'there is lots of work to do and I want you to help us out.'

'No! You can pick those weeds yourself. I won't.'

'Philippe!' Claire had had more than enough of his behaviour and felt anger rising in her blood.

'Stop bossing me around! I don't work for you!'

'Philippe, that's enough!' Claire barked at him. She found him really obnoxious when he was in this mood. But he was not yet finished.

'You can stick those weeds where the sun don't shine!'

'Okay mister, that's more than I'm going to take from you. Out of my sight! Immediately! I don't want to see you around here anymore this afternoon! Go! Now!' Her fury made Philippe realise that he had gone too far, but he was not inclined to give in. He turned away and stepped into the orchard, all the while continuing to curse her.

'I hate this miserable garden, and I hate you too, bitch!' For now Claire was content that he had left as he had been told, and with his foul temper she did not want to push him completely over the edge.

Philippe walked around in the orchard, not knowing where to go or what to do with himself. Taking big steps, as if he were in a hurry, he all of a sudden turned towards the chapel where he was out of her sight. The chapel door was unlocked as usual, so he had no problem getting in. The air was much fresher inside, so it would have been the perfect place to cool down, but Philippe was not going to do that. Once he had got into this mood, he became obsessed with whatever was bothering him.

'Bitch...' he kept muttering, 'bitch... telling me what to do... She has no business... Pascal... he is her darling. I miss Ramón... he would tell her... teach her a lesson... Ramón would...'

He was moving back and forth in the aisle of the chapel. Coming to the podium, which was a slightly elevated square, the two candles on the table caught his eye.

Had someone seen him there at that very moment, they would not have left Philippe alone for one more minute. He was known not to be safe with fire, and was not allowed to have candles in his room. He would not deliberately set fire to anything, but he could not resist the lightning of matches, and was not very careful with extinguishing them before he threw them away.

'Matches... matches...' He went to open the cupboard that stood left of the table against the wall. The door was locked. 'Locked... Ramón... locked... There is a key... Ramón knows... He found it.'

Unfortunately on one of his walks to the chapel Ramón had taken Philippe with him, and without paying attention he had placed a chair next to the cupboard to grab the key that was kept on top of it where it was invisible. But Philippe had seen where the key was hidden, and that was enough. He took a chair, and soon he had the cupboard opened.

The rest was a matter of seconds. It started with the carpet underneath the table, which caught fire, when the flames flared up and reached the chair that Philippe had left standing close to the cupboard. Seeing what was about to happen he tried to kick the chair away, but coming too close to the table his shirt was in flames before he knew. Instinctively he pulled what remained of his shirt from his body, and screaming in pain he ran to the door and out of the chapel. Before he had left the building the first flames were already crawling up the beams that carried the roof.

In the meantime Claire and Pascal had carried on weeding, and she was just beginning to get over her anger when the boy asked her where Philippe had gone.

'I don't know … Why don't you go and look for him?'

Pascal got up from his knees to do as he was asked. Only a few moments after he had turned around the corner of the pottery an alarming scene unfolded before his eyes. Looking in the direction of the orchard he saw Philippe coming towards him, limping. The boy hurried to see what the matter, when he saw flames coming out of the chapel.

'Oh my… Claire!! Fire!! Fi–ire!!! Claire, … Fi–ire!!!' The boy shouted at the top of his lungs. 'The chapel is on fire! …Fi–ire, Fi–ire!!!' When he reached him he saw Philippe's body. 'Oh my God! You're burned… Claire…Claire…Help!! He–elp!!!'

Claire was about to enter the back door of the house when she heard Pascal shouting. Something very bad was happening, she could tell. Turning back she came running around the corner, and saw Antonio coming out of the front door of Lucie's apartment. She saw the boy kneeling on the ground, and only then saw Philippe lying there.

'Philippe… Oh my God… Antonio, the chapel! The chapel is burning … Oh my God, the trees … the trees!' Claire covered her face with her hands in anguish; she didn't know what to do first.

'Pascal, run to the house and tell Sylvia to call the fire brigade,' Antonio instructed the boy. 'Hurry! She should also call Doctor Solares to tell him we have an emergency. Philippe has serious burns.' Next he turned to Claire. 'Go get blankets, as many as you can find. We need to cover him. And we need blankets to put out the fire! Hurry, hurry … before the entire orchard is gone!!'

When Antonio sat beside Philippe, who was now in shock, he saw the roof of the chapel collapsing in a cloud of sparks. The next moment a wild fire began crawling over the ground. Within minutes the two almond trees that were closest to the chapel had caught fire as well. Lucie's apartment would soon be in danger, which meant the workshop, and then … the house!

In the meantime some of the others were approaching the orchard, terrified by what they saw. Antonio quickly moved in their direction to stop them.

'Maria, take the others into the house, quick. And pray for us all! We are going to need it!'

When he saw Pascal coming back from the house, Antonio called him. 'Pascal, you get the water hose in the garden connected and take it as far as you can into the orchard. Fernando you stay here too.'

Maria was pushing Sofia in her wheelchair. Alfredo took Joaquin by the hand, now that his buddy was not with him. Alonso and the girl followed.

Sylvia was bringing blankets to Claire. 'Take these blankets to Antonio,' Claire shouted, 'while I help Pascal with the water hose. Hurry!'

'The fire brigade is on its way!' Pascal reported when he found Antonio back on his knees next to Philippe, who was in bad shape. 'We need to get him out of here before things get worse,' Antonio said. 'Is the doctor coming?'

'Yes, as soon as he can!' Sylvia responded.

'Cover Philippe with blankets, and get him into Lucie's apartment. Find something to carry him on. Fernando will help you. And stay there with him! Pascal you come back to me with Fernando. When you do, bring buckets, as many as you can find.'

'We'll fold one of the blankets and carry him in it,' Sylvia answered. 'Fernando, come help me. I need a strong hand!' She spread a folded blanket beside Philippe and the three of them moved him carefully while he was moaning and clearly in pain. They took him to the pottery, laying him on the floor.

In the meantime Claire had brought the water hose into the orchard. 'What do you want to do?' she asked Antonio.

'See that open space over there?' He pointed to a wide but not too deep corridor running from left to right where the orchard was bare of trees. 'If the wildfire crosses that line, we are in trouble, so that's where will try to stop it until the fire brigade gets here. Claire, you try to keep it wet. I will use blankets to smother the fire when it comes too far. The boy will be here soon with Fernando to help. Sylvia stays with Philippe'.

It was a plan that made sense – except for the fact that wetting a piece of land that hadn't seen a drop of water in weeks was hardly achievable. But it was the only thing they could do.

'Where does the fire brigade get water from?' Pascal wanted to know.

'The water tank, I guess. I hope it has enough water left in it.'

After the two trees closest to the chapel were gone, they were shocked to see the big walnut tree had caught fire. The fire was approaching two pear trees before reaching the line where it needed to be stopped. Claire went up and down with the hose following the imaginary line that Antonio had drawn from left to right, which was about sixty, seventy yards. When Claire saw Pascal and Fernando coming back with buckets she said, 'How many buckets do you have?'

'Four. I only found four!'

'That's fine. I will fill these up. Antonio you tell them where to drop it.'

It soon became clear that they had little or no chance of stopping the wildfire. The soil drank the water in; their efforts were making little difference. Claire was about to warn Antonio when she heard the siren of the fire brigade coming down the road.

'They're here!'

64.

Claire's Regret

Once the fire brigade arrived, the danger of the wildfire spreading towards the garden and Lucie's apartment was soon averted. In no time they had cleared a stretch of about two yards from weeds and grass for which they used a special motorized plow.

'It could have been worse, Señor, you should consider yourself lucky,' the captain of the fire crew told Antonio, 'A fire in this dry weather is difficult to stop. You did well. We have seen things going very wrong in this kind of situation.'

For Claire the arrival of the fire brigade had been a signal to run to Lucie's apartment to find out how Philippe was doing. In the confusion she had not noticed the arrival of Henrique Solares, their local doctor. She found him on his knees beside poor Philippe. Sylvia stood by with tears in her eyes. When Claire arrived Philippe was just about to regain his consciousness.

'Philippe, how are you dear?' She got down on her knees, and gently stroked his face.

'Not yet, Señora,' warned the doctor, 'he will need more time.'

'How is he?'

'He'll be in a lot of pain, but he has been lucky. I think we can treat him here and avoid taking him to the hospital. Do you know what he was wearing?'

'I think he was wearing shorts and a cotton shirt,' Claire responded.

'That would explain the state of his burns. They cover large parts of his upper body, so they must have come from his clothes. Had he been wearing synthetic material his condition might have been much more critical. It melts and would have stuck to his body.'

'What do you prescribe?'

'Painkillers, ointment, and liquids. He must drink a lot. The ointment will ease the irritated skin, but particularly during the nights he will be very uncomfortable. We will be careful with painkillers, given his other medication, but I will make sure you have them in case he needs them.'

'Thank you, doctor.'

'*De nada* Señora Gomez,' the doctor said getting on his feet again. 'I saw the fire as I came in. What's happening out there? No more wounded people, I hope?'

'No, doctor, fortunately not. But our chapel is gone, and so are some of the trees.'

'I don't know about the chapel, but the trees will be back before you know,' the doctor said heartily. He sat down to write a prescription, and then turned to Claire again to say goodbye.

'Keep an eye on him during the night. That's when these kinds of wounds tend to be at their worst. And make sure he drinks a lot. Anything.'

'I will, I will, thanks again.'

As soon as the fire brigade had left and things were more or less back to normal, Claire called Ramón in Sanlúcar la Mayor. She knew he would want to know right away what had happened to Philippe.

'Claire, hello, what a surprise! It's good to hear your voice! How are you all doing?'

'Not so good, I am afraid. I have awful news. We had a fire in the orchard.'

'A fire? …How terrible! Nobody is hurt I hope…?'

She told him the story of how they found the orchard on fire, and Philippe lying on the ground with burns, but immediately added that he was safe.

'Oh, Claire, how terrible… how terrible! How did this happen?'

'That we don't know yet, but we think that Philippe being burned means he must have been in the chapel when the fire started.'

'How is he?'

'Stable for the moment. The doctor says he can recover at home and won't need to go to hospital.'

'Oh, how awful… the poor man… the poor man! How frightened he must have been! You said the chapel was on fire?'

She noticed the alarmed tone of voice in his question, and hated having to tell him what had happened.

'Yes, Ramón. I am so sorry … the chapel is gone.'

'Our chapel is gone…?' He fell silent for a few moments, then asked her if the fire had started in the chapel.

'Yes, it was late in the afternoon and Pascal was going from the garden to the pottery when he saw that the chapel was on fire.'

'You said Philippe is stable for the moment?'

'Yes, that's what Henrique Solares said, but he expects Philippe will be in pain during the night. He is asking for you, Ramón. He wants you to come home.'

The news about the fire had deeply shocked Ramón, and he decided to come to Benacazón that same night.

'I am so happy to know you're coming,' Claire said, 'and I am sure everybody else will be too.'

What Claire had not told him, of course, was why Philippe had been in the chapel unsupervised. The fact that she had sent him out of the garden weighed heavy upon her soul. She had been right in not condoning his foul mouth, but she believed she could have tried harder to keep her irritation with him in check. Usually Philippe had no problem with her and Pascal working together. His position in Bethany did not depend on his connection with her, but with Ramón, and as the latter was no longer among his daily companions, Philippe's position had changed. She felt that should have exercised more patience. It disappointed her that she had not managed to be more thoughtful.

After dinner she went up to Philippe's room to find him asleep. Just when she was about to leave, she heard him moaning. Turning around she knelt beside his bed, and whispered:

'Philippe, are you in pain?'

He opened his eyes, and nodded. She felt his forehead to check whether he had a fever. He felt a bit warm, but not feverish.

'In an hour or so I will give you something the doctor prescribed, so that you won't be in pain, okay?'

'Can I have it now?'

'Of course you can, dear,' Claire responded, 'but the doctor said you would need it during the night. It is a painkiller that might not sit well with your other medication, so I was thinking that if you could wait a bit longer, you could have some that will get you through the night without pain. Do you agree?'

'What time is it?'

'About half past eight.'

'When will I get it?'

'In an hour, but only if you agree.'

'That's fine.' He turned his face towards her with an anxious look in his eyes.

'We are friends Claire, aren't we?'

She felt tears coming up as she looked at him. 'Yes dear, we are … I am so sorry I shouted at you.'

'You're not mad at me, are you?'

'No dear, I am not.' Without thinking she added: 'Do I have reason to be mad at you?' As soon as it was out of her mouth she hated her question. What a bad moment to be quizzing him about the fire!

'No … I couldn't help it.'

To reassure him she put her face close to his, and whispered:

'You know, maybe we should forget about that now. We need you to get better.'

'Yes.' The response sounded as a relief.

'I have some good news for you,' she continued whispering. 'Ramón is coming soon!'

His eyes lit up, and then closed. Looking at him lying there, Claire realized just how much he must have missed his friend.

65.

'The Valley of Achor'

When Claire returned to give Philippe his painkiller and his other medication, she took a chair close to his bed and decided to sit with him until he fell asleep. He was quite restless, which meant she would be sitting there for the next few hours. The day was quietening down after what had been a horrible afternoon. Looking at the bandages on Philippe's chest, her mind's eye put him in flames in the chapel. Before she knew Claire found herself in tears at his bedside, as sorry as she had ever felt that her lack of patience had brought him there.

Sitting there that evening, memories came back from the time they had first met. She remembered his way of addressing her, his dominant presence, always commanding her attention if he could. 'Philippe has an attention deficit; he never gets enough.' At the time, it had been her shorthand description of his character, and it had never really changed. Claire was also aware of the fact that she had never liked him as much as she had liked his buddy Eduardo Villanova.

When she first became aware of her dismissive way of responding to Philippe, she believed it was because she instinctively felt like protecting his subdued friend Eduardo, who never would claim any space for himself. 'A matter of fairness' was how Claire justified her response. Philippe was too much of a loudmouth. When Eduardo was asked a question, he hardly got a chance to answer it. Philippe would leave him no time, and answer it for him.

Then she noticed that she behaved the same towards Philippe when Eduardo was not around, and understood that 'fairness' could not be her only motive. Looking at her irritation she realized there was more to it. One night she had been talking about this with Ramón, and she vividly remembered his response.

'Perhaps you just don't like people asking for your attention,' he had said. She had been rather annoyed by this suggestion. 'Now why in the world would I do that?' There had been much irritation in her voice.

'That I don't know, dear. That is a question only you can answer.' They had never addressed the subject again, but at Philippe's bedside the memory of this exchange came back and now, after all these years, Claire knew the answer.

She recalled that as a child in southern Andalusia receiving attention had grown into an important thing in her own mind. Her father had never paid any attention to what mattered to her. Being at war with the wine farmers – those self-made grand-seigneurs of the Jerez region – had been his main concern. That was the only thing that really mattered to him. The desires of a teenage daughter did not appear on the radar of her father's belligerent interests. The aim of defending his property had made everything else irrelevant.

Her father's lack of responsiveness had put its stamp on his daughter's character more than she had realized. At the time she had not known any better than that this was how grown-ups behaved, and she had resolved that asking for people's attention was a stupid thing to do. She was a sensitive person, and she did not try to shut herself off from responding to people's needs, but she could not tolerate that they would be asking for her attention before she herself had resolved that they needed it. Ramón had been right. Only Claire herself could answer why she would respond in this way. Now, after all these years, she had come to realize that she had been great influenced by her father's behaviour toward her.

After their phone call she had informed Maria and Antonio that Ramón would be coming from Sanlúcar later that night. When he arrived the three of them were gathered in the kitchen to welcome him.

'How is he?' was the first thing he asked.

'He's been asleep for about an hour. I gave him a painkiller. According to Henrique Solares it should take him through most of the night. Hopefully he will feel better in the morning,' Claire responded.

Ramón looked very concerned 'Do you want to go and have a look at Philippe?' Claire asked him.

'No, I'd rather not risk waking him. Let him sleep.'

'Shall we have a look at the orchard, then?'

'Yes, let's do that,' Ramón said, 'though it will be dark out there.'

'I'm off to bed,' Antonio interrupted. Maria too said she was very tired, and left them after saying good night.

Claire would now have Ramón to herself for a little while, which she usually liked, but now she dreaded being alone with him, troubled as her conscience was by her conflict with Philippe.

Standing outside looking into the partly burned orchard, Ramón asked again how the fire might have got started. 'You think Philippe had something to do with it?'

'I am afraid I do, yes.'

'Why?'

'Because he was the only one in the chapel and he was burned by the fire.'

'What business did he have in the chapel?'

Claire told him what happened between them in the garden before Philippe went into the orchard, and then into the chapel. 'It makes me feel awfully guilty to think he got himself into trouble because I pushed him away.'

'I can understand that. I would feel the same,' Ramón said, making no attempt to take the burden of guilt away from her.

'When I sat at his bedside earlier this evening, I was reminded of a conversation you and I had years ago. It was about my dismissive way of responding when Philippe would try to get my attention. You said that perhaps I don't like people who want my attention when I am not ready to give it. I was reminded of it because it seems what to have happened this afternoon.'

Ramón remained silent. She then told him how the conflict with Philippe brought back memories about the way her own father had treated her.

'It is painful to realize but as a child I seem to have told myself that asking for people's attention is stupid, and a waste of time.'

'The Valley of Achor,' Ramón said, more to himself than to her. Occasionally he had these moments when he seemed to be more attuned to his own thoughts than to his company. Claire hated it because it made her feel shut out. But now she was too occupied with her own sense of guilt. Seeing her puzzled look at his obscure remark, Ramón explained.

'Oh … I am sorry, something I came across the other day when I was reading. It's the symbolic name of a place to which painful memories are attached. A place of trouble, the name means. It's a story from the Bible. It seems your father's farm is such a place for you.'

'Hmmm.' Claire was never at ease when her friend was throwing around phrases from his holy book. But this time she considered his learned comments even more out of place. It was one of the very rare moments she was lonely at his side. All of a sudden she felt how tired she was, and felt she needed to get away.

Ramón pretended not to notice, which was not his usual behaviour. Perhaps he was captivated by his own thoughts, or perhaps he was more concerned about Philippe's condition than about hers. Either way, he didn't stop:

'I found a comment on the story of what happened in that valley that completely changed its meaning. The people kept its memory as a place of horror, but one of the prophets speaks of the Valley of Achor as the door of hope.'

'Hope?' There was a tinge of sarcasm in her question that Ramón pretended not to notice.

'Yes … It's a thought that has occupied my mind since I read it. The valley stands for a painful memory that we do not want to be reminded of. Instead of looking it in the face, we are trying to turn away, but in doing so we allow it to continue its destructive work.'

Claire turned her head away from him, and didn't say anything. An empty, awkward silence rose up between them. Claire felt awful. She didn't like the way he was explaining her feelings and felt he was patronizing her, even though he had said nothing to rebuke her. They sat together for a few more minutes and then she got up. Without looking at him she said goodbye. As soon as she was on the stairs she could not hold back the tears that had been burning right behind her eyes.

Twice in her life Claire Gomez Moreno had been running away. The last time had been when she realized that her wish to be a schoolteacher would not be fulfilled in Madrid. But Madrid had not been her Valley of Achor. The place she had left with pain in her heart was her father's farm, precisely as Ramón had described it. She had been a daughter who loved her father dearly, even if he had done very little to deserve it.

That night Claire Gomez was left alone in her room with her memories, and the pain of feeling shut out by her dearest friend. It was a desolate night in which she faced up to what was behind her impatience with Philippe. Whatever had happened in the chapel before it started to burn, she knew that the manner in which she had sent him away had brought him there.

The next morning Ramón was at the breakfast table when Claire came in, later than usual. It was clear that she had spent a rough night. After a quiet 'good morning' they said nothing more, and focused on the others who came in, still full of what had happened the day before. When they wanted to know about Philippe, she told them his condition was stable.

'He has been sleeping quite well, as I hope you all have been doing. Philippe will stay in bed for a few days. I will take his breakfast upstairs in a few minutes, and tell him you wish him well.'

After breakfast Ramón visited Philippe. When he came downstairs he packed his bag and was just about to return to Sanlúcar when Claire caught him at the back door. She held his arm, her eyes cast down. Then she looked at him, her eyes full of sadness. 'How did it become a door of hope?' she asked, almost in a whisper.

66

Rebuilding the Chapel

Presenting the plan of rebuilding the chapel became the highlight of Ramón's homecoming party, just as they had hoped it would be. Antonio had drawn a beautiful picture of Phoenix rising from the ashes that Claire handed over to Ramón when she announced the plan. He was speechless, and it was Maria's good sense to applaud the moment, seeing that he was too overwhelmed by emotion to say anything. 'Hurray for the new chapel!' 'Hurray for Ramón's return!' Everyone had been clapping their hands and shouting for joy.

In the weeks to follow, the task of fundraising for the new project was on their agenda. When they were speaking about it, Claire told Ramón to go and see Maria. He found her in Lucie's apartment looking after her.

'Claire said I should see you about the fundraising for the new chapel.' There was a slight blush on her face. 'What is it that you can tell me?'

'The other day I happened to tell the Reverend Mother about our plan. She said she would soon meet with the archbishop, and would certainly mention it to him and see if he would support it.'

'And did she succeed?'

'I think so,' she said. 'I would be invited to the palace. He wanted to speak about what kind of support was needed.'

'Wonderful! How smart of you! Fundraising seems to be in good hands with you,' Ramón said with admiration

'Well I didn't do much really. But the archbishop has instructed Reverend Mother to make sure I come to see him. He said that the archdiocese wanted to make a contribution for which he needed to consult his financial person. And he also wanted to speak to you.'

'So? Why wait? Let's try to get an appointment in his calendar and go together.' They agreed to make the trip to Seville as soon as the archbishop was prepared to receive them. In the meantime, Ramón was thinking that perhaps he could get Maria involved permanently in his fundraising job, so that she would get acquainted with Bethany's network of important people. In the future someone should be ready to step in anyway, so why not start to prepare her for this task now?

Sooner than he had anticipated the first opportunity to have Maria explore her talents as a fundraiser was a joint visit to the mayor of Benacazón, a woman who some said governed the municipality as her personal domain. They hoped she could make sure that there would be no delay in getting the plan to rebuild approved and obtaining the necessary permissions. When they succeeded in getting the mayor to put her weight behind the project, the next step would be a joint visit to the archbishop.

'We will have to work a little on the mayor's mood,' Ramón said to Maria when they were preparing for the meeting at the town hall.

'And how are we going to do that?'

'I suggest we take Alonso with us, just to put a name and a face to what we are doing. I have seen how this worked when we had the mayor of Sanlúcar la Major visiting us in Benacazón about the second house we wanted to establish in his village.'

There was no doubt that the company of Alonso could be very effective, given his usually joyful demeanor, but Maria paused for a moment.

'I agree, Ramón, but would you not rather take Philippe? He has recovered physically from his burns, but ever since the fire he has been in low spirits. It would greatly help him when he had an active part in getting the chapel rebuilt.'

'You think so?'

'I do. Claire spoke to me about how quiet and withdrawn he is while they are working in the garden. It worries her.'

'Hmmm.'

Maria noticed his hesitation. 'Let me instruct him about how to behave and all that,' she said firmly. 'He will be fine.'

'All right then, you do that. I will be glad to have him with us.'

Two days later the visit to the mayor took place, and it delivered what they had hoped. She promised to make sure all the paperwork for the reconstruction would be ready within four weeks.

'That's the best I can do!' the handsome woman said from behind her desk. Her stern look told them that they were very lucky with this promise, and that further pressure with regard to the timeframe would be considered highly inappropriate. Before Ramón could respond to thank the woman, Maria was quick to announce that Philippe had something to say, if that was permitted. The mayor nodded, and turned towards him with interest.

'What is it you have to say, Sir?'

'Thank you… thank you very much… Madame Mayor,' Philippe began. 'A new chapel will help us to forget about the fire. It was very frightening. Thank you for helping us out.' He reached out to shake her hand with his typical gesture. She took it, slightly surprised.

'It is my pleasure, Mr.…?'

'Philippe, Madame Mayor… my name is Philippe Bousquet.'

'… Mr Bousquet, I hope your new chapel will become a very nice place.'

'Can we ask you to come when it will be opened? I would be mighty glad if you did… and you can bring your family too!'

'Oh… of course you can ask me that, Philippe… And to bring my family too, how nice of you to ask… I will be glad to!'

When they stepped outside, Ramón announced they had earned themselves a cup of coffee on the plaza in front of the town hall. They found a table under the big oak tree that gave the terrace pleasant shade on a sunny October day. As soon as Philippe had left for the restroom, Ramón glanced at Maria with a look of admiration on his face.

'Well done!'

'I promised you I would prepare him for the visit, didn't I?'

'You surely did!'

In the weeks that followed when Ramón and Maria were working on the necessary funds for the new chapel, Claire had taken on the task of preparing for the building process. She had approached the same contractor who had built the original chapel. The man had heard about the fire, and had wondered if there might be a job for his men. When asked to come over to discuss rebuilding the chapel, he remembered what Claire had asked him the first time and anticipated the same questions. So he made inquiries about existing ruins in the area from which they might collect used building materials. Unfortunately, this time he didn't find any.

'But we could use the kind of rough cobblestone that is used in rural buildings. The difference will be hardly noticeable,' the contractor suggested.

'What about the price though? New brick will be more expensive.'

'I will make you a deal,' the man said. 'I will charge you the same price as secondhand brick.'

'Thank you,' Claire said to him, 'that's very generous.'

'Consider it my contribution to Bethany.'

They negotiated the budget for the reconstruction plan as Claire had agreed with Ramón. When this part of the deal was done, there was another concern that the man wanted to discuss with her.

'Are you sure you want it rebuilt exactly the same way as before?' he asked her. 'Because if there were things that could be improved about the old building plan, now is the time to decide.'

'The only thing I can think of was that the temperature in the chapel was often too hot for it be pleasant.'

'We could make it more airy, but that would involve all kinds of adjustments that would increase the building costs. There is another possible solution.'

'What's that?'

'We can change the direction of the building. The old chapel had its door towards the west and its altar pointing to the east. This meant that the roof of the nave was exposed to full sunlight for most of the day. Having the entrance pointing to the south, the new chapel would be cooler.'

'That sounds sensible, but I will have to ask Ramón about changing it, and will let you know.'

When she asked him, Ramón readily agreed with the suggestion to change the chapel's direction. 'Our chapel is not a church,' was his comment, indicating the traditional precept of building churches with their sanctuary pointing east. 'Besides, there is something to say as well for having the entrance visible when you enter the orchard from the garden.'

There was something else on his mind too. 'I think we also should ask for a path to be paved though the orchard to the new entrance. It would enhance accessibility, which is much more friendly, especially for Sofia.'

Claire took the finalized plan to the contractor. He promised their new chapel would be finished by Christmas. Everything was in place now. Within a month Claire was busy supervising the construction process, and making sure everything was done according to the plan she had negotiated.

67.

The Star of the Show

'If you could take the lead together with Antonio in preparing for the celebration of opening the chapel,' Claire proposed to Maria, 'then I will ask Sylvia to prepare for the reception of the guests afterwards.'

'What date did you have in mind? Christmas?' Antonio wanted to know.

'I am not sure. Ask Ramón.'

When they took the question about the opening date to him, Ramón did indeed have a suggestion. 'Christmas might be a bit tricky. If there were only a short delay in getting it finished we would already be in trouble. No, let's do it on the Sunday of Epiphany, January 6.'

'I love that idea, opening the chapel on that day will be special,' Maria said. 'What's 'epiphany'?' Antonio wanted to know.

'It is the last day of the Christmas celebration in the tradition of the Church. It remembers the Three Kings that came to visit the newborn Jesus in Bethlehem.'

'Ah, *los Tres Reyes*!' he said. 'What do we do to make it special?'

'Perhaps we could do a play about the star that guided them on their journey and lead them to the new chapel.'

'Sounds good to me,' Antonio agreed. 'Let's talk about it in the pottery tomorrow morning with everyone present.'

The next day the early morning coffee in the pottery took much longer than usual because of the announcement of the plan.

Everybody loved it, most of all Sofia and Philippe, but it soon appeared that their immediate enthusiasm for having a play was in no small part inspired by their hope to have an important part in it.

'What Antonio and I have in mind is that we make a play about the three kings that followed the star,' Maria began. 'They then find the newborn Jesus and his parents.'

Before she had even finished her sentence, however, the first part in the play was already claimed. 'I have always wanted to be Maria!' Sofia exclaimed.

There were comments about putting herself in the spotlight, but on this occasion she was lucky. 'I too think Sofia should be Maria,' Antonio said and subtly winked to signal he knew what he was doing. 'I don't think we can ask Lucie to hold a baby in her arms for more than half an hour,' he continued. The unlikely alternative to Sofia as leading lady soon settled the matter. There simply were no other competitors for the part of Jesus' mother.

'Well, that's settled then.' Maria concluded. Foreseeing what would follow next Antonio got behind Sofia's wheelchair saying, 'Now don't get overexcited, dear, that's not good for young mothers.' Sofia's excitement about her assignment was not easily tempered.

'Can my mother come to see me?'

'All the relatives of the members will be invited,' Maria said.

The prospect of her mother watching her performance in the play created a wave of red spots on Sofia's neck. Knowing how much all this mattered to her, Antonio was sad to see how quickly her anxiety about failing her mother's expectations once again got the better of her. Keeping her emotionally stable was not going to be easy.

Assigning the other parts in the play turned out to be easier to do. Alfredo, Fernando, and Joaquin would take the parts of the Three Kings. Philippe would be Joseph, Alonso would be a shepherd, and Pascal would be the star.

'How do we get Jesus's mother in a wheelchair on stage?' Pascal wanted to know. It was a very practical question, but the way he put it almost made Sofia burst into tears, seeing her moment of glory slip away. When he noticed her agitated face, Antonio intervened.

'We will put our Mary and Joseph on the stage before people come in to the chapel,' he proposed, 'so she won't have to move at all.'

'And we can dress you in garments that cover your wheelchair completely,' Maria added. Sofia was thrilled. She would be on centre stage during the whole performance! Joseph and Mary would be taking care of their baby. But then the question arose of where the action would be.

'What is the play going to show?' Antonio wanted to know.

'Joaquin, you surely must have an idea about what to do with the Three Kings,' Maria asked to get him involved. 'Where will they be?'

'They could come from outside, so that the chapel would be the destination of their journey,' Joaquin said quietly.

'That makes the chapel into the stable where they find Jesus in the manger!' Sofia said with shining eyes.

'Do we have animals?' Philippe wanted to know. 'I think we should have animals, and bales of straw for them.'

'We don't have a donkey, or a cow,' Sofia responded, finding it a worthwhile suggestion if they had animals.

'A cow…? Is that not a bit too much?' Maria was not sure it was a good idea to have real livestock in the chapel.

'We can borrow a few sheep from the neighbours.' Philippe said. 'I can go and ask them.' Antonio looked with some amusement at their enthusiasm and did not interupt.

'Where do we leave them,' Maria wanted to know. 'How do you know they are not going to run around?'

'Sheep don't run around in a pen when they are behind bars,' Pascal answered, indicating how that problem could be solved.

'Let me think about that,' Antonio said, 'We will find a way to deal with the sheep.' Maria looked slightly upset at him, seeing her concerns go unanswered.

'Two sheep, no more, and only if they are safely penned in, and on straw,' she decided firmly somewhat disappointed that her colleague remained silent.

'Pascal and I can go this afternoon to the neighbours to ask if they could borrow two animals,' Philippe jumped up, as if there was no time to lose.

'First, we should perhaps tell Ramón and Claire about the play, and see what they say, don't you think?' It was Maria's last attempt to temper the excitement about what promised to be an unusual spectacle. Philippe nodded this might be wise. Antonio again refrained from any comments.

There was another question from Pascal.

'If Alonso is the shepherd, why can't Lucie be a shepherd too?' he wondered. 'If we have them watch the sheep, she will also be behind bars. So she cannot wander around and bother other people. Besides, Alonso will be with her. In that way everybody would be taking part, just as it should be.'

Maria could not say she was happy with the proposal, but she knew Antonio would be thrilled, as they of course were.

'That's the spirit this play is about, young man!' Antonio confirmed her expectation. Within seconds the point was accepted, but there was a remaining worry. Sofia wanted to know where the sheep would be placed. Not because she minded the sheep, but because she didn't want to have her prominent presence on stage ruined by Lucie's chaotic behaviour.

'We will have the table removed from the centre, of course, and then put up some bars at one side,' Antonio suggested. 'I can see how that might work out well; I will be in charge of the sheep,' he concluded this part of their discussion. Now there was only the part of the star to be decided.

'We can make a huge star from cardboard and put Pascal in it, so that he is the star,' Maria suggested, which made everybody laugh. Pascal's face dropped, and she quickly decided to leave them with the impression she had been joking.

'I have another idea,' Alfredo joined in. 'We make a star from cardboard and put it on a long stick. Pascal can hold it up so that it will be high in the air.'

Pascal's face brightened up. It was received as a much better suggestion, so that this idea also went down pretty smoothly. Maria augmented it by suggesting that Pascal should be an angel, since the star was the sign for the birth of the new king that the heavenly angels had announced.

'Think of how it will be when the people in the chapel sing a song about angels announcing the great news,' she said, 'while the angel goes around the chapel with a star high up in the air. Then he stops before Mary and Joseph, at that moment the kings enter. Seeing the star they know they are in the right place!'

'Now you're talking!' Pascal exclaimed, 'I am going to be the star of the show!' Immediately Sofia's face dropped a few inches. She seemed to have missed that he was joking and for a moment feared he would be getting in her way.

'Of course not, silly! 'Maria said, when Sofia commented about Pascal taking the leading part.

'Speaking of stealing the show,' Antonio joined in, dryly this time, 'do we have a baby?'

'Yeah, let's borrow a baby too!' Luckily Philippe was not serious this time, so that the point was easily dismissed. They would somehow find a doll to put in the manger.

68.

———

Epiphany

As the final assurance of financial support from the archdiocese was not yet obtained, all these preparations for the celebration of the chapel's inauguration were quite expeditious. But when Maria asked Ramón about it, he was confident that the archdiocese would be generous.

'Don't worry about that,' he said, 'it's going to be fine. But tell me, how is the play coming on. Did people like the plan?'

'Yes, very much so.' She told him about the ideas for the play. Ramón raised his brows.

'Sheep in a pen?'

'I didn't like it either, but it was Philippe's idea, and they were thrilled about it. Antonio never made a move to change their minds.'

'It's not that I don't like it,' Ramón laughed, 'but I had in mind persuading the archbishop to do the inauguration himself. I'm pretty sure he never said mass with a few sheep among his flock.' There was a boyish grin on his face when he said it.

'Very funny,' Maria said a bit impatiently. 'What are you going to do about it?'

'What am I going to do about it? Nothing.' His unexpected lightness surprised her visibly. 'You and I are going to make him take out his chequebook first, and then we are going to prepare him for his first mass celebrated in a barn with animals.'

'Ramón, it's the archbishop!'

Since she became Lucie's assistant Sister Maria had come a long way in negotiating Bethany's profane manners, but this time her respect for the hierarchy of the Church made his casualness hard to swallow. She had learned how to handle Antonio's blunt manner of speaking, but from a man like Ramón she expected more reverence for His Eminence.

'I am sorry dear,' he said laughing, 'don't worry. I will behave myself when we go to visit him.'

'Did you get an invitation then?'

'Yes, it was in the mail yesterday. The archbishop will receive us on Tuesday a week from now.'

The trip together to Seville was cozy, in a way. Maria enjoyed every minute of it, especially since Ramón took the opportunity to ask her about her life in the convent. She told him some of the funny details about the other nuns, which amused him. Time flew, and before they knew they found themselves admitted into the archbishop's quarters.

Monseigneur Manuel Romero was there to welcome them in person, and entered the room with his arms spread.

'Sister Maria, it's wonderful to meet again, and you have brought Dr. Jimenez I see, who I am very pleased to meet, finally.' The archbishop turned to Ramón to shake his hand. 'Welcome, Sir.'

'Thank you, Your Eminence. We're honoured that you want to see us; we're also happy to be able to inform you about how the plan for the chapel is developing.'

The archbishop was eager to have all the details, and when they had told him all about it, he informed them about the treasurer's decision to cover the construction bill.

'The entire bill? That's more than generous, Your Eminence!' Ramón exclaimed. 'Thank you very much!'

'Well, I was informed through Sister Maria about the importance of the chapel for your community. I knew right away it had to be built,' the archbishop said with an avuncular smile to the subject of his praise, who blushed from ear to ear.

Then, in a confidential whisper, he continued, 'Between us, I had to push the treasurer a little, which I did by suggesting that in fact the archdiocese was building a sanctuary in a rural area were people could not afford to build one themselves.' When he saw a brief disquieted glance on Ramón's face, he added jovially, 'That's rubbish, of course, since we will have nothing to do with that chapel, except pay the construction bill.'

'Excuse me, Your Eminence,' Maria interrupted with the same blush on her face, leaving Ramón astonished about her flair, 'here I have correct you, if I may, because we have come to ask you to lead the inauguration ceremony for us.'

'Come to ask me? Inauguration ceremony? That sounds mighty impressive,' Monsignor Romero responded. 'What do you want me to do, and when?'

'We intend the inauguration to take place on Epiphany. If you would be willing to celebrate mass for us,' Ramón said, 'we would be very honoured.'

'The honour will be mine! It will be entirely mine!' The archbishop clearly was in the best of moods, and looked very content with the unfolding prospect. 'But before I make a mistake, what day of the week is January 6 next year?'

'It's a Sunday, your eminence.'

Monseigneur Romero left the office for a few minutes to check with his secretary whether he would be available. The secretary told him he would be celebrating mass in the cathedral on that Sunday morning, but he would be free in the afternoon.

'If the celebration can be held in the afternoon, you can count on me,' the archbishop said when he entered the room again, 'In the morning I have to be in the cathedral.' Ramón and Maria agreed that this would be no problem, so it was settled.

'Very good! You can count on me then.' His acceptance pleased Ramón because it meant the reopening of the chapel of the House of Bethany would not go unnoticed by the media in the region.

Monseigneur Romero asked whether there were any details known about the celebration that he should be aware of. Before he could say anything, Maria made a gesture to Ramón to allow her to answer, which he did, by now astonished by her ingenious way of catching the archbishop.

'We asked the members our community what they wanted to do.'

'Very good, Sister, very good. What did they come up with?'

'A play about the Three Kings from the East following the star and finding the newborn child in the manger.'

'Splendid idea. Is it going to happen?'

'Yes, it will happen. There is one thing perhaps a bit unusual about it.'

'Is there?'

'They decided we should have animals in the chapel.'

'Animals? In your chapel?'

'The play is about the kings following the star, which takes them to the stable where they find Jesus. Since that stable is our chapel, our friend Philippe said there should be animals like in the stable where Joseph and Maria were staying. They all agreed.'

'I must admit I have never before said mass in the presence of an ox.'

'It's going to be sheep, Your Eminence, only two of them.'

'Oh, well that makes all the difference,' the Monseigneur laughed, very pleased with his own joke.

'Everything will be conducted in style, your Eminence,' Ramón said. 'I will see to that in person. We will take care to ensure mass will not be interrupted.'

'I hope so,' the archbishop answered.

'It will be a very special occasion to have *all* our members involved.' Maria said. 'I think you'll agree that this is what the church should be like.'

The archbishop looked at her from behind his glasses, with raised eyebrows. It did not happen every day that he was told by a young nun what the church should be like.

'Yes, Sister Maria, I fully agree.' His secretary came in with an air of importance to signal their visit had come to an end.

A few minutes later they stepped outside the gate of the episcopal palace. Ramón turned towards her, and before she knew he gave her a big hug.

'The entire construction bill!' he shouted. 'And this woman here was telling me she was inexperienced in fundraising!'

'I… I had no idea… Oh Ramón… how wonderful!' Maria was clearly swept off her feet. No doubt it was because of the large donation they had received, but her sparkling eyes said his boyish hug might also have something to do with it.

In the weeks before Christmas, the preparations for the celebration were carried out energetically. Maria had succeeded in finding a set of impressive costumes. The shepherds as well as Joseph and Maria were easy, since they were poor people. But an angel, not to speak of the three kings, that was a different matter. She knew that in Seville there were several churches that would have costumes and other accessories for the occasion, which her former colleagues at the Convent would help her to find.

While securing their assistance, she had also arranged that the musicians among the nuns would be present. In the meantime Pascal had assisted Philippe on his visit to the neighbour requesting the two animals for the Sunday afternoon. Antonio made sure that bales of straw were arranged. Sylvia had provided a baby doll for in the manger, which made all their requisites complete. Nothing was left undone. The inauguration ceremony would be a very special event.

The guests were stunned when they entered the chapel. As the late afternoon sun was turning west, bundles of light entered the small windows and lit the scene as if spotlights had been deliberately placed. There were rays of sunlight lighting up the front where Sofia and Philippe were seated, costumed as Maria and Joseph, he in a brown cotton shirt with a cap on his head, she in robes of the traditional blue and red.

Their guests were even more stunned when in a dark corner they saw a small enclosure with two sheep behind bales of straw, and Alonso and Lucie sitting beside them in shepherd's robes, and

Antonio also clothed as shepherd, hovering within reach in case his assistance was required.

They were all there. Lucie's father Señor Miles; Carina Recuenco, Sofia's mother; Alonso's parents, Mr and Mrs Calderon; Mrs Garcia, Alfredo's mother; Ramón's sister Imelda who was visiting; Sylvia and her family; people from the House of Bethany in Sanlúcar. Mother Chiara was the guest of honour, a dignity also bestowed upon the Mayor of Benacazón, who had brought some members of her family. Finally, Mr and Mrs Solares, the doctor and his wife, were also present, as well as the contractor and his family. Even the neighbours, whose sheep were an essential part of the play, were there.

When Maria started to play the piano, assisted by two nuns playing the guitar, the archbishop came in, followed by two priests he had brought with him, and Ramón, who was to do the sermon. When the Monsignor was seated, the congregation started to sing *La Adoracion de Los Reyes* and the angel Pascal came in, dressed in a white robe. He went around through the aisles left and right in a solemn, slow pace, his eyes lifted up to the star. It was a very special sight, which in conjunction with the lovely hymn created an intense atmosphere.

When the music stopped, Balthazar, Caspar, and Melchior came in. Their colourful headgear and kaftans were beautifully decorated. Alfredo's crooked body walked alongside big Fernando, who guided the slender Joaquin; it was in itself a moving sight.

There was one line of text to speak for Joaquin. Though his voice sounded usually quite timid, he spoke his line with a crystal clear voice so that everybody heard him say, 'Do you see the star, my friends? Take me to the star.'

The Three Kings approached Joseph and Mary and were offered a bench to sit on. Half in the dark in the corner, Lucie and Alonso were guiding their sheep. It was one of those special occasions when the girl was very quiet, as if she felt the solemnity of the moment. Sitting with Alonso on a bale of straw between the two sheep, she stuck out her hands and pulled a few hairs from the sheep's fleece to play with them, while Alonso was leaning with his head on her shoulders, softly caressing her hair, as he would do at their dinner table.

After the archbishop had said a prayer, he invited Claire to read the story of Epiphany from the Bible. She began to read:

> *In the time of King Herod, after Jesus was born in Bethlehem of Judea, wise men from the East came to Jerusalem, asking, 'Where is the child who has been born king of the Jews? For we observed his star at its rising, and have come to pay him homage'....*

Her voice was clear as she read the story that was now unfolding in their chapel. She had positioned herself on a spot lit by sunlight that made her white dress shine like sparkling snow.

> *... When they saw that the star had stopped, they were over-whelmed with joy. On entering the house, they saw the child with Mary his mother; and they knelt down and paid him homage. Then, opening their treasure chests, they offered him gifts of gold, frankincense, and myrrh.*

And while she was reading, the Three Kings did as she said. They opened their bags and offered their precious gifts to Mary and Joseph. It was truly the moment of glory that Sofia had hoped it would be.

After the reading, there was more music. Then Ramón got up from his chair for his sermon. He stepped up to the little podium, and when he saw the vision of complete peacefulness in front of him his face showed that he was deeply moved. The paper he held in his hands was trembling. He wanted to speak, but his voice broke. Before he knew what to do, Maria was at his side. Sensing what was happening she took the glass of water she had put on the table for the archbishop, and gave it to him, while her hand was on his arm. He took the glass and drank from it.

'Thank you, Maria.' Then he spoke.

'Dear friends, when the prophet Isaiah was announcing the birth of this child, he said it would be for the hope of the world, and he named him the Prince of Peace..... That name was not accidentally chosen. The hope of the world is in a newborn child that by its very nature can do nobody any harm.'

'The story of Epiphany that we have just heard tells us there are two ways of responding to this message. The first is the one coming from Herod, King of Palestine. Having received the message of the birth of the Prince of Peace, he was afraid to lose his power to this new prince as he was prophesied to become King of the Jews. One day the newborn child would be his competitor, King Herod feared, so he attempted to get rid of the danger, and had all the newborn boys in his kingdom killed. Thus Herod became what most kings in human history, ancient and modern, have become. Warlords they are, tempting to control the world, as they want it to be, by violence.'

'Then there is a second response. It comes from three kings from the East. The only thing we are told about them is that they were wise men. Their response is to honour the newborn child with precious gifts. The story names the gifts of gold, frankincense, and myrrh. But the true gift of these men preceded these precious goods. We are told they were overwhelmed with joy. The true gift they brought, was a gift from the heart. They were wise men because they opened their hearts for the Prince of Peace.

'In Bethany we are familiar with both kinds of responses. We all have our fears, and our scars that we want to do away with, so that our world remains what we want it to be, a world we can control. But then there is another possibility. We can also try to face our fears, and our scars, and try not to hide them. Trying to hide our fears requires that we pretend to be strong, and invulnerable. It also requires that we put away the cause of our fear. Send it away, kill it, if necessary, like King Herod did when he killed the newborn boys in Palestine.

'Here in Bethany we try to live the other way of responding, the response of peace. We try to understand that the power of violence is a sign of weakness, and that facing our scars is a sign of strength.

A few months ago I moved out of the House for some time as some of you may know. When I did this, I thought it was because I was tired, needed time to re-energize. That wasn't true. I believed I was strong, and could not stand when I failed myself. So I went away because I didn't want to face my fears; I didn't want to look at scars that made me pretend to be strong.'

'That is what I have learned to see. The life of peacefulness isn't easy, but I found that pursuing it is a true source of happiness. I have been blessed with the people that God sent into my life, but it took me some time to understand why.'

'I have been blessed with the presence of the couple here at the front, Sofia and Philippe; I have been blessed with those who embody wisdom in their own right, Alfredo, Fernando and Joaquin; I have been blessed with my companions, Claire, Antonio, Maria, and Sylvia, without whom Bethany would not have existed or survived; I have been blessed with the leading star of Epiphany, our Benjamin Pascal, whose brightness is a blessing to us all; I have been blessed with the presence of Alonso, whose essence is joy; I have been blessed with the presence of Lucie, because she made me look into a mirror I did not want to see.

'I hope and pray that this chapel will always remind us of Epiphany, the day of appearance of the Prince of Peace, that it will help us see us that opening our hearts is the sign of wisdom, and that peacefulness cannot be found behind fences.'

When he stepped down from the podium, Ramón was trembling, but he felt calm. Returning to his chair he caught a glimpse of Claire's eyes; they said 'Thank you,' and her eyes expressed what everybody felt. His words had been a confession that enabled everyone present there that afternoon to join him, and say in his or her own words: 'Amen.'

Part IX

Jonathan's Father

69.

Return to San Francisco

Hannah Harrison left Bethany to return to San Francisco in early January 1983. Two years had passed since the new chapel had been inaugurated. After his mother had left with his brother Josh, Jonathan was anxious to know how things were developing back home, particularly between his parents. He had witnessed the depth of their crisis, and knew that in respect of her feelings his mother was past the point of return. What she had told him about her marriage, after his father had left the hotel room in Seville, could not be unsaid. Now that she had put it into words, there was no way back. It had changed her relationship with her husband in a way that made her realize that her marriage was broken beyond repair.

How quickly things can change! Only a few months before his father's intrusive visit to Bethany, Jonathan had faced Ramón's challenge to find out for himself what he was trying to hide. When he told him that he had left home to escape a future designed by his parents, Ramón had shown him that this was not his real problem. Running away from home would not change the fact that he was his father's son. To figure out what this meant to *himself*, and how to be in peace with it, instead of running from it, that was the question he needed to answer.

Remarkably it had been answered, even without trying, and quite unexpectedly. Looking back at that afternoon in the hotel, Jonathan realized how irrevocably the tables had been turned.

411

Seeing his mother's agony about her confession, he had not allowed himself any longer to act like a boy. He had declared that he accepted his father – even told him explicitly that he loved him – but at the same time he made it clear beyond any doubt that he was his own man, and would not walk in his father's footsteps.

Most surprisingly, however, was that stepping up in this way came to him as a natural thing to do. It had not been like taking a stand against his father, or a deliberate resolve that his father's brutality had to be opposed. It had not been an act of courage, like David facing the towering strength of Goliath.

It had not been like any of this. Jonathan Harrison had simply been himself, and had acted accordingly. It was then, at that very moment that he understood for the first time how very much he was his father's son, and he *was* at peace with it.

Clearly his mother had noticed the same, as became apparent during the final days of her stay at Bethany, when she had leaned upon her son as her stronghold. Jonathan realized that this was what she did. She had told him the truth about what happened on her walk with Ramón in the orchard. Embarrassed because of her guilt she had faked being unwell, after he had asked her what she thought of people like Alonso. She had been utterly unable to face that question, let alone answer it, having a memory on her mind of aborting a child with the same condition.

'You did not tell him, did you?' she had asked.

'Mother!'

'I am sorry, but I was so upset by his question that I thought perhaps ...'

'I think you know I didn't, particularly after I promised you not to.'

His mother almost had been in tears again when she apologized for having been dishonest with Ramón. It had been an act of weakness that he had seen before. Jonathan recalled his surprise in their hotel room when she had appeared to stand beside him in opposing his father, followed by the sadness of seeing her flinch under his rebuke. It reminded him of earlier times when he had witnessed her failed attempts to rise and resist her husband's claim to authority.

These memories weighed heavily on Jonathan's mind after his mother had left for San Francisco. There was reason to fear that once again under the spell of her husband's will, she would again fall into compliance, even though that would not do her any good. She would be extremely vulnerable. Jonathan was far from being at ease with how things would be developing between them.

When Hannah arrived with her youngest son their house was empty. Her husband had moved out. Hannah wondered to what extent this was an attempt not to confront her with the memory of their unhappy showdown in Seville. After all, they had shared so many years in a marriage that had been relatively peaceful. Even when this had been the result of her own submissiveness, her husband was not a malicious character. It had crossed her mind that her husband knew she couldn't afford staying in their house on her own. In view of the possibility that he would force her to leave, she reassured herself, 'You know he wouldn't do that.'

But then she was not sure about her financial future either. Peter had not been a miser in spending money on his wife, but she knew she had deeply offended him by taking sides with his oldest son against him.

None of these worries were communicated with Jonathan. His mother did not want to make him feel he should come home to support her. Had she fully informed him about their situation, he would feel he had no choice but to leave Bethany. It would be the final blow to his intention to stay away for a while. A few days after they were back in San Francisco, Hannah had her son on the phone.

'We're okay,' she said when Jonathan asked her how they were doing.

'How is dad? Have you spoken with him?'

'Your father was not at home when we arrived, nor have we seen him since.'

'You haven't seen him at all?' Jonathan was alarmed. He had hoped that things would be settled, even though he didn't see how they could be, but now that his fear seemed to come true, he was worried.

'No, we haven't seen him. Yesterday he sent me a message; it said he was out of town for a couple of weeks, that was all.' When Hannah had received her husband's message, she was both relieved and upset. She had been afraid of facing him, but now that his absence seemed to confirm her sense of foreboding, she knew hard times were coming her way.

Shortly after Hannah had informed him about his father's absence, she was on the phone with her son again. Expecting more bad news from this unexpected call, Jonathan received notice from his mother that his grandfather was in a hospital. His condition was serious.

'What's wrong with him?'

'He has become a very old man, Jonathan. His doctor told me he had a very weak heart, kidney failure, and respiratory problems. When I asked if he would get better, he said the chances he would recover were slim.'

'Have you seen Grandpa?'

'I visited him yesterday,' his mother said.

'How was he?'

'Very weak, but he said he was not in pain or anything.'

'That's fortunate. Is he in good hands?'

'I think so. At least he had no complaints. But there is something else.' There was a hesitation in his mother's voice that Jonathan found slightly alarming.

'What's that?'

'He said he had one dear wish before he died.' His mother stopped, as if she was considering how to break an unpleasant message. Then she said: 'He wants... oh Jonathan! ... His dearest wish is to see you.'

Jonathan was upset about this message, as was his mother. Being wanted at the bedside of a grandparent who was going to die was sad, but in a sense it was gratifying too. They both realized however that the moment Jonathan set foot back in their house, he inevitably would be involved in the domestic troubles of his parents, and that was what upset them most.

'Can you tell me what he said?'

'He asked me whether I expected you home anytime soon. I said that I didn't and wanted to know why he asked. 'I cannot tell you … how much I would like to see that boy again … before I go,' he said. Then he was silent for a moment and closed his eyes. He seemed very sad. When he opened them again, he took my hand ….'

Hannah hesitated to go on. She knew her son; he was not going to take this lightly.

'Please go on.'

'He spoke with a very weak voice when he said, 'I want to tell him something … about his father.'

Jonathan was alarmed. So far the truth of their family troubles was unsettling, but at least the picture had been clear. His father had crossed the line with his cruel and inconsiderate behaviour. Now it seemed as if that picture was going to be blurred by something about his father that was apparently unknown to him, and that might throw a different light upon what had happened.

'Why did he say that?'

'I don't know what was on his mind, but I am sure he meant what he said.'

'Did you tell him what happened between you and dad?'

'Yes. I believed I ought to be honest with him.'

'Does dad know that you told him?'

'I don't think so. As far as I know they haven't met since he came back from Spain.'

Jonathan had known for some time that there was a family history that was never spoken of. He recalled that in his early teens he had asked his mother why his dad never went to see his own parents even though they were only an hour's drive away. After his mother had died, it had been Hannah's task to maintain the connection with her father-in-law. She had always gotten along quite well with Grandpa Harrison, much more than with his wife. Peter had never even mentioned his mother. As a matter of fact, he had hardly spoken a word to his mother for as long as Hannah knew him. Something had happened between them, that much she understood, but she had never found out what it was. Peter had refused to talk about his mother from the very beginning of their engagement.

'Does it have to do with Grandma?' Jonathan wanted to know.

'I really don't know. When your father and I first started dating, we exchanged family stories,' his mother said, 'which is what people do when they are in love, to get to know one another. Your father hardly ever mentioned the years of his early childhood. When I asked him about it, he said he didn't remember very much of it. When I asked him about his mother, he said he didn't want to talk about her.'

'What can Grandpa want to tell me?'

'I would tell you if I knew, but I don't.'

Later that same afternoon when they had cleaned up the pottery, Jonathan turned to Antonio and asked if he had a minute. As soon as the rest of the crew had left, the two men sat down and Jonathan told his boss about his mother's call.

'You need to go,' was the potter's brief comment.

'You're sure?'

'Of course, after all that happened in your family lately, surely you want to be there, and see your grandfather, don't you?'

'Yes, but … '

'That's settled then, no buts.'

'What about the workshop? You'll need a few extra hands.'

'If I need anything, it will be more than a few extra hands, that's for certain. But that's not for you to worry about. You have other things to do, and from what you've told me about your family, it may take a while. You go now, and tell Maria what's happening. She will tell you exactly the same.'

'I will, tonight after dinner.'

Antonio nodded; he got up from his chair and turned away. Realizing the young man would be gone soon without any idea when, or even whether he would come back, was a depressing thought. But he didn't want to show in his face how much it affected him. After a second, in one of his typical gestures, the potter turned around with a grin on his face.

'Just one more thing. In case Maria forgets to tell you, as I am sure she will, let me add that I would not mind if you showed up some day to finally finish that bead project of yours!'

70.

At His Grandfather's Bedside

When Jonathan arrived at the California Pacific Medical Center in San Francisco to visit his grandfather he still didn't know what to expect. It had been four days after his mother's phone call. Arrangements for his return were made swiftly, and of course caused a lot of consternation in the House of Bethany. He had informed his friends that he had to go home because of his grandfather who was dying. Ramón and Claire, and the others, they all agreed. But only Maria and Antonio knew the full weight of what was on his mind.

He entered the department of cardiac services of 'CPMC', as the hospital was known in the city, and was referred to the room where he found Mr Harrison senior asleep. The nurse who accompanied him gestured that it was all right for him to take a chair, and then she left.

Grandpa Harrison had become very old indeed, just like his mother had told Jonathan. He had never been a tall man, but now curled up in his bed he seemed tinier than ever. His disorderly hair was thin, his face with sunken-in cheeks looked pale. His grandson immediately felt that the decision not to postpone this trip had been right.

Sitting there at Grandpa Harrison's bedside some of his treasured memories of the two of them together came to his mind. Among them were the many fishing trips they had made in the Bay area when Jonathan was a little boy. He had been clumsy with a fishing rod and managed to get into trouble with his line each time, but it never had annoyed his grandfather. 'The fish will love to see you coming,' he would say with a twinkle in his eyes. And indeed, his grandson never succeeded in catching one. But it never mattered. What mattered was the way in which Grandpa Harrison talked to him, asking him endless questions about his buddies and teachers at school, and always answering with anecdotes from his own childhood. Such conversations Jonathan never had with his own father. School talk was only for the dinner table, and the only subject was grades.

After a few minutes Grandpa Harrison's legs stirred in his bed, which announced that he was about to wake up. When he opened his eyes and looked at the person sitting there his eyes remained blank, until all of a sudden he recognized his grandson.

'Jonathan…! My boy! You came to see me…! You did! …All the way from Europe…!' Catching the bony hand that his grandfather stuck out, he felt it was cold. He couldn't help being overwhelmed by the old man's joy of seeing him. He nodded with a smile, but could not speak.

'You came when I asked for you…!' A flush appeared on his face, and there was light in his eyes.

'Yes I did. Mother told me about your illness, and that the doctors had said you were very weak. When she said you wanted to see me, I knew I had to come.'

His grandfather's speech was slow because he had to stop after every few words and take a breath.

'Thank you… my boy… thank you… I am dying, son ….I am,' he said with a soft voice. He looked at the door as if to make sure nobody was eavesdropping, and with a twinkle in his eyes he added in a whisper, 'But don't tell anybody… because… you know what? ….In a fancy hospital like this…. you're not allowed to talk about dying! …. Isn't that funny? …. Doctors and nurses…. they all talk as if death is an alien... You can't take them serious...What did your mother say? .... Did she also say.... that I soon would be well?'

Mr Harrison knew his daughter-in-law well but this time he was mistaken about her. Jonathan told him what she had reported, and that she had not belittled what his grandfather had said.

'She told me what you said about...'

'About what?'

Jonathan hesitated. '.... About that you wanted to see me... and why.'

'She told you that too.... That's good.... that's good.... So you know.... why you came... to see me, then?'

'Yes, Grandpa. I do.'

Mr Harrison folded his hands on his chest, and closed his eyes for a moment. When he looked up again, Jonathan noticed how soft they were. His grandfather started to talk but his voice was weak. What he was about to tell him apparently did not come easily.

'Your father.... is a complicated man, Jonathan.... I know he has not always been kind.... and he has done little.... to make you and Josh feel good.... about yourselves. He could have done much better... But there is something.... that you should know about.... what happened in our family.... when he was still a small boy... I am sure... he never spoke about it.... because as I found out.... even Hannah doesn't know.'

He stopped and took a deep breath, but when he continued he did so with closed eyes. Jonathan could not stop himself from taking his hand while he spoke.

'When Peter was small.... a child of only three.... his mother, your Grandma became seriously ill.... something with her mind.... It was devastating for a little boy.... One moment.... she would yell and scream at him.... for no reason at all.... the next she would smother him.... with kisses and candy.... She was completely unreliable.... I saw it made him very insecure.... and he started to withdraw from her presence.... hiding himself under the table.... or in a closet....' The old man was silent. Jonathan saw there were tears in his eyes.

'I should have protected.... my son.... but I was afraid of her too.... Instead of saving him.... from her rage... I stayed out of her way.... Oh, Jonathan.... What a coward I was....'

Seeing his grandfather reliving these agonizing memories, he squeezed his bony hand, not knowing what to say. When he looked into his eyes, Grandpa Harrison looked infinitely sad. He had witnessed the abuse of a small boy by his wife, and had done nothing to stop it.

'Did she overcome her illness?' Jonathan asked.

'Eventually she did....but it went on far too long for Peter....After a year he became deeply depressed.... had terrible nightmares.... and completely lost his appetite....When I took him to a doctor.... without telling his mother....he told me to send the boy away....if I wanted to save him.... from lasting mental problems.'

'Did you?' Jonathan wanted to know. Grandpa Harrison nodded in silence.

'Where did you bring him?'

'To family in Oregon.... Farmers. Good people....But not for a small boy ....in that condition....'

'How did he come back?'

'He was gone for about a year.... and came back.... when his mother had overcome.... her mental illness.... But by that time.... too much damage had been done.... to become a family again.... In those two years.... we lost our marriage.... and our son.'

When Jonathan left the hospital half an hour later, it had been the hardest goodbye ever. Grandpa Harrison had been exhausted when he had said what he wanted his grandson to know. After he was finished speaking he had been lying again with his eyes closed and his hands folded on his chest, which for a moment made Jonathan fear he was gone. But Mr Harrison only was recovering in order to find the energy to depart from his grandson, which was the last thing he needed to do. He was still lying quiet with his grandson sitting on a chair beside him, when a nurse came in to say that it was time for the patient to rest. Her instruction brought his grandfather back to his wits again. For a brief moment there was that same twinkle again.

'Rest in peace … you mean?'

The nurse protested and was offended, which made Mr Harrison gesture, 'See what I mean?' towards his grandson. It had broken the intense sadness of the moment. Grandpa found the energy to even ask him a few questions about the place where he stayed.

'Are you happy there?' He wanted to know.

'Yes, Grandpa, I am.'

'That's good to hear.' He spread out his hand, which Jonathan took and held till Grandpa nodded that it was time. No more words were spoken. The grandson embraced the dying old man, and left the room. A few moments later he entered the elevator, sobbing like a little boy.

In the days and weeks after this visit Jonathan was revisiting the memories he had from his childhood. What he had learned from Grandpa Harrison could not but affect the way he had come to see his father. The story about what Peter Harrison had been through as a child strongly reminded Jonathan of the story of Pascal Marais. Years before Jonathan arrived in Benacazón young Pascal had come to Bethany with a similar background. When they met for the first time in the pottery Pascal was a clever boy of just eleven years old. In no way did he remind anyone of the frightened little boy they saw when he first came to their house.

Jonathan's father had not been so lucky. Returning from Oregon when he was six, he had found his mother recovered from her illness, but the bonds of love had been broken, and were never healed. Peter Harrison had grown up without trust in the people surrounding him. It was like he had made an agreement with himself never again to have his affection denied, and wasted.

71.

A Saddening Message

In the back of the orchard the first blooming almond tree announced a new year had just begun. Claire asked Sofia if she would care to join her after lunch to enjoy the sight of it.

'I would love to, but you have to push my wheelchair.'

The air outside was crisp. After a few minutes they found the tree. It was simply gorgeous, not only the sight but also the scent of its blossom. Claire managed to pick a few twigs so that Sofia could smell the blossom too.

'Here, let me put these in your hair. It will make you look lovely,' she said, and succeeded in sticking a small bundle of white blossom with patches of pink in the young woman's hair.

'How does it look?' Sofia wanted to know. 'I will need a mirror.'

'Lovely. Trust me. Shall we sit down a moment before we get back?'

'Yes, but it will get chilly soon.'

'Just tell me when you get cold, and we will return.'

Not far from the almond tree there was a bench, at the side of the chapel. Claire pushed the wheelchair close to it, and they sat down. As Sofia had been the first female member to join Bethany's community, before Lucie and Maria came, it had fallen upon Claire to assist her with her personal care. This had created a bond of confidentiality between them that expressed itself in intimate moments of 'girl-talk' that not only Sofia, but also Claire always enjoyed. Their chat on the bench in the orchard was one of such moments.

'Has there been any news from Jonathan? When will he come back to Bethany?' Sofia wanted to know.

'I haven't heard anything from Maria,' Claire said. 'She would know, because Jonathan promised that he would call her as soon as he knew what his plan was going to be.'

'He will come back, won't he?'

'To be honest, I don't know dear.'

Sofia's face grew sad. There was a melancholy look in her eyes when she said,

'I miss him.'

'I know you do, honey. We all do.' Claire had heard from Antonio about Sofia's infatuation regarding the young American, and being aware of her delicate sensibilities with regard to affection, she didn't want to stir any emotions.

'Do you like him?' Sofia wanted to know. Claire's intention to generalize the appreciation for Jonathan apparently had missed its target. She now was asked about her own feelings. But she was not to get caught in this way.

'You mean like a woman likes a man?' Sofia nodded to affirm that this was indeed what she meant.

'No, not particularly.' Claire deliberately pretended a lightness in her response, as if she really didn't care all that much. There was no deceit in this regard. Claire had greatly appreciated Jonathan's presence in Bethany because of what he had brought to its community, particularly to the pottery. But it was not different in kind from the way she appreciated Maria's contribution, or anybody else's for that matter.

'I do.' It was spoken softly, but earnestly in a way that Claire sensed she could not but take as a precious confession of love. Instinctively she didn't respond, at least not in words, but bent over to Sofia's wheelchair. She stroked her hair, and then kissed her on the cheek.

This was a few weeks after the evening of his mother's call. Jonathan had spoken with Maria, as Antonio had summoned him to do. He had indeed promised her to keep them informed about his plans once he was back in San Francisco. Maria had understood he didn't know yet exactly what would happen having just received the message about his grandfather's illness.

'You take all the time you need, you know, but you will be missed dearly. In more than one way, as you know,' she added.

'You mean Sofia?'

'Among others. I am sure your unexpected departure does not leave Antonio indifferent either, as it does no one here, to be honest.'

He had been silent for a few moments after these words. Maria remembered the day he arrived at her office. She had liked something about him the moment he entered the door. He had tried to mislead her with his cocky behaviour, which she had taken as a sign that he wasn't nearly as sure of himself as he pretended to be. He had been a committed young man who hadn't figured out yet where to direct his commitment. She had then thoroughly enjoyed calling his bluff.

'I don't know what's going to happen. From what she told me, my mother left me with the impression that Grandpa Harrison does not have months, perhaps not even weeks to go. Apparently he is very ill.'

'Of course, I understand that. But can you at least tell me whether you plan to return after the funeral.' Noticing that her words might be seriously misunderstood, she was quick to add, 'Please don't hear me say I hope you will be back soon. It's just that with regard to the coming months I need some kind of indication what we need to plan for.'

'I understand that.' Jonathan hesitated to continue with what he had on his mind. Going back home for his grandfather's funeral was only one thing. And though it was the most urgent and important thing right now, he was aware that after the funeral, were that to come to pass, the troubled marriage of his parents would almost certainly prevent him from returning right away.

'Is there something else on your mind?' Maria asked quietly.

Jonathan took a deep breath, 'Yes there is.'

'Do you care to tell me about it?'

He nodded but then stopped. He wasn't sure what Maria knew about the episode in the hotel in Seville, and why his parents had been separated for Christmas. 'You must have asked yourself why my mother and my brother Josh showed up quite unexpectedly to celebrate Christmas with us,' he started.

'Ramón has told me something,' she said. Not to leave the impression of being talked about behind his back, she added carefully, 'He thought I needed to know that your father had come to tell you to come back to the States and work for him.'

'Which left you only more curious about what my mother had to do with all that, and why she had to stay with us for Christmas.' He put it as an observation, not seeming annoyed.

Maria looked at him with the beginnings of a smile. 'I don't want to pretend I didn't ask myself that question, yes. But then I figured that if you considered it any of my business you would tell me. So apart what Ramón told me about your father, I haven't heard anything. It must have been a not-so-merry-Christmas for your family, that much was clear to me.'

'It wasn't. What happened may immediately affect my answer to your question about returning to Bethany, so I'd better tell you something about it.'

'If you think you should, I am listening. I hope you trust me when I say that what is between assistants and myself as their supervisor remains confidential.' She had not yet finished this sentence before she saw a shadow passing over his face. 'Oh, I am sorry,' she quickly added, 'I didn't mean it to sound as formal as that. I just want you to know whatever you want to tell me stays between us.'

'That's all right.' Inadvertently Jonathan said it with some reservation in his voice. He might have mentioned the cause of his parents' deep crisis, but now he was sure not to mention his mother's abortion. Maria noticed his tone, but said nothing.

'The thing is, my parents' marriage seems not to work any longer, which means it will be hard for me to turn my back on them, particularly my mother, and return to Spain when Grandpa is gone. I hate to talk about him this way, but that's what I am facing.'

'I see. You think you will be needed home.'

'I do. If you had asked me a few days ago, I would have said that I was very worried about my mother's future. Were their marriage to break down for good, she would be in a very vulnerable position without a career, or even a job.'

'You mean you're worried your father might not sufficiently provide for her?'

'I would have said so, had you asked me before my mother's call. But now....' He told Maria about the message that his grandfather had passed to him through his mother.

'He wants to tell me something about my father. I cannot stop thinking about what this means,' he said.

'You are wondering whether your father is after all the kind of man you take him to be. Is that it?'

'Something like that.'

'In which case your family situation might be much more complicated than just blaming your father for the breakdown of their marriage.'

Sister Maria might not be a woman of the world, but she did understand a few things about the human heart, particularly when it came to the complex feelings of broken relationships between parents and their children. To be sure, Jonathan Harrison was not a child anymore, but if what he anticipated were to come true it might throw a different light upon his father, and pent-up feelings from his childhood would have to be reconsidered.

Jonathan nodded but did not respond. What Maria had just said was put quite bluntly, but it was exactly what he felt.

'I see. In that case I'd better be prepared that we won't see you back soon.'

72.

Jonathan Finds His Father

His grandfather's funeral was the first time Jonathan Harrison had seen his father since the meeting with his mother in Seville. Grandpa had lived for another three weeks after Jonathan had visited him, and in that time he had seen him twice. Once he went to accompany his brother Josh to say goodbye, and the second time he went with his mother.

It was on this latter occasion that Hannah learned what Grandpa Harrison had told her oldest son. He had kept it to himself, not knowing how to share the horrible story about his father's childhood. But the secret was revealed when Grandpa broke the silence between them. Very much weaker than before, he hardly spoke during their visit. When he finally opened his eyes, he moved his hand asking them to come closer.

'Did you tell your mother what I told you?'

'No Grandpa, I didn't. Not yet.'

'I think you should … It might help.'

The old man had felt his daughter-in-law was grieving, and he had guessed that her marriage was the cause of it. Hannah had said nothing at his bedside other than trying to make him as comfortable as she could, but Jonathan felt she was not at ease. As soon as they left the hospital to enter the parking lot, she began,

'Jonathan, I….'

'I understand … I will tell you, but not here. Let's go for a coffee, and take our time.' His resolute tone left her no choice but to agree.

Some time later they were sitting in a quiet corner of a coffee bar, when Jonathan finally told her what she needed to know. It was an awkward moment, listening to her husband's unknown past, unraveled by a child they had raised together. Hannah was devastated by what she heard, and felt utterly powerless to do anything but weep. Why had Peter never told her this? It was not like a secret to be ashamed of! Why had he kept this to himself? The times she had asked him why he always behaved so coldly towards his mother! The times he was just as cold towards her, when she had wondered about his feelings for her! Endless memories pressed in on her, and she was forced to relive many moments when she had been in despair about his aloofness and heartlessness, as if he could not be touched by anything, or anyone.

Having finally been told the truth Hannah Harrison realized how her husband had been trying to get away from the pain of an abusive childhood. She felt drawn to forgive his shortcomings instantly. It had seemed to her that the coldness of the insurance industry had changed her husband into an insensitive man of business, but the true cause of his detachment went much deeper.

Jonathan guessed at what was going on in his mother's mind, and tried to comfort her as much as he could. The many memories that had been on his own mind, after he had first visited Grandpa, were to some extent similar to his mother's, but his feelings were not shot through with guilt. She had come to think of the man she had once loved as heartless but she wondered, had she known the truth, if would she have thought of him in that way.

Jonathan, meanwhile, felt sorry for the true father he had missed, but there was no misguided regret on his part. He had been a boy who felt his father let them down, him and his little brother, and in fact that was what had happened. Josh and he could not in any way be held responsible for their grandparents' sin. Jonathan was wise enough to realize this. But even so he felt the pain of knowing that young Peter Harrison had coped with finding his way in the world by hiding his loneliness behind impenetrable fences. But his sadness was not without hope; Jonathan wanted to meet with his father. He hoped that once his father knew what Grandpa had told his son, things between them would change. The funeral created the possibility of taking the first step.

It was a rainy day in San Francisco and the funeral ceremony had been brief. There had not been extensive communications between Hannah and Peter, nor had he expressed any interest in meeting with his two sons. He was about to leave when the ceremony was over, but Jonathan was at his side before he could jump into his car.

'Dad!'

His father stopped, and turned around slowly. The expression on his face could not have been more annoyed had the police stopped him. But now that he knew his father's story, Jonathan was not intimidated as he once would have been.

'What do you want?' his father snapped.

'I want to say I am sorry that you lost your father....' Jonathan began.

'Thank you,' his father said, and turned to get into his car.

'....And also that Grandpa told me about what happened to you when you were a little boy.' Of course he would never have chosen this frontal attack, had his father been more forthcoming. As it was, Peter Harrison stood frozen to the spot.

'He told you ... *what?*'

'You heard me.'

Peter Harrison composed himself, recovering from the blow he had received, and soon the same emotionless expression was back on his face: 'So?'

'Well, it may not mean much to you, but it meant a great deal to me.'

'What do you want?'

'I want to talk to you.'

His father looked away, as if to weigh up his options. But behind his usual intimidating demeanor, Peter Harrison was shaking. Looking at him from the outside one would have thought he couldn't care less about his son approaching him, but inside he was scared to death. He wanted to run, but he instinctively knew this could be the last chance he would get to be reunited with his two sons. If Jonathan came first, Josh would follow. But at the same time he was frightened. When he turned his face back to look at his son, he wasn't sure what to say. Before he could say anything, Jonathan spoke again:

'You're my father; and I am your son.' Jonathan could not have chosen a better way to blow a hole in his father's defences than speaking these empathic words. They did what was needed. There was a brief moment when he saw his father's face turn pale, then he seemed unable to find the words with which to respond. When he remained silent, Jonathan felt his father was thrown off guard.

'Eh, yes…. What….' Seeing his father's confusion, Jonathan jumped in, 'I have your phone number. I will call you.'

'Yes, you do that…. That's okay…. Yes. Call me.' He turned around, got into his car, and slowly drove away, leaving his son behind with a sense of relief. Jonathan knew he was going to meet his father, but it was not going to be easy.

That he was correct in foreseeing a difficult meeting was confirmed the next day when he called his father to set up a time and place to talk. Jonathan felt he wanted to have this conversation as soon as possible, but his father said he was too busy. They finally met a week later in a restaurant in downtown San Francisco. His father had suggested meeting him in his office, but Jonathan had declined saying that business surroundings did not suit what he hoped their conversation would be.

The last time the two men had spoken with one another, apart from the brief encounter in the cemetery, had been when Peter Harrison arrived in southern Spain to summon his son to come home. Obviously the memory of that occasion did not leave much room for chatting before they got to the real subject. His father looked far from relaxed, in marked contrast to Jonathan, who was actually quite happy to see him.

'It's good to see you, Dad, how have you been?'

'I've been okay.'

'Christmas was not what you had planned it to be, I guess?'

'I didn't plan anything.' Seemingly not intent upon giving him an inch, his father's responses were curt. It was clear that Harrison Sr. had not yet grasped the extent to which his son had changed in the last two months.

'Have you spoken to Mam at all?' Jonathan started.

'I met her briefly in the hospital.'

'So you did see Grandpa before he died?'

'Hmmm.' Jonathan was not consciously aware of it, but the more he tried to get close to him, the shorter his father's answers were.

'How was it?'

Shifting nervously on his chair, his father clearly was not happy with where this was going. He put both his hands flat on the table in front of him as if he had made a decision.

'Look, son, I don't know what you want from me, but I'd rather keep my last words with my father to myself.'

'I don't want anything from you; I just want to tell you that I am very sorry about what happened to you.'

This self-composed manner of speaking was completely new to Peter Harrison. It was not the kind of exchange between father and son that he was familiar with. Used to putting brief questions to which he demanded clear answers, he always had managed to make Jonathan feel like he was an assistant from his company rather than his son. Yet, he did not fully see that his mode of command was no longer working for him. This time it was his son who was asking the questions. What confused him even more was that Jonathan was not at all interrogative; he just was interested.

'It's okay, Dad,' Jonathan said softly when he saw the man struggling.

Not ready yet to give in, his father cleared his throat, and said, 'I saw Grandpa two days before he died. He was barely conscious.'

'He didn't notice you were there?'

'Hardly. There was one brief moment … 'Talk to your son' … that's all he said.' He looked out of the window. He stopped.

'You must have felt lonely.'

Being his father's son, Jonathan Harrison could be very direct and just fire away whatever he had on his mind, but this time it was not a shot in the dark. He knew exactly what he said, and why he said it. His grandfather had not said anything personal to his own son when he had visited him in the hospital to say goodbye. How could this not have hurt him? Jonathan assumed that after all these years Peter Harrison still needed a word from his old man, and he was right. He had been hurt, had been hurt deeply.

His father took a deep breath, and said: 'You're right. I left the hospital without a word from him.'

'I remember Grandpa when we went out fishing together as an affectionate man, funny most of the time....'

'He never took me out fishing together, if that's what you're getting at.'

'What did he do then?'

'Nothing. My father and I went separate ways. After I came back from Oregon, when I had been sent away for a year, I was only six years old. There was no way my father would try to reconnect.'

'He never talked to you about what had happened?'

'I know you don't think much of me as your father ...'. Jonathan made a gesture to object, but this time his father was persistent. 'No, don't. I know that's true – but I can assure you that in my whole life I never had anything with my father that came close to being what you would call a "father-to-son-conversation".' Jonathan smiled. For years when his father wanted to talk to him, which was mostly about school, Jonathan would respond by saying 'Time for another father-to-son-conversation'. It was aptly put for the one-way-street these exchanges had been.

'Yeah, I know you spoiled me,' he said. Without being aware of it, he had slipped back into his old self again. He meant it to sound funny, but there was a sting. When he saw his father's face frozen, he realized what a stupid joke it was.

'I am sorry, Dad, I shouldn't have said that.'

Peter Harrison was stony faced, ignoring his son's apology. 'What did my father actually tell you?'

Jonathan gave a brief summary of what he had heard. There was neither a response nor a comment, which was why after a few moments he ventured a further question:

'Do you want to tell me about your mother?'

Once more his father's gaze wandered to the street outside. It was several minutes before he turned back, his face emotionless. He then took a deep breath, and said:

'There is not much to tell. She was a nightmare. But she was sick, mentally ill. That doesn't change what she did to me, of course. One might say that she killed me emotionally ... In view of how it felt ... not feeling anything was the only way to survive....'

'How was the family you were sent to?'

'Being sent away to Oregon was a relief, in the sense that I did not get worse. But they were farmers, not talkers.... They were as open as the forests that surround them, so things were not any better there either.'

His father still showed little emotion when he spoke, but the brief silences that interrupted his words bespoke his feelings that apparently were still very strong even though what had happened was more than fifty years ago.

'I came back from Oregon after the doctor declared my mother healed ... but I did not trust her condition enough to ever allow her to be my mother again.' As a matter of fact Peter Harrison had been convinced for most of his life that his rejection of her was what got his mother killed before she was forty. 'I did not detest my mother. On the contrary, but I just knew she meant danger, so I kept away from her ... But my father ...' He fell silent, and closed his eyes for a moment. When he looked up, he said, 'My father could have ... He could have reached out, but he didn't ... I shut down emotionally ... I was not sad. Nor was I angry with him ... I was just cold.' There was a chill running down Jonathan's spine when he heard his father say this.

Peter Harrison had stopped talking, and now it was time for his son to be silent and look out of the window. He remembered his mother had talked about how her husband could shut off his feelings. It was not the moment to bring this up. He let his father's words sink in, and could almost feel the benumbing pain of loneliness. When he looked back again, there were tears behind his eyes. He laid his hand on his father's arm. The face he saw was quiet, perhaps even peaceful, and the eyes were softer than he remembered having seen them in a long time. It wasn't until the waiter came a few minutes later that they spoke again.

'What are your plans?' his father wanted to know. Jonathan noticed the timid voice raising that question. He could not help a faint smile appearing on his lips.

'I would like to go back again to Andalusia,' he said quietly. His father nodded, as if he had anticipated the response. 'But I will postpone my departure to stay around for a few more weeks. From what I've heard they are doing quite well without me, so a few weeks more won't hurt anybody. Perhaps you and I can find an opportunity to meet again before I go. At the very least I do not want to leave without saying goodbye.'

73.

Welcome Back!

The community of Bethany was very excited when Sister Maria received the message that several people in Bethany had been waiting for: Jonathan Harrison would come back to Benacazón in a few weeks. It had been much longer than they had anticipated, and there had been doubts whether he would return at all.

Maria was elated when she got the news. Pascal had been running an errand for Antonio in the village, and stopped by her office to ask whether there was anything to could get for her.

'There is some news that I think will make you all in the pottery very happy!' she said. 'I had Jonathan Harrison on the phone this morning.'

'What did he say?' Pascal wanted to know.

'He will be coming back to Bethany in a couple of weeks.'

'Really! Yeah! That is great news! They will all be very happy, particularly Sofia!' the boy said with smirk on his face.

'That includes you?'

'Yeah, sure, if he doesn't start messing around with those beads again!' Maria saw Pascal was acting out his 'big boy' character that he had assumed lately, and grinned. 'I am sure you will tell him that when he gets back.'

Sofia was very happy to have Jonathan back in Bethany. The reason was the deep sense of comfort that he gave her. Had anyone asked, she would not have said she was in love with him, but the treasure she kept was a secret of her heart. It was the memory of the beads project. 'Do you allow me, my lady?' he had said with a gracious smile before he put the necklace of beads around her neck. Rarely had she been treated the way he did that afternoon, so courteously, and with such tender consideration for her feelings.

Antonio was someone else in Bethany who had missed Jonathan dearly. From the very beginning he had been pleased to have him around in the pottery. When he heard that Jonathan would not return immediately after his grandfather's funeral, Antonio was quite certain he would not return at all. Being reunited with his family again, he would not be able to tear himself away for a second time, or so Antonio believed.

What his boss couldn't know, of course, was the change that the young American had gone through since he returned to San Francisco. Once he had really taken in what Grandpa Harrison had told him, he couldn't help but see his father in a different light. Surely he could have done better at supporting his sons and acting like a true father, rather than a supervisor. But then Peter Harrison had never had someone to show him how that was done, parenting his two sons in such a way that they learned to trust the world and become their own person. Whatever Jonathan and his younger brother had managed to learn in this respect had been their mother's doing.

Jonathan's father was a different man now, at least in his son's eyes, and the unforeseen result was that the son had freed himself from the need to live up to his father's expectations. If Jonathan were to come back to Bethany it would be very different from the first time. He wouldn't be running from anything, or anybody.

It was a windy Friday afternoon in April of 1983 when he arrived at the railway station in Benacazón. Walking the tree-lined lane towards the house the dry southern wind was blowing in his face, making his arrival not as pleasant as he had anticipated, after an exhausting trip from San Francisco. When he stepped into the kitchen he found Claire and Sylvia busy. There were of course hugs and kisses, but the first exchanges on how they had been were brief. Most of all, he said, he wanted to rest for a while.

The Second Calling

'We have prepared your room,' Sylvia said. When they had been on the phone, Maria had already told him that he could have his old room, which she hoped would make his return to Bethany feel like coming home.

'You go, and lie down for a while,' Claire said, 'because you will need some energy tonight.'

'Why is that? I have no plans, I can assure you.'

'Perhaps you don't, but we do!' Sylvia said with a twinkle in her eyes. Before he could ask how that would involve him, Claire gestured that they were busy. 'You go and get some sleep, we have work to do here.' Without further comment he went upstairs for a nap.

The celebration of his homecoming party was to be that same night. They would start with a meal together; afterwards there would be music and dancing. Entering the dining hall that evening was a treat in itself. Flowers decorated the tables, garlands were hanging down from the ceiling, and candles lit up the room. The guests were received by Claire who was assisted by Alonso; together they acted as masters of ceremony. Claire pointed out where their seats were located, and Alonso would lead them to the chair she directed him to. He did it very graciously, with his big smile, and everybody felt as if they were the guest of honor.

Jonathan was seated next to Antonio and Maria. The seat opposite him was kept open for Ramón.

'Ramón is not here?' he asked unable to hide his disappointment at this news.

'Why? No, he will come, but he will be a bit later,' Maria said. Her answer faded away in a whisper because the master of ceremony was calling upon the guests.

'May I have your attention for a moment please,' Claire started while Sylvia was serving out sodas and drinks.

'When everyone is seated, we would like to start with a toast. Ladies and gentlemen, I give the floor to Don Antonio Ardiles from Galicia who together with Lucie will welcome Jonathan back into our community.' As she spoke, Alonso cheered her announcement, and was joined with hurrahs and bravos from everyone. With his arms up in the air he went over to Lucie, and gave her a hug.

'Friends, we are all very happy that the prodigal son has returned,' Antonio started, which immediately elicited a frown from Sister Maria. 'Never mind if you don't know what that means,' he continued. 'We lost him, and now he's back,' upon which the audience reacted with enthusiasm.

'To welcome Jonathan back home, Lucie wants to say something!'

'She can't speak!' Philippe yelled at him, as if he might not be aware of the fact.

'Can she not? Well you know that people speak in many different ways, don't they? And Lucie here has a very clear message.' While he said this, his hand went into his pocket from which he got a little paper bag. He gave it to Lucie. 'You go, and bring it to him,' he said, pointing her in Jonathan's direction. For once Lucie reacted by doing what she was told. She went over to Jonathan's chair and held up the little paper bag for him.

'That's for me?' He got up from his chair and accepted her gift. 'Thank you Lucie,' he said and gave her a kiss on her cheek. When he opened the bag a laugh appeared on his face before anyone could see what was in it. Out of the bag came a necklace made of beads!

A general excitement filled the dining hall, accompanied by many compliments and cheers. Jonathan looked at Antonio to signal his gratitude for the surprise gift, but his boss put up his usual blank face as if he had nothing to do with anything. Then he noticed Sofia's beaming eyes, and turned to her.

'I suspect you know more about this, don't you?' he said with a big smile. The young woman was thrilled by his attention, having feared for a moment that Lucie would get all of it.

'Hmmm,' she nodded conspiratorially, and produced one of her nervous giggles.

'Thank you all very much for this gift. It means a lot to me.' He turned again to Antonio who was still standing aside with both his hands on Lucie's shoulders. 'You may not know this, but when I left in January Antonio said he wouldn't mind when I came back to finish the beads project that we started after I first came to the pottery. I now find that you already have been working on it! What a nice surprise!'

'Okay, people, glasses up in the air,' Antonio commanded. Everybody followed his example and held their glass up to toast Jonathan's return. 'Here's to our friend, who was lost and now is back again!' he repeated.

When they had delivered their toast, the master of ceremony announced there were more speakers to welcome Jonathan, and Sofia would begin. Claire thought it wise to let her go first, noticing the level of excitement on the girl's reddened face. He gestured her assistant Alonso to go and move Sofia in her wheelchair to the middle of the room. When everybody was seated again, Sofia managed to get a piece of paper out of her bag, and kept it up to read what it said:

> *Dear Jonathan. We have missed you terribly since you went home. And now that you are back we are very happy. Thank you for returning to Bethany. We hope that this time you will stay forever!*

Everyone noticed the trembling voice with which this short speech was made, which occasioned a guarded response to Sofia's words. A few hands applauded, but without any comments. She had taken the opportunity to tell Jonathan of her feelings for him, which created a slightly awkward moment. Jonathan noticed it too, and thought it wise to stay on the safe side.

'Thank you, Sofia, for these kind words,' he said. 'Forever is perhaps a bit long, but I am definitely not planning to leave Bethany any time soon.'

'All right,' Claire jumped in, 'before we serve our dinner, there is time for one more. Who's next in line?'

'I will be next,' Maria volunteered.

'Of course our official supervisor needs to speak.' Antonio remarked with a quasi-serious look on his face.

'Be quiet, you,' Claire ordered him.

'Jonathan,' Maria started, 'I know you had a difficult time when you were in San Francisco with your family. You lost a beloved grandfather, which made us all pray for you when we heard the sad news. But from what you have told me, I also understood that when you left to return to Spain, it was in a different way than when you first came here. We are very glad that we have kept your room for you, and we hope you will soon feel that Bethany is your second home. Now I want to hand over this as a sign.' As a token of their appreciation for having him back she handed him over the set of keys that he had returned before he left.

For a brief moment Jonathan's memory went back to the conversation in his father's office a year-and-a-half ago that made him run. How different the second time had been! His father well understood that his son would not be working in his firm, at least not for the next few years, and he had not objected to his plans. 'If that's what you need to do,' he had said in a supportive manner, 'I won't keep you from it.' In fact, the father envied the son for having a place where friends were waiting for him to return. He had never enjoyed such friends, a fact about his life that he had dismissed by telling himself he didn't need anybody. How untrue! But it was only when he looked at himself with the eyes of his oldest son that Peter Harrison began to consider what he had missed.

'Thank you, Maria, for your kind words, and for these,' Jonathan said while holding up the keys she had given him. 'A house cannot be your home without a set of keys,' he continued, 'so with these in my pocket Bethany cannot be anything but my home!'

While he sat down Claire announced that it was time to start with their dinner if they didn't want to have cold food. 'So let's say grace and get started!' she said inviting them to join her. But before she could say anything further she was interrupted.

'Do I not get a chance to say something to our returning friend?'

'Ramón!'

As they had been listening to Maria's welcome speech, no one except Sylvia had noticed that Ramón had silently waited just outside the door before he entered. As soon as he saw him, Alonso was up on his feet and hugging him with his biggest smile. He took his hand to bring him to the empty seat opposite Jonathan. But before Ramón could even get started with what he wanted to say, the assistant master of ceremonies decided his time was up! He laid his hand on Ramón's face so as to seal his lips, and then turned to the crowd. In his inimitable language he announced the main course:

'Wadies an gen'men. Naw eat. Pasta!' Spreading his arms as to embrace all the spaghetti dishes that were brought into the room, Alonso cheered the food in such a way that the others could not help but follow him. Spreading their arms smiling they affirmed and made it sound like a blessing: 'And now we eat pasta!'

When they had finished their dinner, Sylvia produced her accordion, and it was time for songs, funny songs, silly songs, and spiritual songs. Though he barely managed to stay on his feet Jonathan was very happy. He had taken his life into his own hands instead of running away from it, and he felt this place and its people would not be easily abandoned this time. The evening went by with singing and dancing, accompanied with much laughter and joy. When the time had come to end the party Alonso placed himself in the middle of the room with his biggest smile, and pointed his two hands to the door: 'And naw, get out!' Everybody laughed, and applauded Claire, Alonso, and Sylvia for what had been a lovely evening.

74.

'You Can Always Bring Me Flowers!'

Various people in the House of Bethany each in their time were supplicants of unanswered prayers. One of them was Sofia Recuenco who was clearly infatuated with Jonathan Harrison. Knowing the girl quite well Antonio had noticed it, almost from the very first day. He was worried about Sofia's wounded heart, especially since the object of her admiration was not focused on her but to the one she in this respect considered her rival: Lucie Miles.

During Jonathan's 'six-weeks' interview, he had been challenged by Ramón to regard his zealous interest in the girl with different eyes. Now, after his return Jonathan tried to be more observant than his engaging ceramic beads-project had allowed him to be. But the enigma of Lucie's life continued to absorb his attention, mainly because of the question regarding the girl that Ramón had raised, which was what it meant for Lucie to be herself.

It didn't take long for Antonio to notice the change. Rather than figuring out ways to make Lucie part of their work in the pottery, Jonathan was no longer trying to mould her into something he considered more 'meaningful' than what he had previously called her 'impulse'.

But his relationship with Lucie was not Antonio's only concern, for he keenly observed that Sofia was once again continually attempting to please the young man whenever she could. Perhaps it was his own soft spot for the girl, feeding upon his own unhappy experience with her mother, that made Antonio anxious to protect her from being hurt. While he did not blame Jonathan for keeping her at arm's length, he wanted to avoid a situation where once more in her life Sofia would have reason to feel rejected, and become depressed because of it.

'Maybe you should give in a little,' he said to Jonathan when they were talking about Sofia. 'I have noticed how she tends to claim you, and how you respond by trying to keep your distance.'

'You think I should try to engage more?'

'That wouldn't hurt.' Antonio said. 'Instead of simply turning the other way you might say how you want to work with her and when. That might put her at ease, and stop her feeling left out. You've seen the source of her anxiety,' he said, meaning the incident with Sofia's mother the very first week after Jonathan had come to know the girl.

It was some time later that Sofia developed a troublesome wound on one of her feet. They had been consulting Doctor Henrique Solares who prescribed herbal ointment to massage her swollen foot, and keep it warm. It had to be attended daily in order not to cause lasting damage, he said.

'The most important thing is to activate blood circulation in her foot in order to help it heal itself. Without that I can prescribe anything I want but it is not going to work,' the doctor had instructed them. Ordinarily, assisting the girls with their personal care was Maria's and Claire's task, but Jonathan suggested that during her hours in the workshop he could look after Sofia's foot, when necessary.

One morning after their coffee time when they were ready to start work she bumped her wheelchair against the table she was trying to move away from, and her painful foot got caught in between.

'Shoot, stupid girl!' she shouted, furious with herself. 'That hurts!'

'Oh, dear, I am sure it does!' Jonathan said, turning around to bend over in order to look at her foot. Having obtained her permission, he touched it and found it was cold.

'Your foot feels much too cold,' he said looking up at her. 'That's not good at all.'

'What do you want, it's too swollen to put on my shoe. A sock on its own is not going to keep it warm.'

'Is it okay if I take your sock off and warm up your foot? Do you have the ointment with you?'

'Yes, of course. The ointment is in my bag at the back of the wheelchair,' she said. The prospect of having his undivided attention for more than a few minutes was itself sufficient for raising the girl's temperature, if not that of her foot then that of her soul. Red spots came up around her neck accompanied by the habitual nervous giggle.

'You know my feet are ticklish,' she said in a flirtatious manner. Jonathan noticed it, and did not respond. He kept a distance when she acted this way towards him. It reminded him too much of the way her mother had been trying to take him in.

'Tell me about your legs, dear.'

'What about them?'

'Tell me what happened that you cannot walk.'

'You know what happened!'

'Tell me again.'

His tone was serious, but not cold. He wanted to support her in getting out of her 'mother's darling' attitude that made her behave like a child. Behind this façade she could be a very different person as he had learned from working with her on the beads project. Then she had surprised him with a few casual remarks regarding Lucie. She had pointed out that Lucie's obsession with the paper balls in her hand might be just a game to deal with her anxiety of not knowing how to be Lucie. 'A bird with a broken wing,' she had said.

Sofia shrugged her shoulders. 'There is not much to tell,' she started. 'When I was little an infectious disease did something to my nervous system, and one of its effects was that I lost control over my legs. They stopped responding, and though I had been walking I lost the ability within a few weeks.' In the meantime Jonathan had anointed her foot and was rubbing it carefully. When he looked up to her face he noticed the red spots were gone.

'That must have made you very sad. Did it hurt a lot?'

'No, not really. From what I remember it was more like when you have a sleeping arm. The same numb feeling when you want to lift it but it doesn't respond. Weird rather than painful.'

'You must have been frightened.'

'No, not that I recall. I was only five years old. What did I know about things mothers hope for their daughters? But I remember being sad, very sad actually.'

She fell silent, and sat quiet for a while. Feeling she needed time, Jonathan focused on his massage with all the tenderness his hands could pass on to her aching soul.

'It wasn't about my legs. When the doctor said I was not going to walk any more, my parents changed. Especially mother. When I needed a wheelchair, she complained about it. I was like a favourite doll that had had a leg torn off.'

'What about your father?'

'I loved him very much, and he loved me. Whenever we were together he would soothe me, and say that being in a wheelchair was not the end of the world. But he was not a strong man in her presence. He never said a word when she was complaining about me.'

'What was she complaining of?'

'All the trouble my stupid legs caused her! I was the apple of her eye but you know, everything needed to be perfect. You've seen her. I always feel awkward when she calls me "mummy's darling". I feel like I am a china teacup with a broken handle that can no longer be displayed on the tray of perfect things.'

Jonathan let her words sink in. Then he asked, 'I recall hearing her say she hoped you would walk again some day. What was that all about? I did hear her say that, didn't I?'

'Rubbish! She knows perfectly well that's not going to happen, has known it all along. She's acting out the compassionate mother. I hate it.'

Jonathan was surprised to see her nervous behaviour was now gone completely. Look at this self-composed young woman! he thought. Being attached to her narcissistic mother must make her weak, at least in her presence. Carina Recuenco had no talent for dealing with imperfection. Any daughter of hers was supposed to be beautiful, not disabled!

Now that Jonathan had seen Sofia in this way, he realized that even Antonio's habitual manner of responding to her in a protective way came from a presumption of weakness. No doubt he was really fond of her, but apparently this was a remainder of his past together with her mother.

'How is that foot of yours coming along? Does it feel any better?' he asked while continuing his gentle massage.

'I was just going to say my other foot feels quite cold too.' He looked up and saw a grin on her face.

'Yeah, I bet it does,' he smiled. Then, after a second, he thanked her for sharing her story with him. But she made a dismissive gesture.

'I should thank you for asking me these questions. And for rubbing my foot, of course, that was very nice.'

'Any time! If there is anything I can do for you, just let me know,' he said. He rose from sitting on his knees during the foot massage and he looked her in the face just in time to see a twinkle in her eye. She had put up her girlish face again.

'You can always bring me flowers!' she said, and produced one of her nervous giggles.

Part X

Earthen Vessels

75.

The Gift From the Pottery

After the difficult year when Lucie Miles had arrived, culminating symbolically in a disastrous fire, the community of Bethany entered into a new life with Ramón's return from his sabbatical, no less symbolically celebrated with the inauguration of its new chapel. Bethany had changed in how its life together was experienced. 'Celebrating the lives that God has given us to live', they had learned, did not only mean the lives of those who came because they needed assistance. If Bethany was truly a sign, it was only because there was no unequal division between them in the economy of giving and receiving. There were different roles and responsibilities, to be sure, but the differences did not concern the soul of their community.

Philippe and Alfredo were now the seniors among its members. Even though Alfredo was much younger than Philippe, who was already in his late-forties, his crooked bones made him appear much older than he was. Fernando and Alonso, had been boys when they first came to Bethany. They were now sturdy youngsters. The first of them, Fernando was now twenty years old; Alonso was one year his elder, Joaquin was eighteen. Only Pascal, now twelve, was still a boy, even though he would dispute it, Lucie was thriving, which was an achievement in its own right. She had grown into a young woman, of now nineteen years of age. Finally there was Sofia, who continued her love-hate relationship with the other girl, behaving as her big sister of twenty-three.

So it happened that after these years of growth, *La Casa di Bethania*, as was its official name, had arrived at the end of its second lustrum. Since previous anniversaries had passed without celebrations, mainly because of lack of money, they didn't want to let another anniversary go by unnoticed, and planned a celebration.

It was a truly impressive event. Maria had put together a picture book with snapshots of all the people who in one way or another had been part of Bethany's history. There were visitors and gifts from all over the country, and even a few from abroad. The House of Bethany had obviously been drawing many people's attention.

The highlight of the celebration had been a very special gift. It was a gift for the chapel from the pottery, and its presentation had been a special moment. Ramón had put his hand over his mouth when he first saw it; he had been in awe, and with tearful eyes he had thanked each one of them from the bottom of his heart.

Antonio and his crew had outdone themselves in craftsmanship. They had produced a mural of ceramic tiles, and placed it on the wall of the chapel, to the left of the entrance. It was the first thing that caught the eye when people were walking towards the chapel through the orchard. When they were close enough they could see it showed a biblical scene: Jesus visiting a place called Bethany.

It had taken months of preparation. In fact they had started it as soon as the plans for rebuilding the chapel had been confirmed. Keeping the secret of what was going to be their anniversary gift was a great burden on those who were in on it. Producing the tiles for the mural had been by far their biggest project together. They treasured its story and when the anniversary was over they recalled what a wonderful time working on it had been.

The idea of this gift had come about in conversation over coffee about six months before the actual anniversary, on a Monday morning in November 1984. Jonathan was going with them through the round of sharing weekend experiences while Antonio was preparing the kiln for some pots to be finished. Pascal was telling them about his trip to Seville with an uncle who had visited him for the weekend. When his uncle noticed the pride he took in his work in the pottery, he had suggested paying a visit to one of the great Andalusian potteries in the city.

'Wow!' Antonio said, as he arrived just in time to join them in learning about Pascal's trip, 'checking out the competition hey? Where did you go?'

'To a factory, I think it was named *Cerámica Santa Isabel*. It specializes in pots and jugs.'

'They're very good, the best, and famous all over the world,' Antonio said with great authority, 'that is the place to be in our trade.'

Pascal had been delighted with his visit to this factory. It was in Triana, in a part of the city across the river. It was not only known for its pottery, but also for its *flamenco* music and dance. But the pottery had been his main interest.

'The jugs they make are about the size of a tall man, someone like Señor Miles,' Pascal said, 'but with your belly!' he added, pointing to Antonio. The target of his joke made a dismissive gesture with his hand. Everybody laughed. 'They're just huge,' Pascal continued. 'Even more exciting were the paintings on tiles. You see them everywhere in the city. I wish we could make some of those in our pottery.'

Antonio raised his brows. 'Become a real *ceramista*, you mean?'

Pascal's face glowed. 'I would love to learn much more about it.'

'Maybe we can try a few tiles,' the artist had responded, boldly. Jonathan looked at him with surprise, not used to his boss being ready to try new things.

That was how they got started. Everybody had been fired up about it, and their first attempts at painted tiles were sufficiently successful to keep everybody going. They were six coloured tiles with simple geometrical motifs. Antonio was pleased to discover he still had the skill to do it, and was extremely proud of the first results. When they had brought them into the house to be shown at the dinner table, everybody who had not seen them yet was excited.

The next day, Antonio announced that the time had come to take on a bigger project. 'You know that in a few months' time, we will have a big celebration?' he said while they were having their coffee.

'What celebration? Someone's birthday?' Sofia had asked.

'A birthday all right, but not someone's,' Jonathan pointed out. 'The House of Bethany will have its tenth anniversary in May next year.'

'Who told you so?' Sofia wanted to know.

'Claire did,' he answered.

'What makes the tenth birthday a special occasion?' Pascal asked. The tone he brought to the question was quite sceptical, but several inquisitive faces around the table suggested they also wanted to know.

'Uhh…,' Jonathan started, 'because….'

'Because we didn't celebrate any of the nine anniversaries that preceded it!' The authority Antonio gave to his response was sufficient for everyone to leave it at that. He immediately captured their attention when he continued:

'I was thinking about surprising our friends with a special gift for the chapel, something only we can do.' He could have chosen no better words to get everyone on the edge of their seats. Even Jonathan's curiosity was rising now that he saw the artist was serious about what he said.

'What is that?' they wanted to know.

'We know we can make tiles, because we have proved it. Now I was thinking we could make a picture of painted tiles.' He picked up a book from the table next to him. 'Here is an example of what I have in mind.' He showed them the picture.

'Alfredo would you be so kind as to tell Joaquin what you see.' Alfredo did as he was asked and described in words a stunning tableau showing Cervantes' hero Don Quixote and his aide Sancho Panza. It was the very same tableau that had brought Antonio and Ramón together. The tiles were beautifully coloured. 'It is from one of the famous factories in Seville,' Antonio added.

'We cannot make something as beautiful as this,' Pascal said in awe of what he saw. Sofia looked disappointed, apparently taking Pascal's remark as a final verdict on their boss' audacious suggestion.

'No, we perhaps cannot. But we can make something that may come close,' Antonio responded. Pascal and the others only had a vague notion of his past in one of the great ceramic factories in Seville, where he had made such tiles. 'Do you want to give it a try? We all keep it a secret. If it doesn't work out well, we forget about it, and nobody will ever know we couldn't do it. What do you think?'

Everyone had been in favour. Pascal and Sofia were elated. 'We need a design, or a picture to copy.' Alfredo's eyes sparkled, thinking of a possibility to make a drawing for Ramón. Only Joaquin was quiet. Jonathan immediately noticed it and hinted in his direction. His boss nodded that he saw what he meant, and continued,

'Well, let's see who can do what. We need someone to make the tiles. They have to be cast in moulds before the paint can be put on. Joaquin, could that be your job?'

Joaquin's face brightened. 'Yes,' he said. 'If Pascal and Fernando will assist me, I can produce moulded tiles.'

'Then we need someone to put on the drawings. A very precise task, I think that is Alfredo's job. I will assist him with the colours. All agreed?'

Sofia did not respond wholehearted to this proposal as she had hoped she would be assigned this important task. Antonio saw her disappointment. 'We also need someone to glaze the tiles. It needs to be done very carefully. Is that something that you could do for us, Sofia?'

'Oh, sure! Yes, sure!' her mood instantly changed and her face flushed with excitement.

'Pascal and I will bake them. If everybody tries hard, I am certain we will make something that will please Ramón and the others very much,' Antonio concluded.

'Excuse me,' Jonathan interrupted him, 'And where do Lucie and I fit in, if I may ask?' His quasi-indignant face did not entirely succeed, which made the pottery crew ready for a joke from their boss.

'You will have the most important job, without which there won't be any tiles!'

'Now what might that be?'

'Keeping Lucie away from smashing them on the floor!' Although the prospect of the girl spoiling their work was potentially alarming, even Sofia couldn't help laughing at him.

'You think this is funny?' Jonathan continued his play, upon which the young woman started giggling uncontrollably. When she had calmed down, Pascal, with his usual down-to-earth attitude, had another question.

'The only thing left is to find a picture,' Pascal commented. 'What would be a nice scene that would suit our chapel?'

'Does anyone know why the house is called Bethany?' Jonathan wanted to know.

'I don't,' Sofia said. 'Me neither,' Joaquin added. It turned out that among the members only Alfredo knew something about the story.

'What story?' Sofia wanted to know.

'Ramón once told it, a long time ago. I do not really remember it well. It had something to do with Jesus visiting a place called Bethany.'

'Not bad for a start,' Antonio said. 'It's a story from the Bible. Now, why don't I read it to you, so that we all know it?'

'Yes, do! I want to hear it.' Sofia was thrilled about having the story read. So were the others. Antonio went into his messy office to get the copy of an illustrated Bible he had somewhere. He found it on a dusty shelf hidden between lots of other forgotten things. When he got back to his seat, he started to flip the pages of the book, but he had no idea where to look, or how to find what he was looking for.

'Sorry, can't find it in here.'

'Give it to me, I will ask Maria,' Jonathan suggested, 'she will know.' Having found Maria and Lucie in her apartment she had shown where to look. When he came back he told them, 'It is in the Gospel of John.' He gave the book opened to Antonio and sat down with the others to listen.

'No, why me? You read it!' He handed the book back to Jonathan, who began:

> *Six days before the Passover, Jesus came to Bethany, where Lazarus lived, whom Jesus had raised from the dead.*
>
> *Here a dinner was given in Jesus' honor.*
>
> *Martha served, while Lazarus was among those reclining at the table with him.*
>
> *Then Mary took about a pint of pure nard, an expensive perfume; she poured it on Jesus' feet and wiped his feet with her hair.*
>
> *And the house was filled with the fragrance of the perfume.*
>
> *But one of his disciples, Judas Iscariot, who was later to betray him, objected, 'Why wasn't this perfume sold and the money given to the poor? It was worth a year's wages.'*
>
> *He did not say this because he cared about the poor but because he was a thief; as keeper of the moneybag, he used to help himself to what was put into it.*
>
> *'Leave her alone,' Jesus replied. 'It was intended that she should save this perfume for the day of my burial. You will always have the poor among you, but you will not always have me.'*

When he was finished Jonathan closed the book. Everybody was silent.

'What does it mean?' Sofia asked, looking around.

'Fortunately that is a question the artist does not have to answer,' Antonio replied dryly. 'The question for us is, do we see a picture?'

'Sure, I do. I see a house with Jesus and the two women, and the man Judas.' Pascal reacted.

'It seems we have our picture!' Antonio concluded triumphantly indicating that now all was set to start the work.

'That will be a fine picture,' Alfredo said, just in case someone had forgotten that he was supposed to be the one to draw it. 'Where are we going to put the tableau?'

'Imagine how it will look when placed on the chapel wall beside the entrance,' Antonio responded. Everyone agreed. There could not be a better place for it!

76

The Anniversary

After the celebration of the anniversary the house was full of memories of what had been a great event. The celebration lasted for three days. It was indeed a feast of gratitude for all they had received. Everywhere signs of congratulations and presents, pictures, drawings, and cards covered the walls of Bethany's dining hall. Many people came to offer their gifts, gifts for the house itself, gifts of recognition of what they were trying to do.

Among them was the mayor of Benacazón who came with a special mission, which was to make Ramón an honorary citizen of her village. She had helped them to the municipal permissions they needed for starting the pottery, and later for building Lucie's apartment, then again for building and rebuilding the chapel. Each time she had personally intervened to speed up the application procedures, and now she had come to collect her reward as the mayor whose vision had foreseen that this community was special and had helped it to survive and thrive. On every occasion that the local media reported about the event, she made sure she was in the picture, even to the point where Claire and Maria started to comment on her omnipresence.

Ramón would have none of it, however, and persistently excused her.

'She is a politician and politicians need attention. It's part of their job.'

'The woman meddles in everything!' Claire said.

'That's why she has been appointed mayor. She's just good at her job.'

'Oh, you're such a noble man,' Claire retorted. 'You would even excuse Beelzebub for being good at his job.' Occasionally Claire's southern temper would play out, and when it came to dealing with local authorities her past made itself felt.

The celebration of Bethany's anniversary went by with receiving dignitaries of various ranks and colours, all of which were cleverly used by Ramón to get support for their bank accounts, which were always short of funds. He made a great deal out of the invitation to visit the archbishop's palace in Seville again, to which he took Pascal, Alfredo, Alonso, and Sofia with him.

Sofia was beside herself with pride that she had been chosen for this visit, and got a new dress for the occasion. The archbishop was very pleasant. He had asked questions to each individual about how they were doing. When they left, Monsignor Romero gave them his blessing. 'It was a pleasure to meet with all of you again. Please, come back some time,' he said as they left.

'How did we do, Ramón?' Sofia wanted to know as soon as they were on their way home.

'You did very well. I think the archbishop was impressed by you all.' They were in high spirits, and on the train back to Benacazón they were singing and laughing. Ramón smiled his gentle smile. 'No doubt there will be difficulties ahead,' he said to himself, 'but we certainly have learned how to celebrate.'

By the end of the third day everybody was very tired. There had been so many gifts that it would take at least another day to really appreciate them and send thank you cards to all the people who had given them. On the programme that night was a party with music and dance for anyone who happened to be around.

In the afternoon the team assigned with decorating the dining room headed by Maria was busy with garlands, flowers, and candles. Others were assisting Claire and Sylvia in the kitchen to prepare the meal they would have together to start the evening. Antonio was in the pottery, keeping an eye at Lucie together with Jonathan.

Ramón was taking a nap in his room upstairs, which Claire had insisted upon. 'You will wear yourself out, then you're no good to anybody.'

'That will make two of us then,' he had retorted. He had planned to spend some time alone in the chapel. But nonetheless he had obeyed her, because he was indeed exhausted after days of receptions and interviews.

Maria was just passing the hall with a bucket of flowers from the garden when there was a knock on the front door. Thus far they had managed to keep the number of unexpected visitors to a minimum. As it was, the programme had been stimulating enough, and they had to work hard to keep Lucie calm. Philippe had also been excited more than was good for him. Maria said to herself, 'Oh, please, not now!' when she heard that knock on the door.

She took a deep breath to open it, still undecided whether to invite the unexpected visitor into the house. The man in front of her was a farmer; that much she could see. He had his straw hat in his hand, and was looking down at his boots. He seemed very timid. She could not see his face, but immediately felt that this was not an ordinary visit.

'Sir?' Maria asked, slightly alarmed. 'What can I do for you?'

The man in front of her remained as he stood there for a moment, then he spoke. 'Uh… Hmmm… I am…'

She did not hear the name he gave her, since it was spoken almost in a whisper, with his face still to the ground. When he finally lifted it, she saw the man had tears in his eyes. Then he took a deep breath.

'I am… Fernando's father,' he said softly.

Maria tried but could not speak. Inadvertently she put a hand for her mouth. She was usually a very composed woman, but his introduction made her knees go weak. From the very first day they had met Fernando had been special to her. Of her friends in Bethany only Ramón knew that since her early childhood Maria herself had been an orphan, which was why she had a soft spot for the young man. That children lose their parents is bad enough, but that their parents could just dump them? This had always escaped her. 'How could he?' she had said more than once to Claire about Fernando's father. Now, after more than ten years he had decided to show up at his son's house. She was simply shocked.

'Oh my…. Fernando's father,' she said while her voice cracked. Unsure whether she was about to cry, shout, or yell at him, she turned away from the door, leaving him standing there, and ran into the kitchen.

'Claire… Claire… Oh, Claire!' Maria cried.

'What is it? What happened?' Claire asked alarmed that something was seriously wrong. Her first thought was that something had happened to Ramón.

77

Fernando's Father

'There is a man ... He says he is Fernando's father. Fernando's father is on the doorstep.'

Claire let out a sigh of relief. 'Really? Surprise, surprise. Well, did you leave him there? Bring him in.'

'But ...'

'Come on, dear,' Claire put an arm around her shoulders, 'you can handle this.' She knew about Maria's bond with Fernando. 'Invite him into my office, I will wake up Ramón.'

When Ramón entered the room a few minutes later, the farmer was still standing with his hat in his hands, even though Maria had offered him a chair. Both had been silent, finding no words to share.

'Señor Linares,' Ramón said with both hands stretched out. 'What a pleasure to meet you!' The man had clearly not expected this welcome for one who had dumped his child at their doorstep. Even Maria was taken by surprise by his gesture.

'I... uh... I...' he stammered.

'Please, let's sit down first,' Ramón offered him a chair. 'Maria could you perhaps get something to drink for Señor Linares? What would you like? Coffee? Lemonade? Something stronger perhaps?'

'Oh... no... thank you, no I am fine,' the man said, still overwhelmed. 'I heard about the celebration of the anniversary of this house, and...'

'And?'

'And what you all had done… and then I saw pictures in the newspaper, and… I… I felt such a bastard!' He broke down and sobbed terribly. Ten years of suppressed guilt were running down his cheeks. Maria couldn't help being moved when she saw Ramón getting up from his chair, and laying his arm around Mr Linares' shoulder.

'It must have been very hard on you, I reckon.'

'He was a sweet boy, my Fernando,' Mr Linares spoke softly, while the tears were running from his eyes. 'But it took so much time…. and I had to work so hard …. so that we could eat, but…'. Again he broke down. Now that he was finally opening his heart, Ramón thought it was better to have it all out before he clammed up again, like his son had done. He encouraged him to continue.

'But…?

'I had no patience with him…. as I should have had.'

'Hmmm.'

Mr Linares began to calm down. 'I saw on TV what they reported about this house. Then I knew what I had known all along… A good father doesn't send his son away … because of ….his lack of patience.' He broke down once more and sobbed again. The man was in bad shape, his misery almost too unbearable to witness. In spite of her strong condemnation of him as a father, even Maria could not help feeling sorry for the man.

'Do you want to take him home?' Ramón asked. He didn't seem to be alarmed about the idea; at least he did not show it.

Mr Linares cleared his throat. 'Oh, no. I don't think I have a right to. He is a grown man now…' He hesitated a moment. 'But I would love to see him. You think I can see him?'

'We don't see any harm in that, do we, Maria? Though I think we should first ask Fernando.' Maria kept her silence, feeling that Ramón was not done yet.

'Maybe we should prepare your son a bit for seeing his father after all these years, don't you think?' Mr Linares seemed to agree as he vaguely nodded.

'May I ask where you are staying?'

'I am staying in Benacazón.'

'Could you come back tomorrow?'

Since Mr Linares had not planned a longer stay, he did not immediately respond. He understood that he could not just burst into his son's life after ten years at his own convenience, so after a brief hesitation he responded positively.

'Good. I am glad. That's settled then,' Ramón said kindly. 'We will see you tomorrow, let's say about eleven.' Mr Linares took his hat when Maria and Ramón got up to show him out. They shook hands at the doorstep. When they saw him leaving Bethany, he appeared a bit taller to Maria than when she had first seen him.

'How are we going to prepare Fernando for this?' she asked Ramón.

'We are not going to, at least not tonight. Everyone is preparing for a wonderful evening, that's preparation enough for one day, don't you think?'

'What about tomorrow then?'

'I am not sure yet, but my sense is that we tell Fernando shortly before Mr Linares arrives that there is someone important for him to see.'

'That's all?'

'No; I will speak to Joaquin beforehand, maybe even tonight. He will be the one to handle this, better than anyone else could. Trust me, you'll see.'

Before Fernando's father arrived the next morning, they took the two buddies into Claire's office. Ramón had indeed informed Joaquin the evening before. He was someone who would rather not be taken by surprise in a situation like this. They sat down and Joaquin laid his hand on Fernando's arm as he always did when they walked together.

'Fernando, there is something important I have to tell you,' his friend began. There was no response to this message on Fernando's face. 'There is a visitor coming for you this morning.' This time Fernando's eyes were moving nervously up and down.

'Fernando, your father is coming to visit you.' Joaquin spoke very carefully and slowly. His friend's face lost all its colour, which Joaquin could not see, of course, but he felt the trembling arm. He searched for his friend's hands, and when he found them, he noticed Fernando was close to panicking.

'It's all right ... I will be with you. It's all right.' Fernando's face showed he was terribly frightened. When Ramón noticed this, he stepped in.

'Do you want to see your father, Fernando? You don't have to if you choose not to.' When there was no response, Joaquin repeated Ramón's question. 'Do you want to see him?' Again there was no response.

The scene touched Maria in a way that made her shiver, probably because she had never been so close to her own pain. She got up from her chair, laid her arm around Fernando's shoulders and without saying a word she kissed him on his cheek. He looked at her with downcast eyes. At that moment Claire came in.

'Fernando's visitor has arrived. Shall I show him in?'

'Do you want to see him?' Joaquin asked again.

Then, barely noticeably, the big man nodded. He would see his father. When a moment later Mr Linares stepped in the room, Maria saw the same shrunken man again that she had found on their doorstep the day before, his head bowed down, holding the rim of his straw hat in both hands. He didn't dare to look up.

Fernando's face looked almost grey when he saw him, as if the pain had sucked all his blood. He was trembling. Then, just when Joaquin was trying to find his hands, there was a whisper.

'Dad.'

Fernando had spoken his first word in ten years. Though hardly audible it struck his friends in the room like lightning. His father, who could not know what was going on, saw Maria rooted to the spot. Joaquin's mouth fell open, and even Ramón, despite his usual composure, had a bewildered look on his face.

'Fernando.' When his father took a step forward and stretched out both hands, his son hesitated, but then he took them. The two men fell into each other's arms. The atmosphere in the room was filled with grief and sorrow. Maria felt her heart aching and wept. When she looked at Ramón she saw he had laid his hands upon Joaquin's shoulders to comfort him.

78.

A Colleague in Heaven

Why was the house they shared together called Bethany? It was a question that was on Pascal's mind from the moment they had decided to try a *mural de azulejos* as a gift for its tenth anniversary. They had picked the story of Bethany for a picture, a story that Alfredo had heard many years ago. But why this name had been chosen for their house Pascal still didn't know. The week after the celebrations were over he had a chance to ask Ramón about it. They happened to be walking together on their way to Sanlúcar. It was a warm day late in the spring, and the fields around them were filled with wild flowers.

'I have a question for you,' the young man began. 'When we were preparing for the mural on the chapel we found a story about Bethany that was taken from the Bible, but nobody knew exactly why the house is called Bethany?'

Ramón did not answer right away.

'You gave the house this name, didn't you?'

'Hmmm.'

'Why?'

'Do you remember the story?'

'Vaguely. We read it before we started to work on the mural.'

'It's from one of the books in the New Testament that tell us about the life of Jesus. Bethany was a small village, just a few miles away from Jerusalem. At the time it was probably no more than a colony of lepers.'

'What's that?'

'When people were infected by a dangerous disease that might affect a whole town they were sent away. Leprosy was such a disease. People who suffer from it are called lepers. In those days they often gathered in a place outside the city walls where they could stay and hope to survive. Bethany might have been such a place. The people who lived there were probably very poor, and were more or less ignored. On their way to Jerusalem Jesus and his friends were often among such people, so it is not unlikely they probably knew some of the villagers in Bethany.'

'They weren't afraid to become ill too?'

'That the story doesn't tell, but I guess they didn't have much of a choice since they were poor themselves, and they were strangers from Galilee, which is the northern part of Israel. Without money and power they were not very welcome in Judea, so they had nowhere else to go to. It is quite surprising that we even know the story of such insignificant people.'

'Why do you think is that?'

'Hard to say. Most likely their preaching had a lot to do with it. They told people God loved them and would be with them if they did not despise and abandon one another – as they were despised and abandoned by the rest of their society – and if they would share whatever means they had. That was the one treasure they had, the love of God.'

Pascal had to let this sink in for a moment. They went on in silence. Ramón glanced at his earnest face. Then he continued.

'There is a saying about this treasure that connects it to your pottery,' he said. The boy turned his face with a curious look towards him.

'How is that?'

'The followers of Jesus spoke of themselves as having this treasure in earthen vessels.'

'Earthen vessels, why?'

'They compared their own bodies to earthen vessels that were easily broken. Life was not very secure for these people, you see.

Powerful rulers could do away with them, scare them off their land, take their women, and rob them of the scant livestock they had. But they knew their faith in God would save them from living in fear. That was their treasure, not having to live in fear because they had faith. "We hold this treasure in earthen vessels",' they said, knowing they could be smashed as easily as a damaged pot.'

Pascal shivered in the fresh morning sun, and fell silent again. Ramón very well understood why. When he came to Bethany as a little boy he had known more about living in fear than was healthy for a child of his age. Even though he didn't speak about his memories from that time, he remembered a dark and cold room in his mother's house. It had been a gloomy house. No light, no warmth.

Suddenly he turned to Ramón and said, 'That is why the house is called Bethany, isn't it?' It came out of the blue, as if he had seen in a flash what Ramón was telling him. 'You gave the house this name because you think we too are earthen vessels that are easily broken.'

'That is a part of it,' Ramón said in a gentle voice, 'but I like the treasure part better. When we trust that we are loved, we do not have to live in fear.'

'I also like that part better,' Pascal said softly, and looked up towards the man walking beside him. They went on with their hands in their pockets, and didn't speak for a while. The boy kicked a stone away that was lying on the road at the point where the dirt road began. Soon they would be able to see the house.

'There is yet another link with your pottery,' Ramón started again.

'Why do you call it *my* pottery?'

'Nothing in particular, I just think it is the place where you belong, just like Bethany is your house, even when you share it with the rest of us.'

'So, what's the other link?'

'God is also named as a potter.' Ramón made this remark sound mysterious. Pascal looked at him confused.

'Who says so?'

'Several people. Jeremiah, Isaiah, Paul.'

'Who are they?'

'There are books and letters from them in the Bible. When they compare people to vessels they name God as the potter. 'God is like a potter who moulds his clay to make a vessel, and if when working at his wheel he spoils it, he will rework it into another vessel, as pleases him.' That's from Jeremiah; he is called a prophet. Something similar is found in a letter by Paul, one of the apostles, 'Cannot God do with his clay what he wants, and make different things from the same lump of clay?' I think he means people. God moulds different people, as it pleases him.'

'Why are you telling me this?' Pascal wanted to know.

'I thought you might like to know you have a colleague in heaven,' Ramón said it as if he was joking. 'It proves what a serious business you're in!'

'No kidding, seriously.'

'The image is telling us that we are in God's hands. He has made us as we are. We don't need to be different, as long as we don't forget he has made us like earthen vessels with a treasure inside, the treasure of his love.'

'And this I need to know?'

'It kind of helps me in times of trouble. It might help you too.'

'Like when you had your troubles with Lucie?'

'Like that, yes.'

Now it was Ramón's turn to remain silent for a few minutes, which made Pascal wonder whether he had asked the wrong question. When he asked him, Ramón said it was all right.

'Your question reminded me of something. No, I am actually glad you asked me this.' he said without further explanation.

Pascal had no clue what his friend was telling him, but he was used to Ramón speaking in riddles. Responding with a grin on his face he said:

'Oh, don't mention it. I am happy to clear up your puzzled mind any time!' Ramón laughed and patted him on the shoulder. 'Where would my puzzled mind be without you?'

In the meantime they had arrived at the gate. When a few moments later Pascal entered the workshop, he greeted Antonio and Jonathan together with the pottery crew with a joyous remark about what he had just learned.

'Friends, you probably did not know this, but it appears we have a colleague in heaven!' he boldly looked at their puzzled faces.

'How so?' Alfredo wanted to know.

'God has made us earthen vessels with a treasure inside,' Pascal responded.

'Well that explains everything!' Antonio said having no clue what the boy was talking about. Pascal told them about his conversation with Ramón, and how he had explained the choice of 'Bethany' as the name of their house. When he was finished Antonio spread his arms to gesture that it confirmed what he had always known.

'The Good Lord moulding his creatures like earthen vessels! Haven't I always told you pottery is a divine art?'

79.

The Market Fair

When Jonathan was past his 'six weeks' interview he had spent a late afternoon together with Antonio at the *cantina* in Benacazón. Both of them had enjoyed it so much that after Jonathan's return they decided to go there once a week, whenever possible. Usually they went on Friday afternoon after the work in the pottery was finished. Occasionally they took some of the men with them.

Alfredo especially loved to join them, even though walking to the village was far from easy for him. On these occasions he turned out to be a great storyteller, which he proved more than once after a jug of beer.

It was on one of these Friday afternoons that Alfredo told them about how as a little boy he used to visit market fairs with his mother. The family on his mother's side were farmers, so the month of October was the busiest time of the year for them. His mother was frequently asked to help out when they were short of hands with harvesting or picking fruits.

Since the old days, harvesting fruits, corn, or grain went hand in hand with the slaughter of animals in order to provide the family with food through the wintertime. With all these activities came harvest festivals and market fairs in autumn. There was music and dance, and as a child he used to like watching the festivities.

'October was often the best month of the year,' Alfredo concluded with a note of nostalgia in his voice.

'Do they still have these market fairs?' Antonio wanted to know.

'Sure they do. Why?'

'Hmmm. I was thinking that maybe we could go and try to sell some of the stuff that comes from Bethany. You know we did so years ago here in the village, but then we stopped going when they took the fair to Olivares. Listening to you I am just wondering if we shouldn't join the market fair in Olivares this year.'

'I am sure Claire would love it,' Jonathan agreed. 'The other day I heard her wondering what to do with all the produce that will come from the garden and from the orchard in the next few weeks.'

Over the years issues like this had come up several times. Thus far Antonio had refused to take on commissions for pottery work because he thought the pressure to deliver might easily become too much. Not only because of the presence of Lucie, but also because members like Sofia and Alfredo were quite vulnerable when it came to their energy, and he wanted to avoid putting any pressure on them. As a result, the pottery's products – pots, bowls, vases – were everywhere in the house, some of them used in the kitchen, others in people's own rooms. The rest went to relatives and friends for birthday gifts. Occasionally Antonio shipped a collection of the better pieces to a shop in Seville to be sold, but the revenues were modest. The ability to produce *azulejos* for tableaus like they made for Bethany's anniversary showed that its potters had much more potential than this arrangement suggested.

Something similar was true of the garden and the orchard. Claire had been very efficient in getting at least two crops from the garden most of the time, and the trees in the orchard in an average year had more fruit than they could eat, while she lacked the time for jams, juices, and other products. A substantial sale at an autumn market fair would be very welcome.

When the men came back for dinner from Carlos's *cantina* there was the usual hustle and bustle in the kitchen.

'Okay, Sylvia, we can start to serve dinner, the beer brothers have arrived.' Claire knew they loved her innocent jokes on their camaraderie, which for quite different reasons were hugely boosting the egos of characters like Philippe and Pascal.

'Alfredo kept us hanging out with his stories, don't blame me,' Antonio would say to increase the effect of her jest.

'I don't blame you. I know you must follow when you're out with real men.'

Still a boy Pascal would grow an inch in self-esteem when Claire said things like that, even though he knew she was joking. Looking at his bold manners she remembered her first thought the day he came to Bethany: 'the eyes of a wounded deer.' Look at him now!

At the dinner table that evening the men brought up what they had discussed about the market fair. As Jonathan had predicted, Claire was thrilled.

'Oh, yes, what a great idea!' she said. 'We could sell a lot of stuff to local people, which is important, you know. We need strong connections with the local community.'

The market fair of Olivares would be in four weeks and soon the house bristled with activity. This year the harvest of plums turned out to be especially good. There were also tons of pears to be picked.

But not only the garden and the orchard were the center of all this activity. The pottery was also preparing for a big sale. The first attempt to produce *azulejos* had resulted in single tiles with geometrical motifs that were used in the kitchen. They could produce many more of those, apart from the pots and bowls they had made, not to speak of the ceramic beads that Jonathan had found.

The fair was held on a Saturday at the end of October. Remembering the adventure with the wagon a few years ago, when in returning from the music festival in Olivares they had hit a huge stone in the middle of the road, it was decided that Jonathan would rent a van for the occasion. On the Friday afternoon before the fair, the van was loaded with boxes with the things they had wrapped up and priced to be sold. Jonathan would set off early, taking Pascal and Philippe with him. Antonio and Claire and the others would go later by train.

The day started pleasantly. After a long hot summer, the first month of autumn usually was a lovely time of the year in Andalusia, with clear skies, a fresh breeze, and a pleasant temperature. The market square in Olivares was normally a cozy place where men and women of the village met in the evening under the elms to chat and gossip about the day's events, while small children were playing and running around. The buildings surrounding the plaza were a mix of family homes and businesses, mainly hotels and restaurants.

On the Saturday morning of the fair the square was filled with market stands that were lined up for farmers and craftsmen who had bought a permit in the town hall on the day before. To secure a place for the people of Bethany, Maria had visited the village on her way to Seville to get two of these permits, one for the pottery, the other for the garden. Jonathan had left very early in the morning to be able to secure a fine spot. Pascal and Philippe were busy with laying out all the goods with Jonathan's assistance when the train passengers arrived. It was eight thirty in the morning.

'Good morning guys,' Antonio greeted them, 'this is a quite nice place you've got us here.'

'Hello,' Claire joined in, 'look how hard they have been working!'

'Hi, Jonathan,' Sofia said with a nervous giggle, 'the stand looks mighty fine, I am sure we will sell a lot of things today.'

'Good morning you all,' he greeted them, 'taking a late train so you knew the work was done, hey?'

'No we didn't,' Sofia protested. 'I had to get up at six this morning!'

'All right, all right,' he said. Looking at them gathered in front of the two stands, Jonathan pointed to a dozen chairs that were piled aside of them. 'I went to the bar over there,' he pointed out, 'and asked them whether they had party seats. They did, ten euros for the day. I took them. No objections I hope?'

Of course Antonio knew his way with this. 'Spending our money even before we have sold anything, did you? And you were supposed to be a business man?' His broad smile made Jonathan laugh.

'Okay, people,' Antonio said, 'here is how we are going to organize this. These guys have laid out this wonderful display of our things, now we need to make sure we sell them. I suggest Claire, Pascal and Philippe will run the garden stand; Jonathan, Sofia, Alfredo, Joaquin, and Fernando will run the pottery.' All the members were happy with this proposal, not noticing Antonio had left himself out.

'Wait a minute. What are you going to do?' Claire wanted to know.

'Me? I will sit in the shade over there, smoke a cigar, have a beer, and watch your trading skills!'

80.

Lucie Finds Her Vocation

By ten in the morning the market square was full of people wandering around, looking, asking questions about prices, bargaining, and buying, or leaving without any bags in their hands. Claire had found Sofia willing to volunteer for a very special job. She got one of the larger bowls from the pottery display, and placed on it a bunch of plums. She had cut them in half and removed the stone so that people could pick one without bothering about sticky fingers. The bowl was put on the tray that was fixed to Sofia's wheelchair.

'Your job is to offer people a plum with a napkin, and this with the most lovely smile you have, and tell them that the plums are sold over here,' she said, pointing to the garden stand, 'and the bowl on which you present them is sold over there,' pointing to the pottery stand.

As her flushed face and neck showed, Sofia was excited, to the point that made Claire patted her shoulder and spoke soothingly to her. 'Easy, easy, girl, don't get too excited.'

'Where do I go? What if nobody wants them?' Sofia asked anxiously.

'That doesn't matter a dime.' Antonio said. 'We're here to have a good time and meet people. You like to talk to people. Go and do so; leave selling our stuff to us. You go wherever you like; just make sure you can see and hear us, and we you. So we will be close if you need anything.'

Claire's plan worked as she had anticipated. Being able to speak to so many people Sofia couldn't help producing her most lovely smile. Moreover, she got a lot of attention from potential customers who she skillfully directed towards the two stands of her friends. Business was going well.

When they had been planning how to get their market sales organized, Antonio had insisted that Lucie should be present too. 'In one way or another, we want to have her there. We won't go without Lucie.' He stated it in a matter of fact way, making clear there was no room for dispute about this. Discussing how to get this organized, they agreed that Jonathan would drive the van back to Benacazón. Maria would be ready with Lucie at ten thirty when Jonathan would pick them up and return to Olivares.

Everything proceeded according to plan. When upon returning to the market square he had parked the van, they took Lucie in between them to stroll to the Bethany stands. Having arrived there, Lucie was welcomed with cheers.

'Hi, Lucie,' Pascal said, 'Do you care for a pear? You better be quick because they are almost gone!'

After Jonathan had Lucie seated on a chair he placed a box at her side. He had been thoughtful enough to bring some of her own things so she could feel more comfortable. He also put a small basket with scraps of paper in front of her. For the time being Lucie seemed content. Maria was looking at the two of them, and when she saw that Claire had been observing them too, she winked as if to say, 'This is special.' Claire nodded.

Around noon market transactions reached their peak. Pascal was selling almost more plums than he could have picked, and the pottery crew saw their plan of making more of their ceramic tiles rewarded. When they had priced them Antonio had said, 'Start selling them for half the price if they don't go.'

'Alfredo, how are our tiles doing?' the potter wanted to know.

'Going as fast as Pascal's plums,' was the response.

'Really? How many do you have left?'

'From the three boxes we brought, two are gone,' Alfredo said. He looked at Antonio with the pride of a successful salesman. 'We don't need to go down to half the price, I think.'

'Wow! You've done great, man!' Alfredo's face glowed. Antonio looked at the crooked man. His backbone will never rise, he thought, but his spirit certainly has.

Having been on her chair for half an hour, Lucie made attempts to get up, which was a quite alarming initiative given the display of things in front of her she could lay her hands on. Once again Jonathan Harrison outdid himself.

'Look at you!' he said, taking her by both hands, 'Sitting on a chair for half an hour!' Then, much louder than was needed for the Bethany stands to hear, 'People, can I get your attention. This is for the *Guinness Book of Records*. Today on the market fair in Olivares, Lucie Miles sat on a chair for more than thirty minutes.' There were cheers and 'hurray's'. Even Joaquin, usually the quietest of them all, shouted, 'Bravo, Lucie!'

'I better have a walk with you now, before we stretch it too much,' Jonathan said to her, looking at Antonio.

'Do you need company?'

Jonathan saw Maria was busy selling a vase to a potential buyer and replied, 'Not really. In case it gets difficult, I will come back. Tell Maria to be ready to take over in about fifteen minutes.' Antonio gestured 'thumbs up' to show he understood and would make sure Maria was ready.

The two of them wandered to and fro around the market square without any clear plan or destination. Jonathan tried to let Lucie go as much as he could without letting the situation get dangerous. At the other end of the square they came across a small patch that was fenced and covered with straw. It was a small coral with sheep and goats. The Olivares' market was not officially for cattle or other animals, but there was a small corner with half a dozen of them.

As soon as Lucie saw there were animals, Jonathan could hardly manage to keep her at his side. Instead of putting up a fight in the middle of all the people around them, he let go of her and kept his fingers crossed about what would happen next. Lucie ran straight away to the fence of the pen, and stuck her hand out. She was just able to touch a dark sheep that was standing close enough to her to touch it. In two steps Jonathan was beside her and trying to get her away from the animal.

One of the farmers had been watching him. 'Let her,' he said, 'She won't hurt that sheep.' Then he came up towards Lucie, took her hand and said, 'Come with me, there is a better way.' Jonathan noticed a faint surprise on the girl's face, but she followed the man. He brought her to what seemed to be the gate to the pen. Once she was in, she sat down on a heap of straw trying to get to stroke one of the animals. Having shied away at first, some of the animals got back a few moments later, curious to see who had joined them.

'You wouldn't believe what happened,' Jonathan said later to Antonio when they got back. 'The black sheep she had stroked through the fence came over to her, and what did she do? She bowed down over its back, while paying no attention to the animal whatsoever, and pulled out a few hairs. She put them in her mouth to wet them, and then started to roll a little ball in the palm of her hand. It was a Lucie-like thing to do.'

'Really? How did people react?'

'Most of them didn't see anything. Those who did just smiled. No one saw any need to interfere. She sat there for about ten minutes among these animals.'

'What did you make of it?'

'Me? Honestly? I think we buy a few goats and put them in the orchard, and let Lucie look after them.'

'Good Lord! Lucie the goat girl! Brilliant!'

Antonio was thrilled and looked very happy. In fact he was happy about many things. Being here on this beautiful day, spending his life with these people, teaching them how to make a decent pot, having this American guy around, having insisted on bringing Lucie to Olivares, and many, many other things. He grabbed Jonathan by his shoulders and hugged him firmly.

Having noticed something was going on between them, Claire came over, 'What's cooking guys?' Jonathan told her briefly about what happened with Lucie, but before he was finished she interrupted him.

'Sorry to interrupt you, but I think you need to pay attention to Sofia.' When she said it she gestured nodding with her head in Sofia's direction. When Jonathan looked over her shoulder, he saw Sofia fretting in her wheelchair, not a shadow of the bright young woman she had been an hour ago. Without answering Claire he passed her and approached Sofia.

'Now look who's here being sad that all her apples and plums are gone!' he said with a smile.

'Don't make fun of me!'

'I am not making fun of you, sweetheart.'

'Don't call me your sweetheart,' Sofia said, now really angry. 'If I were your sweetheart, you would at least pay some attention to me!' she screamed. Before he knew what was happening Sofia had started sobbing. Jonathan understood he needed to back off. 'I am sorry Sofia. Tell me, what's bothering you.'

'You're always busy with her, Lucie, that stupid girl! I hate her, I really do!'

'Oh, Sofia,' Jonathan sat back on his heels so as to have his face on the same level as hers. 'I am sorry, I had to get Maria and Lucie with the car. But you're right; I should have paid attention to how you were selling our plums.' He was wiping her tears when he said it, which was a much-appreciated gesture. When she calmed down he said,

'Now I have to think of a way to make it up to you.'

'Don't go away,' she said firmly, finally controlling her tears.

'Don't go away? I think I can do better than that.' Without explaining himself any further he went behind her and turned her wheelchair around. Without her noticing it, he gestured Claire behind her back not to mind. 'Back soon,' he mimicked without making a sound. Claire gestured 'okay'.

'Where are you taking me?' Sofia wanted to know.

'That's for me to know and for you to find out,' he said playfully.

'Oh, Jonathan, you're teasing!'

'I am not teasing! I am just telling you not to be nosy but wait and see where we are going. That's all.' The crowd had lessened at that point in the afternoon, and he succeeded in finding a seat on the terrace of one of the restaurants. He placed her wheelchair right before his own chair, so she could look him in the face. Within a minute a waiter came on to serve them.

'Good afternoon. What can I bring you?'

Without looking at her, Jonathan said, 'The lady here would like to try the chef's sorbet. Could you bring it, please? Oh, and don't forget the whipped cream. For me you can bring a beer.'

'Certainly, Sir.' Having placed his order, Jonathan looked at her. Her radiant face suggested happiness that far exceeded what he had anticipated. 'Be careful, now,' he said to himself.

'This is to congratulate you with the successful sale you helped with this morning,' he said. Fortunately she didn't take it as a diversion.

'It was good, wasn't it?'

'It was terrific! I heard you spoke with a lot of people.'

'Yes, I did,' she was still glowing with all the attention she had received.

'What did you speak about'

'Oh, you don't want to know,' she said carelessly. 'Of course about prices, but some also asked questions about me.'

'What did they want to know?'

'Stupid things. Like why I am in a wheelchair.'

'What did you say?'

'You don't want to know.'

'Sure I do.'

'There was one younger guy, who asked me,' then she started to giggle.

'Then what?'

'I said to him: I used to walk on my hands but then they got tired, so I had to sit down and decided this wheelchair was as good a seat as any.'

'You did not!'

She nodded affirming the audacity of her attitude and giggled. The waiter brought what Jonathan had ordered and he asked instantly for the bill. Sofia had finished her ice cream when he had hardly touched his beer, but that didn't bother him. 'We need to go back, dear,' he said, 'they might be waiting for us.'

When they returned to the section of the market stands there was the usual noisy jesting and joking after a profitable day of hard work. Most of the stands were getting empty, the sales people already packing what was left from their merchandise. The same was true of the two stands of Bethany.

Being busy boxing up what was left from the pottery's products, Antonio gestured that he had understood what Jonathan had been doing. Claire was assisting Pascal and Philippe in deciding what could be taken back in the van and what had to be thrown away. Looking around, Jonathan noticed Maria anxiously was waiting for him. Lucie really needed to get back.

'You will excuse me now, Sofia, I need to help out Maria,' he said. Sofia nodded, understanding that she had had her moment and that it was now over.

Except for Lucie and Maria, everybody was busy with getting things ready to go home. They had sold most of their pottery and fruits, which meant the van would not even be half full.

'Maria, let me drive Lucie and you back to Bethany,' Jonathan said while he was looking for his bag with the car keys in it. 'We can take a few others. Fernando, why don't you help Alfredo and Joaquin to get in the back of the van, and drive with us.'

'Yeah, you go Fernando.' Antonio supported the idea. Turning to Jonathan he continued, 'If you wait for half an hour you can take everyone.'

'I don't think we should stretch it any longer, she is really done with it.'

Maria nodded in agreement. 'She has had it for today, and she did great.'

'All right,' the potter conceded. 'We will clean up here, and then I will leave with Claire and Sofia for the railway station. We will tell Pascal and Philippe to wait here and watch our things till Jonathan gets back to pick them up.'

As they drove back to Benacazón, the men in the back were talking. What a lovely day it had been! In the front, Maria was quietly humming a tune to set Lucie at ease.

'Look,' Jonathan said. With her head against Maria's shoulder the girl had fallen asleep. 'The sleep of the innocent.'

Liv May/17

Sources

Jean Vanier, *Community and Growth*. Darton, Longman and Todd, London.
  Revised Edition, 1989.

Jean Vanier, *Becoming Human*. Darton, Longman and Todd, London, 1999.

Jean Vanier, *Our Life Together. A Memoir in Letters*. Darton, Longman and Todd,
  London, 2008.

Jean Vanier, *Befriending the Stranger*. Paulist Press, Mahwah NJ, 2010.

Jean Vanier, 'What Have People with Disabilities taught me'. In: Hans S.
  Reinders (ed.), *The Paradox of Disability. Responses to Jean Vanier and
  L'Arche Communities from Theology and the Sciences*, William B. Eerdmans
  Publishing Company, Grand Rapids MI, 2010, 19-26.

Michael Hryniuk, *Theology, Disability, and Spiritual Transformation*. Cambria
  Press, Amherst NY, 2010.

Hans S. Reinders, 'Being with the Disabled: Jean Vanier's Theological
  Realism'. In: Brian Brock and John Swinton (eds.), *Disability in the
  Christian Tradition*. William B. Eerdmans Publishing Company, Grand
  Rapids MI, 2012, 467-511.

Hans S. Reinders, 'Transforming Friendships. An Essay in Honor of Jean
  Vanier'. *Journal of Disability and Religion*. Volume 19, 4, 2015, 340-364.
  (journal title italicized).